METROPOLIS GROVE

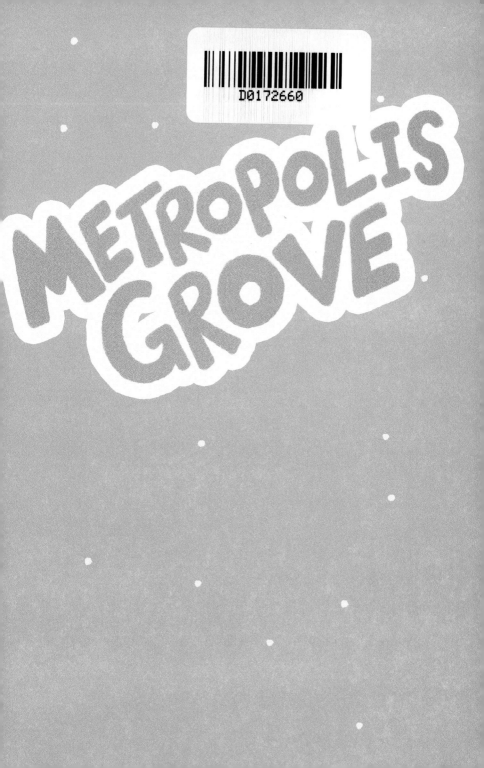

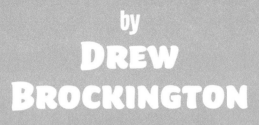

by
DREW BROCKINGTON

colored by Wendy Broome

SUPERMAN created by Jerry Siegel and Joe Shuster.
By special arrangement with the Jerry Siegel family.

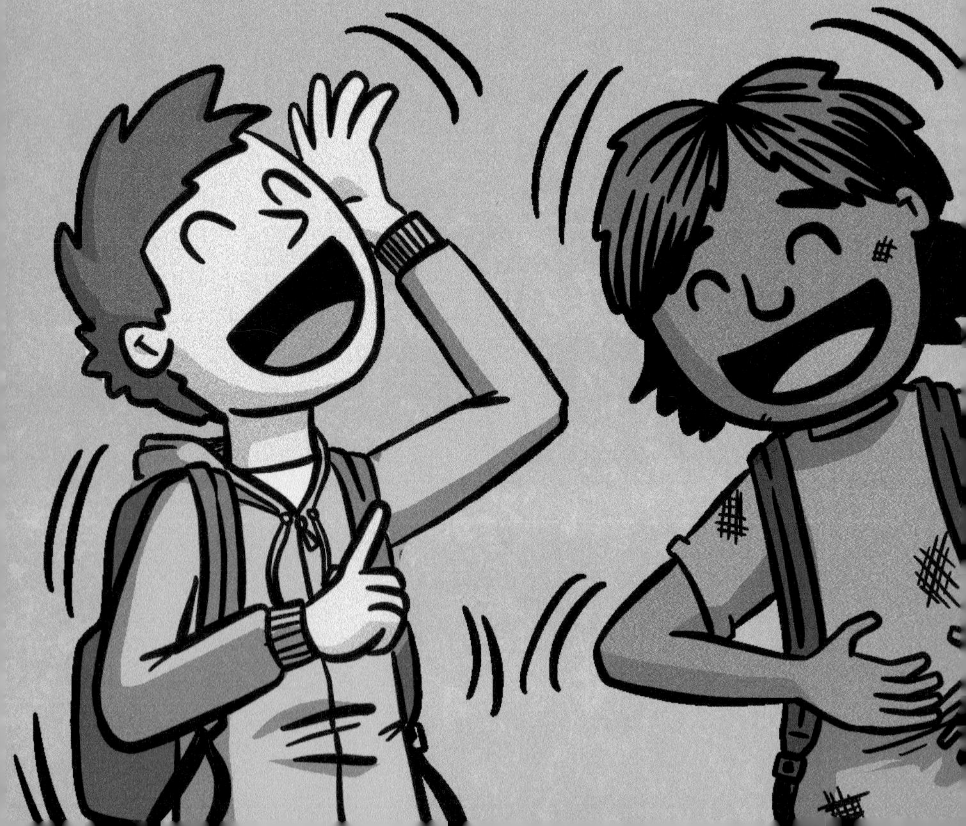

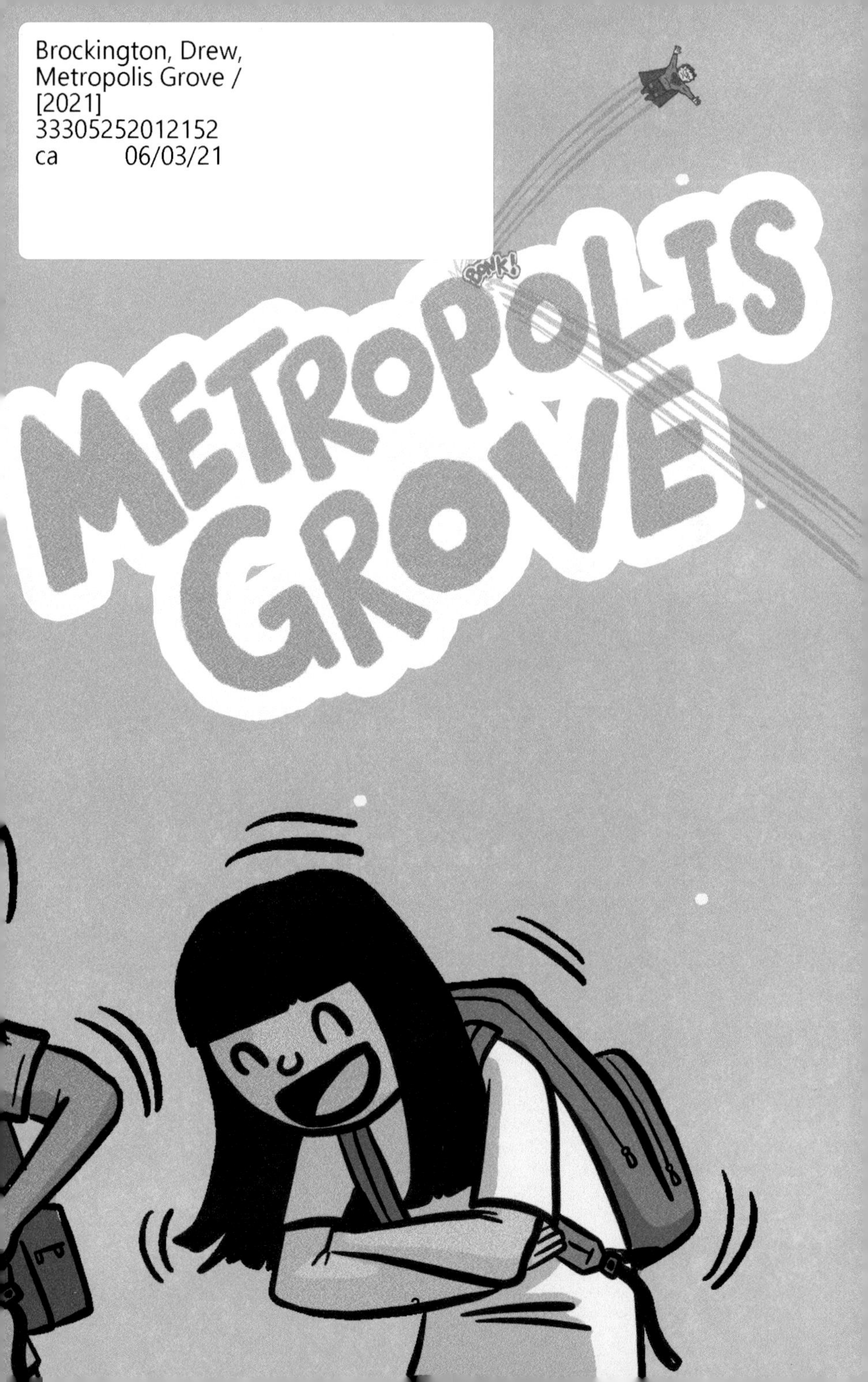
BONK!
METROPOLIS
GROVE

KRISTY QUINN Senior Editor
STEVE COOK Design Director – Books
AMIE BROCKWAY-METCALF Publication Design

MARIE JAVINS Editor-in-Chief, DC Comics
MICHELE R. WELLS VP & Executive Editor, Young Reader

DANIEL CHERRY III Senior VP – General Manager
JIM LEE Publisher & Chief Creative Officer
DON FALLETTI VP – Manufacturing Operations & Workflow Management
LAWRENCE GANEM VP – Talent Services
ALISON GILL Senior VP – Manufacturing & Operations
NICK J. NAPOLITANO VP – Manufacturing Administration & Design
NANCY SPEARS VP – Revenue

METROPOLIS GROVE
Published by DC Comics. Copyright © 2021 DC Comics. All Rights Reserved. All characters, their distinctive
likenesses, and related elements featured in this publication are trademarks of DC Comics. DC logo is a
trademark of DC Comics. The stories, characters, and incidents featured in this publication are entirely
fictional. DC Comics does not read or accept unsolicited submissions of ideas, stories, or artwork.
DC – a WarnerMedia Company.
DC Comics, 2900 West Alameda Ave., Burbank, CA 91505
Printed by LSC Communications, Crawfordsville, IN, USA. 3/26/21. First Printing.
ISBN: 978-1-77950-053-3

Library of Congress Cataloging-in-Publication Data
Names: Brockington, Drew, author, artist. | Broome, Wendy (Comic book
  illustrator), colourist.
Title: Metropolis Grove / by Drew Brockington ; colored by Wendy Broome.
Description: Burbank, CA : DC Comics, [2021] | "Superman created by Jerry
  Siegel and Joe Shuster, by special arrangement with the Jerry Siegel
  family" | Audience: Ages 8-12 | Audience: Grades 4-6 | Summary: Sonia
  Patel hopes having a full summer in her new house in Metropolis Grove
  will let her make friends before school starts, but new pals Duncan and
  Alex do not believe her when she tells them she has actually seen
  Superman in their town.
Identifiers: LCCN 2020057748 (print) | LCCN 2020057749 (ebook) | ISBN
  9781779500533 (trade paperback) | ISBN 9781779508584 (ebook)
Subjects: LCSH: Graphic novels. | CYAC: Graphic novels. |
  Friendship--Fiction. | Superheroes--Fiction. | Adventure and
  adventurers--Fiction. | Superman (Fictitious character)--Fiction.
Classification: LCC PZ7.7.B76 Me 2021 (print) | LCC PZ7.7.B76 (ebook) |
  DDC 741.5/973--dc23
LC record available at https://lccn.loc.gov/2020057748
LC ebook record available at https://lccn.loc.gov/2020057749

PEFC Certified

This product is from
sustainably managed
forests and controlled
sources

PEFC

PEFC/29-31-337   www.pefc.org

CHAPTER ONE

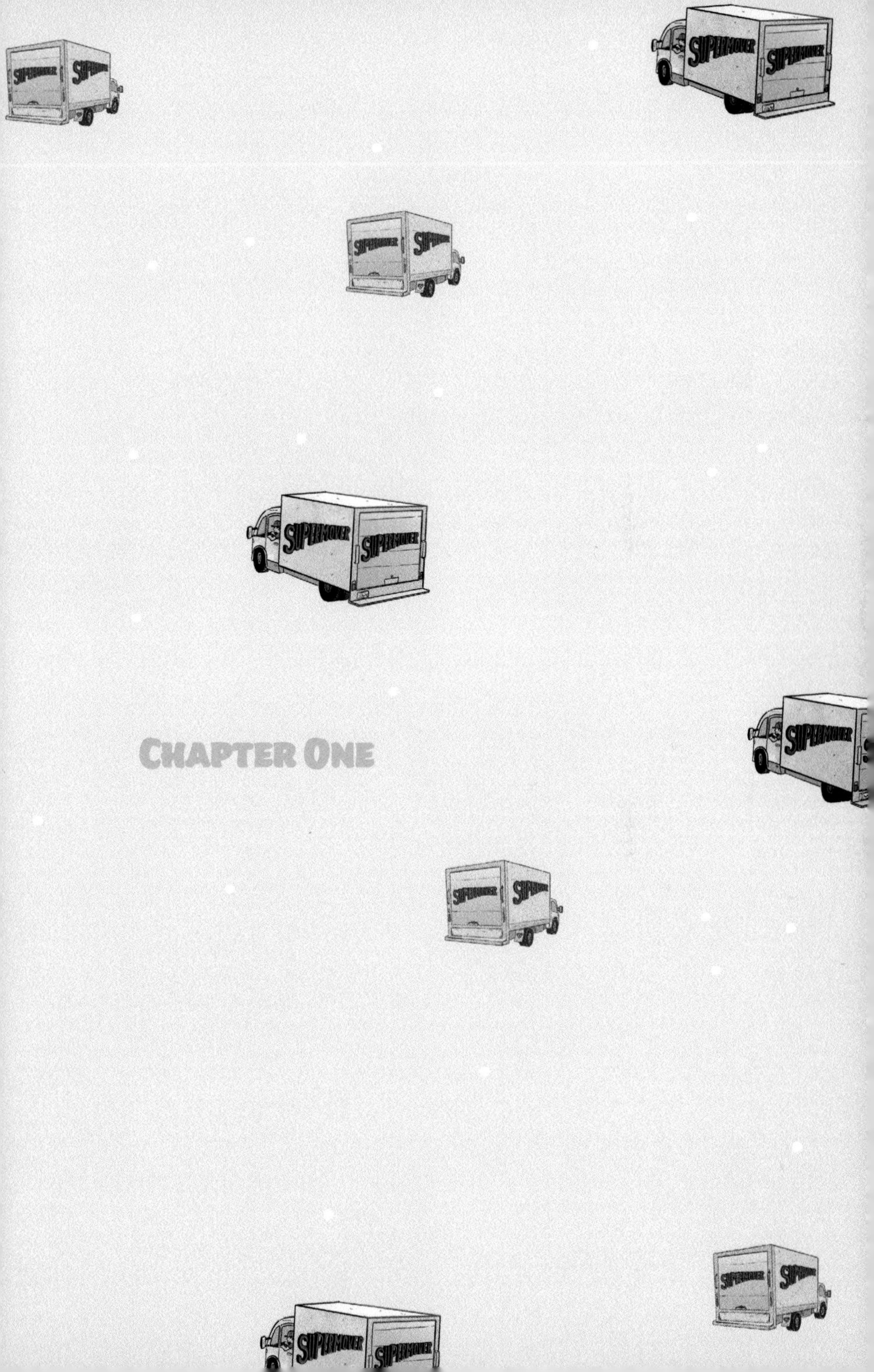
SUPERMOVER

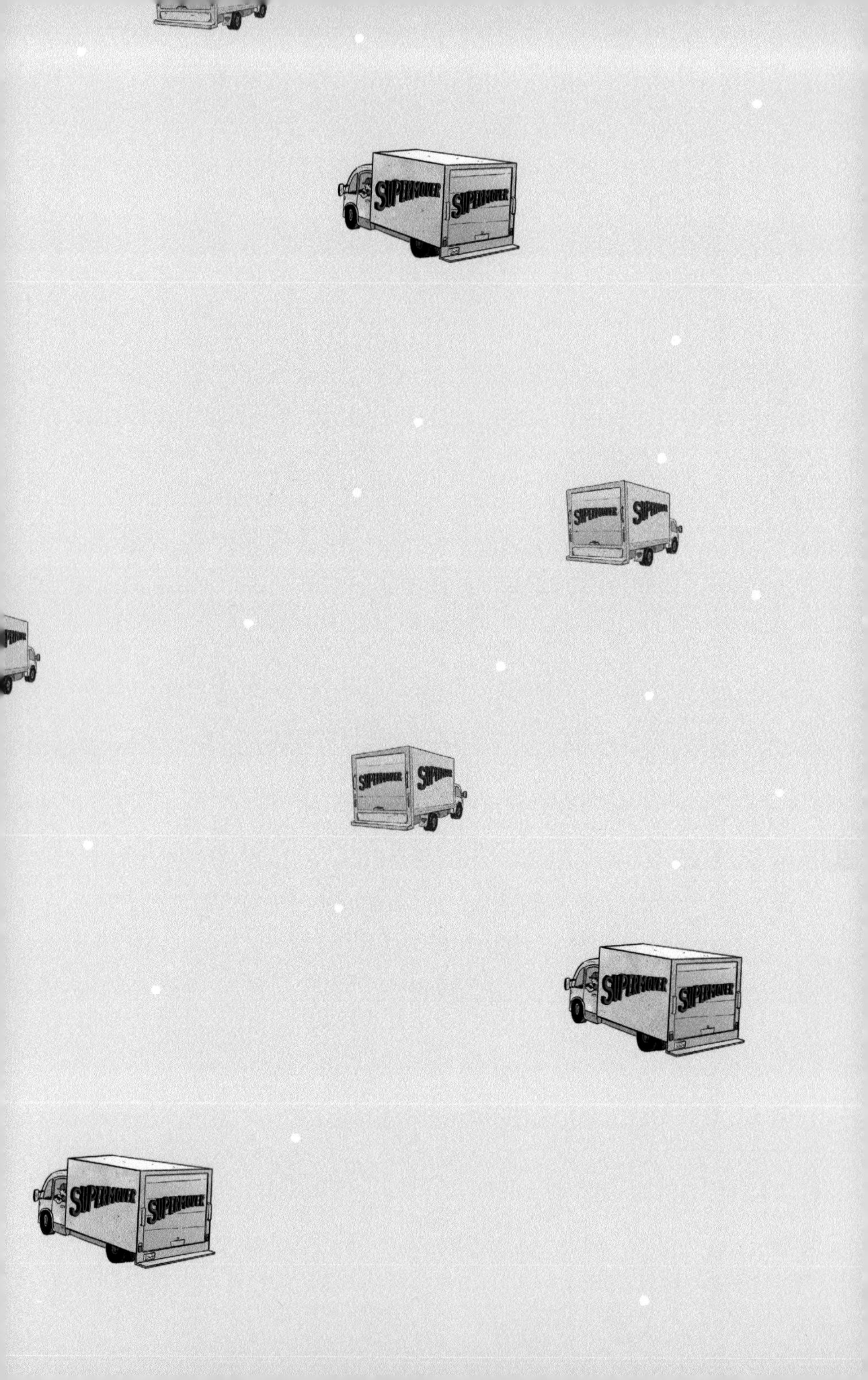
SUPERMOVER

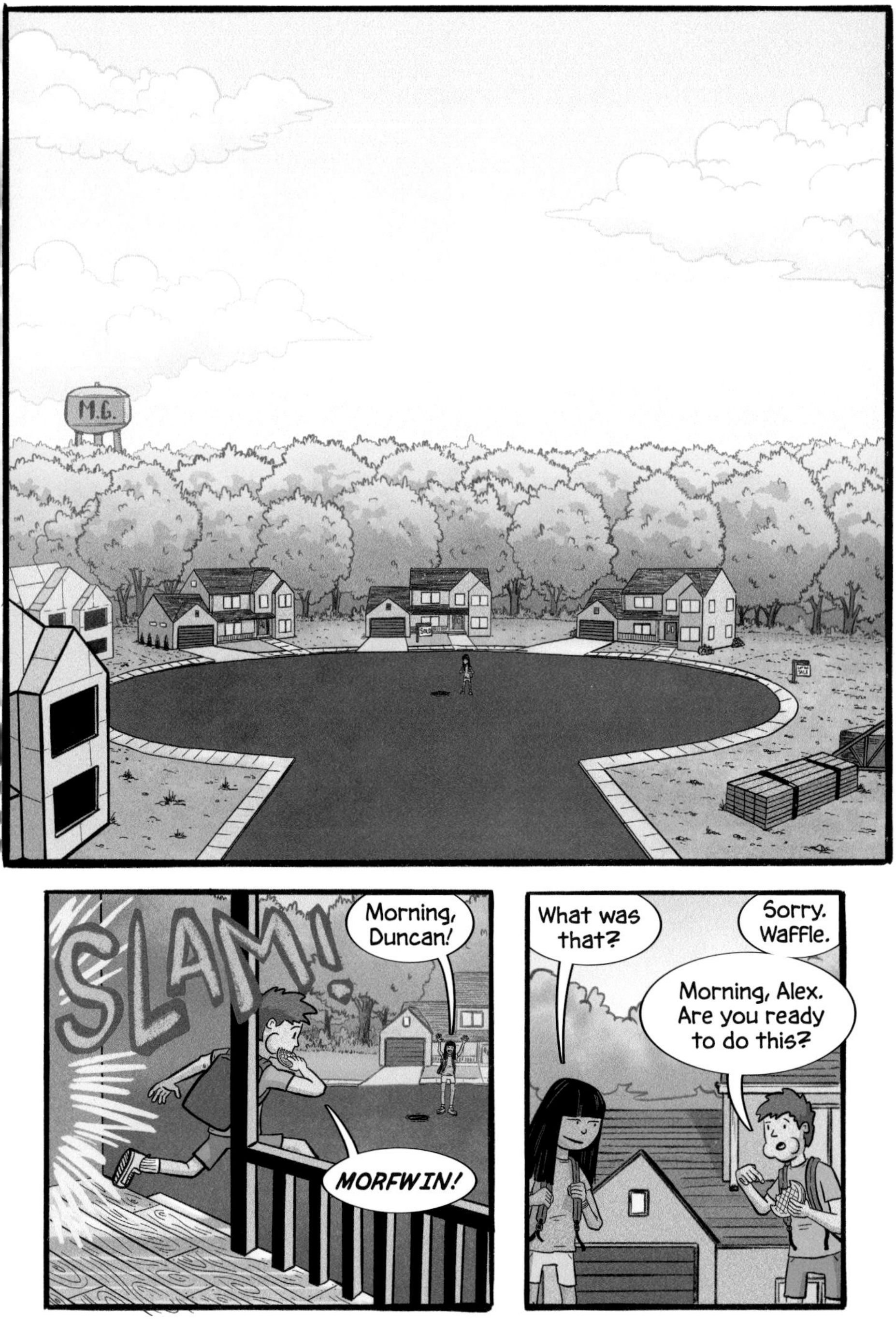
M.G.
SLAM!
Morning, Duncan!
MORFWIN!
What was that?
Sorry. Waffle.
Morning, Alex. Are you ready to do this?

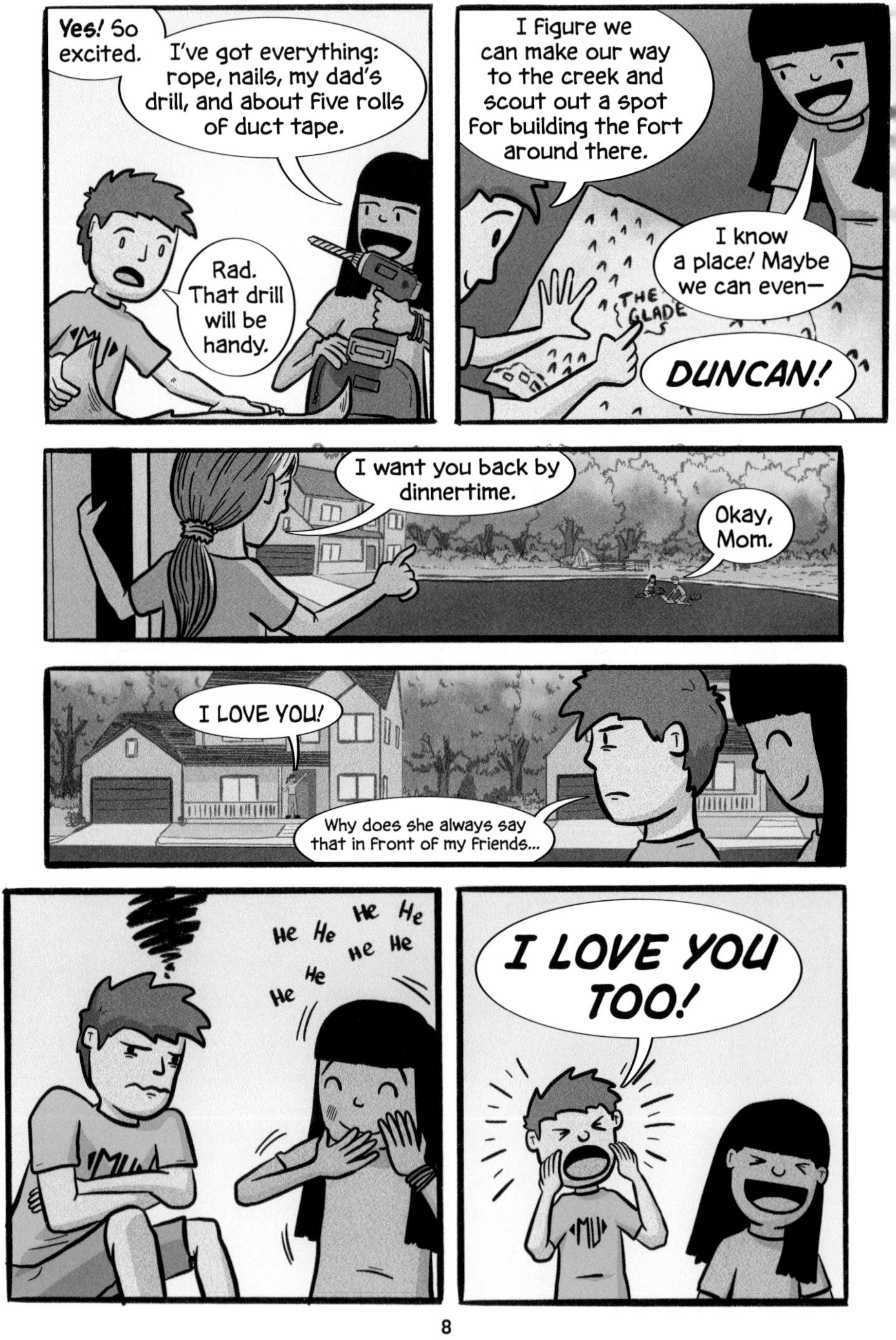
Yes! So excited.
I've got everything: rope, nails, my dad's drill, and about five rolls of duct tape.
Rad. That drill will be handy.
I figure we can make our way to the creek and scout out a spot for building the fort around there.
THE GLADE
I know a place! Maybe we can even—
DUNCAN!
I want you back by dinnertime.
Okay, Mom.
I LOVE YOU!
Why does she always say that in front of my friends...
He He He He He He He He
I LOVE YOU TOO!

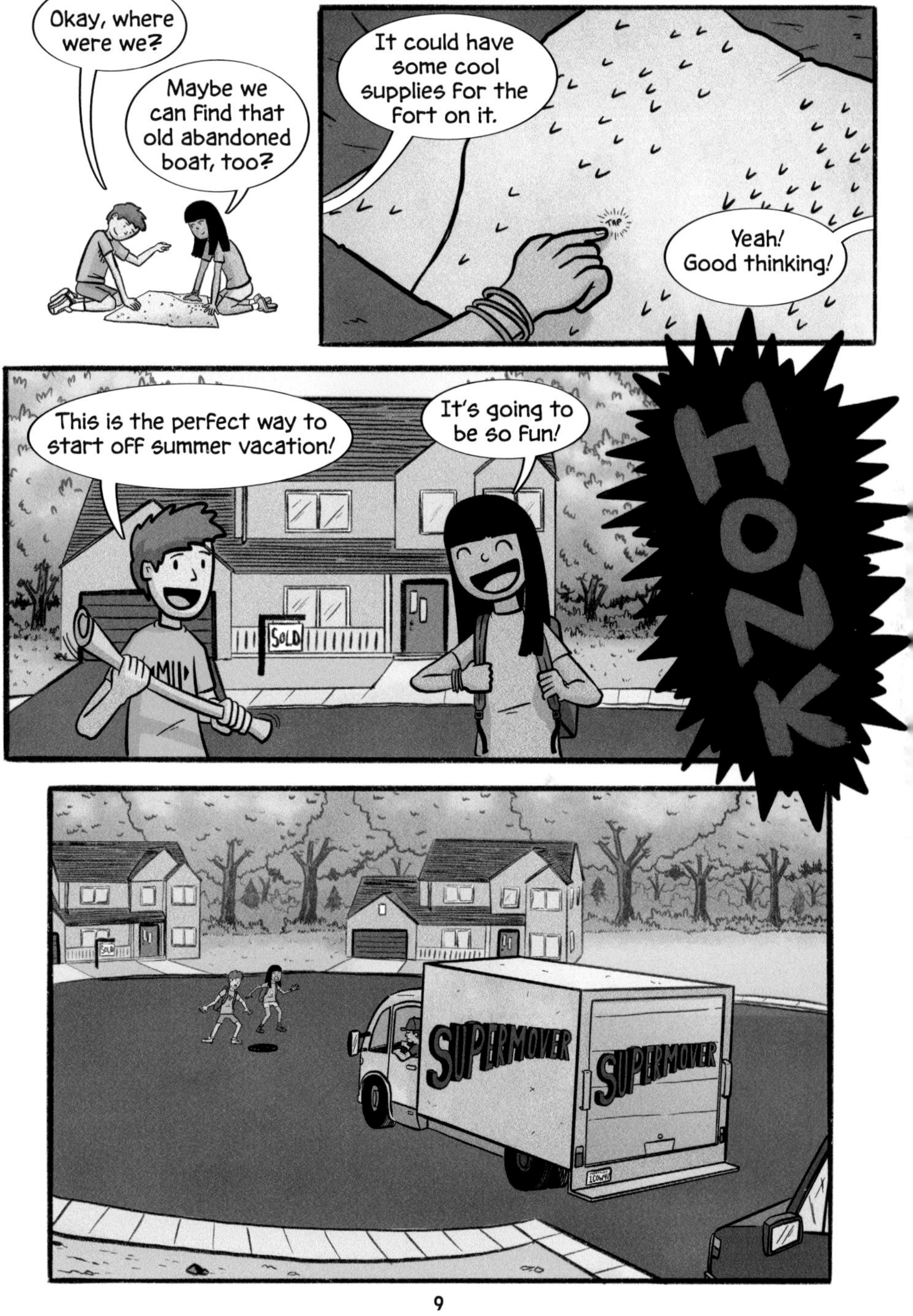

Okay, where were we?
Maybe we can find that old abandoned boat, too?
It could have some cool supplies for the fort on it.
TAP
Yeah! Good thinking!
This is the perfect way to start off summer vacation!
It's going to be so fun!
HONK
SOLD
SUPERMOVER
SUPERMOVER

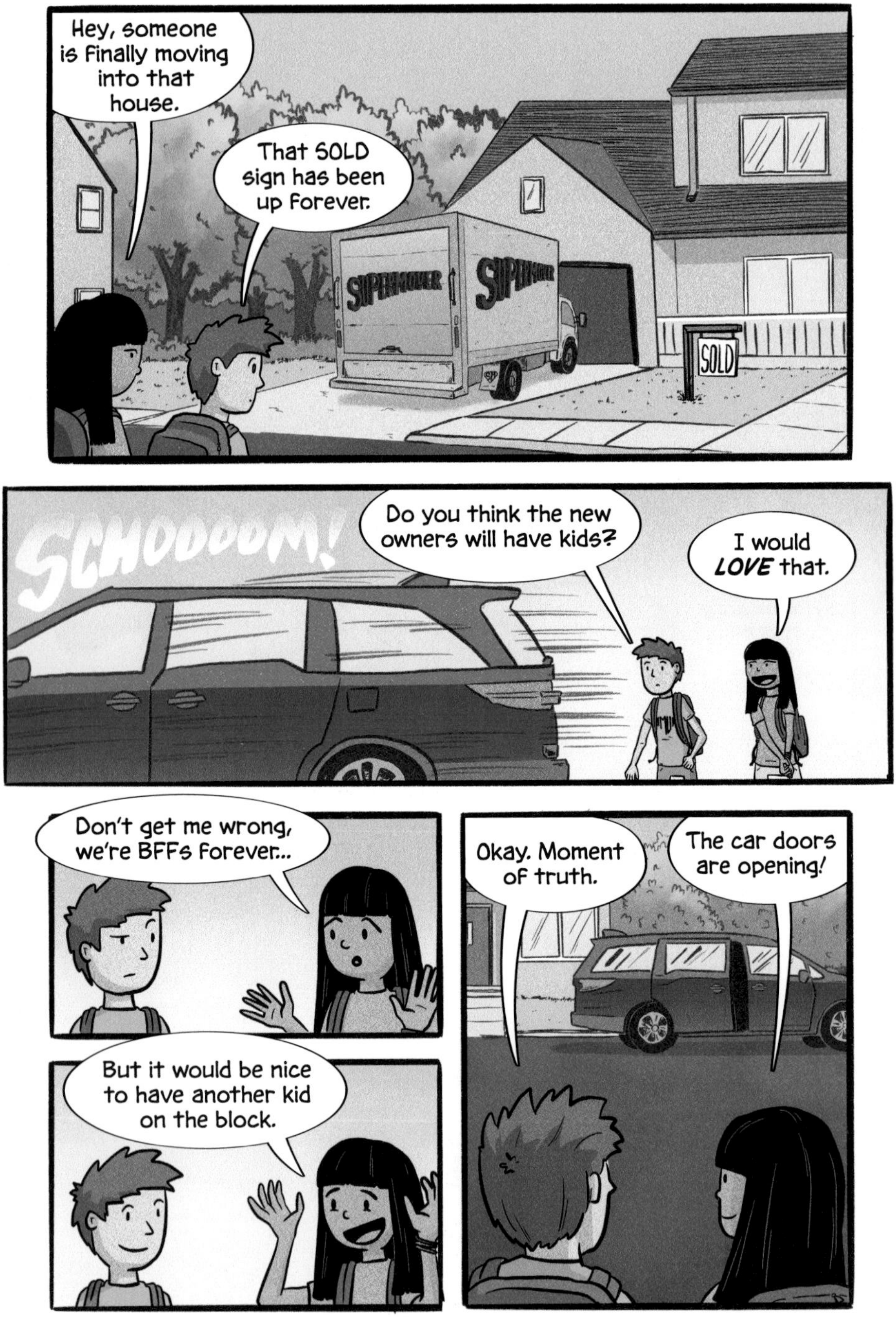
Hey, someone is finally moving into that house.
That SOLD sign has been up forever.
SUPERMOVER
SUPERMOVER
SOLD
SCHOOOOM!
Do you think the new owners will have kids?
I would *LOVE* that.
Don't get me wrong, we're BFFs forever...
But it would be nice to have another kid on the block.
Okay. Moment of truth.
The car doors are opening!

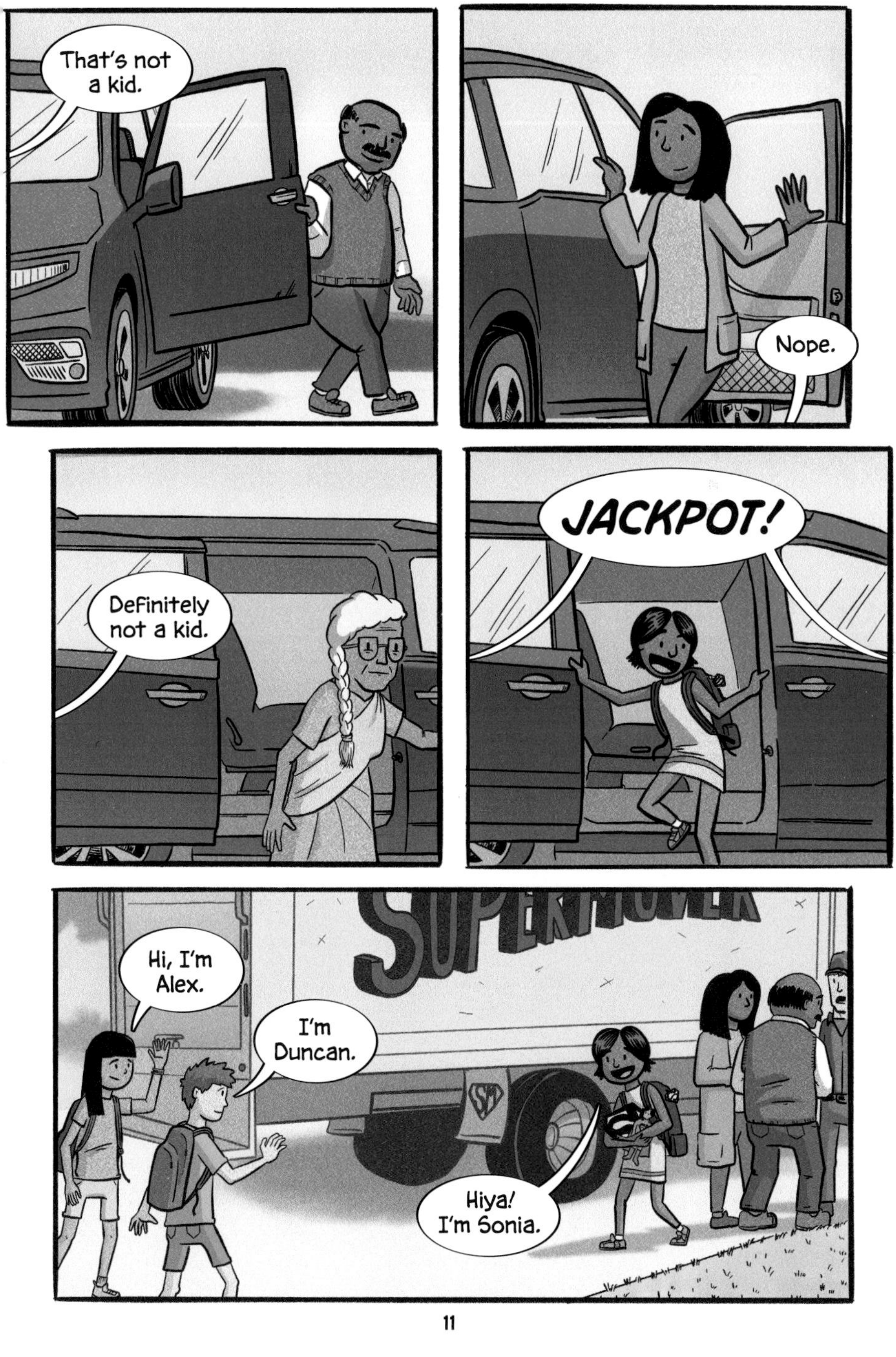
That's not a kid.
Nope.
Definitely not a kid.
JACKPOT!
SUPERMOVER
Hi, I'm Alex.
I'm Duncan.
Hiya! I'm Sonia.

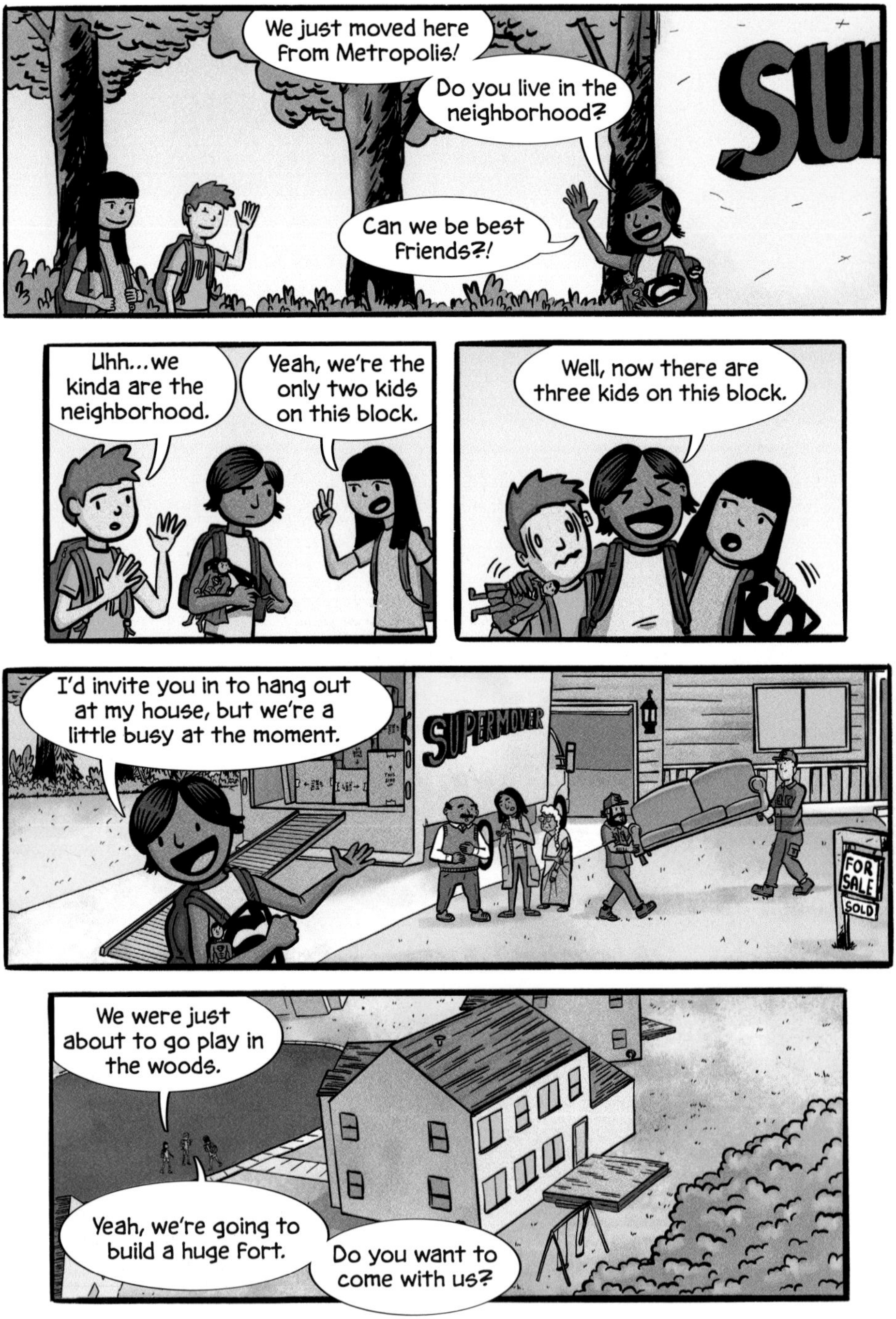
We just moved here from Metropolis!
Do you live in the neighborhood?
Can we be best friends?!
SU
Uhh...we kinda are the neighborhood.
Yeah, we're the only two kids on this block.
Well, now there are three kids on this block.
I'd invite you in to hang out at my house, but we're a little busy at the moment.
SUPERMOVER
FOR SALE
SOLD
We were just about to go play in the woods.
Yeah, we're going to build a huge fort.
Do you want to come with us?

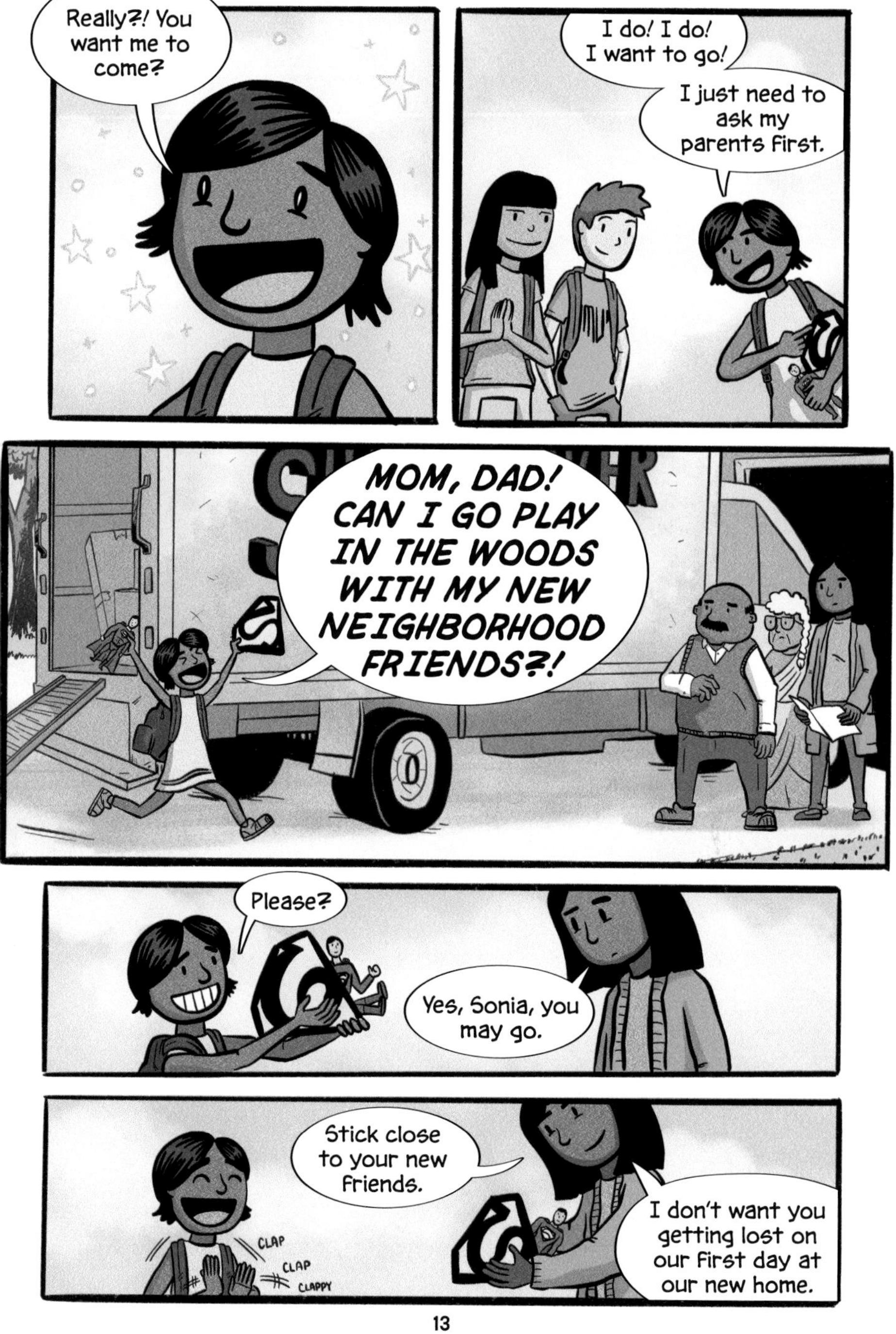
Really?! You want me to come?
I do! I do! I want to go!
I just need to ask my parents first.
MOM, DAD! CAN I GO PLAY IN THE WOODS WITH MY NEW NEIGHBORHOOD FRIENDS?!
Please?
Yes, Sonia, you may go.
Stick close to your new friends.
I don't want you getting lost on our first day at our new home.
CLAP
CLAP
CLAPPY

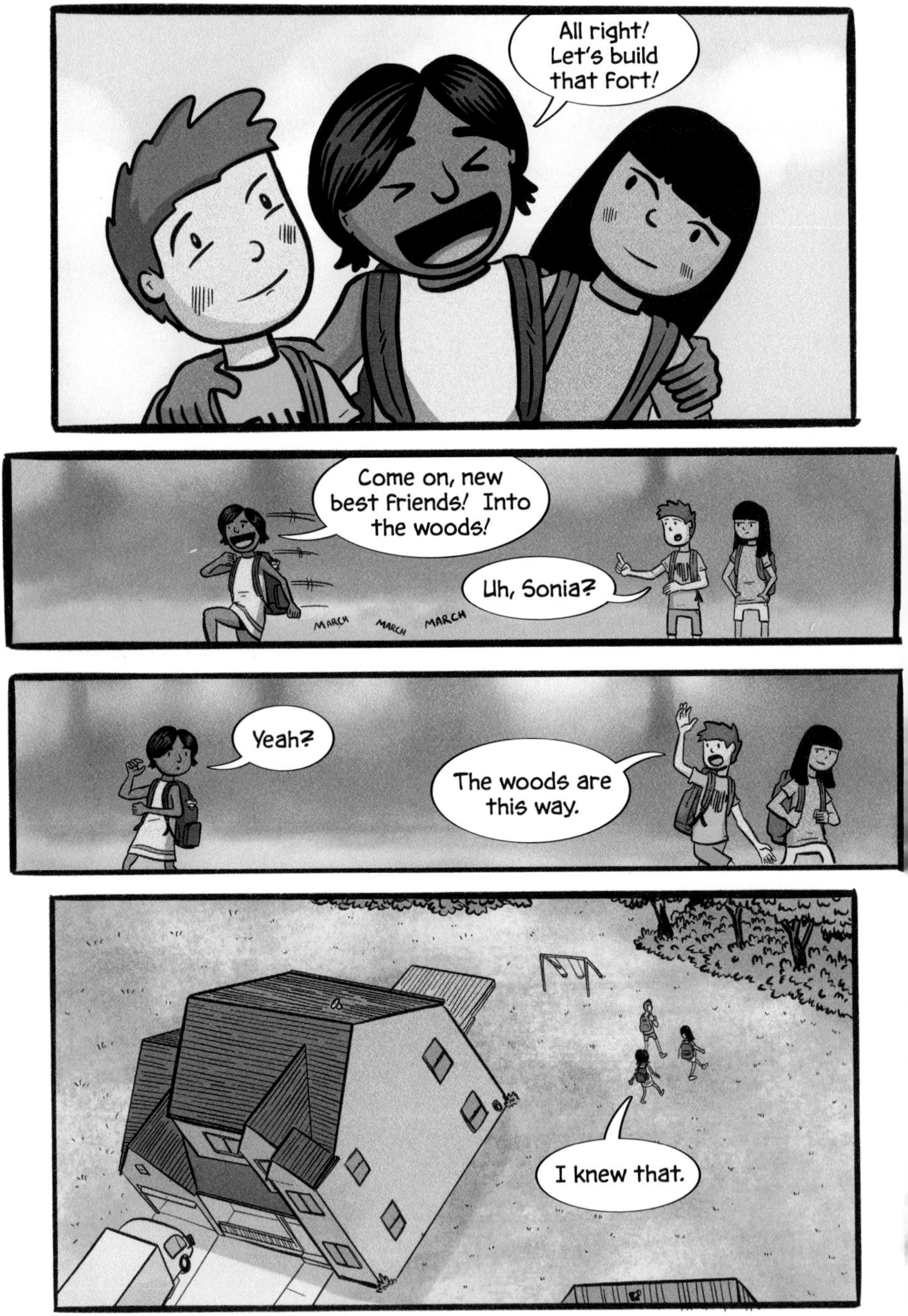
All right! Let's build that fort!
Come on, new best friends! Into the woods!
MARCH MARCH MARCH
Uh, Sonia?
Yeah?
The woods are this way.
I knew that.

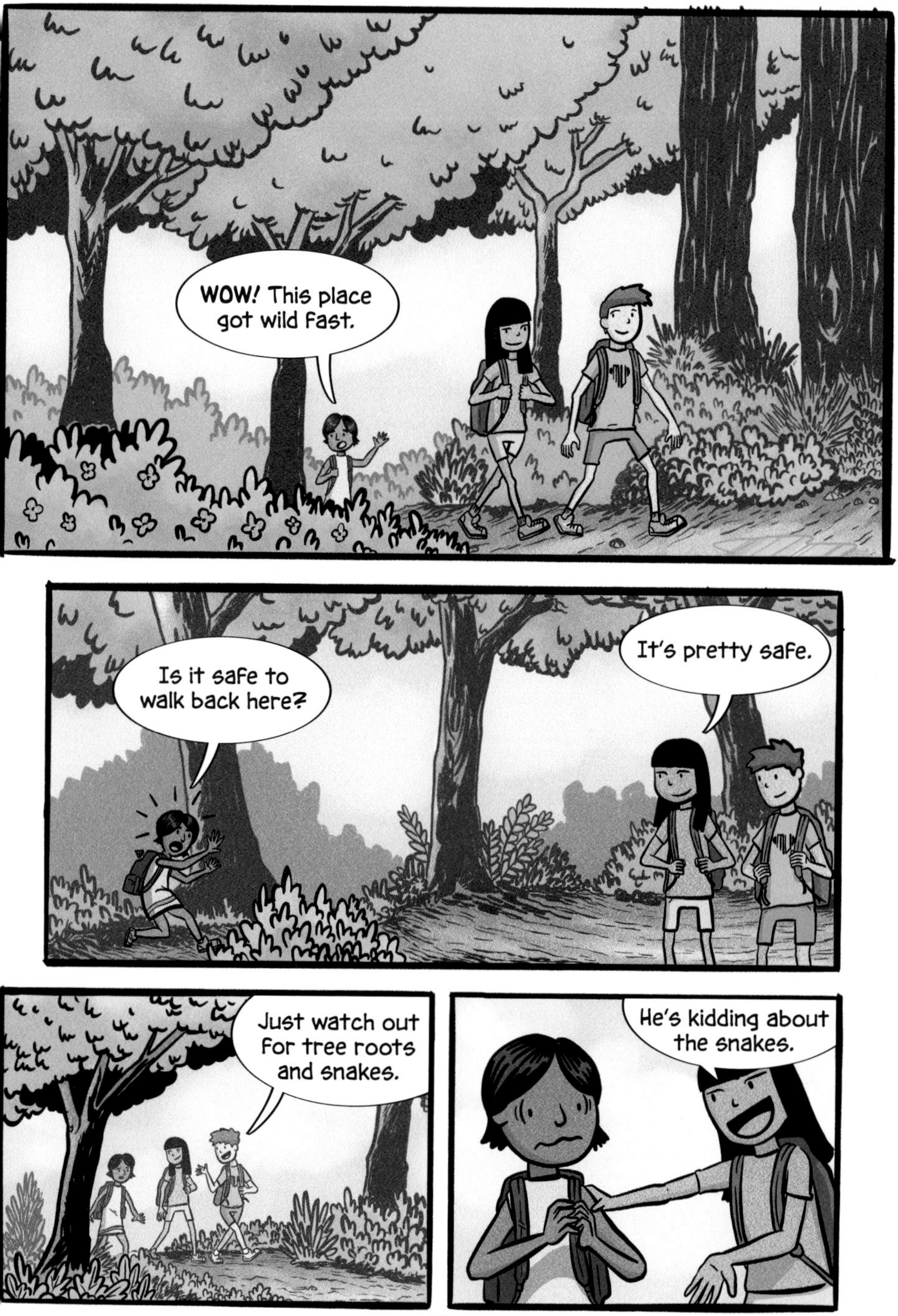
WOW! This place got wild fast.
Is it safe to walk back here?
It's pretty safe.
Just watch out for tree roots and snakes.
He's kidding about the snakes.

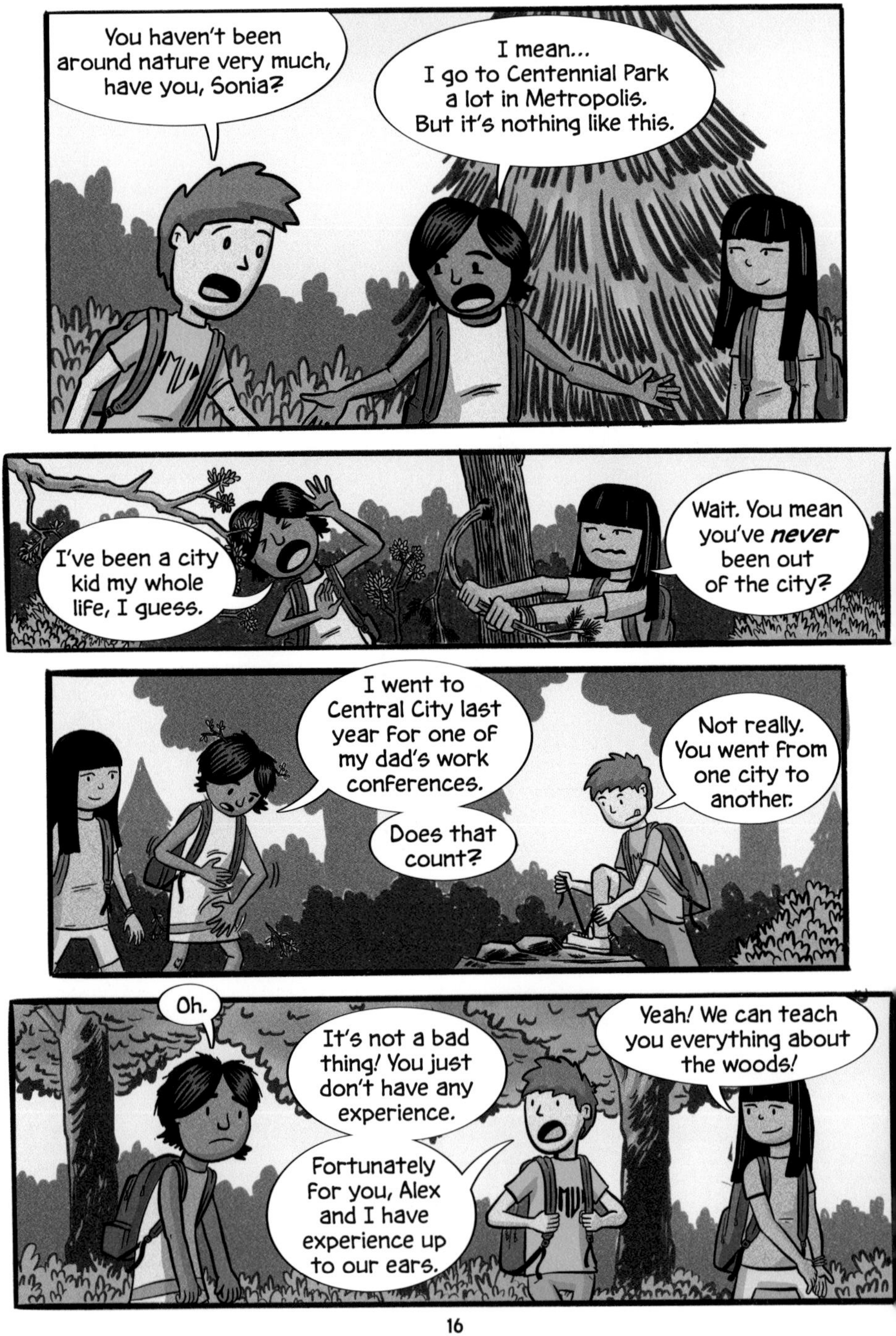
You haven't been around nature very much, have you, Sonia?
I mean... I go to Centennial Park a lot in Metropolis. But it's nothing like this.
I've been a city kid my whole life, I guess.
Wait. You mean you've ***never*** been out of the city?
I went to Central City last year for one of my dad's work conferences.
Does that count?
Not really. You went from one city to another.
Oh.
It's not a bad thing! You just don't have any experience.
Fortunately for you, Alex and I have experience up to our ears.
Yeah! We can teach you everything about the woods!

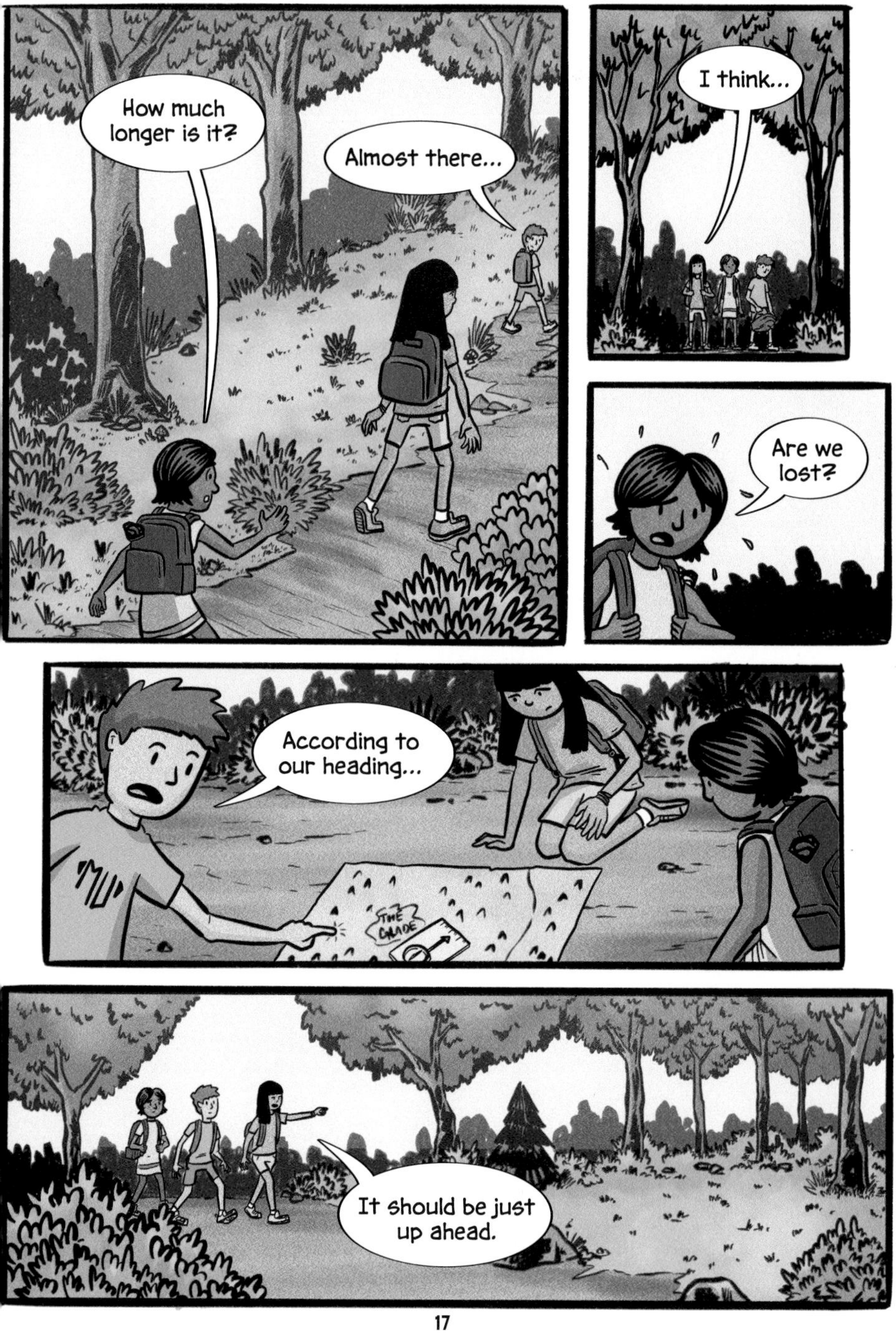
How much longer is it?
Almost there...
I think...
Are we lost?
According to our heading...
THE GRADE
It should be just up ahead.

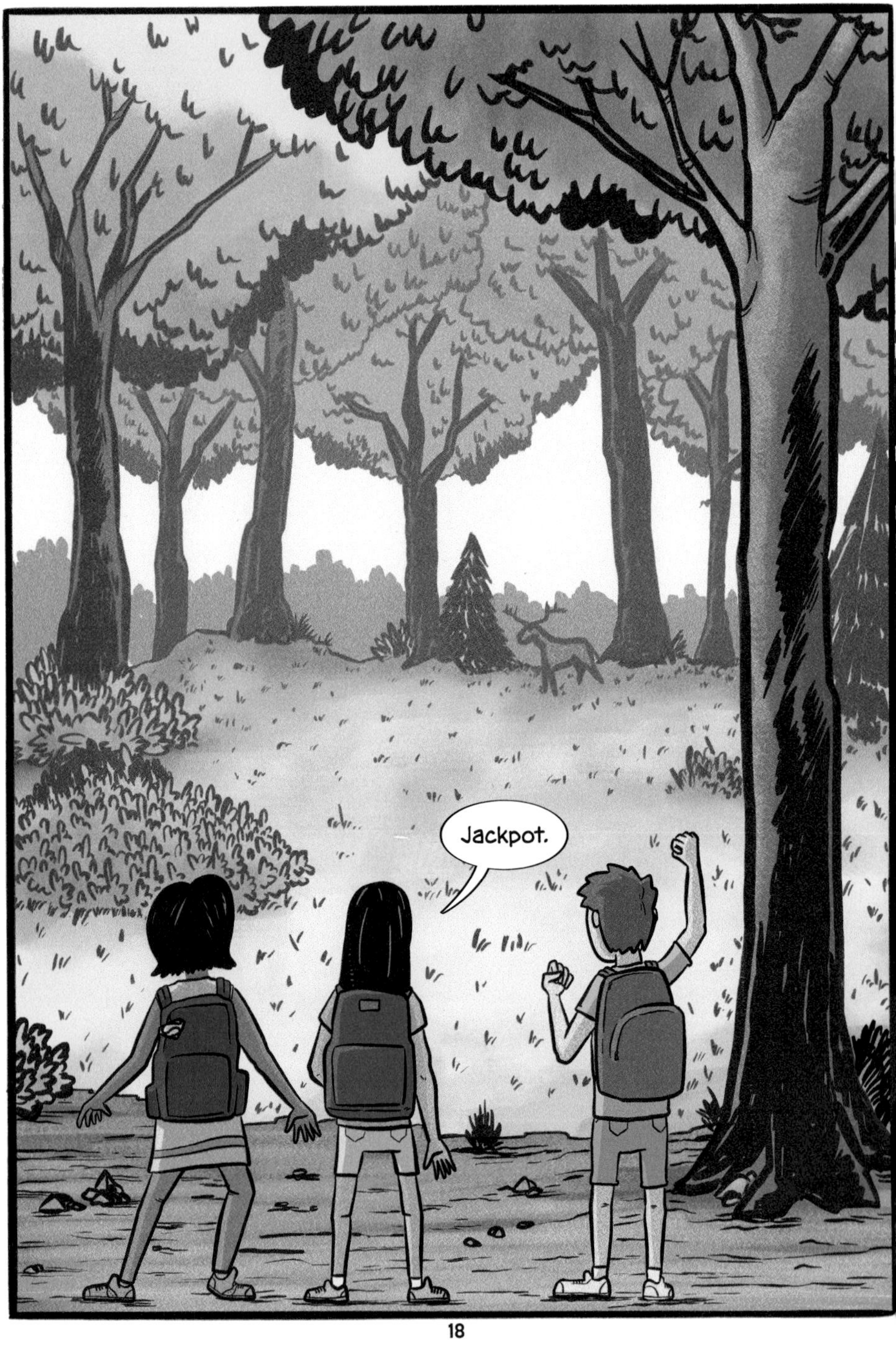
Jackpot.

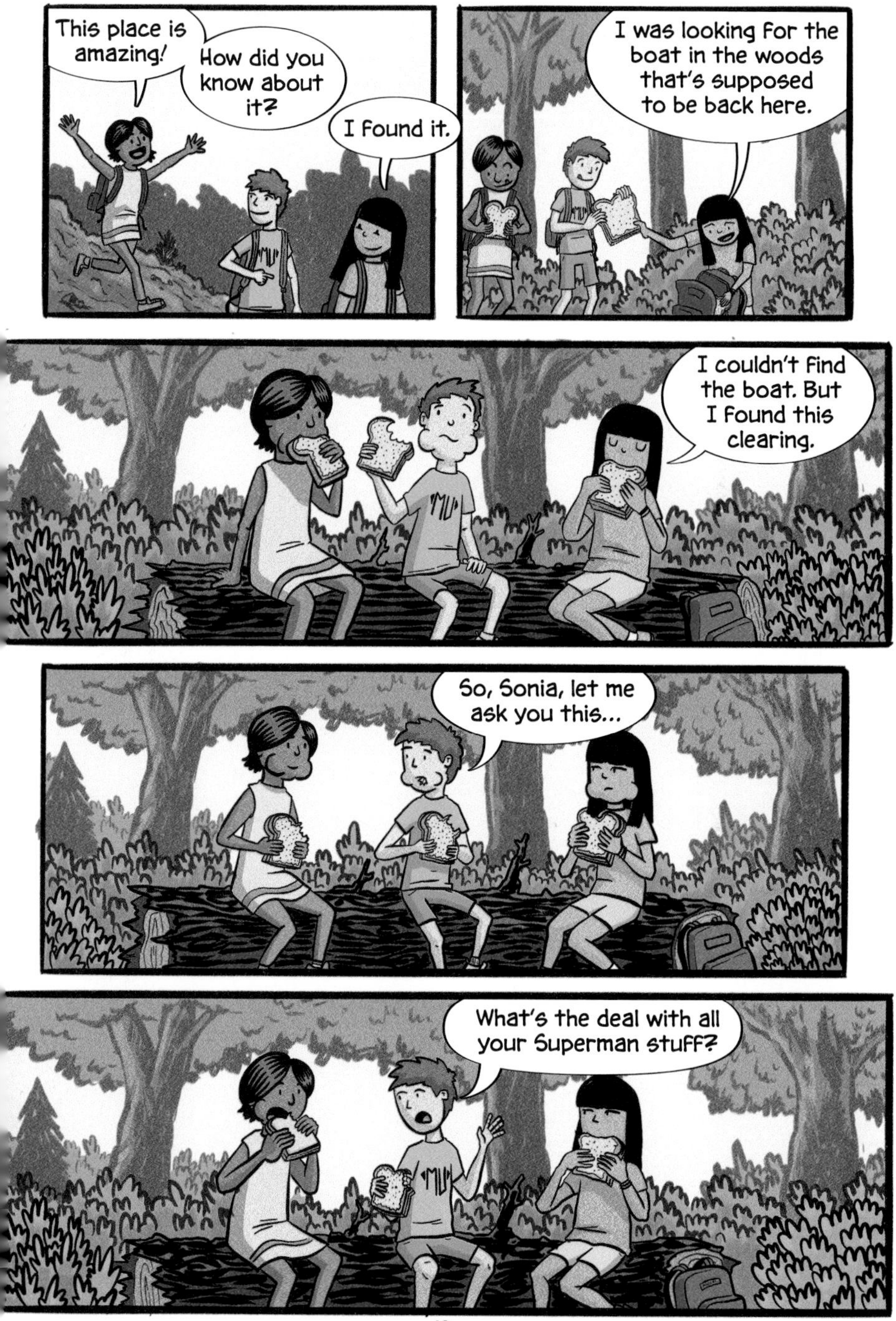
This place is amazing!
How did you know about it?
I found it.
I was looking for the boat in the woods that's supposed to be back here.
I couldn't find the boat. But I found this clearing.
So, Sonia, let me ask you this...
What's the deal with all your Superman stuff?

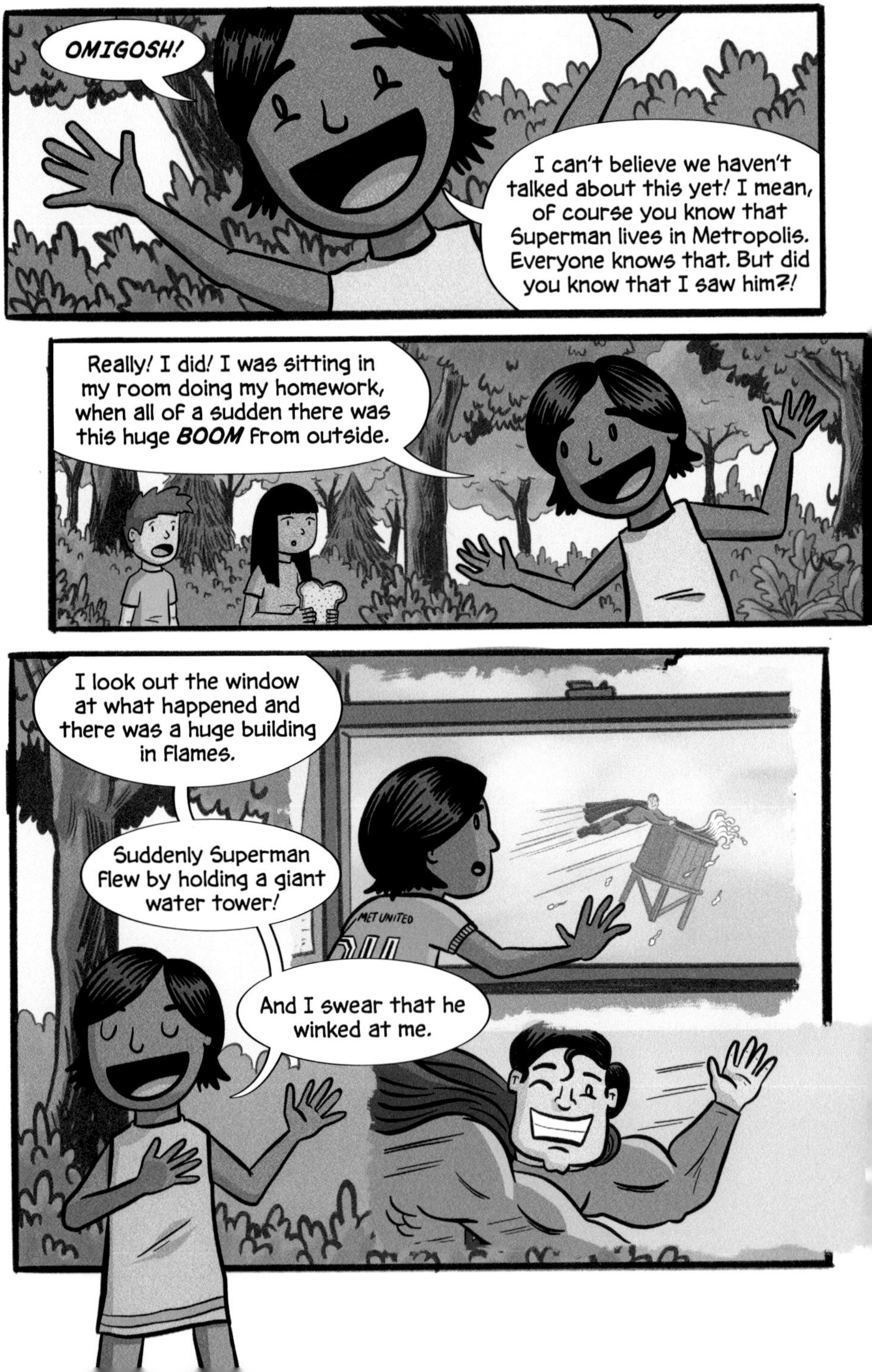

OMIGOSH!
I can't believe we haven't talked about this yet! I mean, of course you know that Superman lives in Metropolis. Everyone knows that. But did you know that I saw him?!
Really! I did! I was sitting in my room doing my homework, when all of a sudden there was this huge BOOM from outside.
I look out the window at what happened and there was a huge building in flames.
Suddenly Superman flew by holding a giant water tower!
MET UNITED
And I swear that he winked at me.

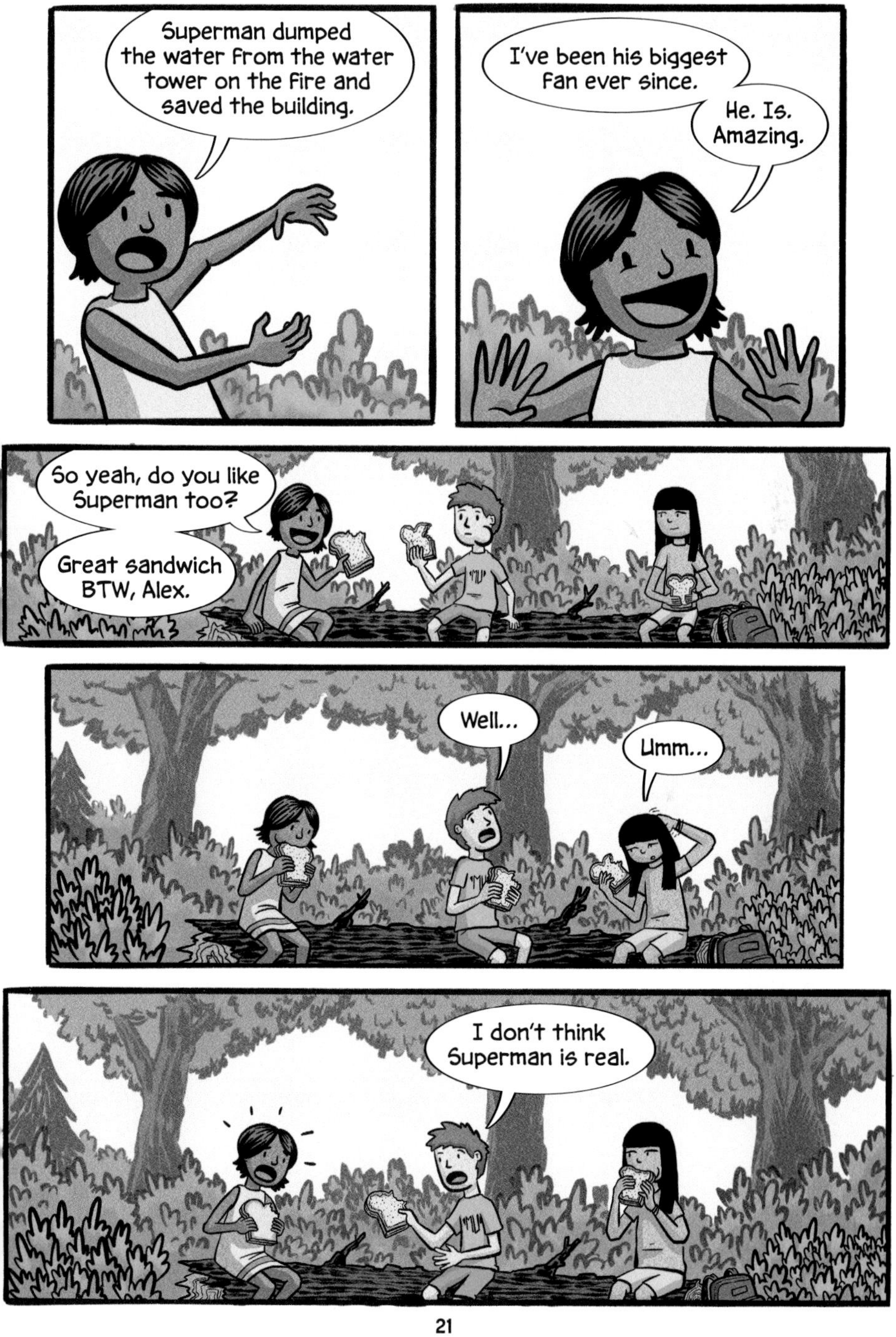
Superman dumped the water from the water tower on the fire and saved the building.
I've been his biggest fan ever since.
He. Is. Amazing.
So yeah, do you like Superman too?
Great sandwich BTW, Alex.
Well...
Umm...
I don't think Superman is real.

CHAPTER TWO

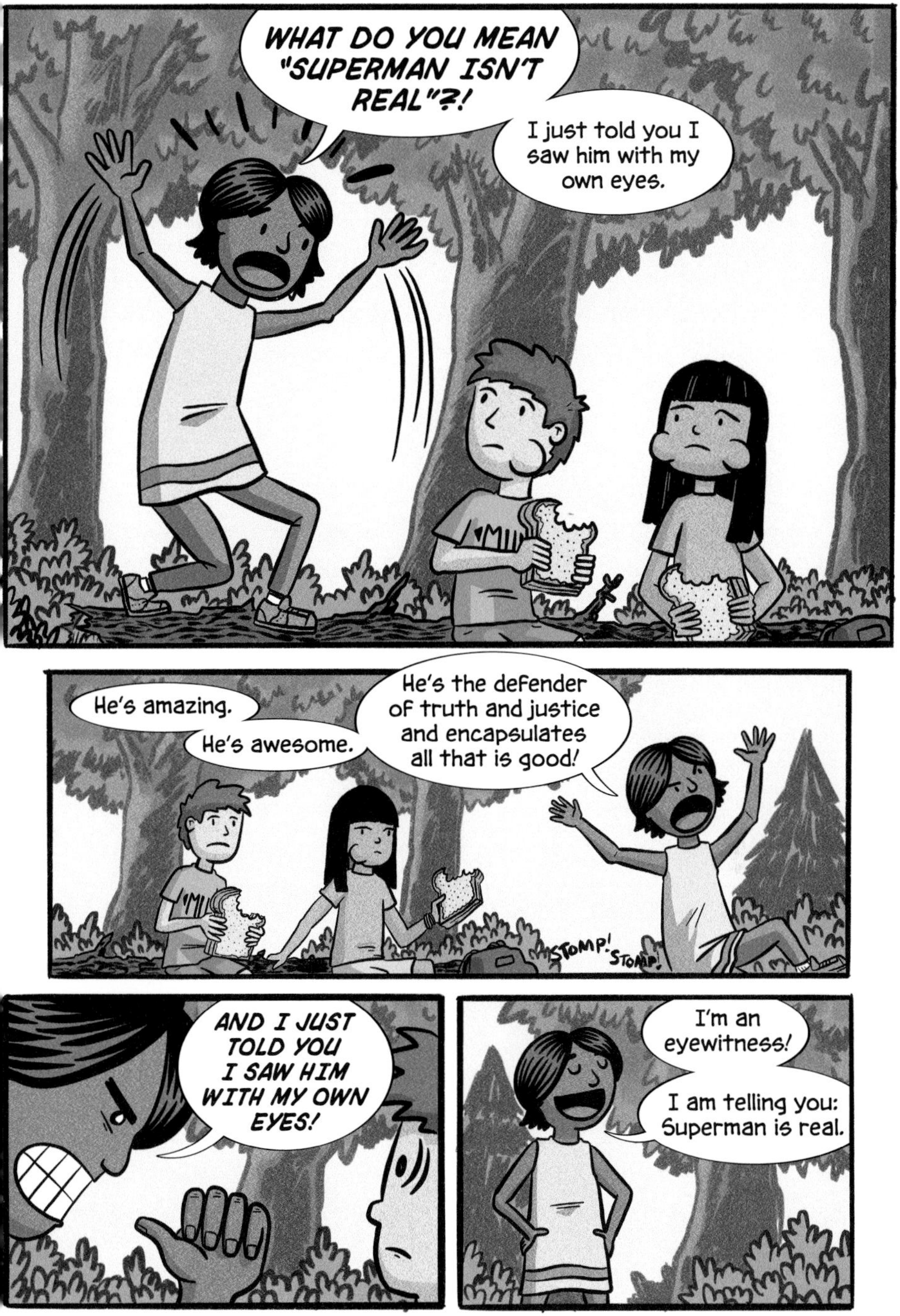
WHAT DO YOU MEAN "SUPERMAN ISN'T REAL"?!
I just told you I saw him with my own eyes.
He's amazing.
He's awesome.
He's the defender of truth and justice and encapsulates all that is good!
STOMP! STOMP!
AND I JUST TOLD YOU I SAW HIM WITH MY OWN EYES!
I'm an eyewitness!
I am telling you: Superman is real.

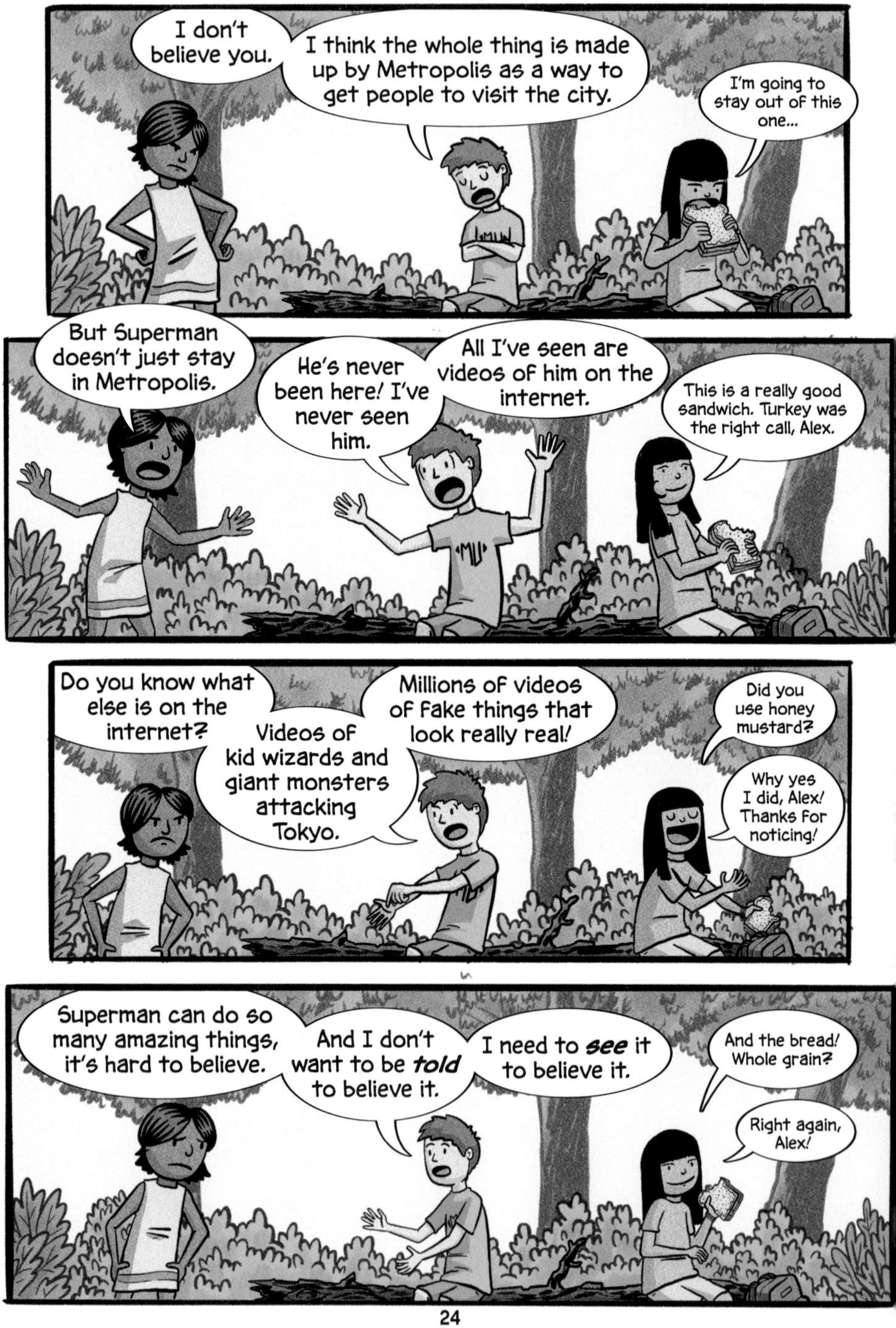
I don't believe you.
I think the whole thing is made up by Metropolis as a way to get people to visit the city.
I'm going to stay out of this one...
But Superman doesn't just stay in Metropolis.
He's never been here! I've never seen him.
All I've seen are videos of him on the internet.
This is a really good sandwich. Turkey was the right call, Alex.
Do you know what else is on the internet?
Videos of kid wizards and giant monsters attacking Tokyo.
Millions of videos of fake things that look really real!
Did you use honey mustard?
Why yes I did, Alex! Thanks for noticing!
Superman can do so many amazing things, it's hard to believe.
And I don't want to be *told* to believe it.
I need to *see* it to believe it.
And the bread! Whole grain?
Right again, Alex!

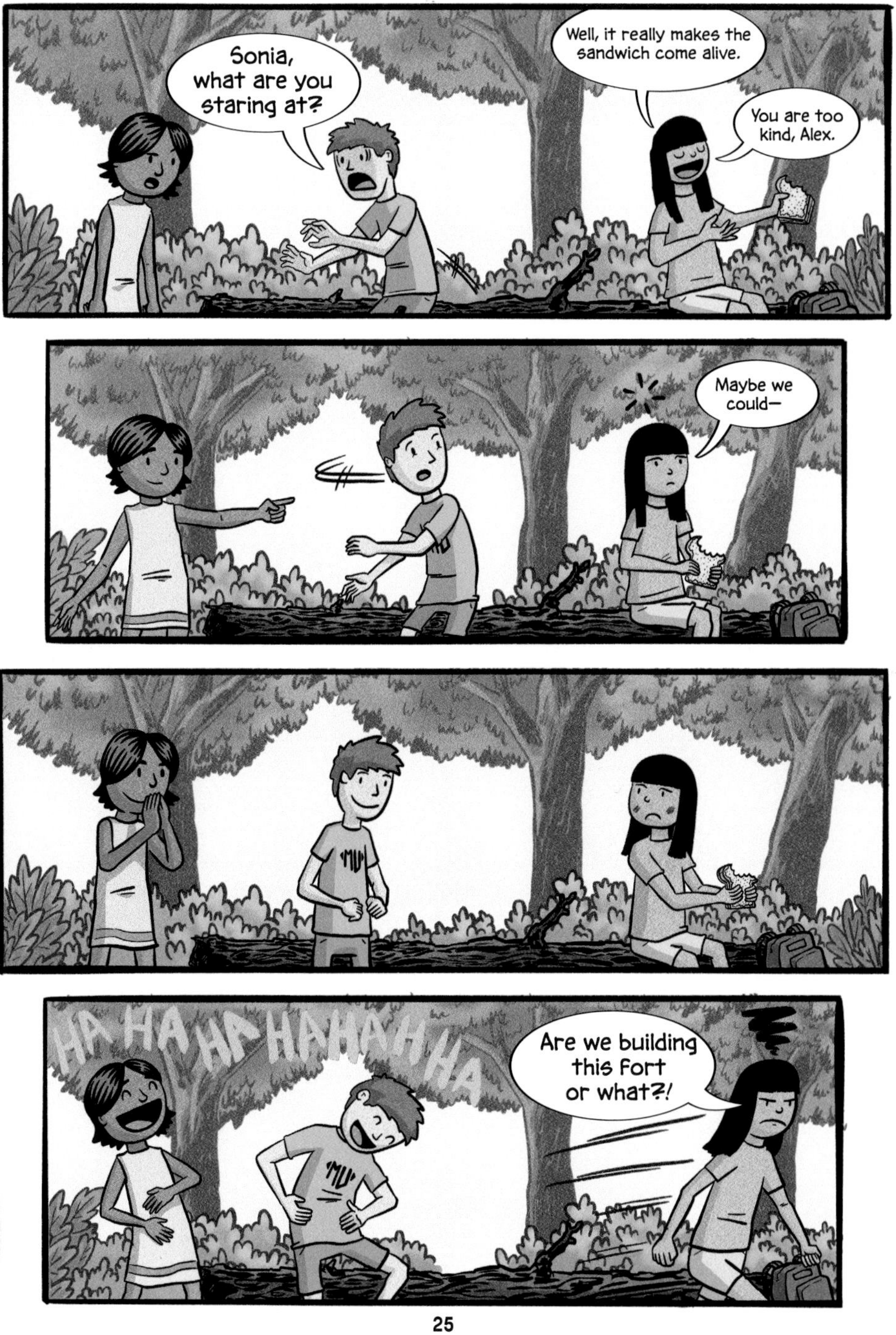
Sonia, what are you staring at?
Well, it really makes the sandwich come alive.
You are too kind, Alex.
Maybe we could—
HA HA HA HAHAHAHHA
Are we building this fort or what?!

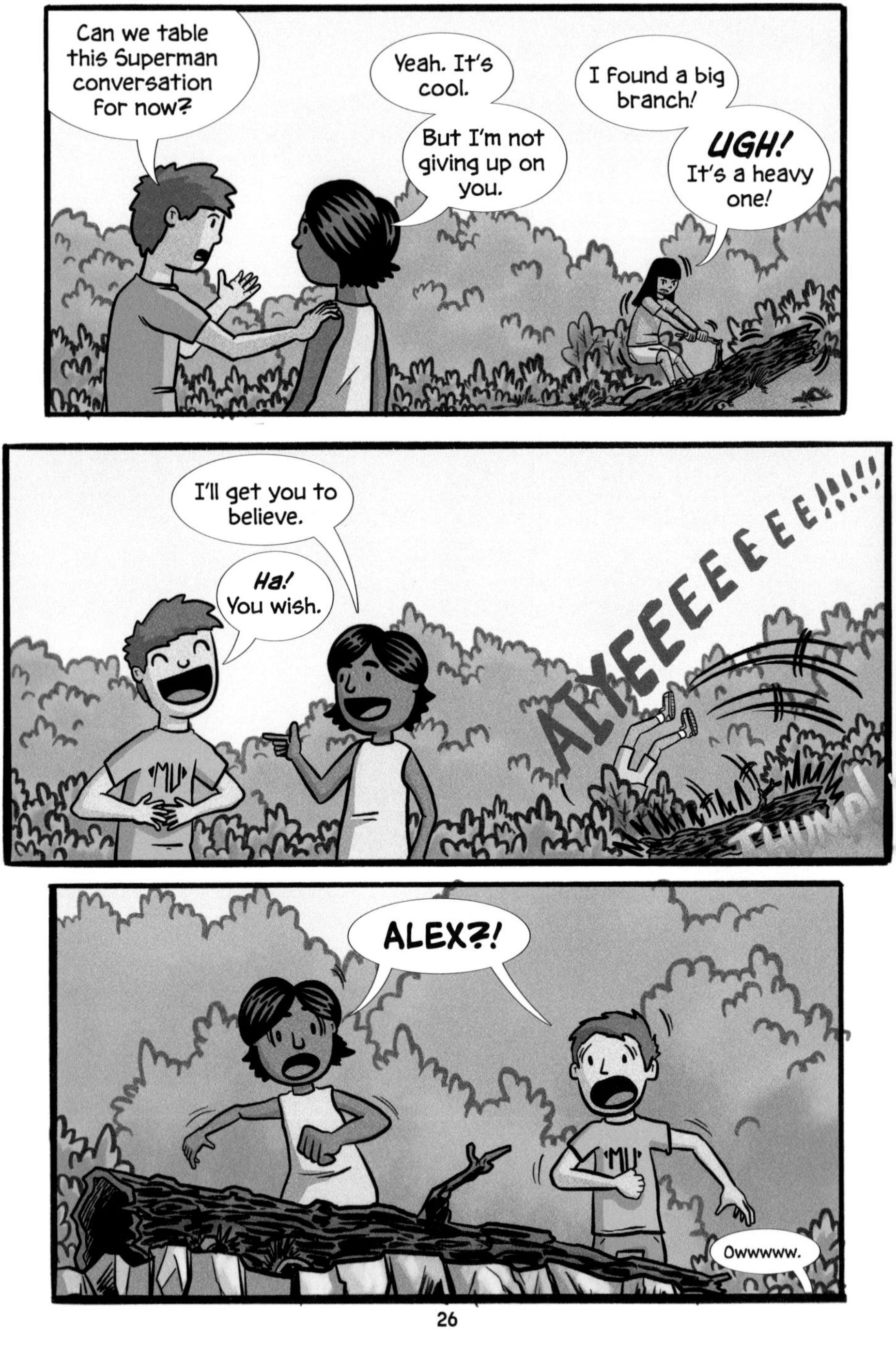
Can we table this Superman conversation for now?
Yeah. It's cool.
But I'm not giving up on you.
I found a big branch!
UGH! It's a heavy one!
I'll get you to believe.
Ha! You wish.
AIYEEEEEEEEE!!!!!
THUMP!
ALEX?!
Owwwww.

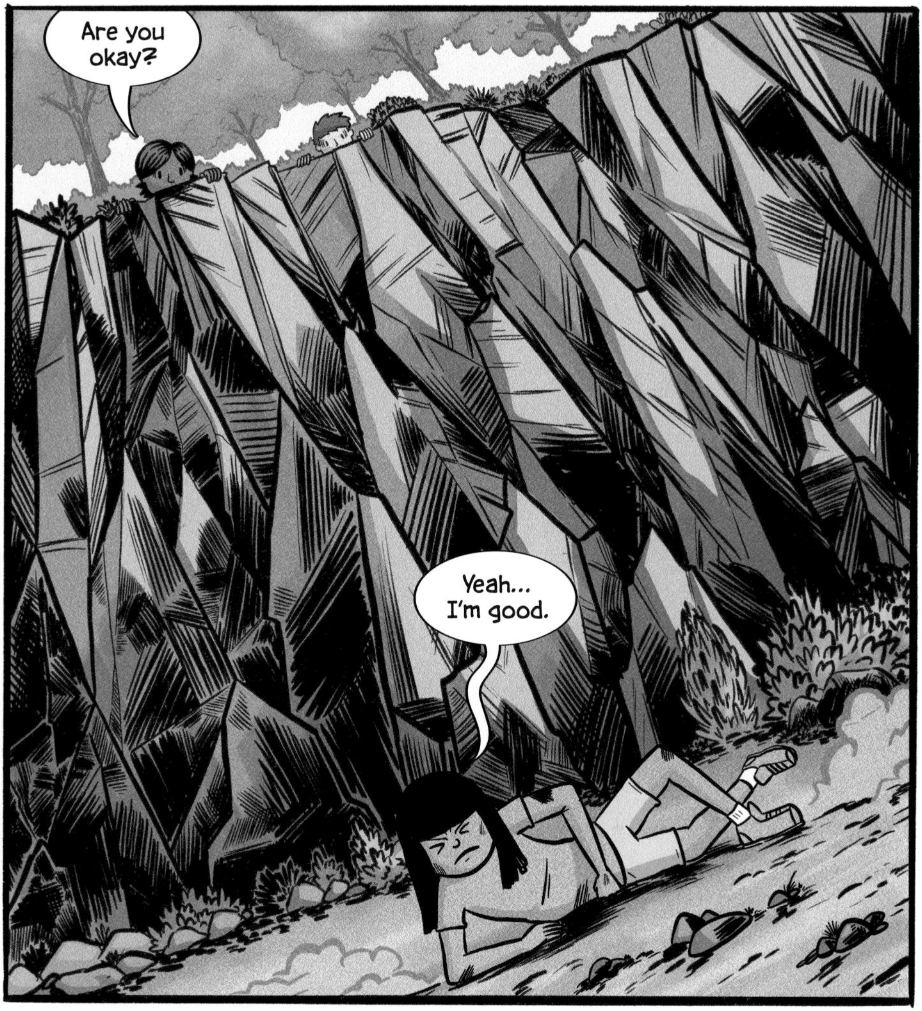
Are you okay?
Yeah... I'm good.

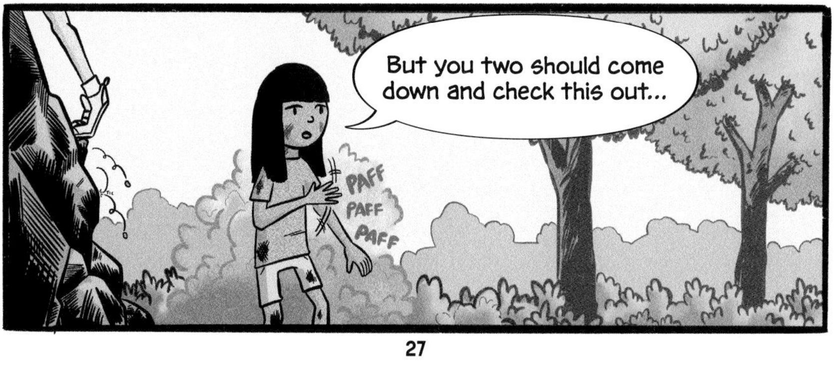
But you two should come down and check this out...
PAFF
PAFF
PAFF

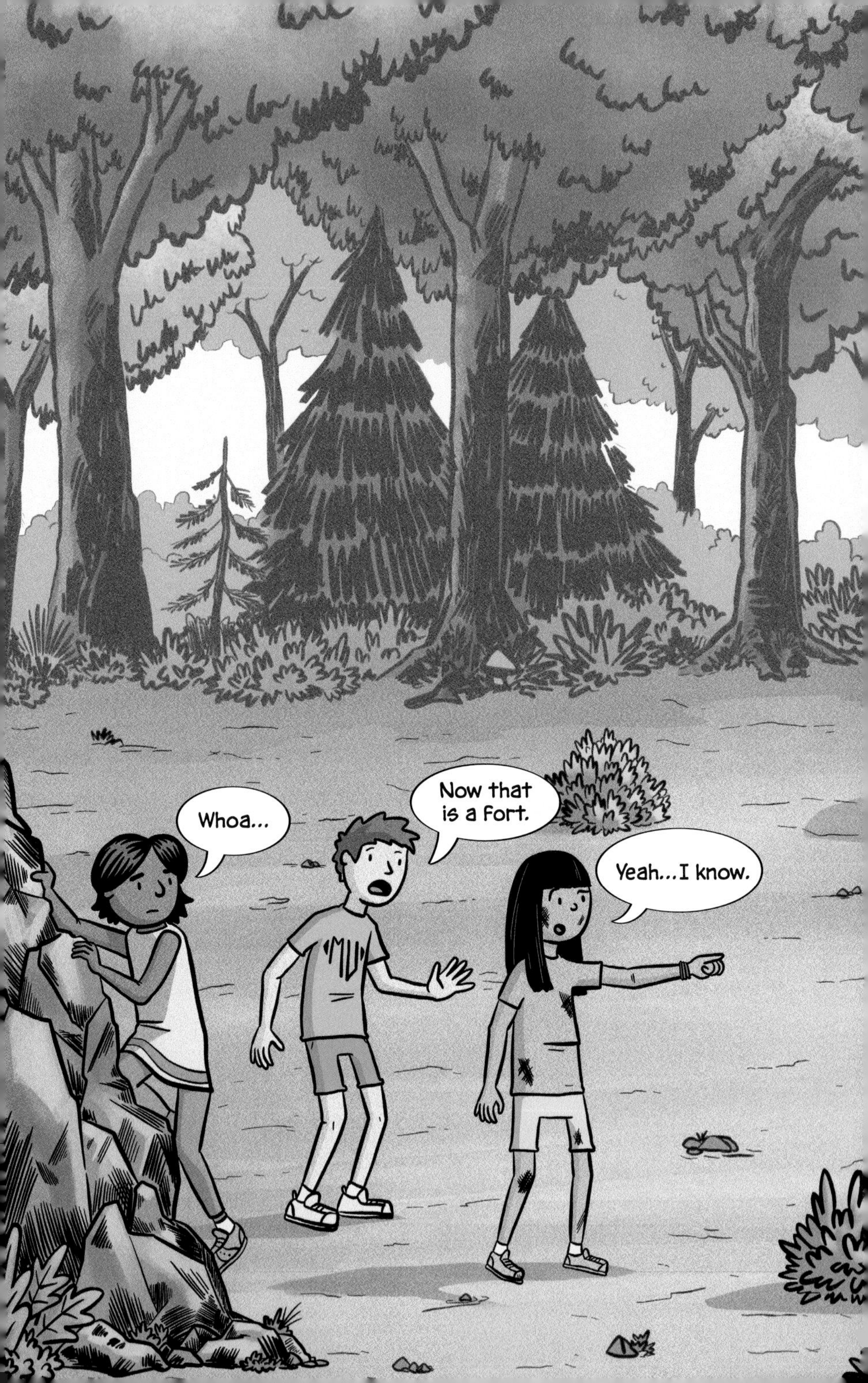
Whoa...
Now that is a fort.
Yeah...I know.

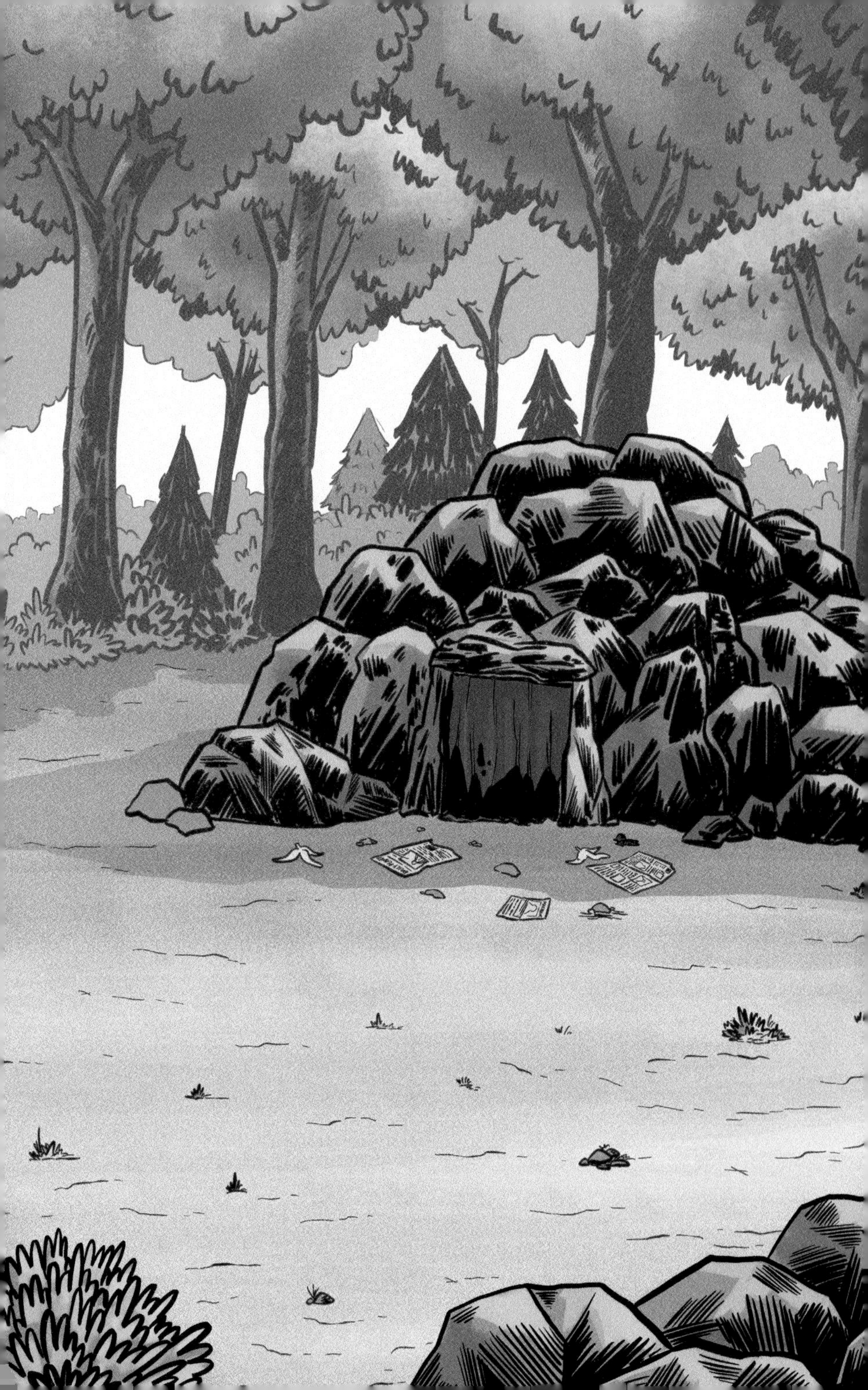

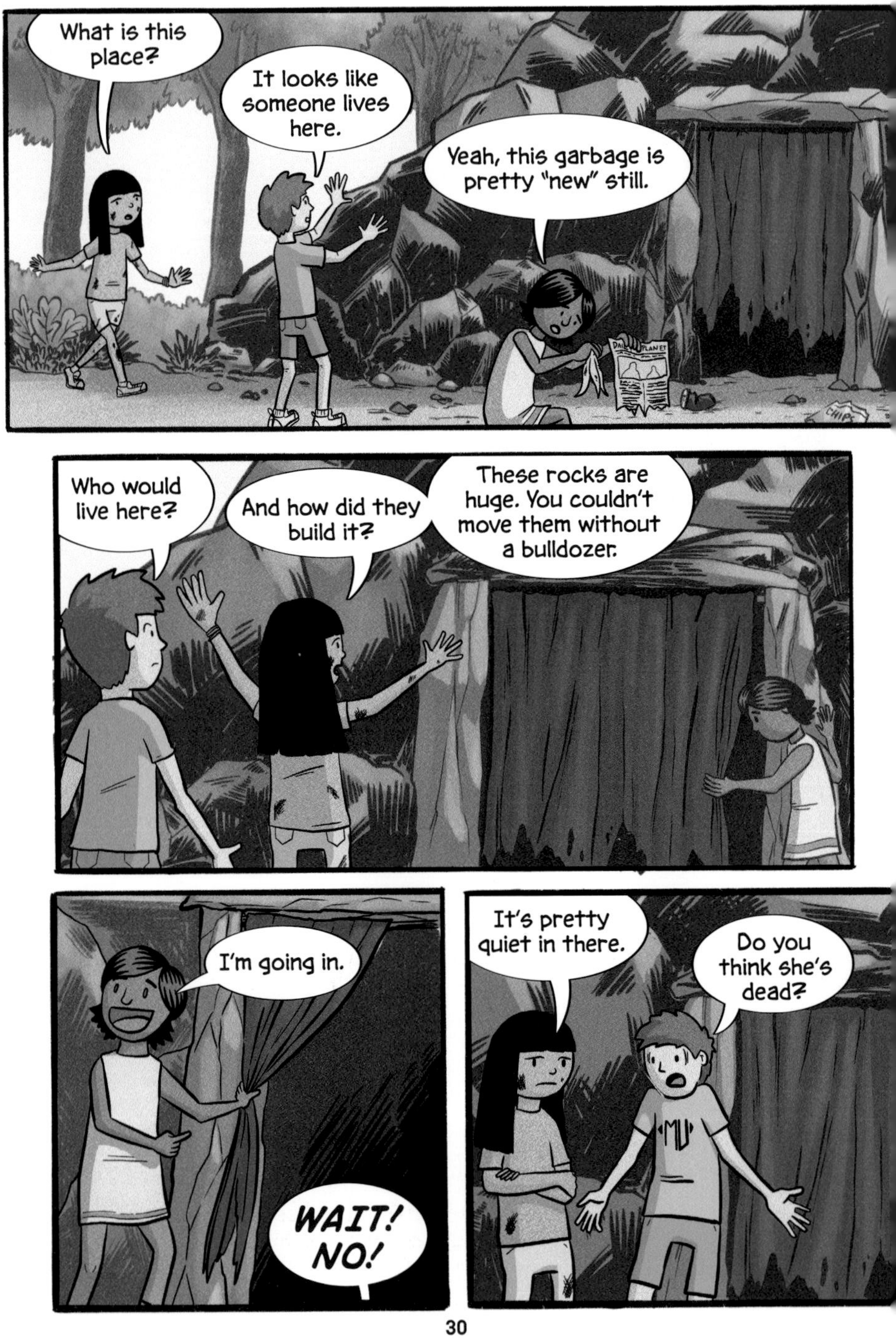
What is this place?
It looks like someone lives here.
Yeah, this garbage is pretty "new" still.
Who would live here?
And how did they build it?
These rocks are huge. You couldn't move them without a bulldozer.
I'm going in.
WAIT! NO!
It's pretty quiet in there.
Do you think she's dead?

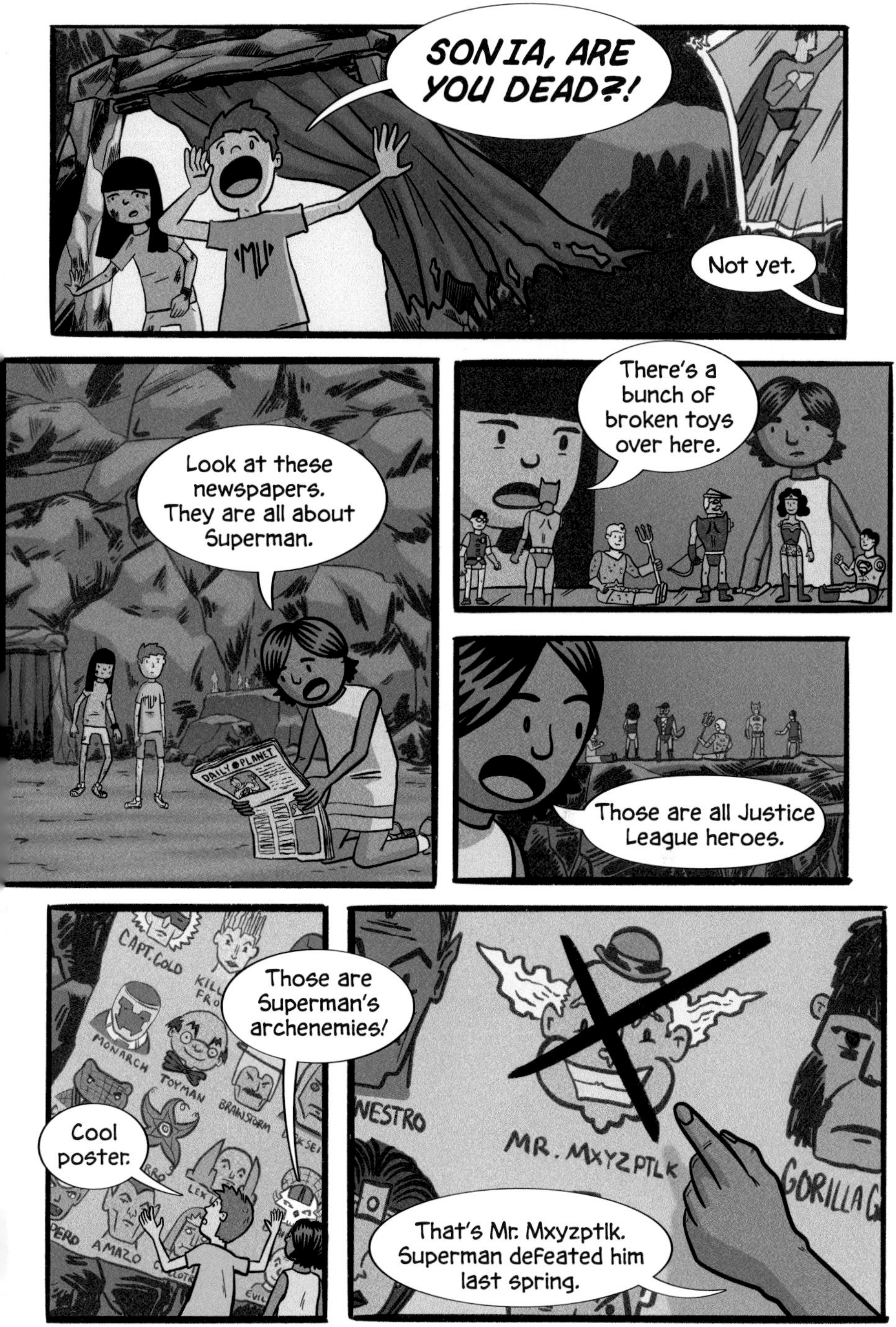
SONIA, ARE YOU DEAD?!
Not yet.
Look at these newspapers. They are all about Superman.
DAILY PLANET
There's a bunch of broken toys over here.
Those are all Justice League heroes.
CAPT. COLD
MONARCH
TOYMAN
BRAINSTORM
AMAZO
Those are Superman's archenemies!
Cool poster.
MR. MXYZPTLK
That's Mr. Mxyzptlk. Superman defeated him last spring.

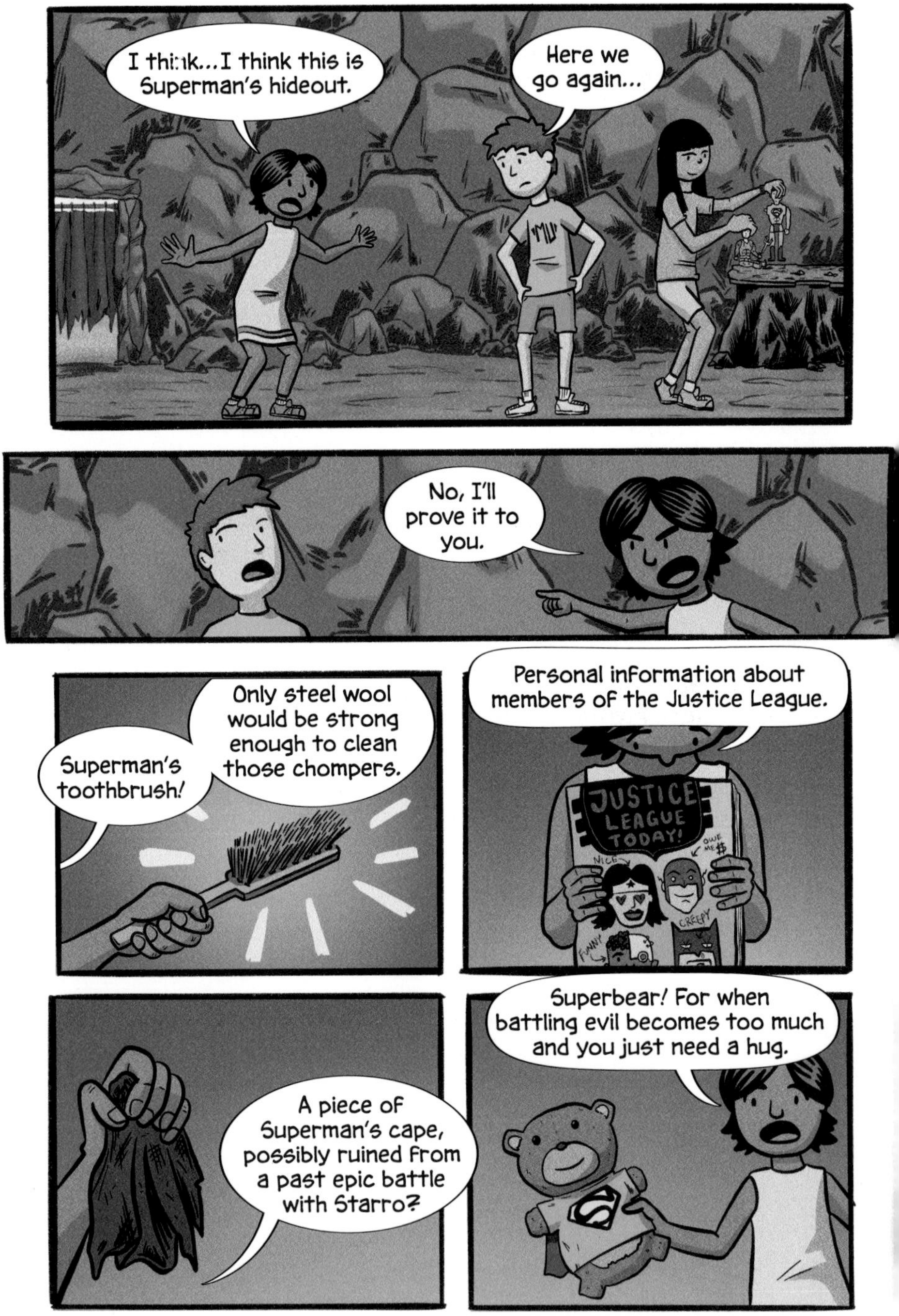
I think...I think this is Superman's hideout.
Here we go again...
No, I'll prove it to you.
Superman's toothbrush!
Only steel wool would be strong enough to clean those chompers.
Personal information about members of the Justice League.
JUSTICE LEAGUE TODAY!
NICE
CREEPY
FUNNY
A piece of Superman's cape, possibly ruined from a past epic battle with Starro?
Superbear! For when battling evil becomes too much and you just need a hug.

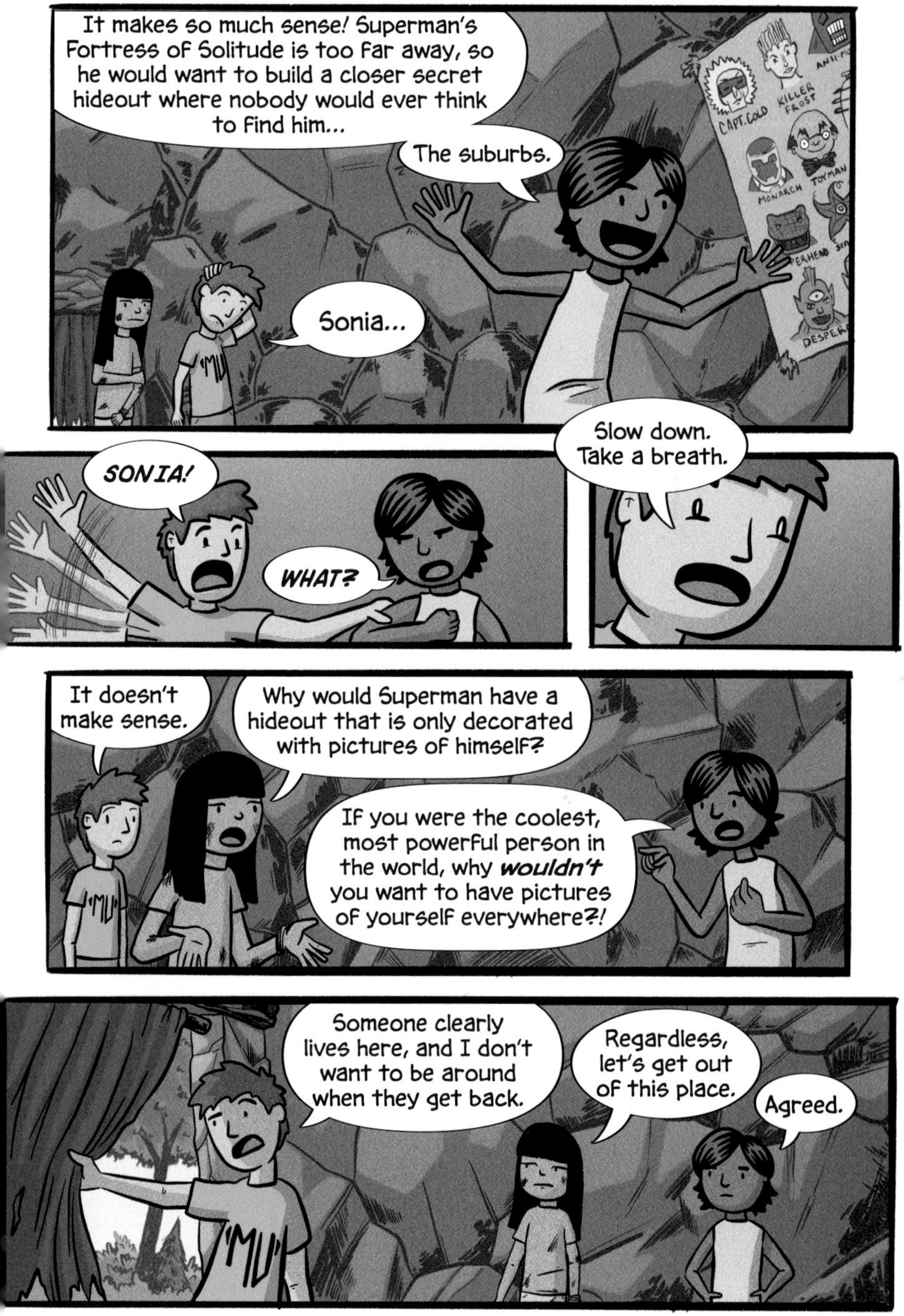
It makes so much sense! Superman's Fortress of Solitude is too far away, so he would want to build a closer secret hideout where nobody would ever think to find him...
The suburbs.
CAPT. COLD
KILLER FROST
MONARCH
TOYMAN
Sonia...
SONIA!
WHAT?
Slow down. Take a breath.
It doesn't make sense.
Why would Superman have a hideout that is only decorated with pictures of himself?
If you were the coolest, most powerful person in the world, why *wouldn't* you want to have pictures of yourself everywhere?!
Someone clearly lives here, and I don't want to be around when they get back.
Regardless, let's get out of this place.
Agreed.

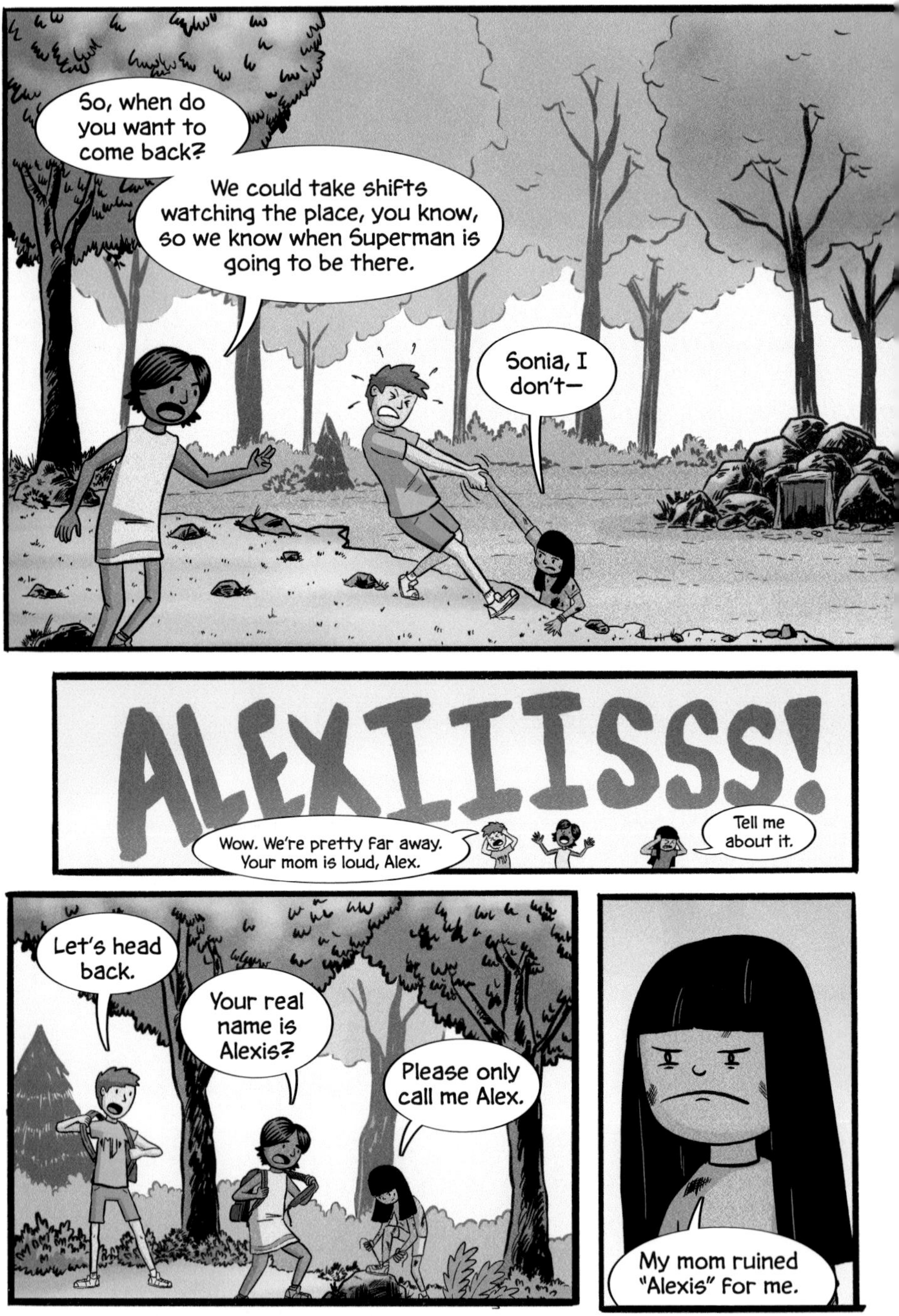
So, when do you want to come back?
We could take shifts watching the place, you know, so we know when Superman is going to be there.
Sonia, I don't—
ALEXIIISSS!
Wow. We're pretty far away. Your mom is loud, Alex.
Tell me about it.
Let's head back.
Your real name is Alexis?
Please only call me Alex.
My mom ruined "Alexis" for me.

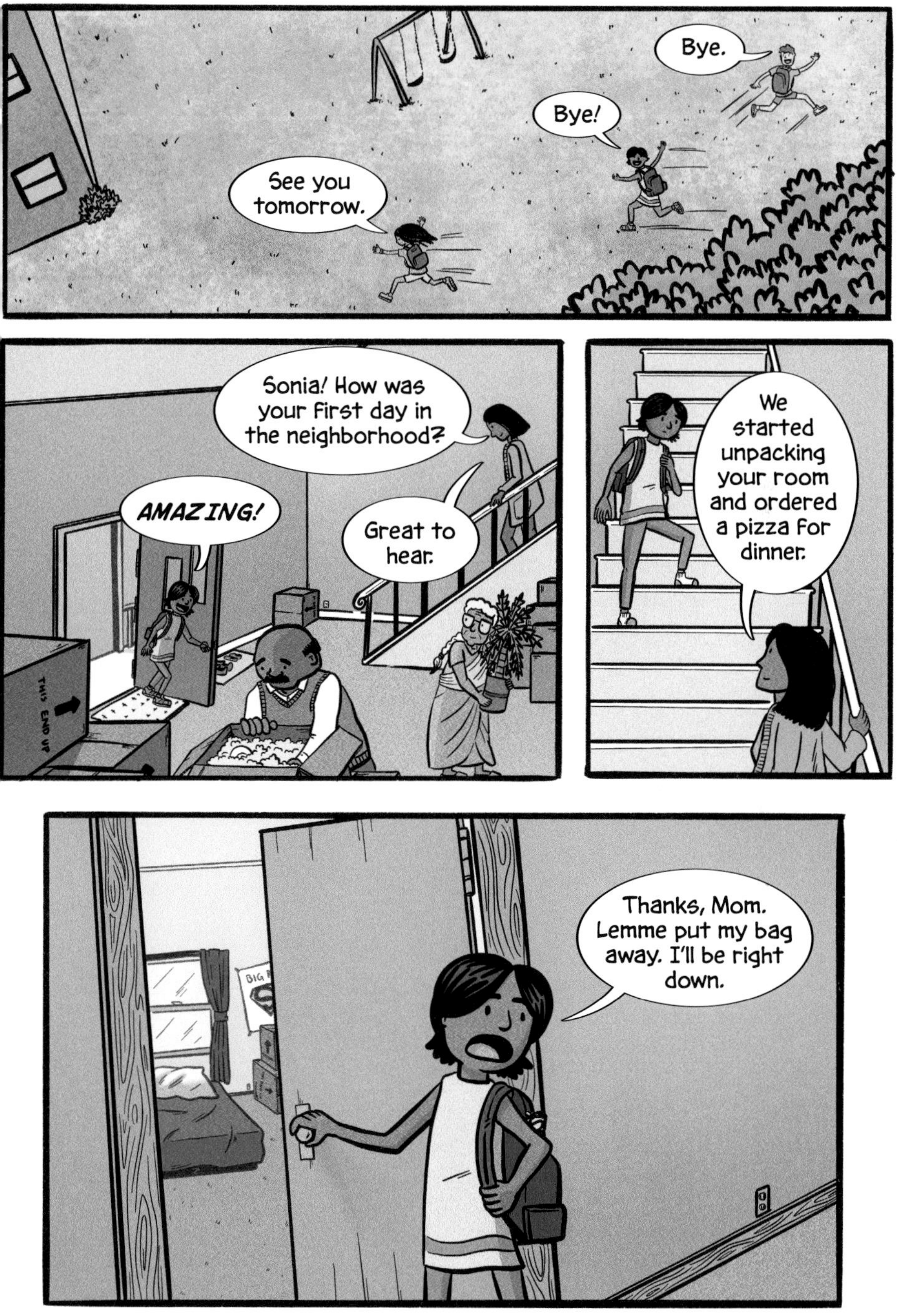
Bye.
Bye!
See you tomorrow.
Sonia! How was your first day in the neighborhood?
AMAZING!
Great to hear.
THIS END UP
We started unpacking your room and ordered a pizza for dinner.
Thanks, Mom. Lemme put my bag away. I'll be right down.

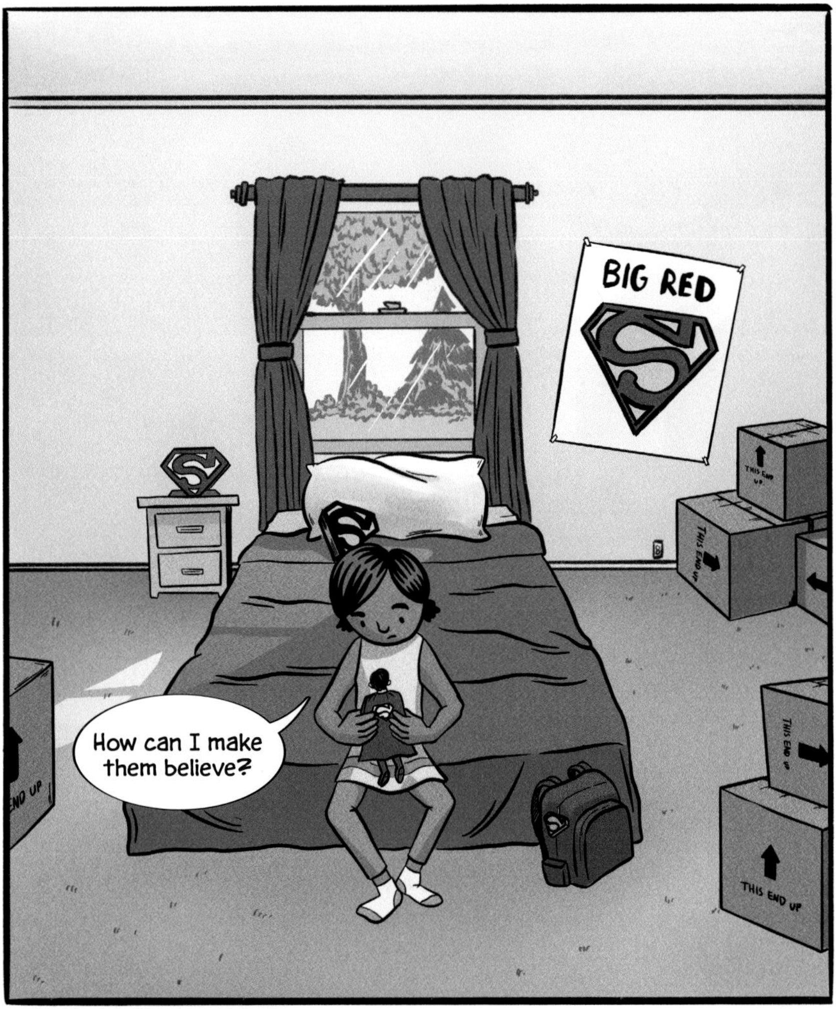
BIG RED
THIS END UP
How can I make them believe?

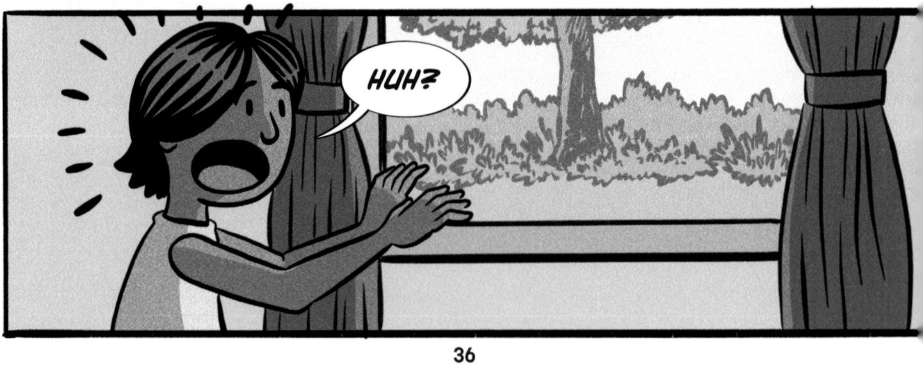
HUH?

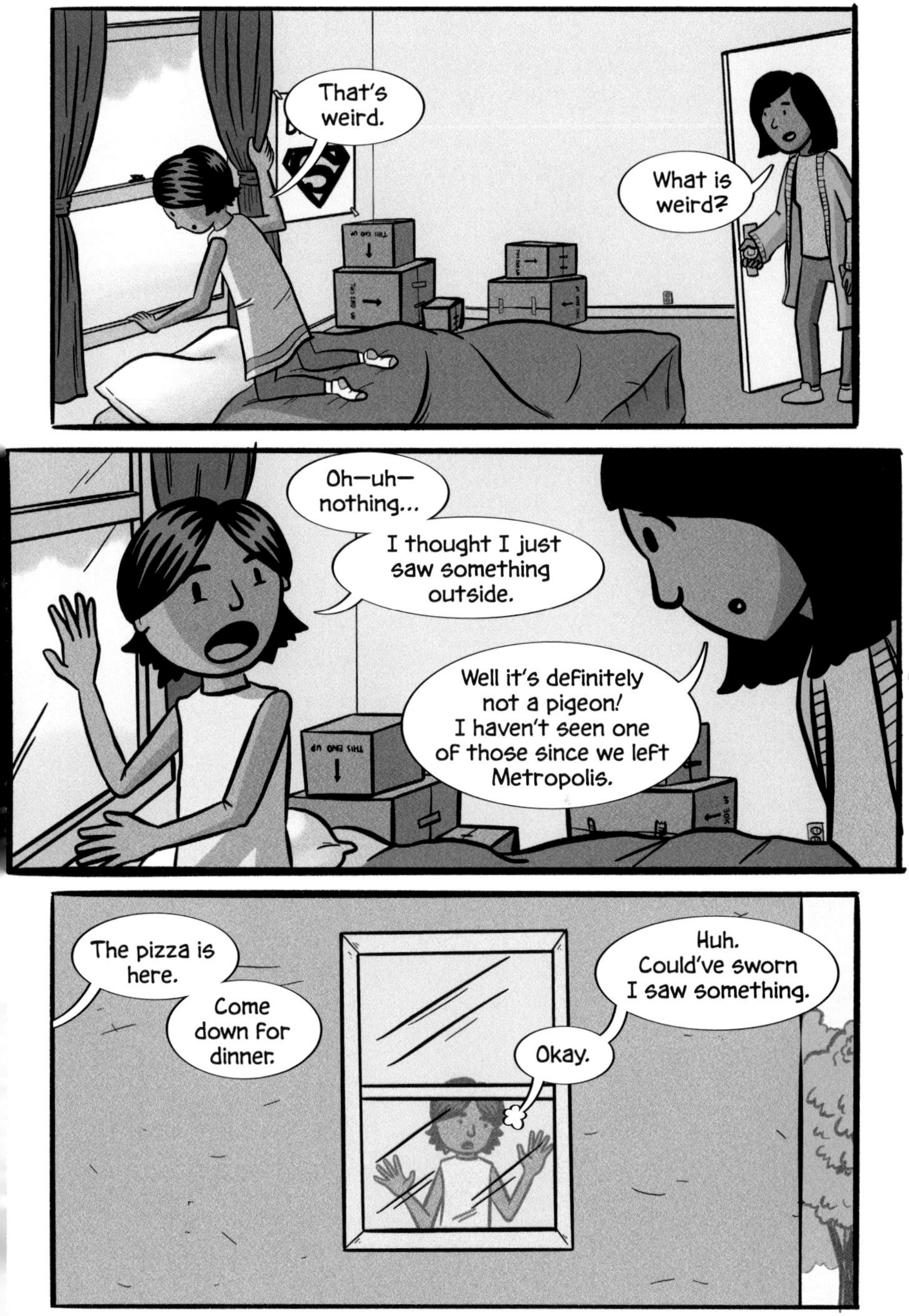
That's weird.
What is weird?
Oh—uh—nothing...
I thought I just saw something outside.
Well it's definitely not a pigeon! I haven't seen one of those since we left Metropolis.
The pizza is here.
Come down for dinner.
Huh. Could've sworn I saw something.
Okay.

CHAPTER THREE

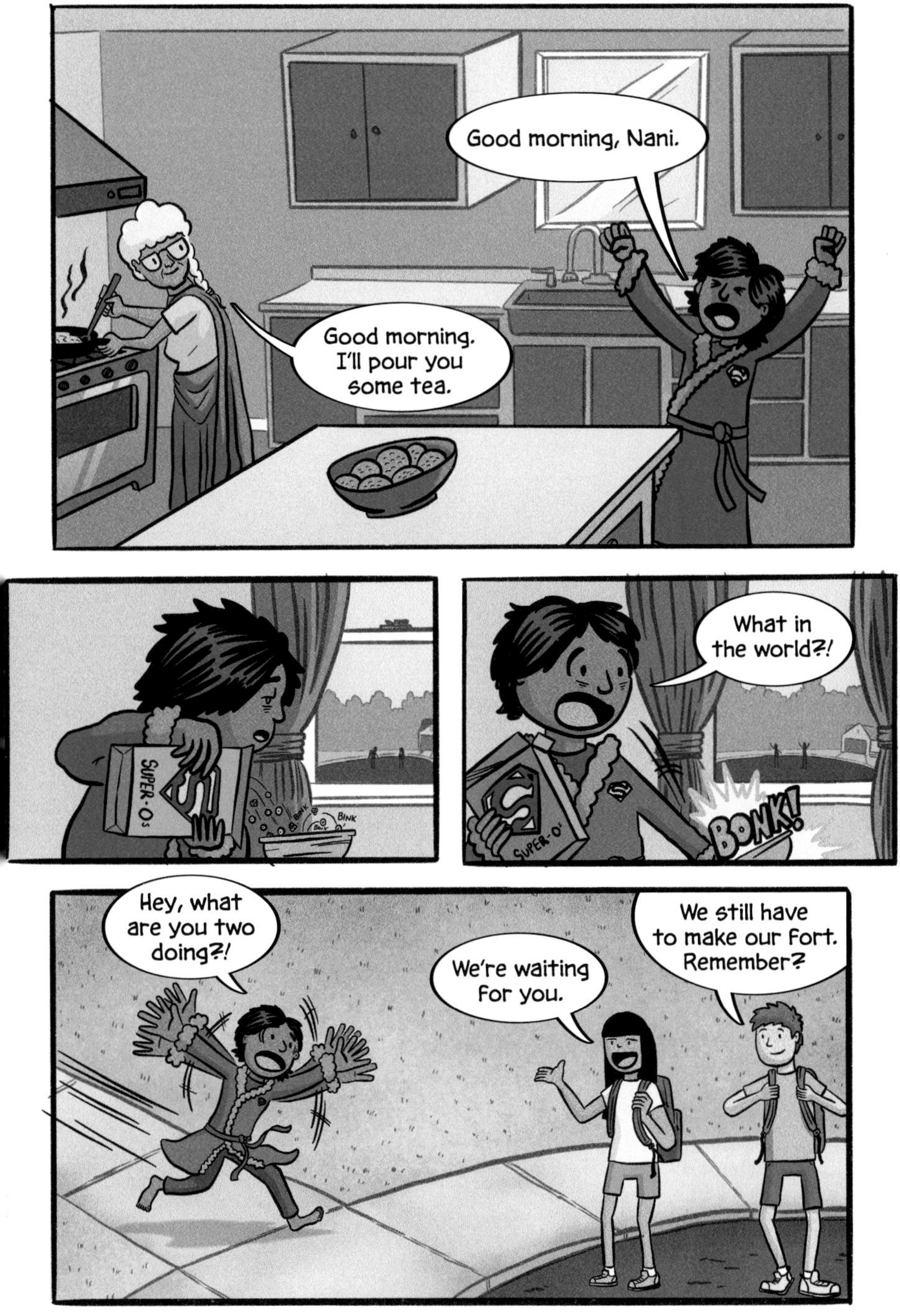
Good morning, Nani.
Good morning. I'll pour you some tea.
SUPER-Os
BINK
BINK
BINK
What in the world?!
SUPER-O's
BONK!
Hey, what are you two doing?!
We're waiting for you.
We still have to make our fort. Remember?

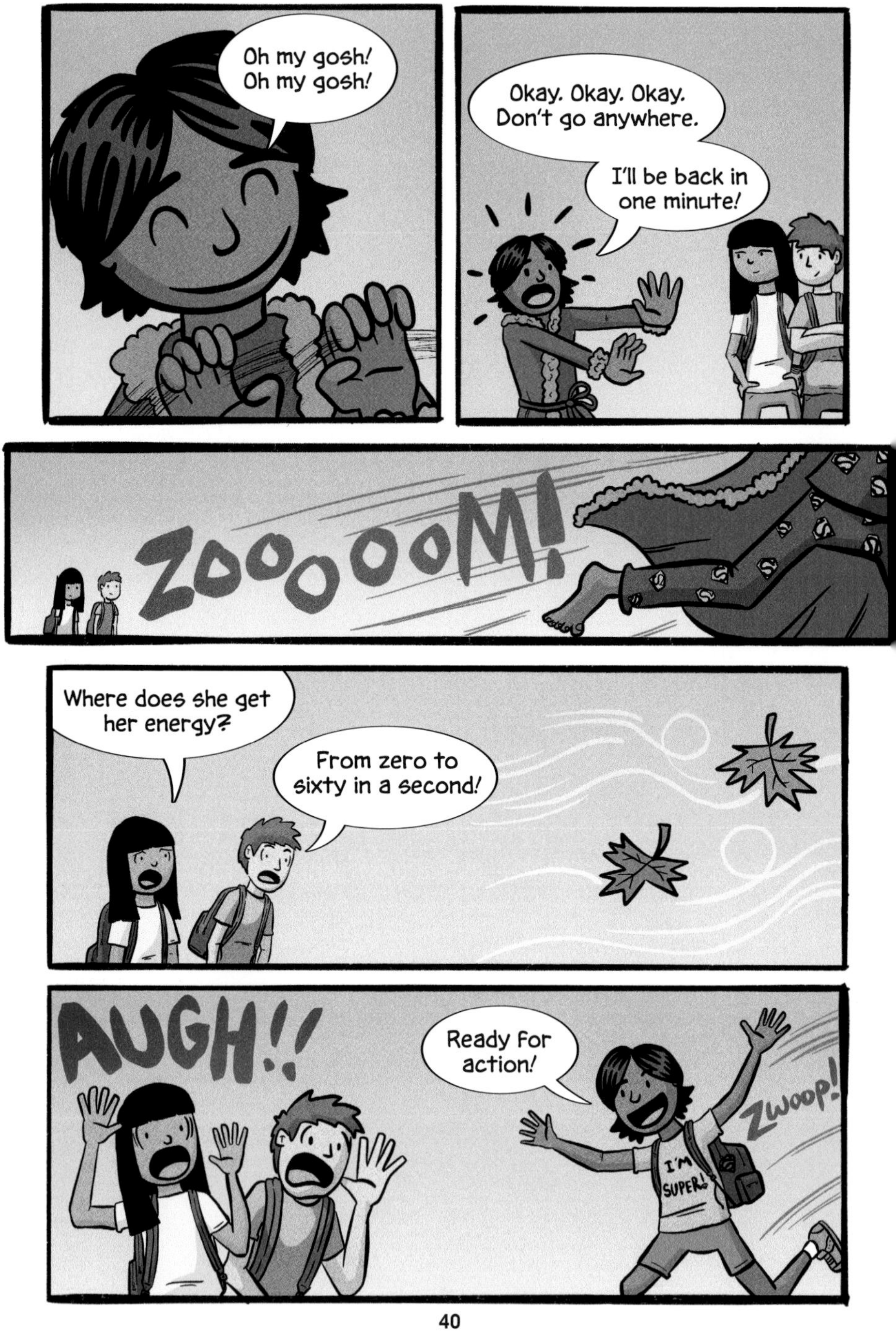
Oh my gosh! Oh my gosh!
Okay. Okay. Okay. Don't go anywhere.
I'll be back in one minute!
ZOOOOOM!
Where does she get her energy?
From zero to sixty in a second!
AUGH!!
Ready for action!
ZWOOP!
I'M SUPER!

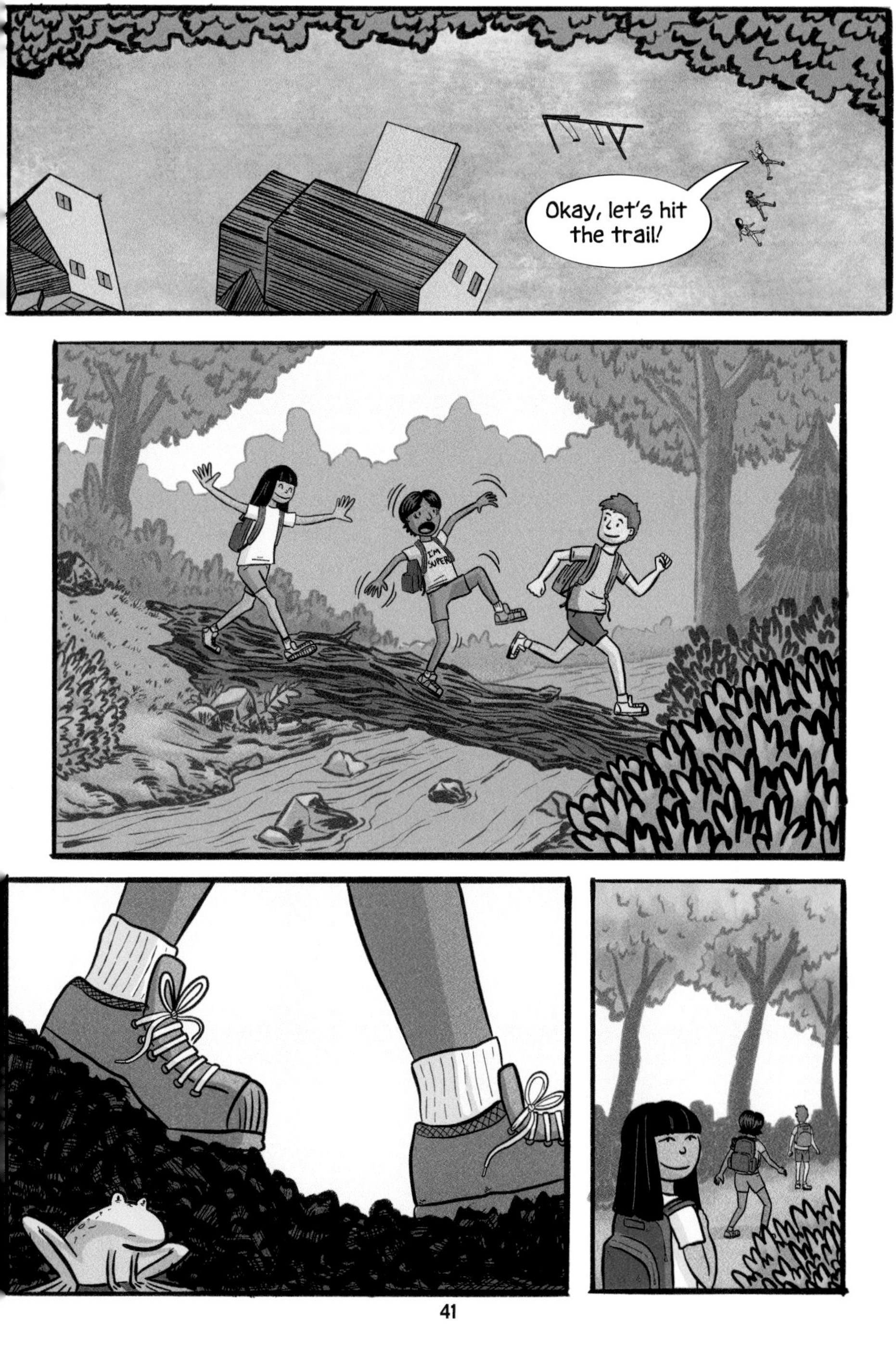
Okay, let's hit the trail!
I'M SUPER

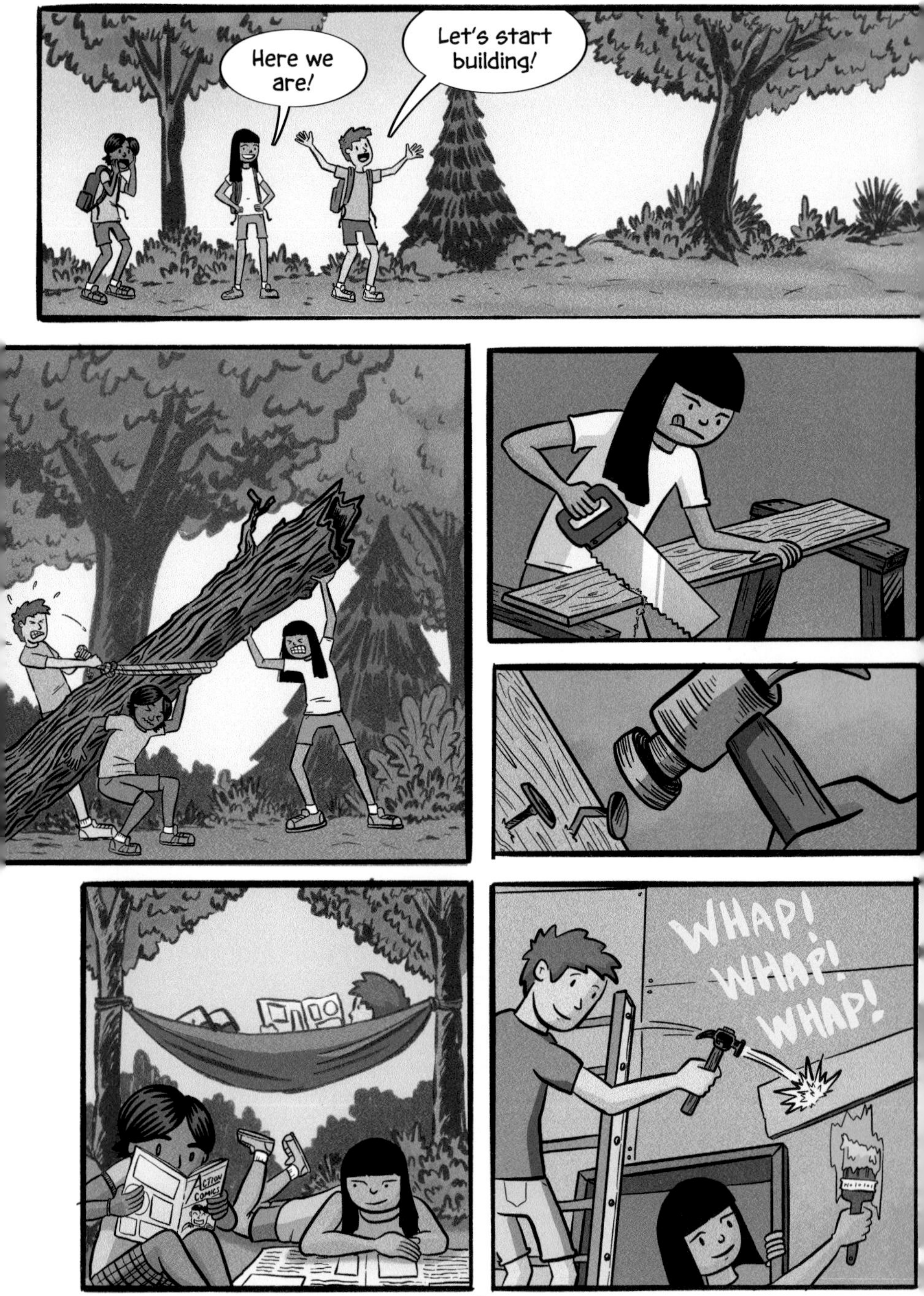
Here we are!
Let's start building!
WHAP!
WHAP!
WHAP!

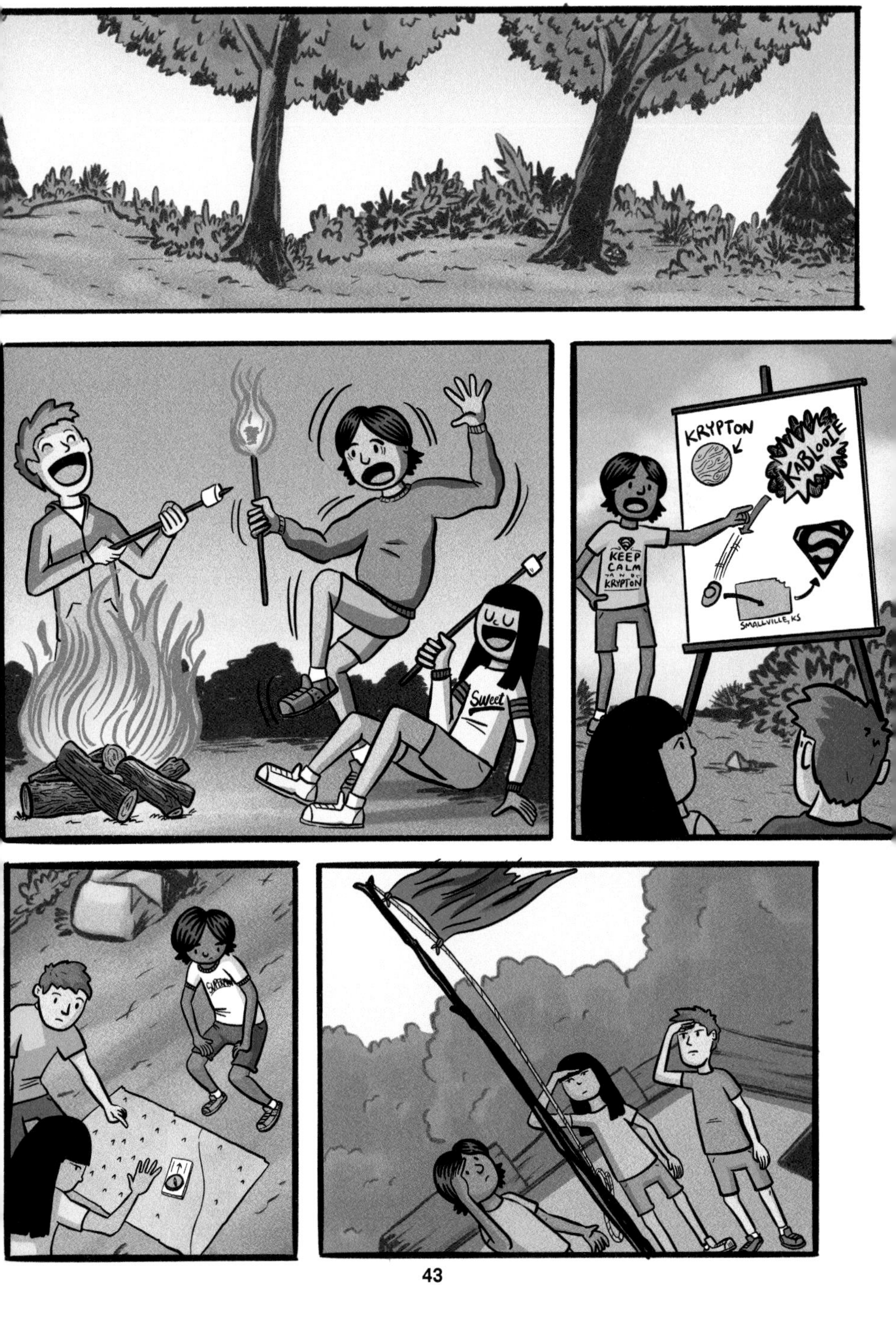
Sweet
KRYPTON
KABLOOIE
KEEP CALM AND KRYPTON
SMALLVILLE, KS

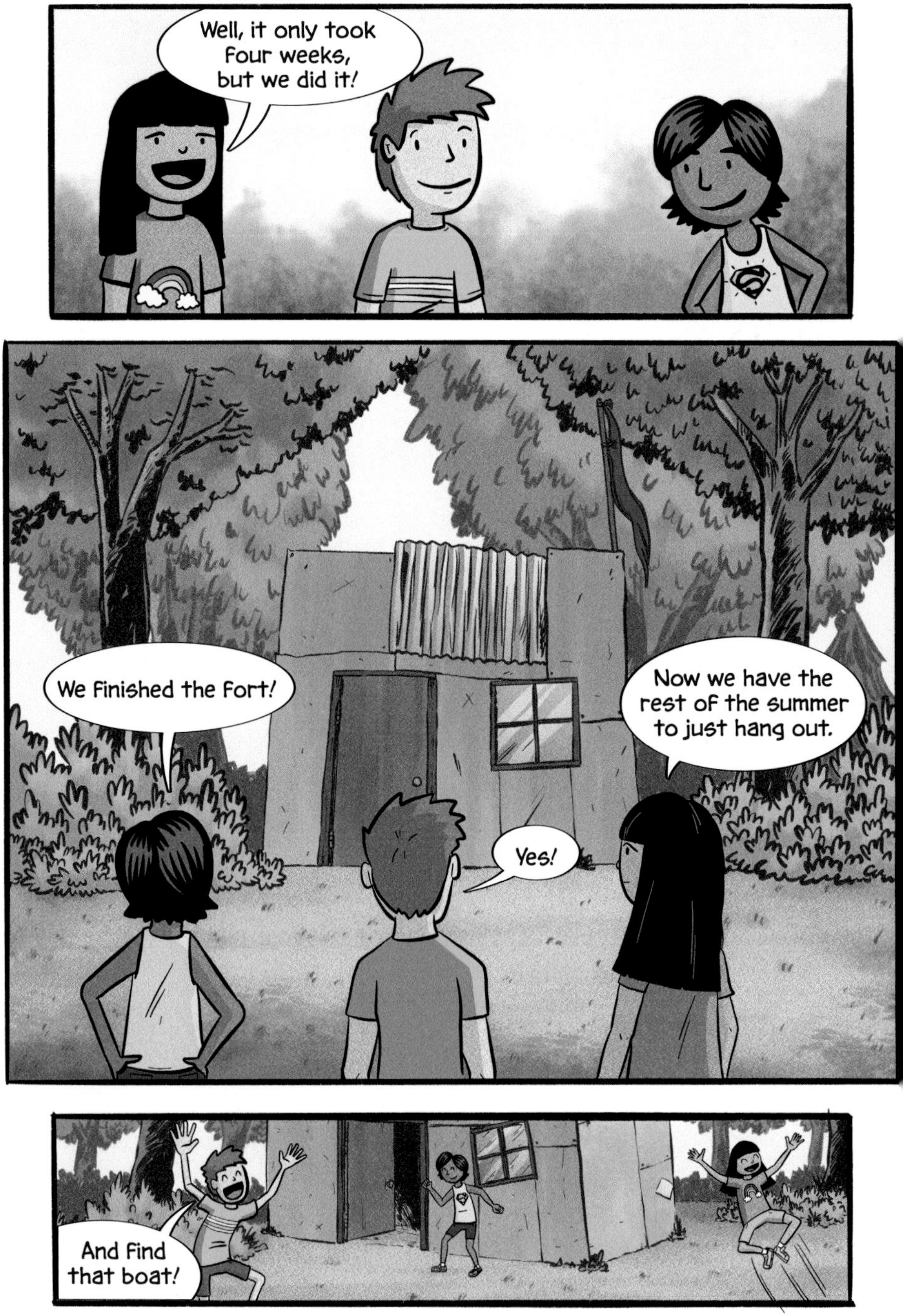
Well, it only took four weeks, but we did it!
We finished the fort!
Now we have the rest of the summer to just hang out.
Yes!
And find that boat!

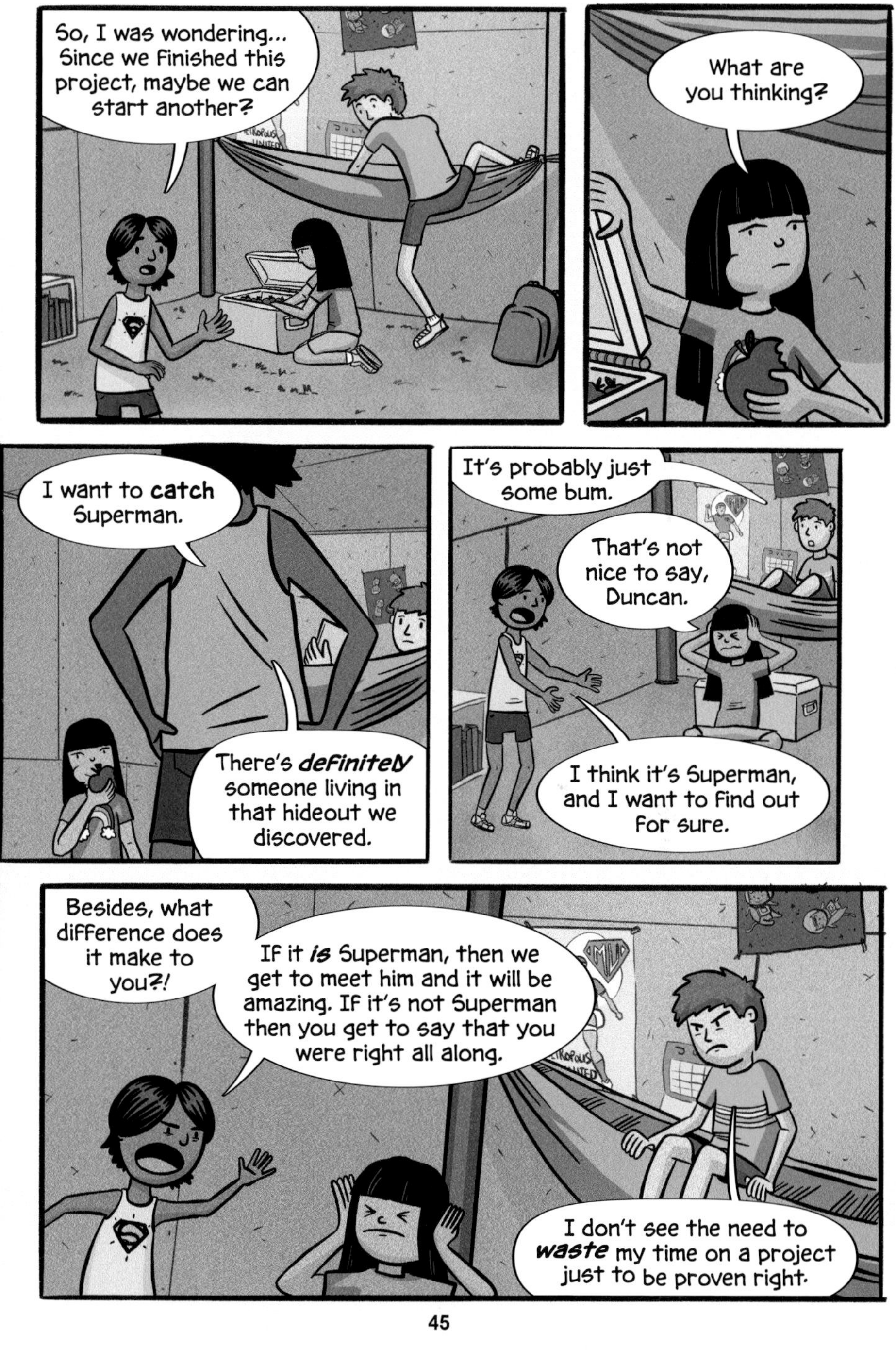
So, I was wondering... Since we finished this project, maybe we can start another?
What are you thinking?
I want to **catch** Superman.
There's ***definitely*** someone living in that hideout we discovered.
It's probably just some bum.
That's not nice to say, Duncan.
I think it's Superman, and I want to find out for sure.
Besides, what difference does it make to you?!
If it ***is*** Superman, then we get to meet him and it will be amazing. If it's not Superman then you get to say that you were right all along.
I don't see the need to ***waste*** my time on a project just to be proven right.

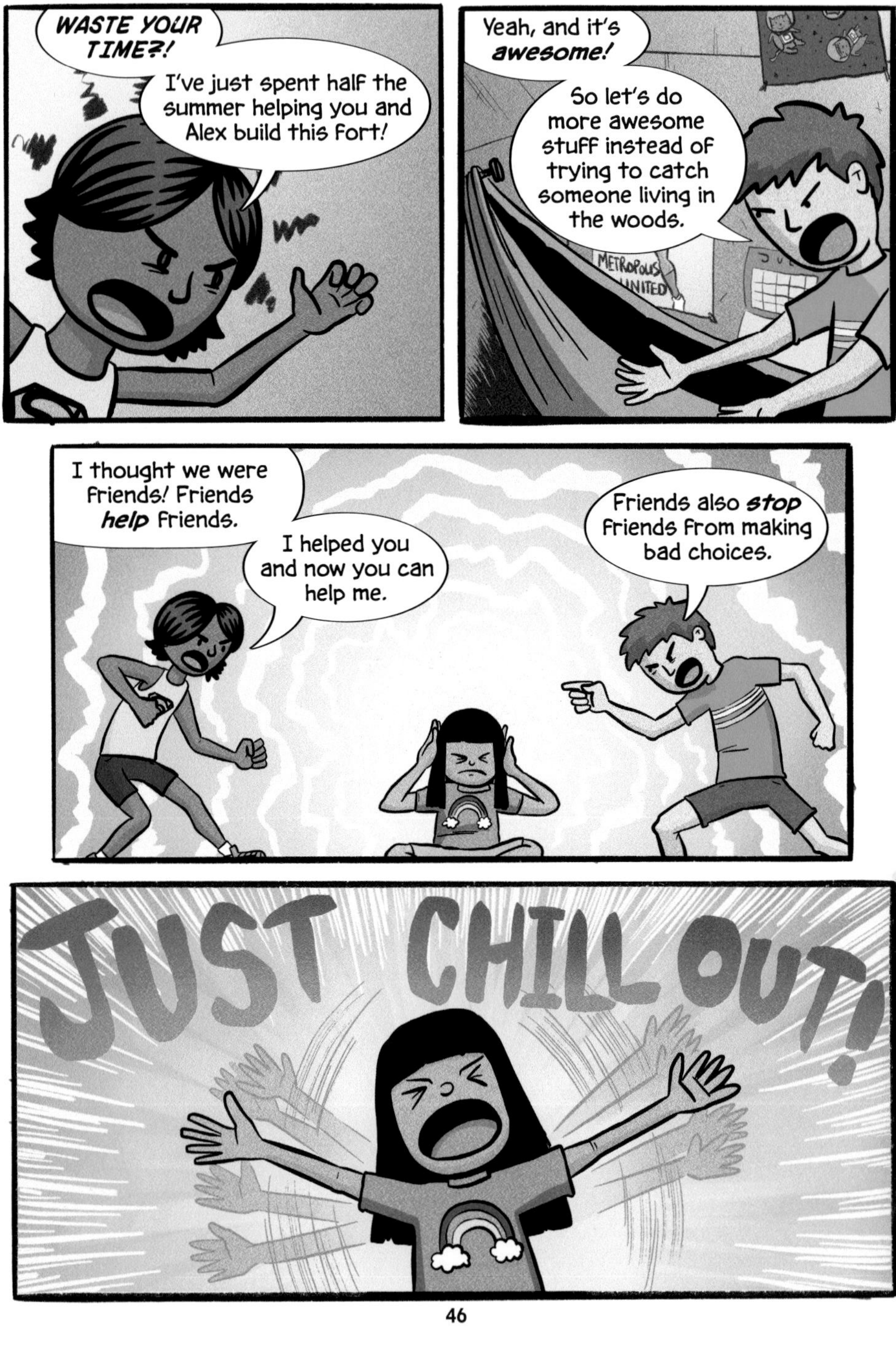
WASTE YOUR TIME?!
I've just spent half the summer helping you and Alex build this fort!
Yeah, and it's *awesome!*
So let's do more awesome stuff instead of trying to catch someone living in the woods.
METROPOLIS UNITED
I thought we were friends! Friends *help* friends.
I helped you and now you can help me.
Friends also *stop* friends from making bad choices.
JUST CHILL OUT!

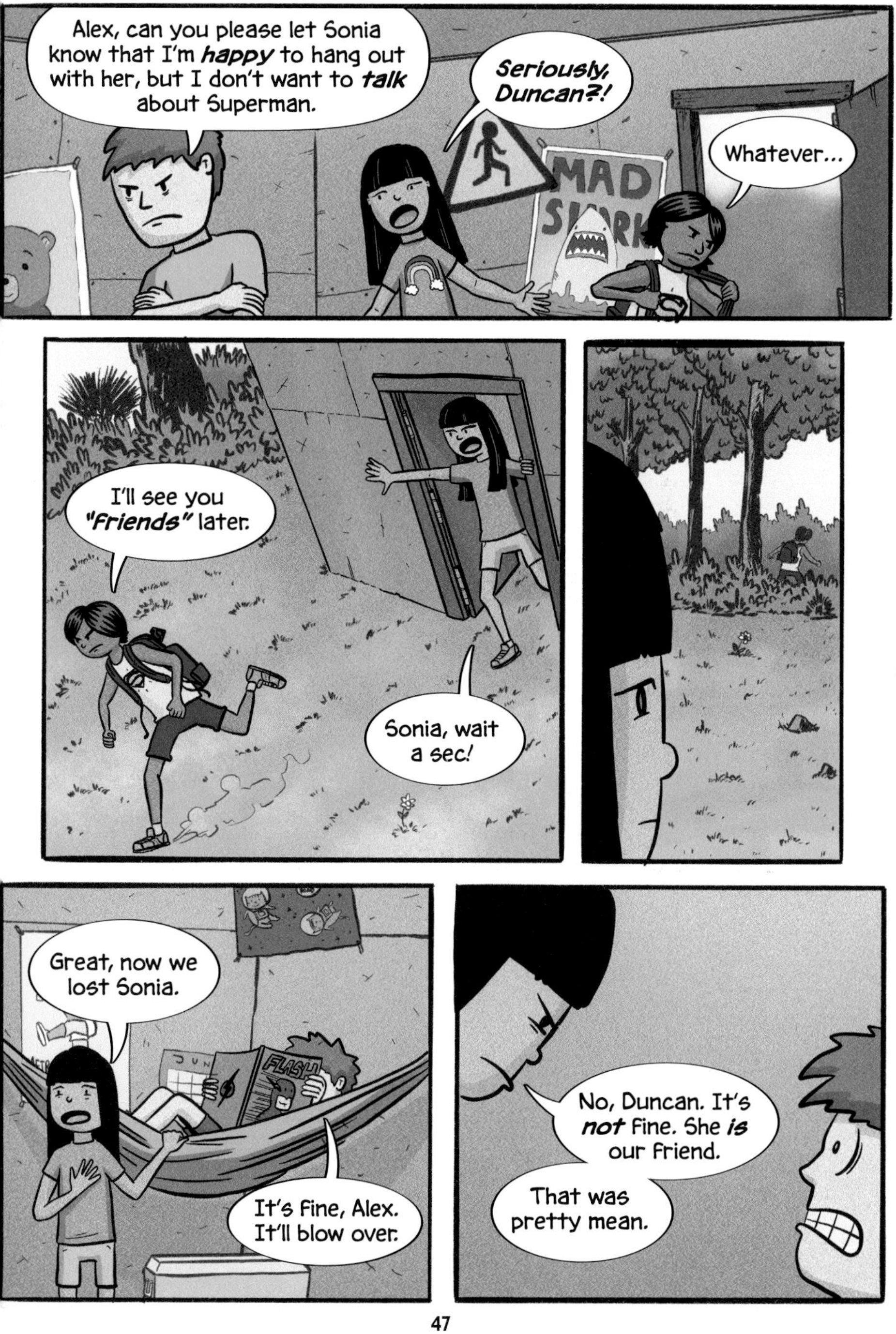
Alex, can you please let Sonia know that I'm *happy* to hang out with her, but I don't want to *talk* about Superman.
Seriously, Duncan?!
MAD
Whatever...
I'll see you *"friends"* later.
Sonia, wait a sec!
Great, now we lost Sonia.
FLASH
It's fine, Alex. It'll blow over.
No, Duncan. It's *not* fine. She *is* our friend.
That was pretty mean.

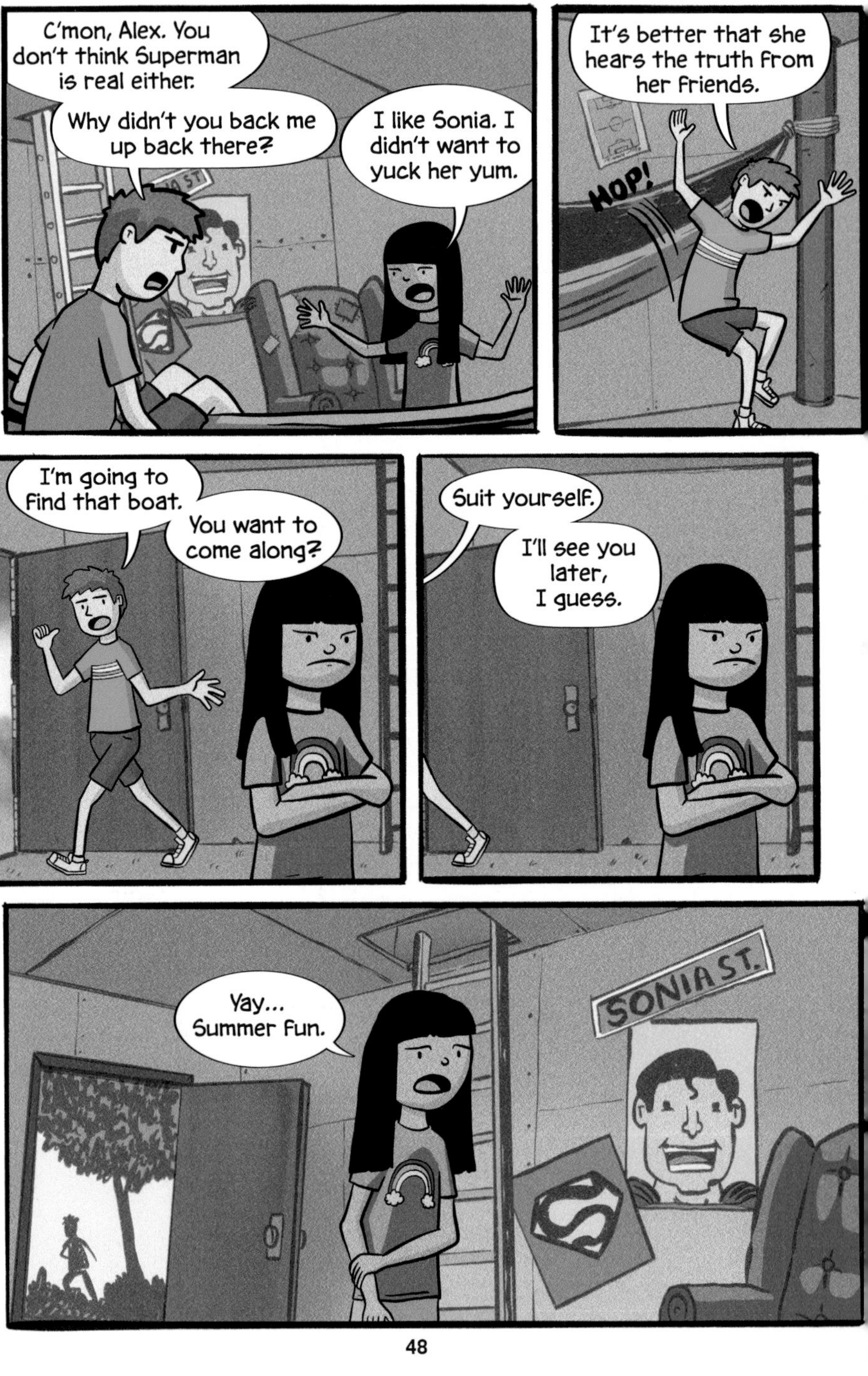
C'mon, Alex. You don't think Superman is real either.
Why didn't you back me up back there?
I like Sonia. I didn't want to yuck her yum.
It's better that she hears the truth from her friends.
HOP!
I'm going to find that boat.
You want to come along?
Suit yourself.
I'll see you later, I guess.
Yay... Summer fun.
SONIA ST.

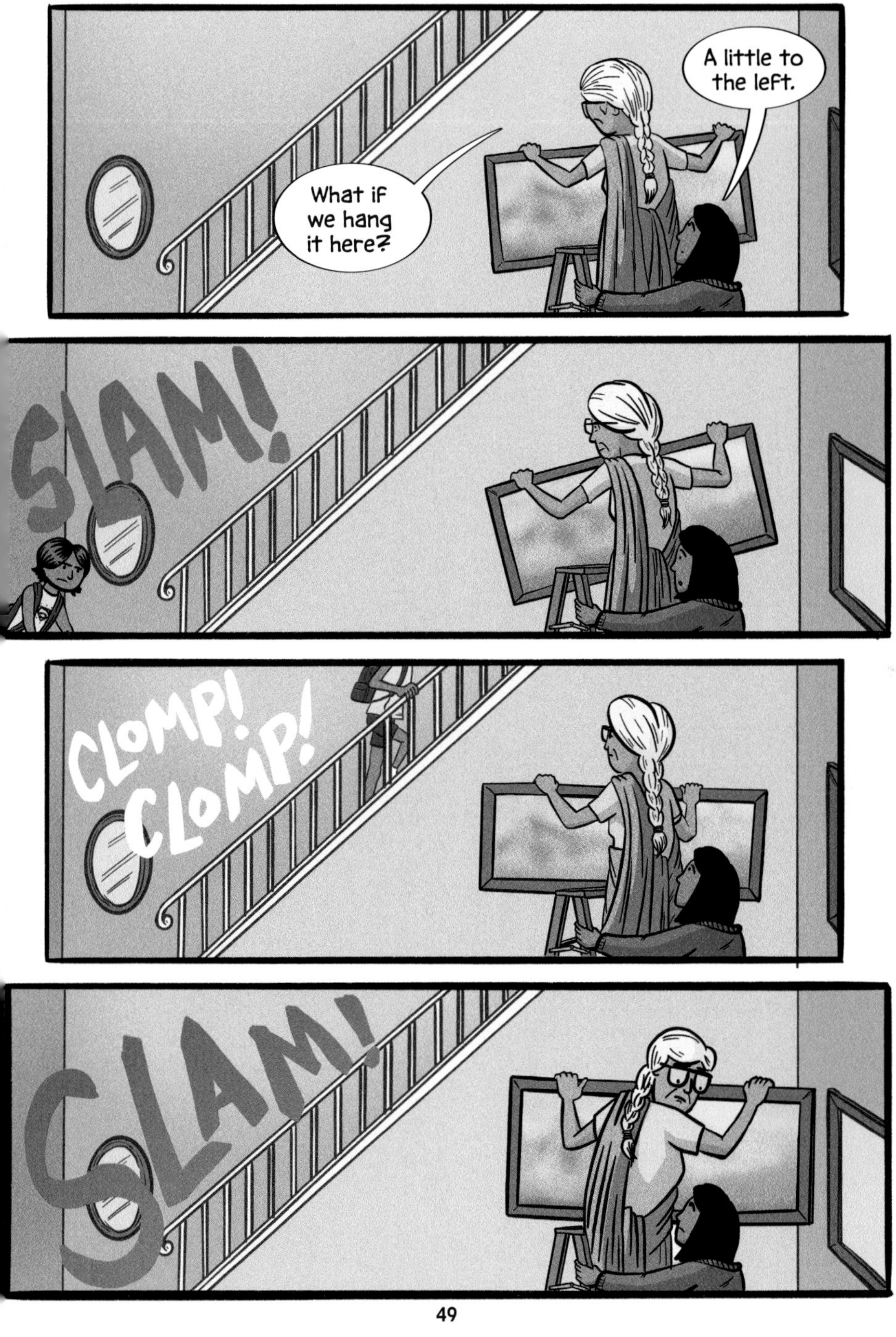
What if we hang it here?
A little to the left.
SLAM!
CLOMP! CLOMP!
SLAM!

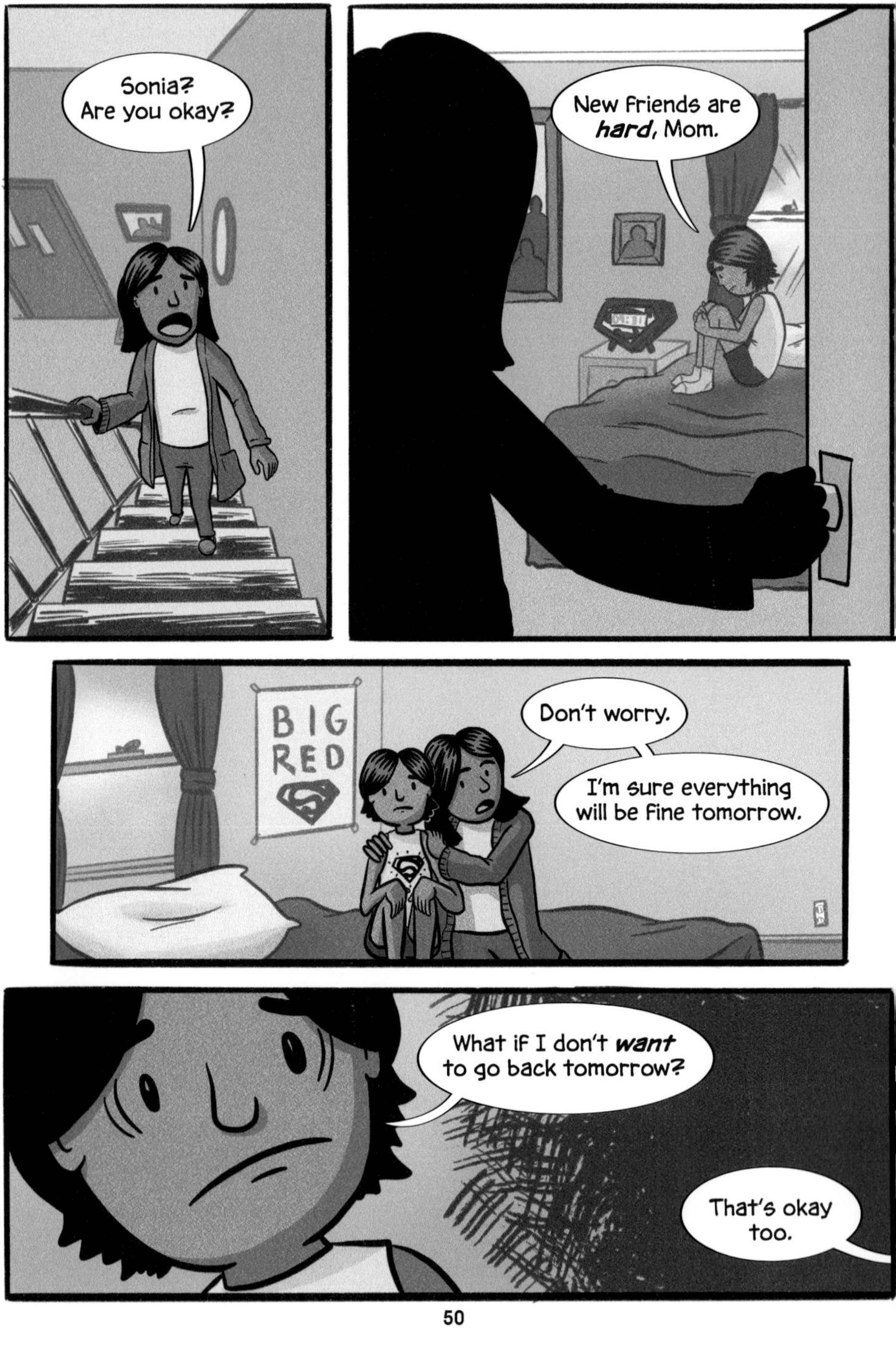
Sonia? Are you okay?
New friends are *hard*, Mom.
BIG RED
Don't worry.
I'm sure everything will be fine tomorrow.
What if I don't *want* to go back tomorrow?
That's okay too.

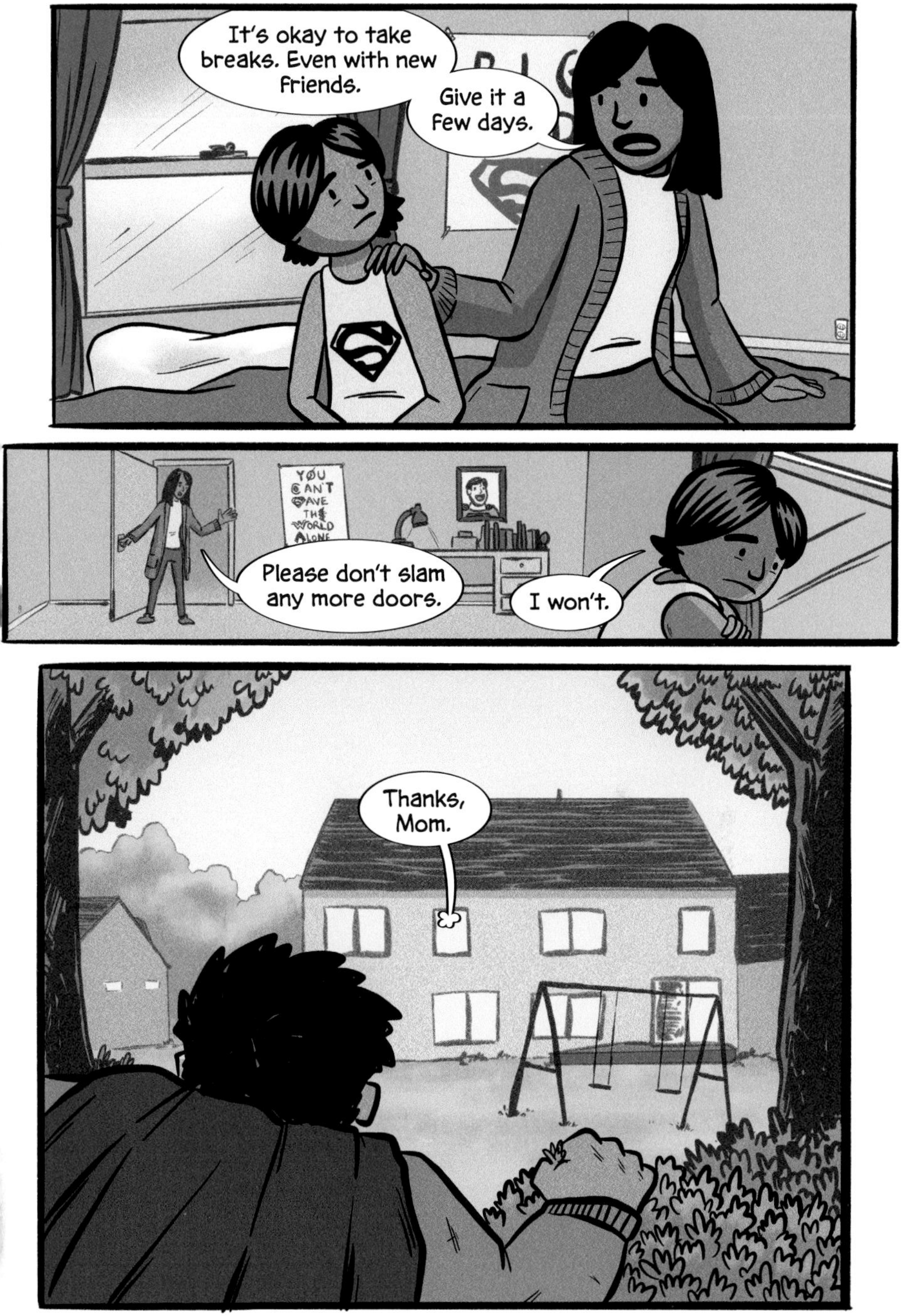
It's okay to take breaks. Even with new friends.
Give it a few days.
Please don't slam any more doors.
I won't.
Thanks, Mom.

CHAPTER FOUR

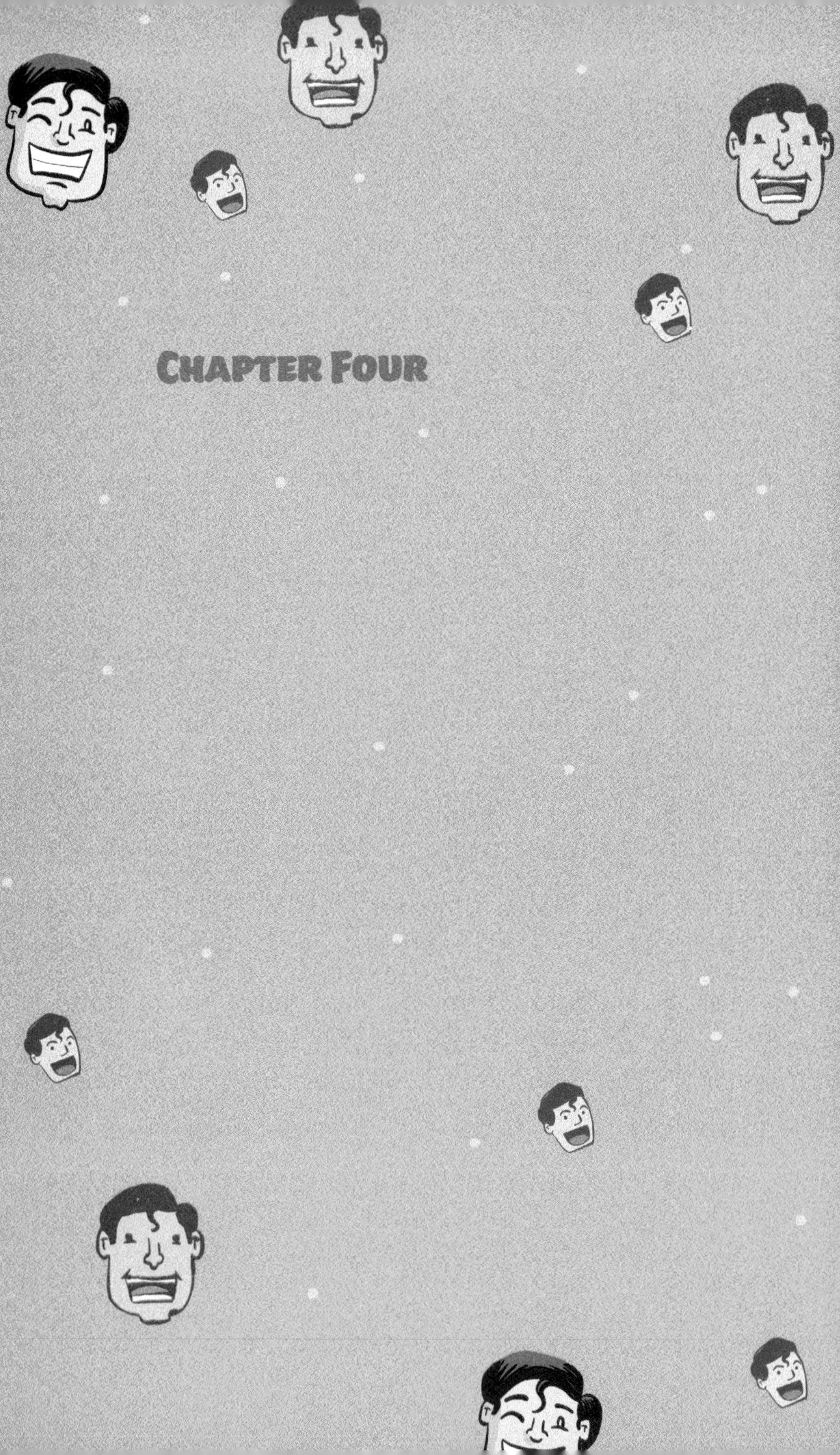

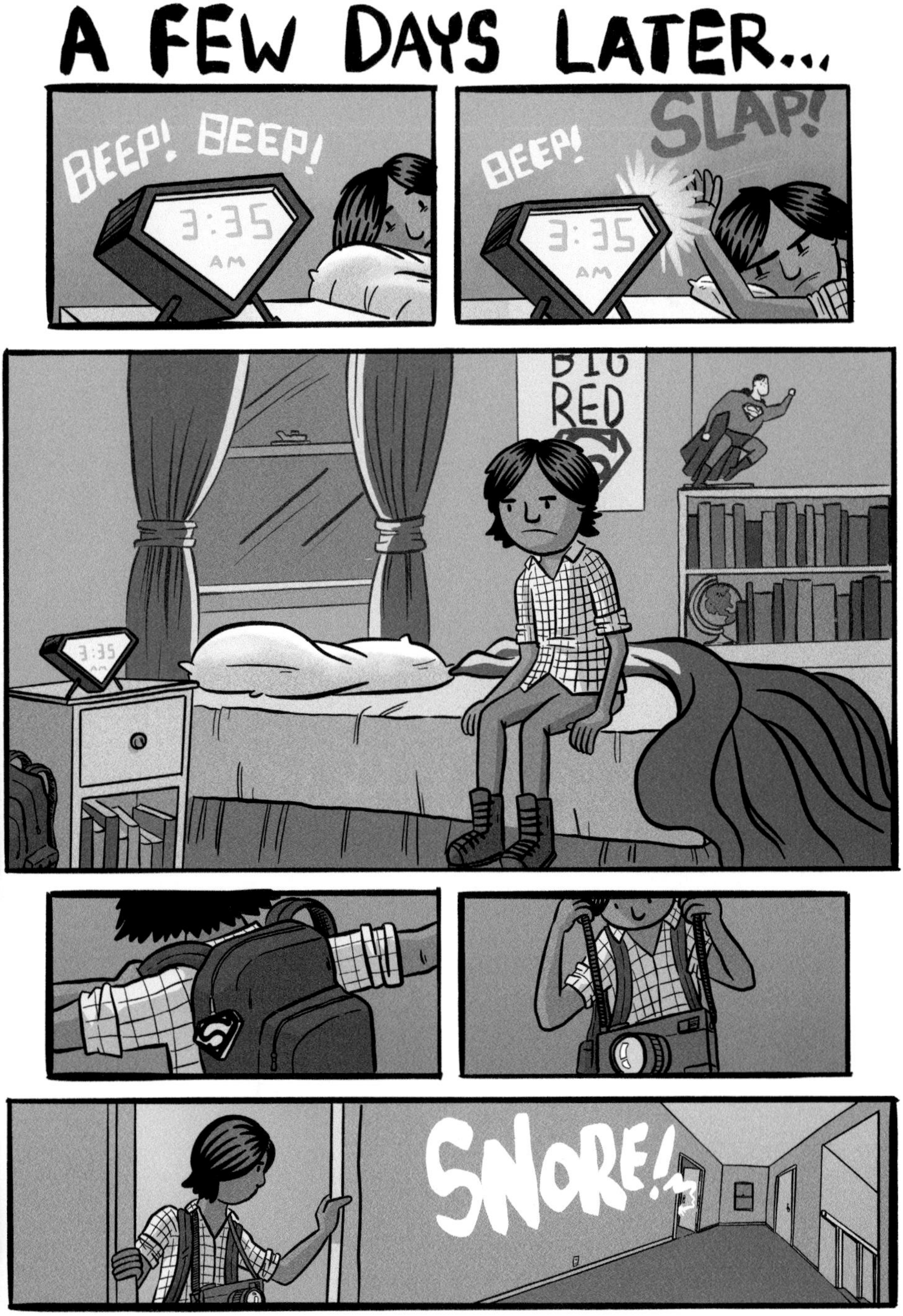
A FEW DAYS LATER...
BEEP! BEEP!
3:35 AM
BEEP!
SLAP!
3:35 AM
BIG RED
3:35 AM
SNORE!

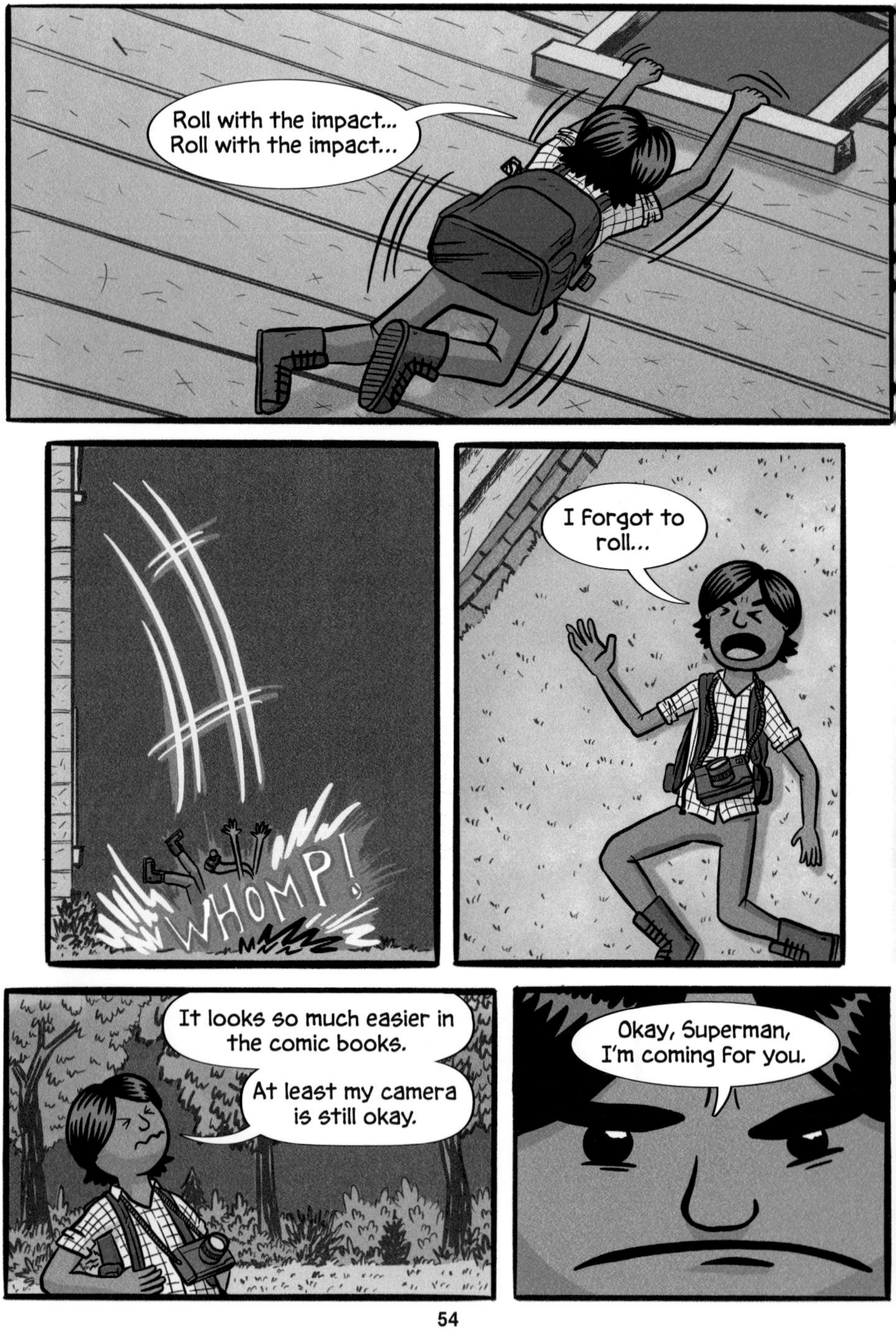
Roll with the impact...
Roll with the impact...
WHOMP!
I forgot to roll...
It looks so much easier in the comic books.
At least my camera is still okay.
Okay, Superman, I'm coming for you.

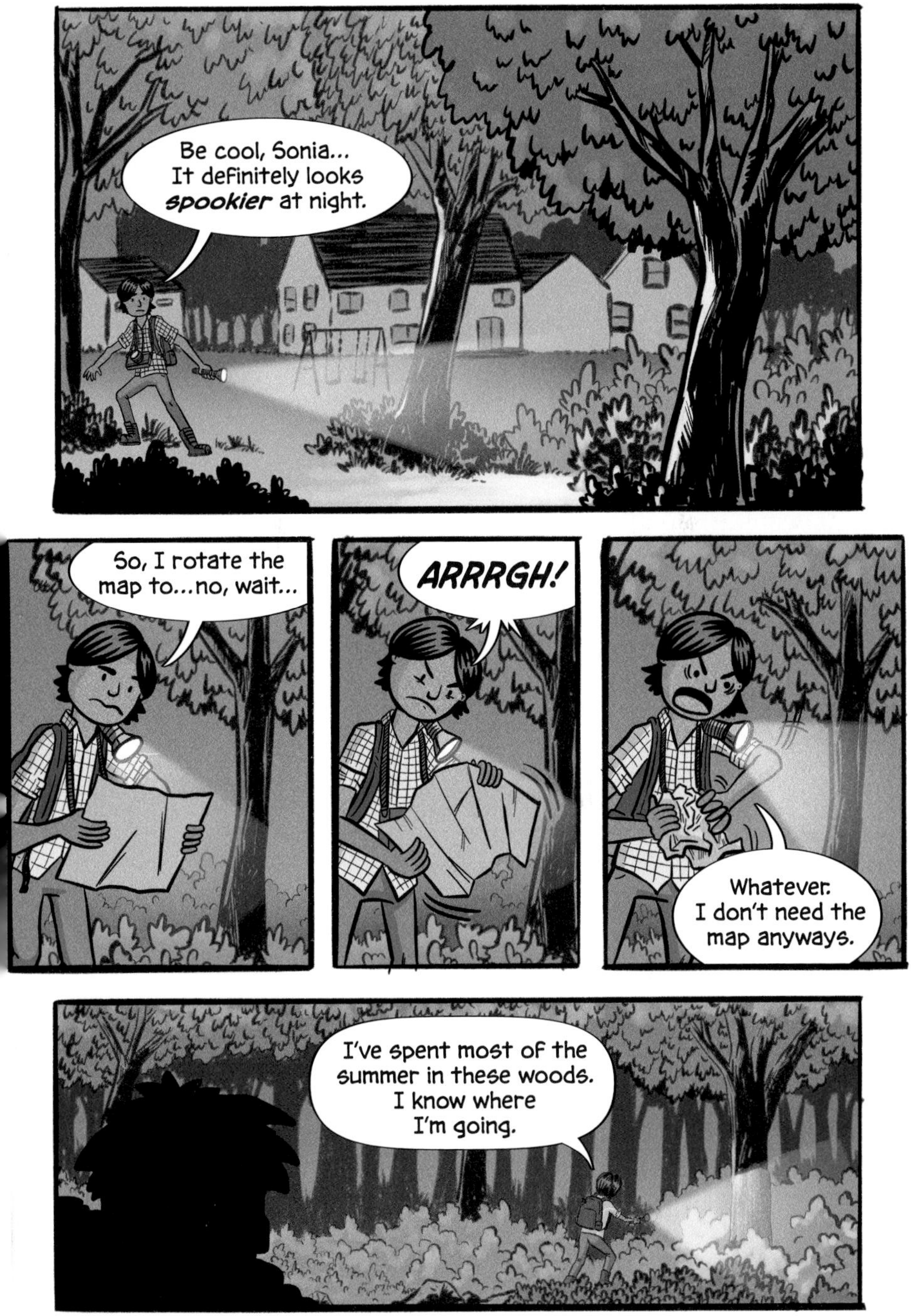
Be cool, Sonia... It definitely looks *spookier* at night.
So, I rotate the map to...no, wait...
ARRRGH!
Whatever. I don't need the map anyways.
I've spent most of the summer in these woods. I know where I'm going.

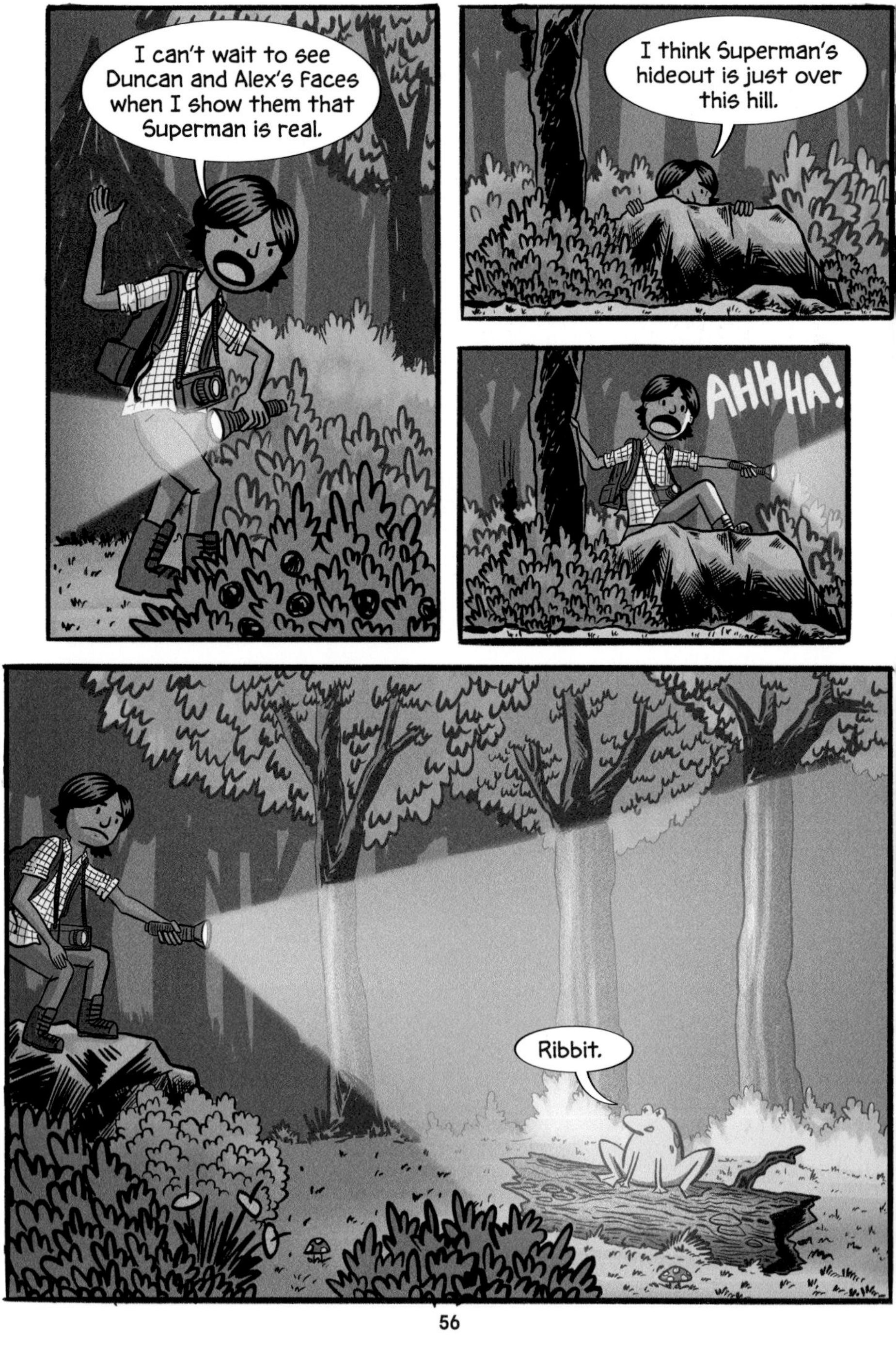
I can't wait to see Duncan and Alex's faces when I show them that Superman is real.
I think Superman's hideout is just over this hill.
AHHHA!
Ribbit.

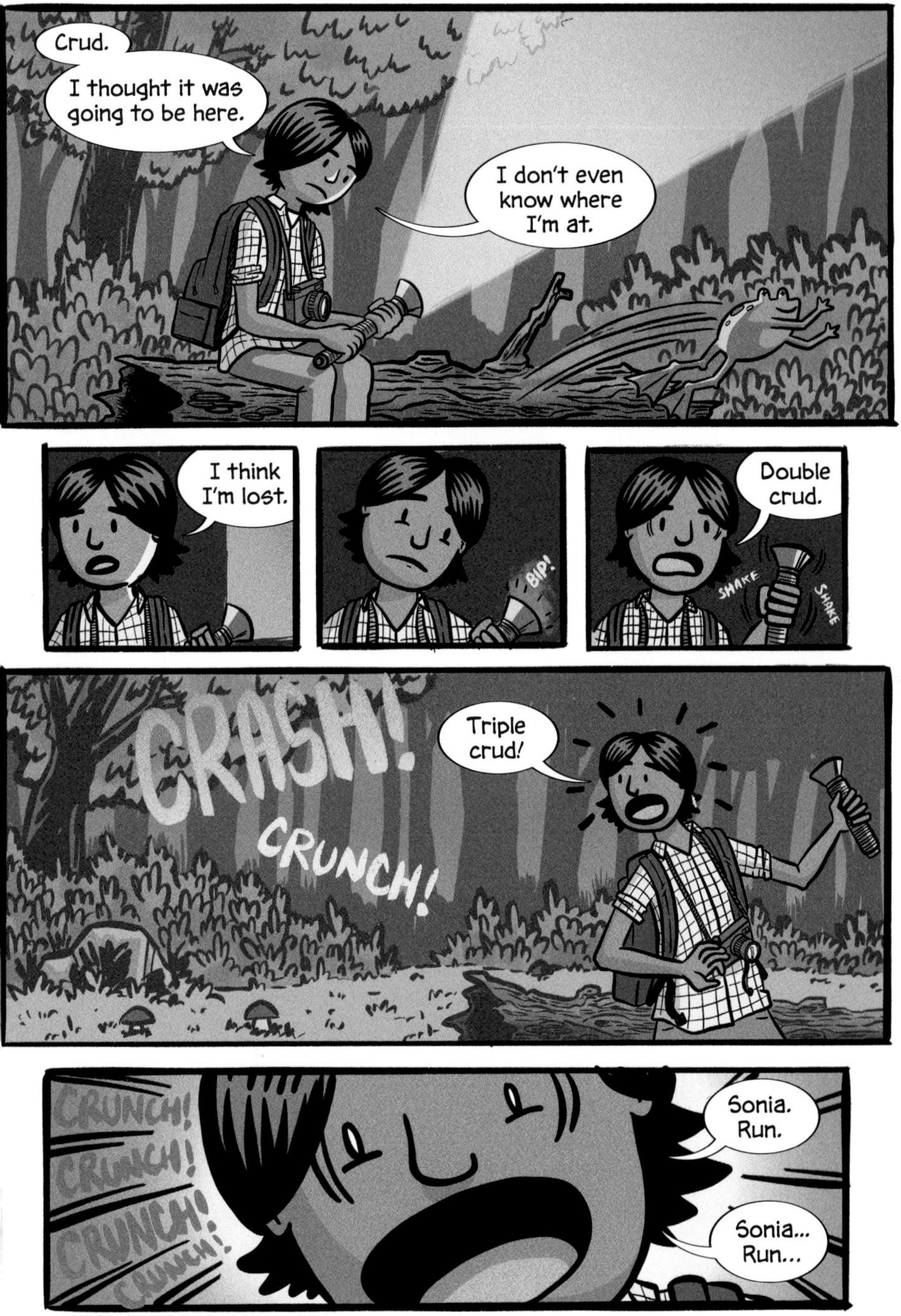
Crud.
I thought it was going to be here.
I don't even know where I'm at.
I think I'm lost.
BIP!
Double crud.
SHAKE
SHAKE
CRASH!
CRUNCH!
Triple crud!
CRUNCH!
CRUNCH!
CRUNCH!
CRUNCH!
Sonia. Run.
Sonia... Run...

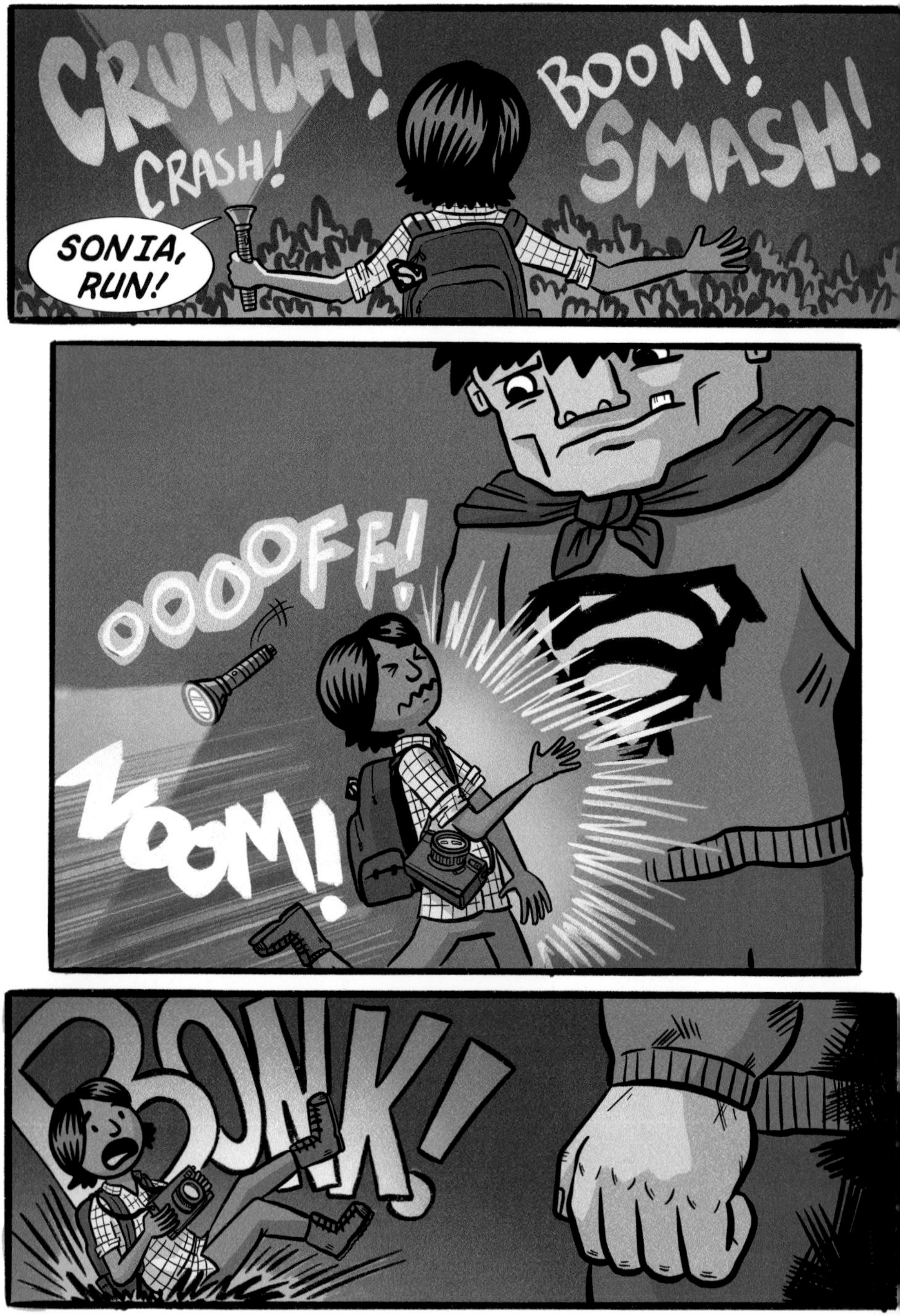
CRUNCH!
CRASH!
BOOM!
SMASH!
SONIA, RUN!
OOOOFF!
ZOOM!
BONK!

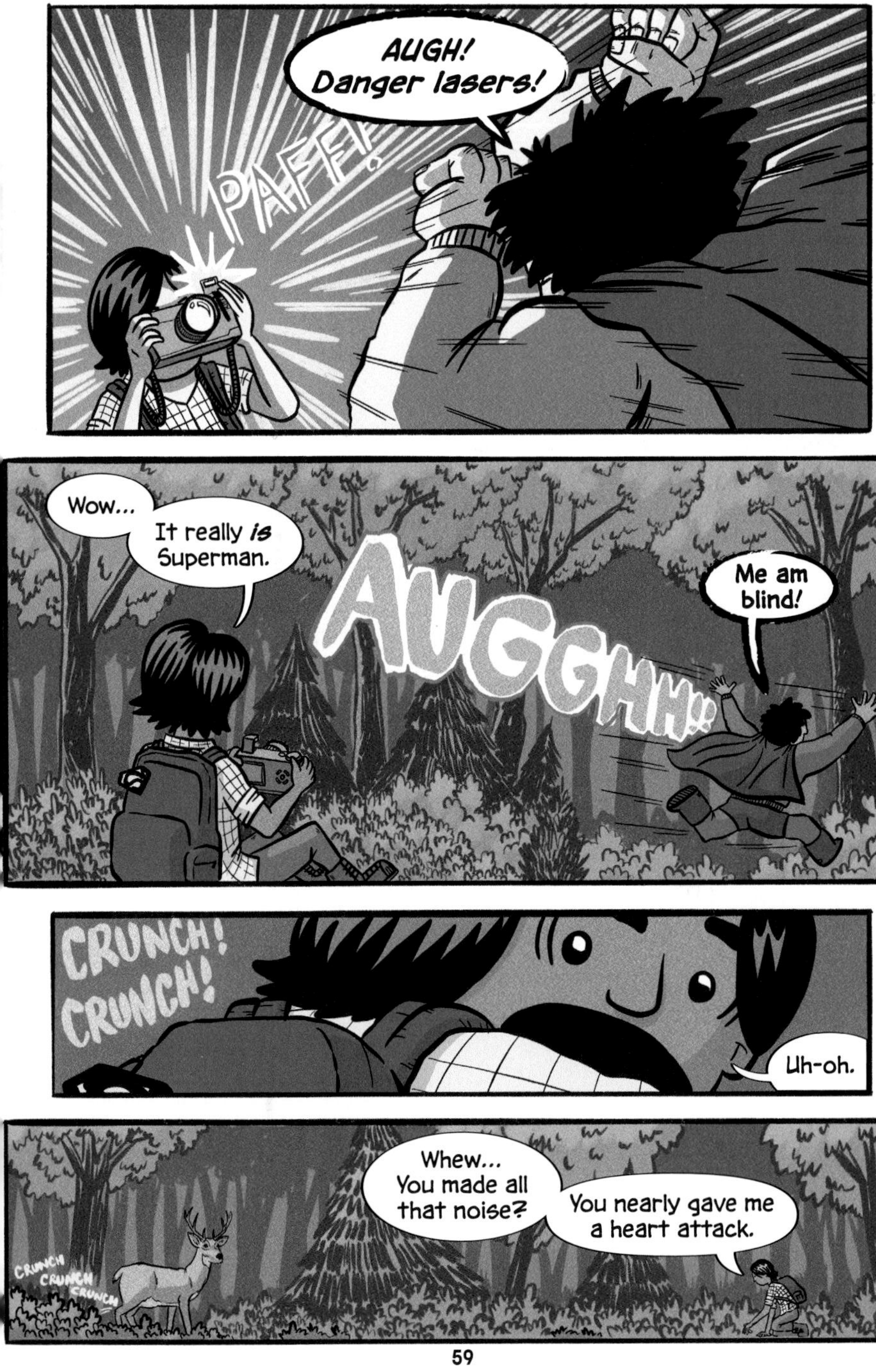
AUGH! Danger lasers!
PAFF!
Wow...
It really *is* Superman.
AUGGHH!!
Me am blind!
CRUNCH! CRUNCH!
Uh-oh.
CRUNCH CRUNCH CRUNCH
Whew... You made all that noise?
You nearly gave me a heart attack.

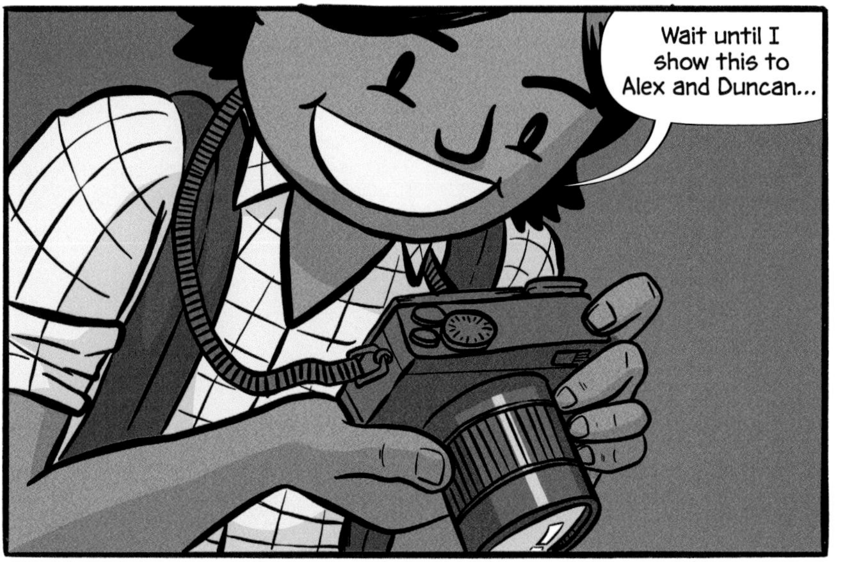
Wait until I show this to Alex and Duncan...

THE NEXT DAY...

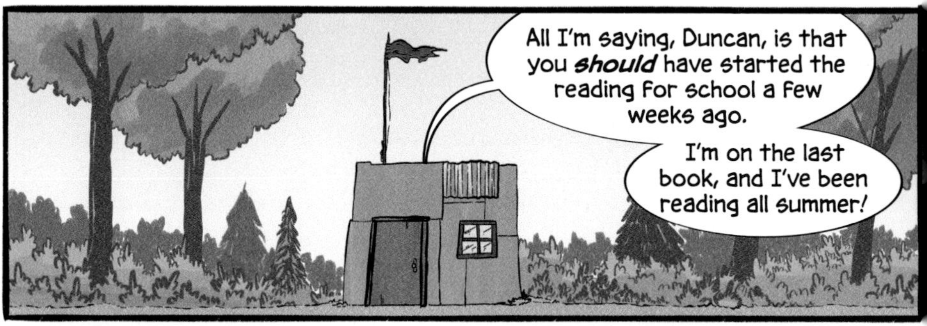
All I'm saying, Duncan, is that you *should* have started the reading for school a few weeks ago.
I'm on the last book, and I've been reading all summer!

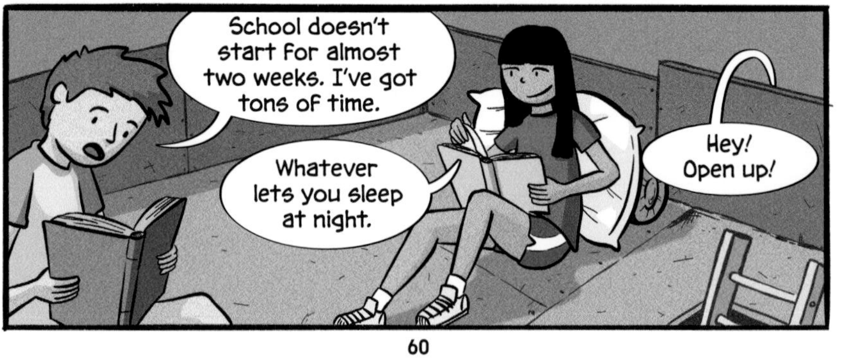
School doesn't start for almost two weeks. I've got tons of time.
Whatever lets you sleep at night.
Hey! Open up!

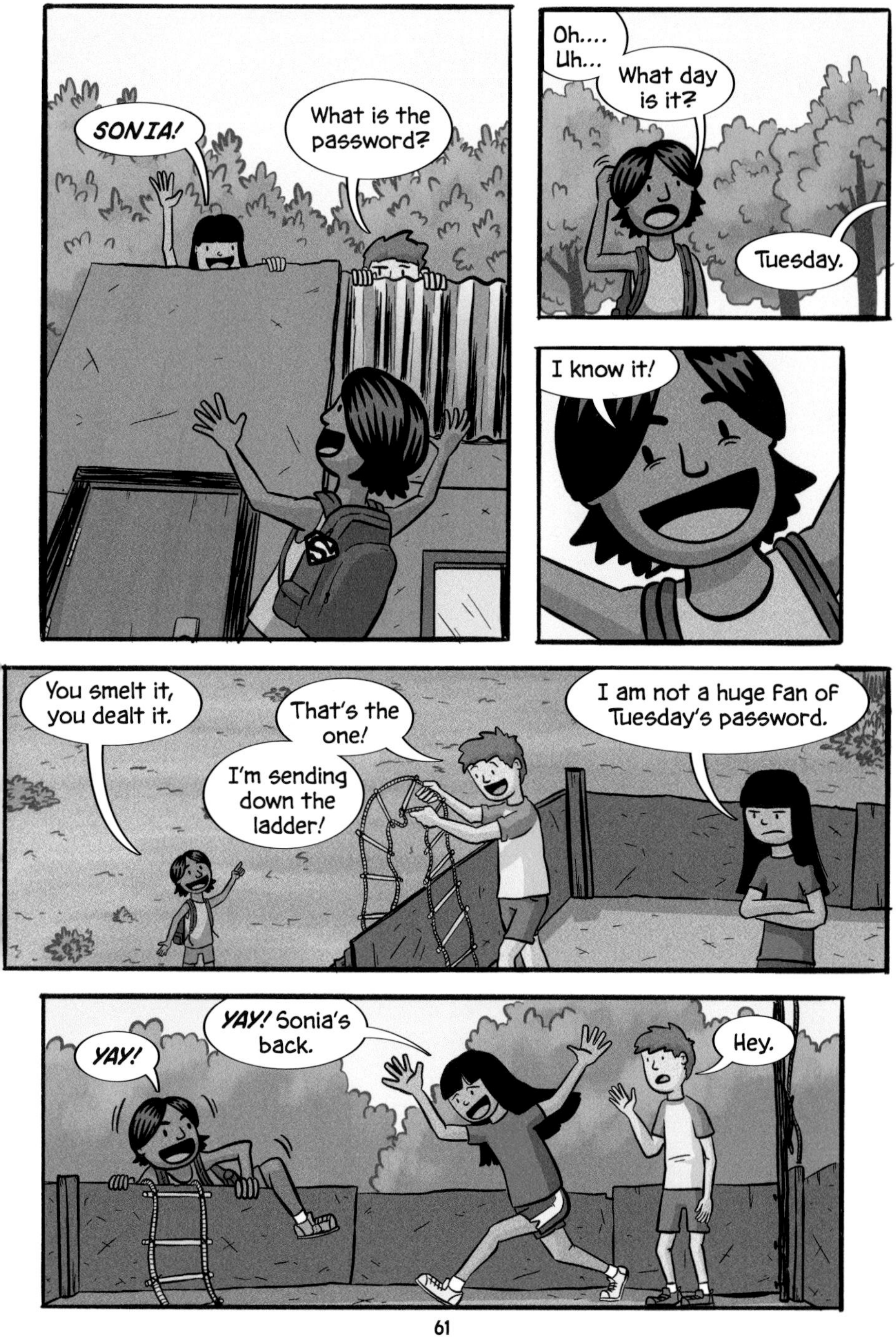
SONIA!
What is the password?
Oh.... Uh...
What day is it?
Tuesday.
I know it!
You smelt it, you dealt it.
That's the one!
I'm sending down the ladder!
I am not a huge fan of Tuesday's password.
YAY!
YAY! Sonia's back.
Hey.

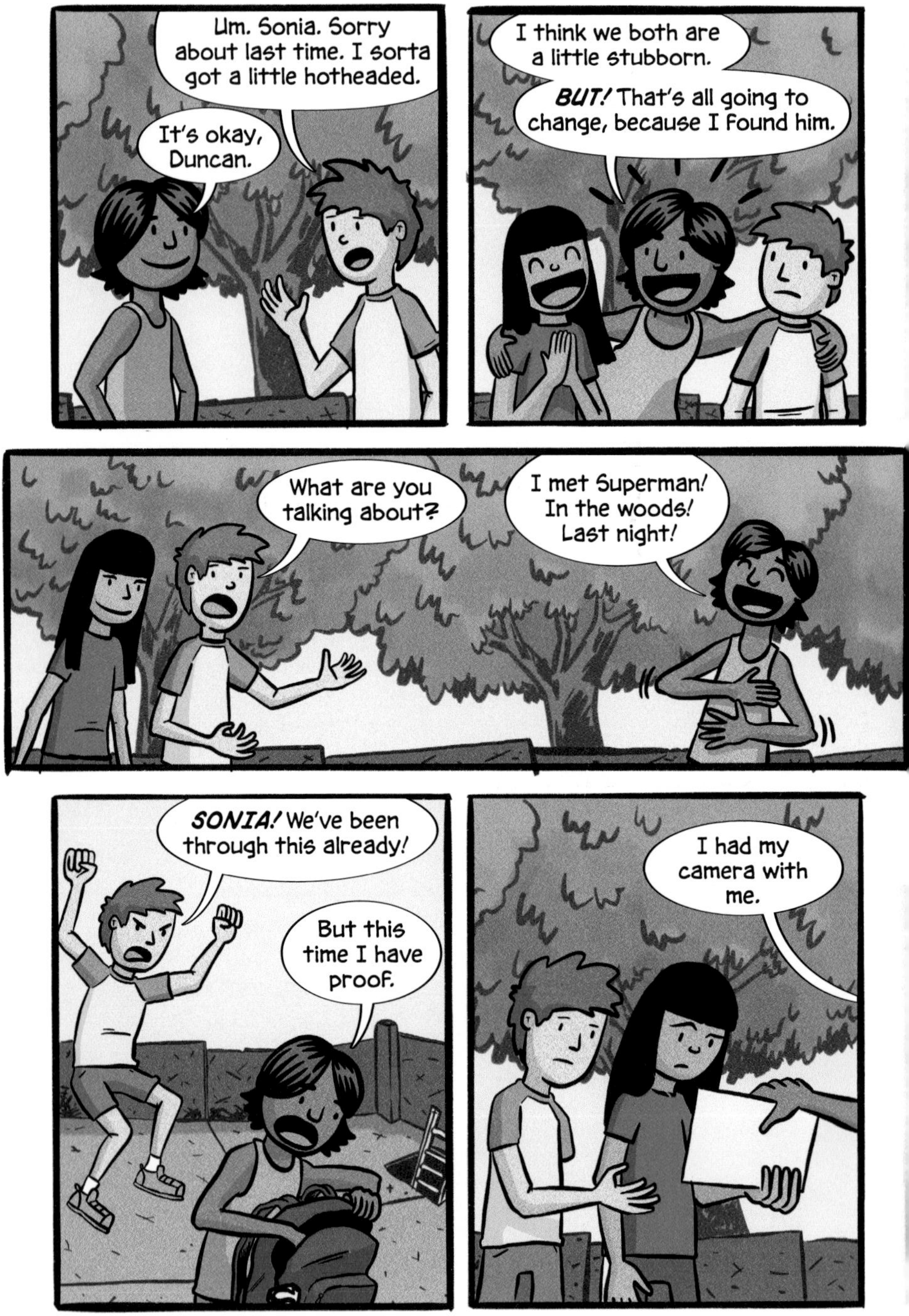
Um. Sonia. Sorry about last time. I sorta got a little hotheaded.
It's okay, Duncan.
I think we both are a little stubborn.
BUT! That's all going to change, because I found him.
What are you talking about?
I met Superman! In the woods! Last night!
SONIA! We've been through this already!
But this time I have proof.
I had my camera with me.

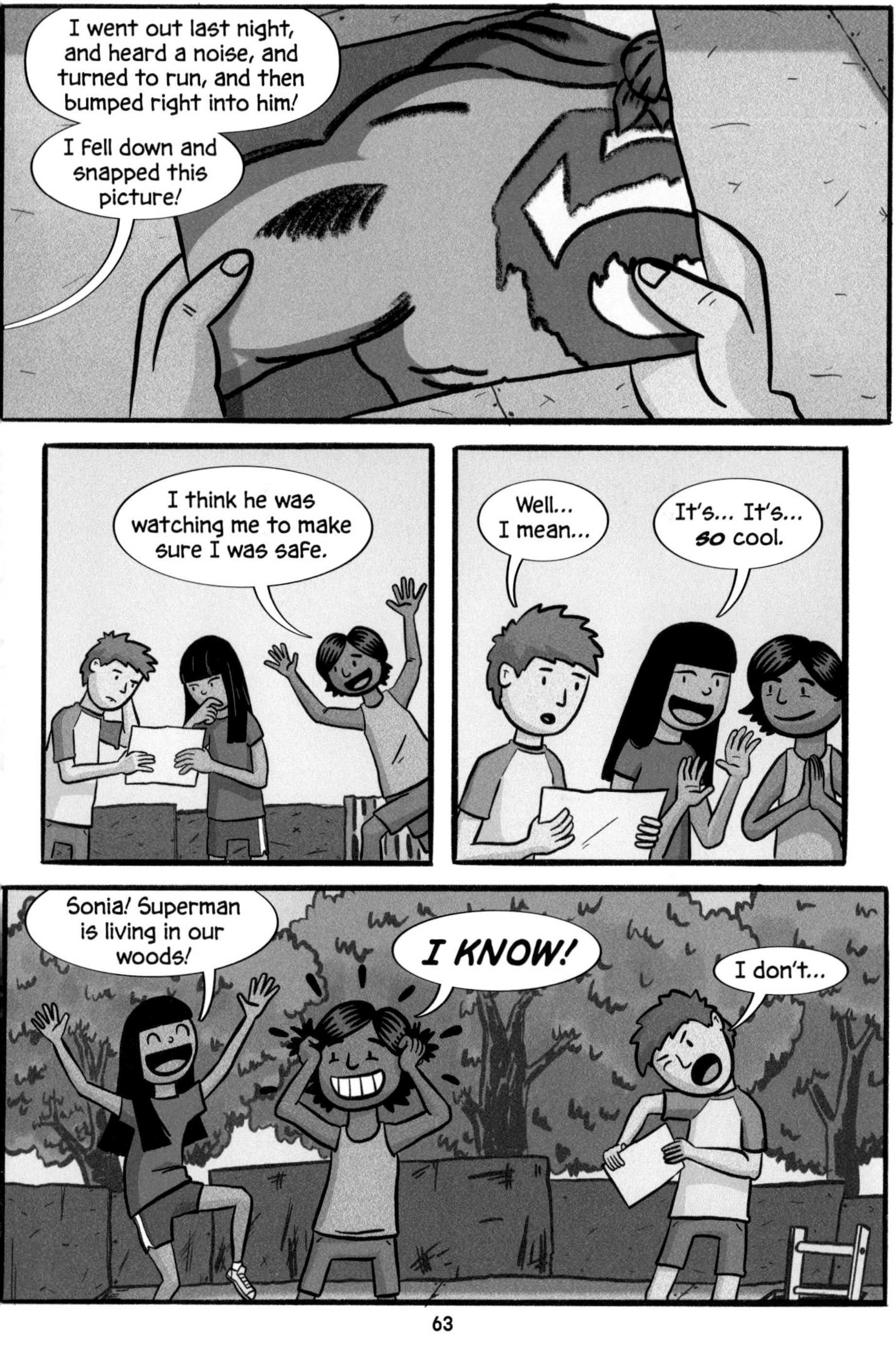
I went out last night, and heard a noise, and turned to run, and then bumped right into him!
I fell down and snapped this picture!
I think he was watching me to make sure I was safe.
Well... I mean...
It's... It's... *so* cool.
Sonia! Superman is living in our woods!
I KNOW!
I don't...

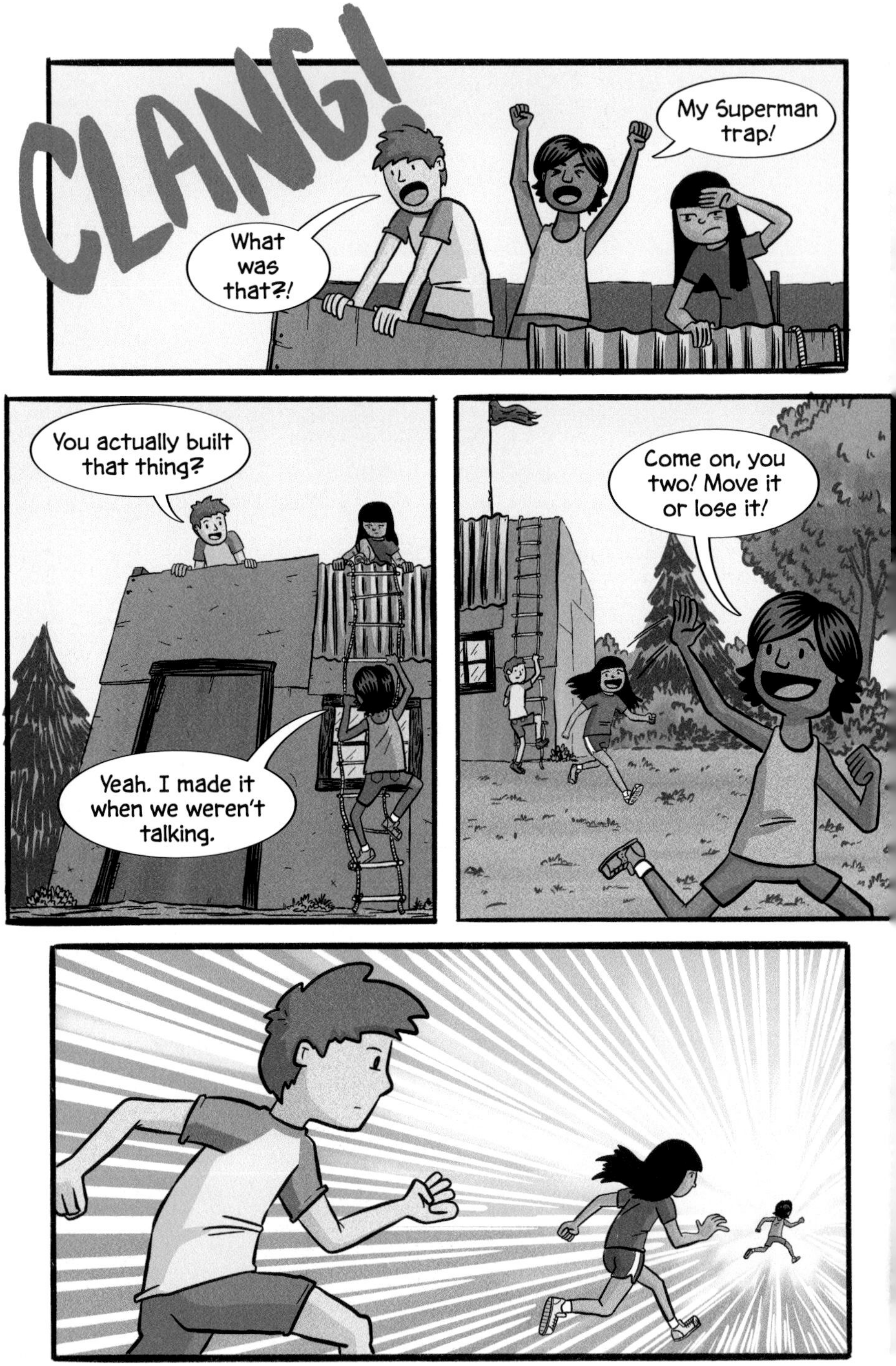
CLANG!
What was that?!
My Superman trap!
You actually built that thing?
Yeah. I made it when we weren't talking.
Come on, you two! Move it or lose it!

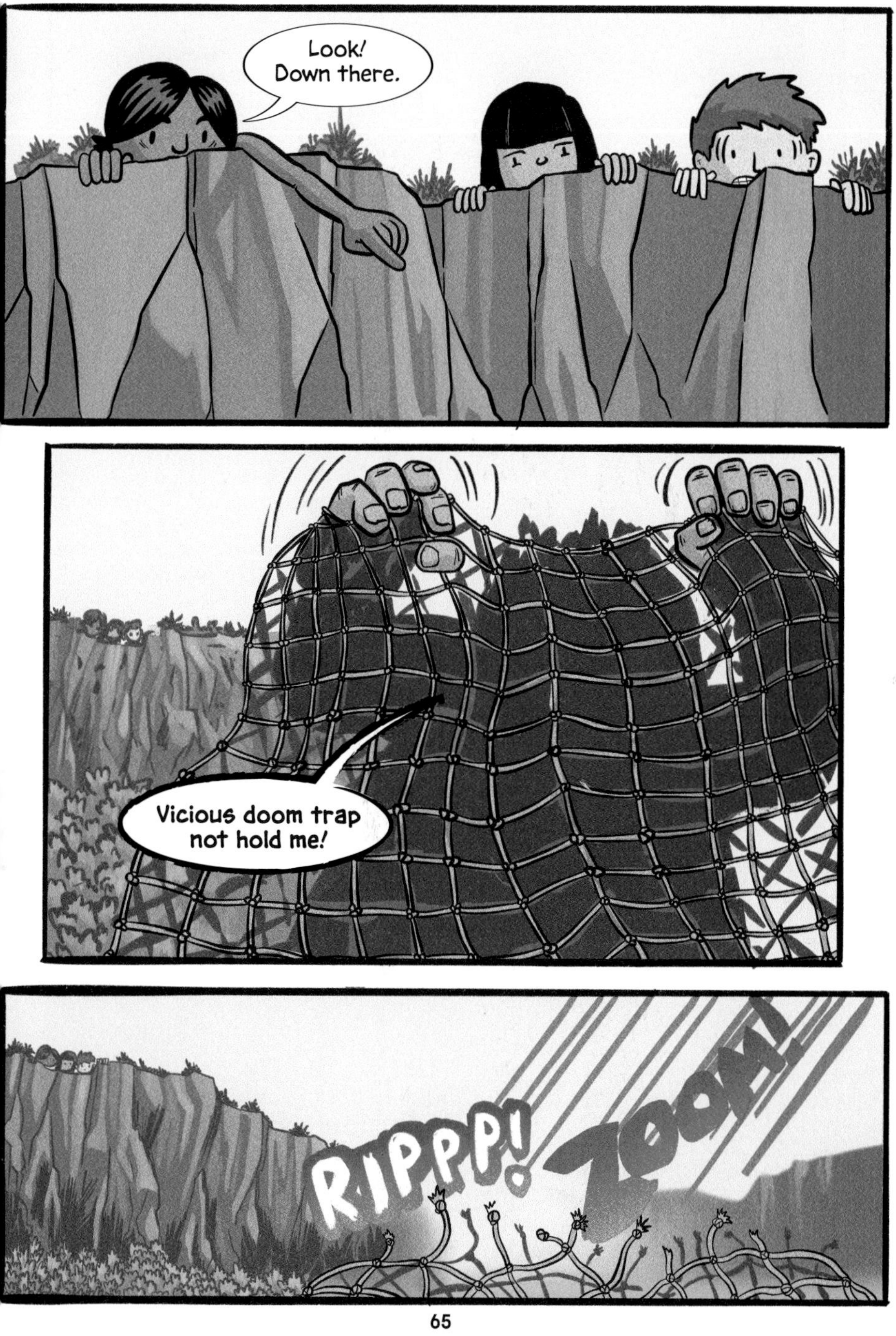
Look! Down there.
Vicious doom trap not hold me!
RIPPP!
ZOOM!

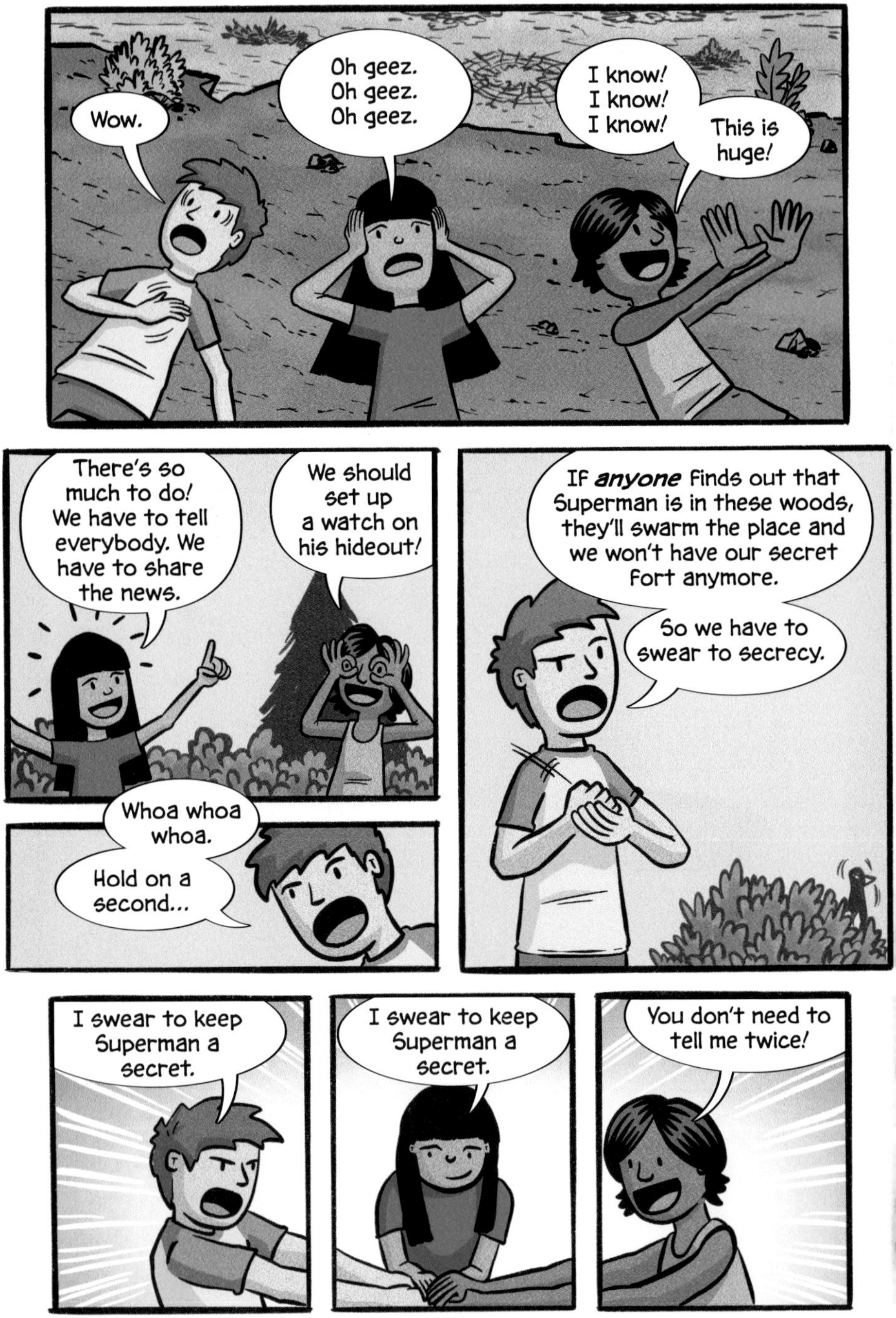
Wow.
Oh geez. Oh geez. Oh geez.
I know! I know! I know!
This is huge!
There's so much to do! We have to tell everybody. We have to share the news.
We should set up a watch on his hideout!
Whoa whoa whoa.
Hold on a second...
If *anyone* finds out that Superman is in these woods, they'll swarm the place and we won't have our secret fort anymore.
So we have to swear to secrecy.
I swear to keep Superman a secret.
I swear to keep Superman a secret.
You don't need to tell me twice!

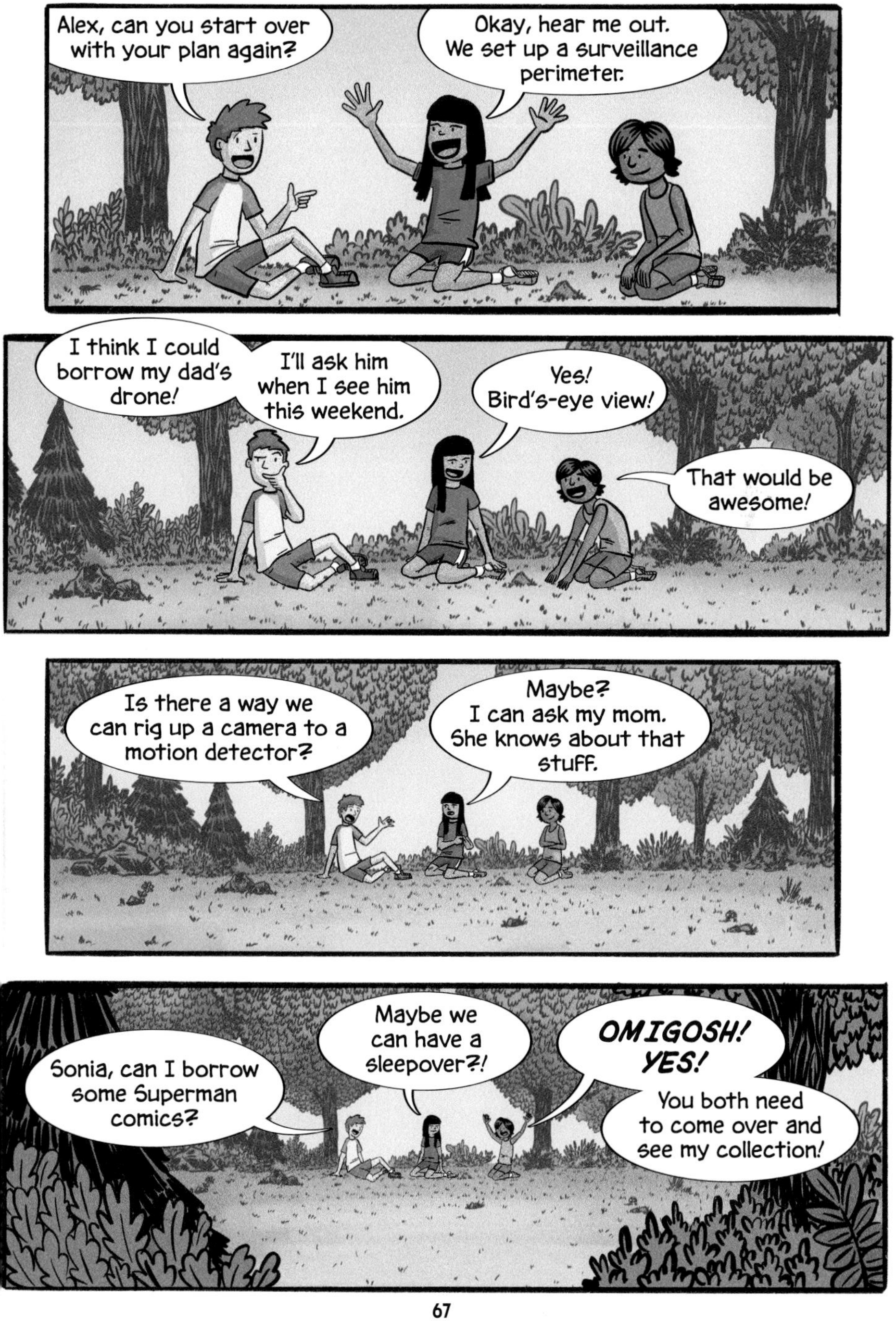
Alex, can you start over with your plan again?
Okay, hear me out. We set up a surveillance perimeter.
I think I could borrow my dad's drone!
I'll ask him when I see him this weekend.
Yes! Bird's-eye view!
That would be awesome!
Is there a way we can rig up a camera to a motion detector?
Maybe? I can ask my mom. She knows about that stuff.
Sonia, can I borrow some Superman comics?
Maybe we can have a sleepover?!
OMIGOSH! YES!
You both need to come over and see my collection!

CHAPTER FIVE

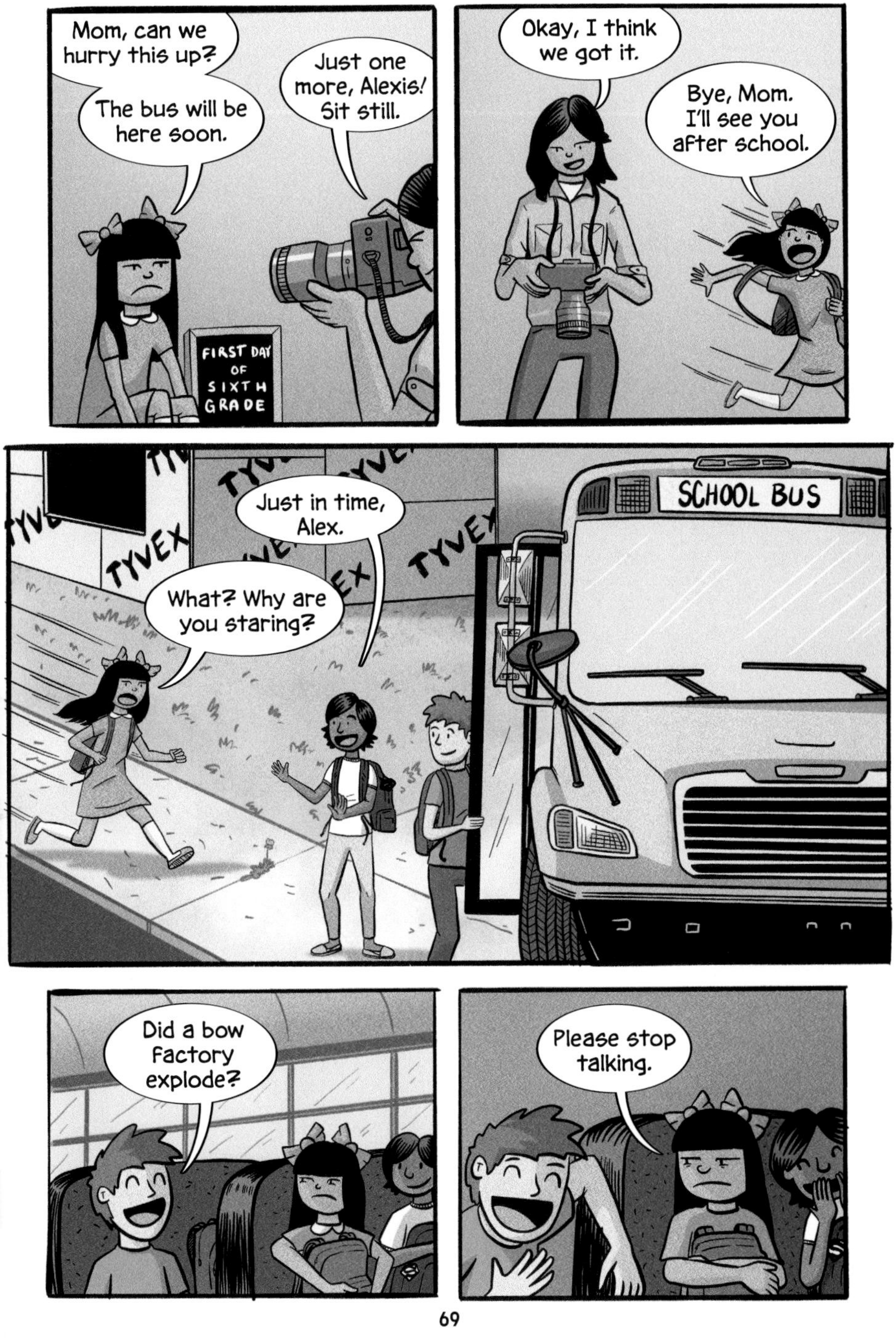
Mom, can we hurry this up?
The bus will be here soon.
Just one more, Alexis! Sit still.
FIRST DAY OF SIXTH GRADE
Okay, I think we got it.
Bye, Mom. I'll see you after school.
TYVEX
SCHOOL BUS
Just in time, Alex.
What? Why are you staring?
Did a bow factory explode?
Please stop talking.

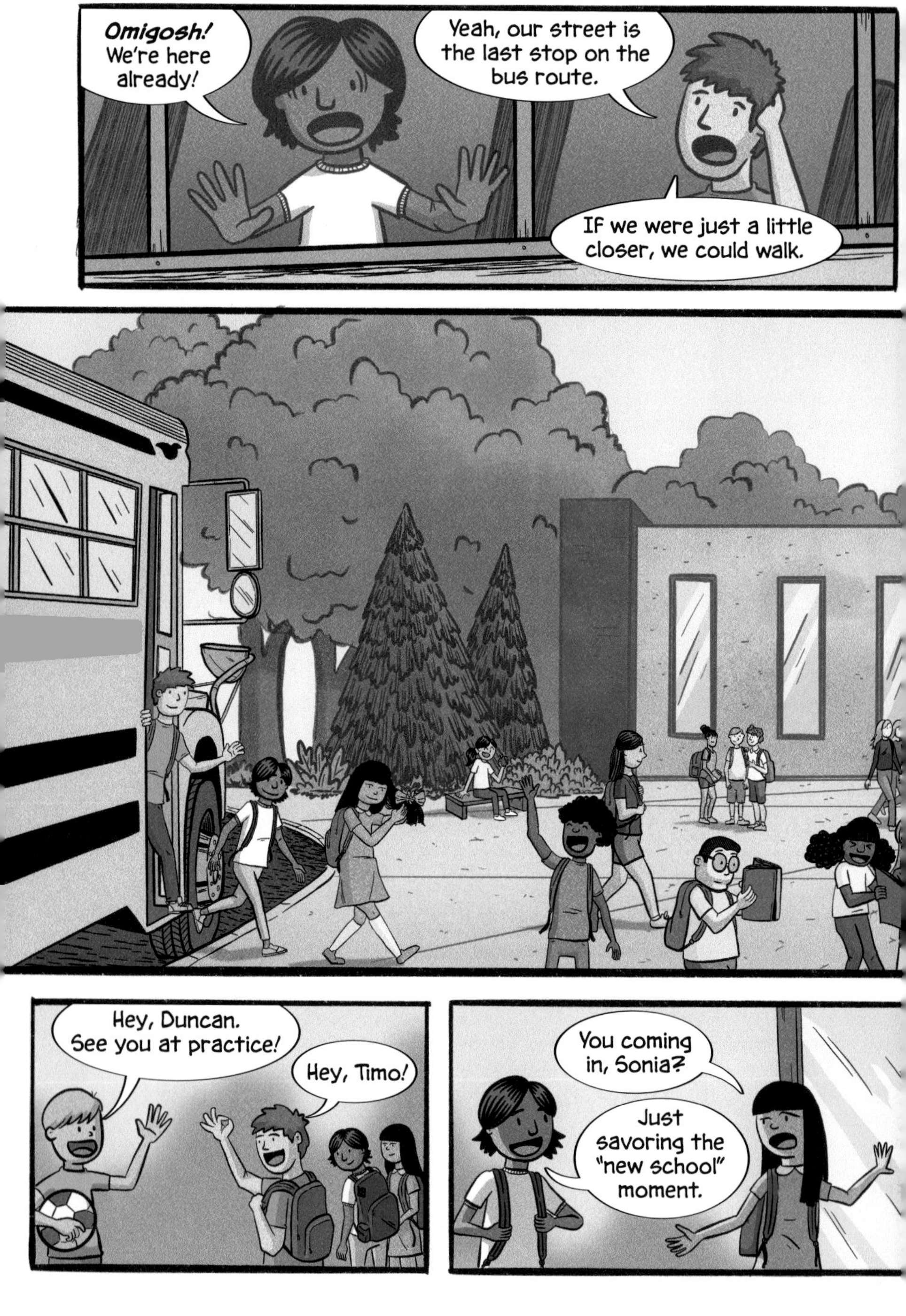
Omigosh! We're here already!
Yeah, our street is the last stop on the bus route.
If we were just a little closer, we could walk.
Hey, Duncan. See you at practice!
Hey, Timo!
You coming in, Sonia?
Just savoring the "new school" moment.

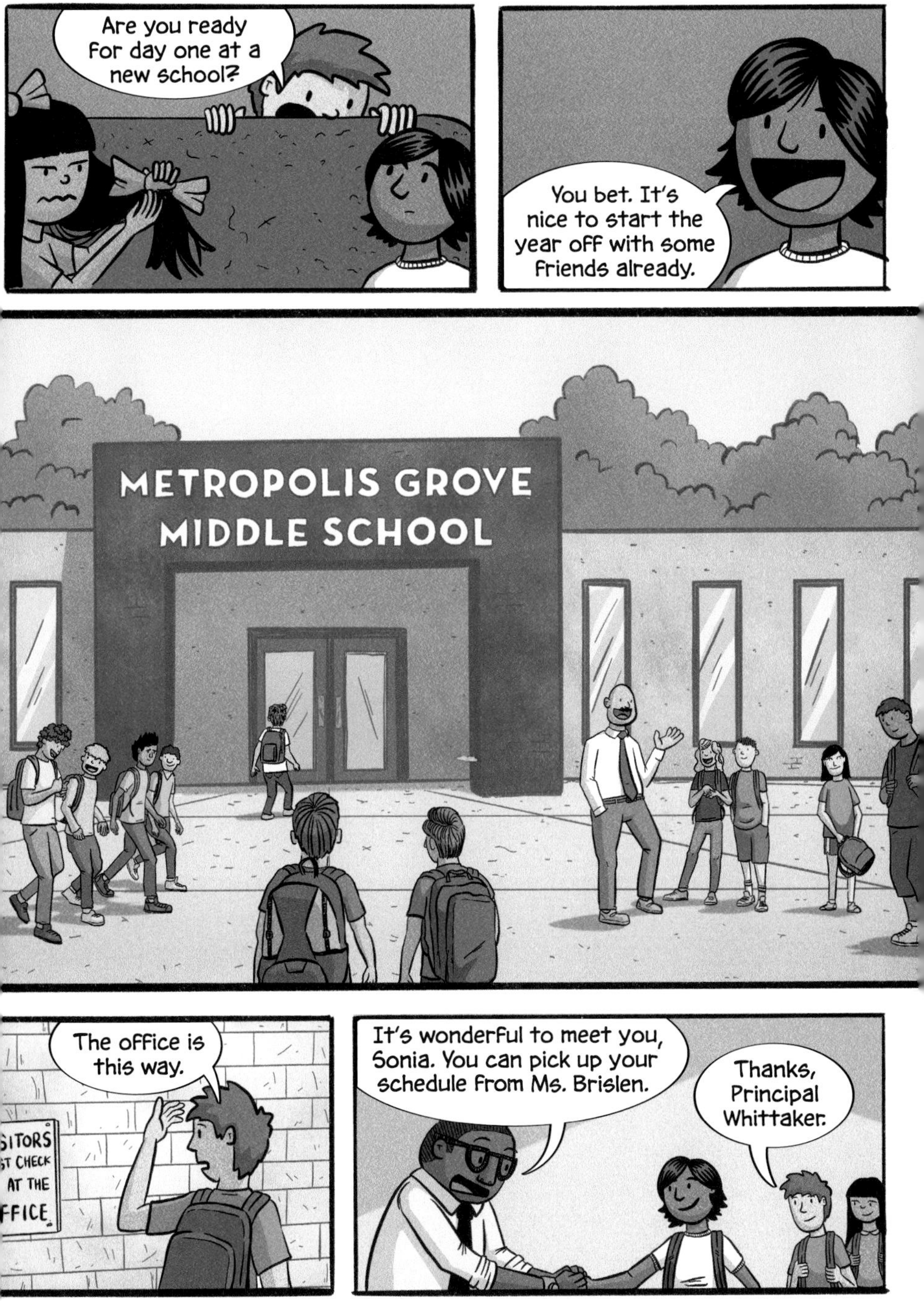
Are you ready for day one at a new school?
You bet. It's nice to start the year off with some friends already.
METROPOLIS GROVE MIDDLE SCHOOL
The office is this way.
SITORS
ST CHECK
AT THE
FFICE
It's wonderful to meet you, Sonia. You can pick up your schedule from Ms. Brislen.
Thanks, Principal Whittaker.

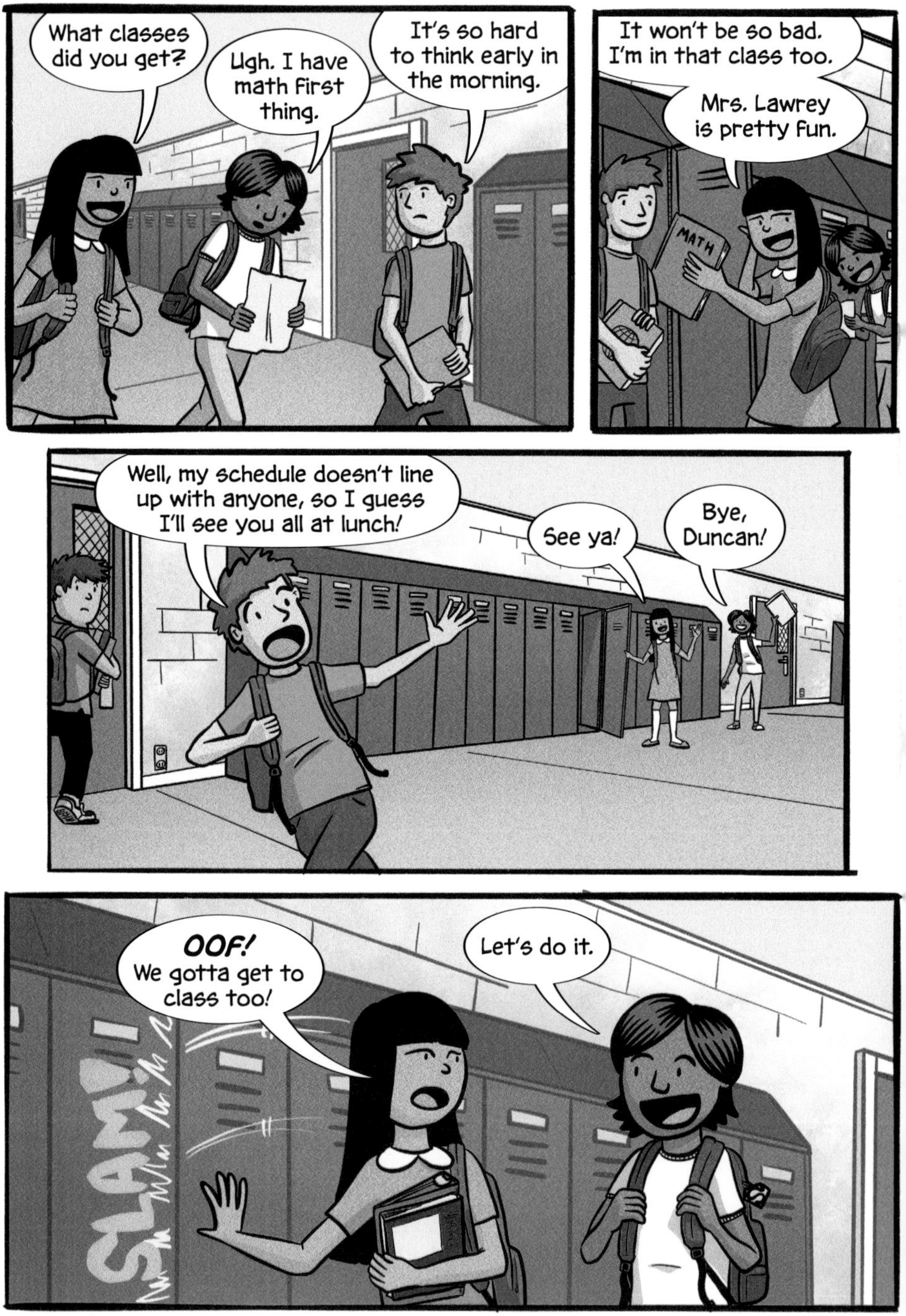
What classes did you get?
Ugh. I have math first thing.
It's so hard to think early in the morning.
It won't be so bad. I'm in that class too.
Mrs. Lawrey is pretty fun.
MATH
Well, my schedule doesn't line up with anyone, so I guess I'll see you all at lunch!
See ya!
Bye, Duncan!
OOF!
We gotta get to class too!
Let's do it.
SLAM!

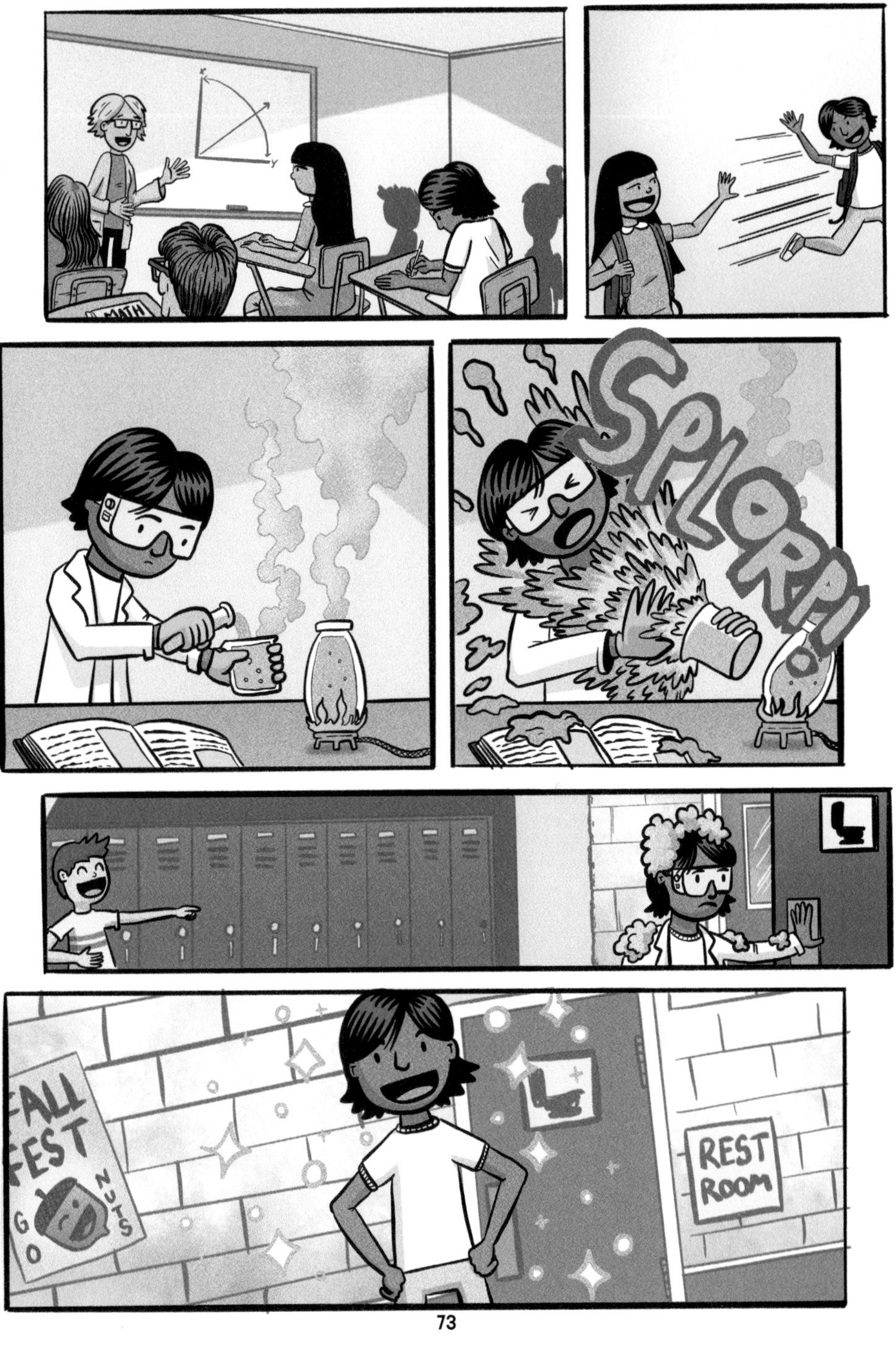
MATH
SPLORP!
REST ROOM
FALL FEST
GO NUTS

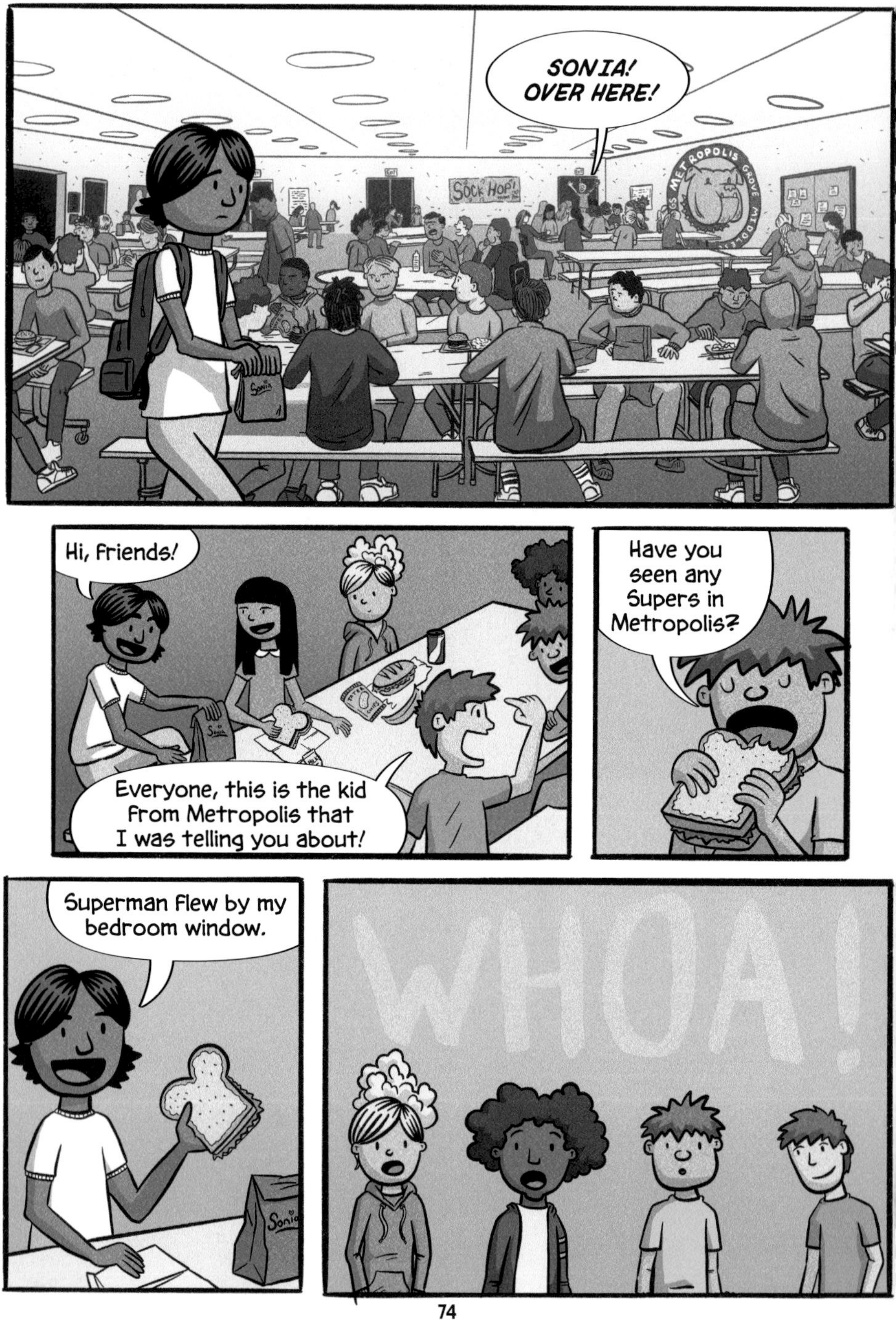
SONIA! OVER HERE!
SOCK HOP!
METROPOLIS GROVE MIDDLE
Hi, friends!
Everyone, this is the kid from Metropolis that I was telling you about!
Have you seen any Supers in Metropolis?
Superman flew by my bedroom window.
WHOA!

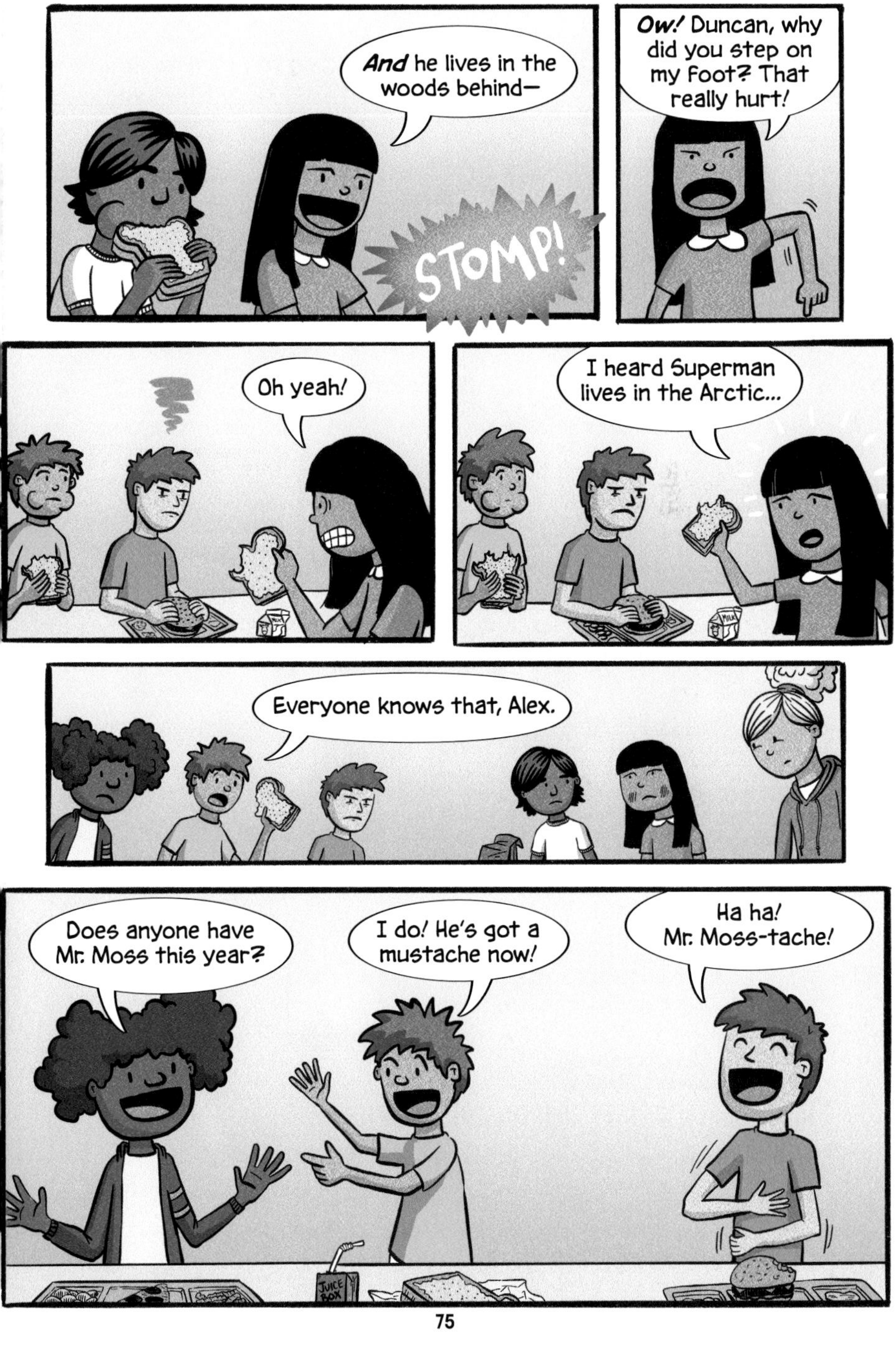

And he lives in the woods behind—
STOMP!
Ow! Duncan, why did you step on my foot? That really hurt!
Oh yeah!
I heard Superman lives in the Arctic...
MILK
MILK
Everyone knows that, Alex.
Does anyone have Mr. Moss this year?
I do! He's got a mustache now!
Ha ha! Mr. Moss-tache!
JUICE BOX

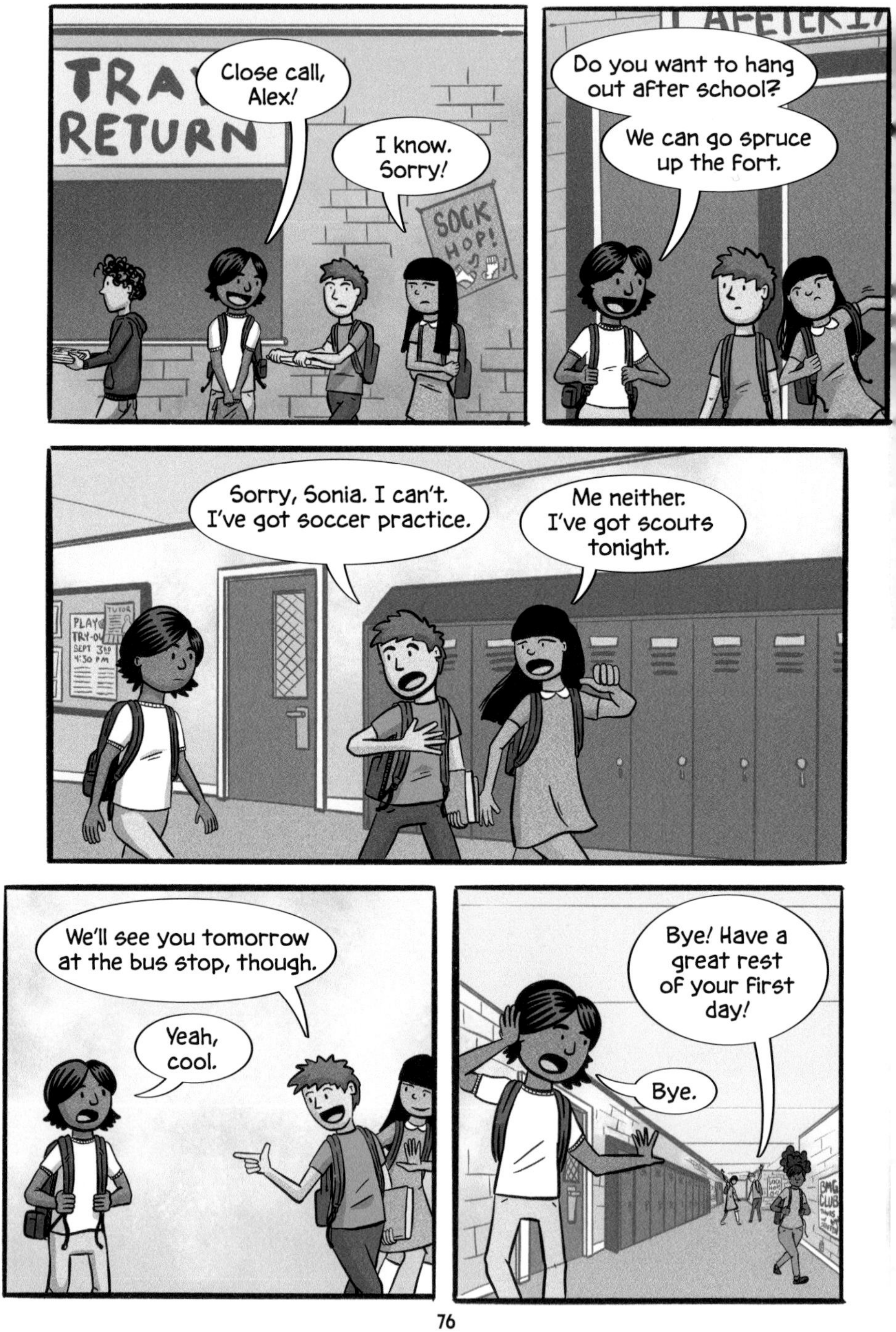
TRAY
RETURN
Close call, Alex!
I know. Sorry!
SOCK HOP!
Do you want to hang out after school?
We can go spruce up the fort.
Sorry, Sonia. I can't. I've got soccer practice.
Me neither. I've got scouts tonight.
PLAY TRY-OU
SEPT 3RD
4:30 PM
TUTOR
We'll see you tomorrow at the bus stop, though.
Yeah, cool.
Bye! Have a great rest of your first day!
Bye.

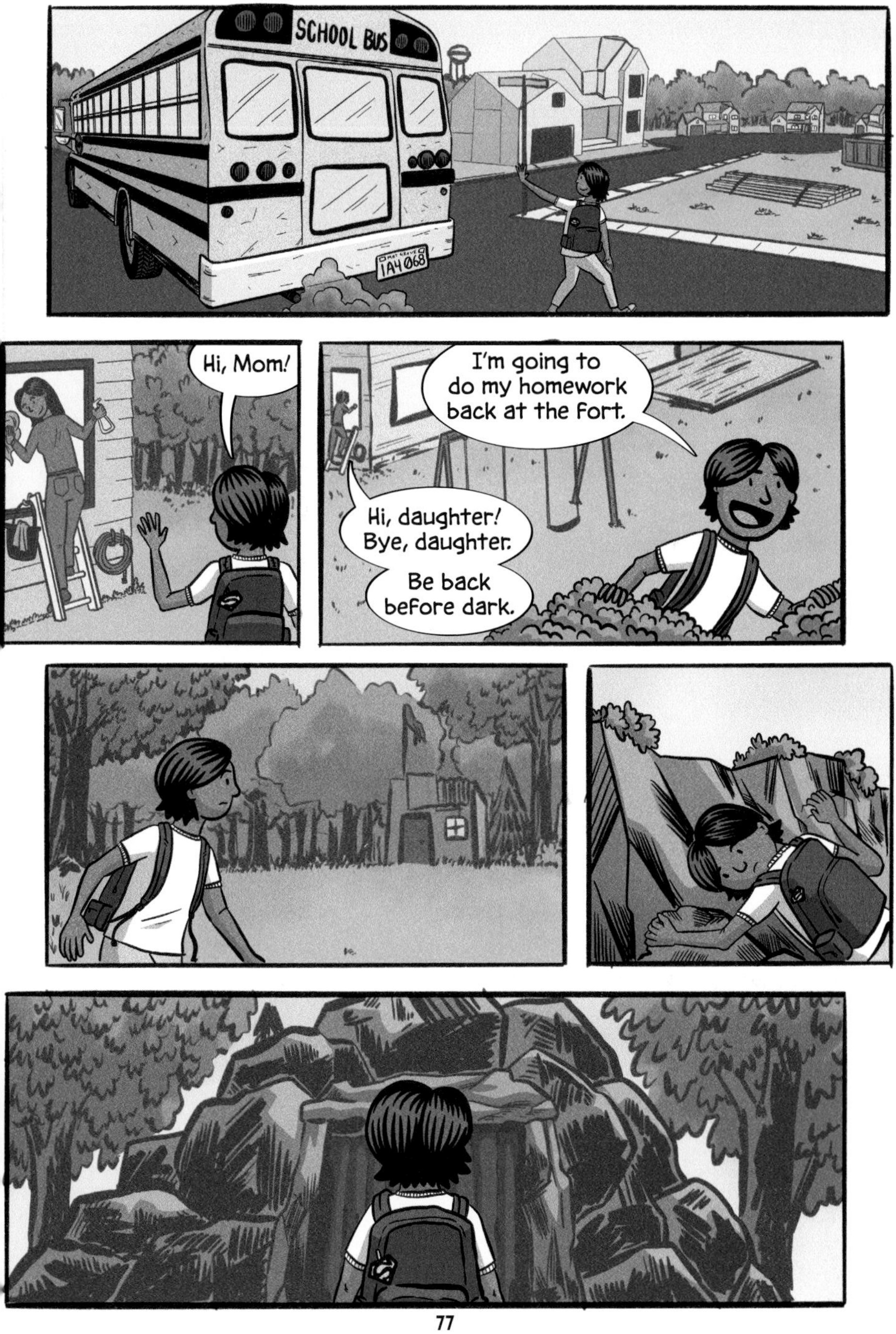
SCHOOL BUS
Hi, Mom!
I'm going to do my homework back at the fort.
Hi, daughter! Bye, daughter.
Be back before dark.

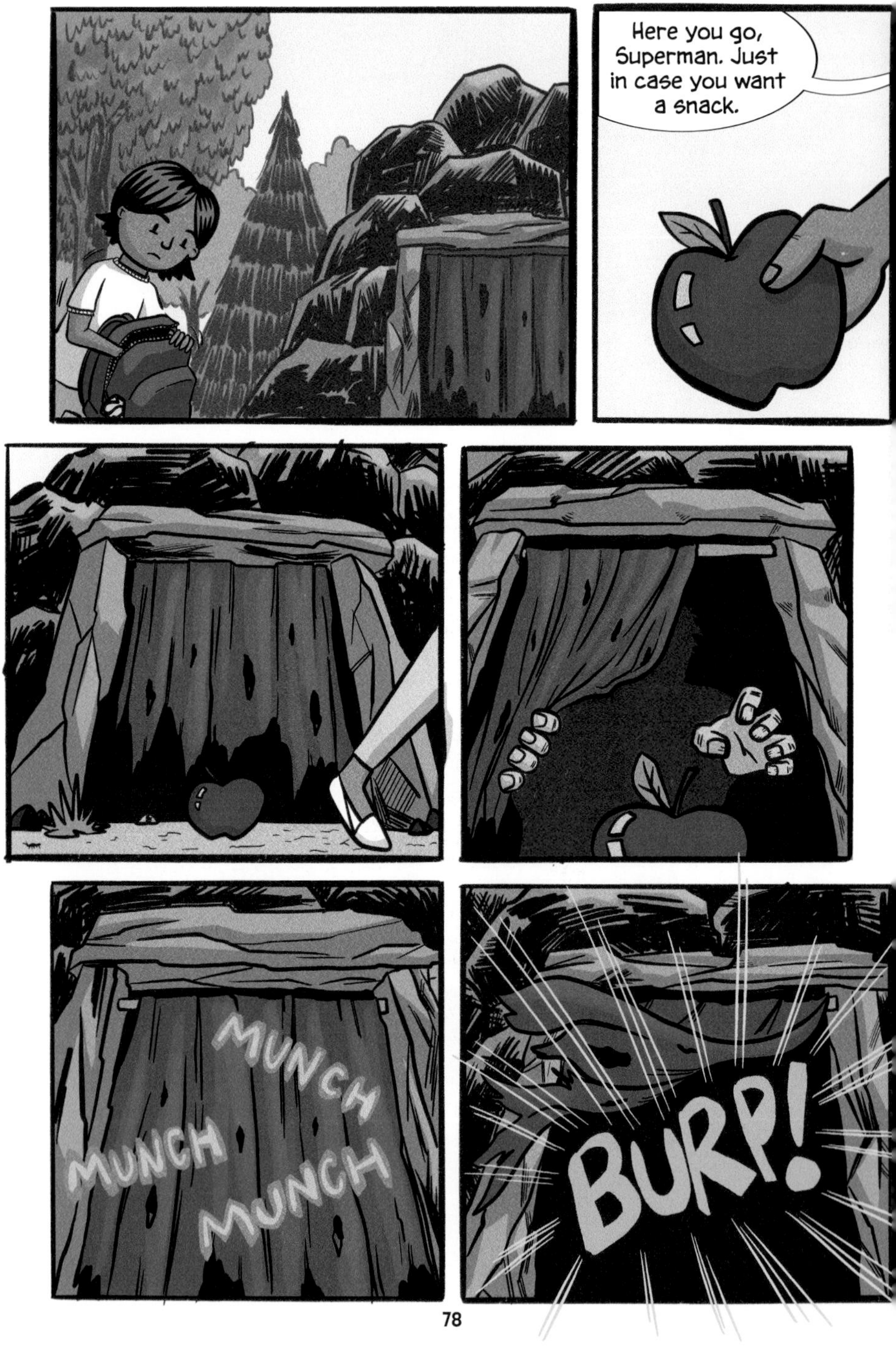
Here you go, Superman. Just in case you want a snack.
MUNCH
MUNCH
MUNCH
BURP!

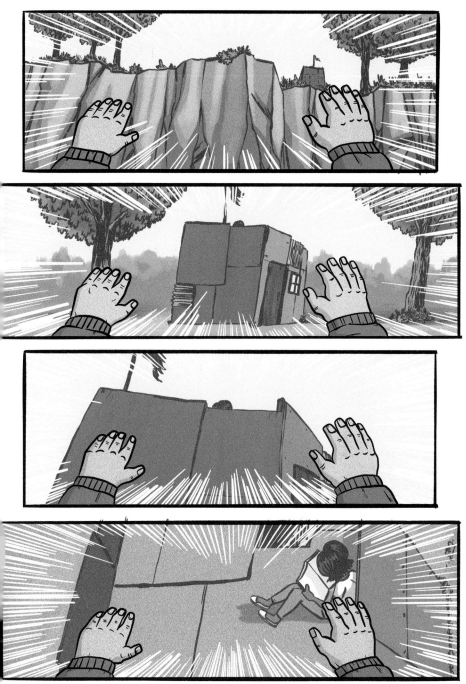

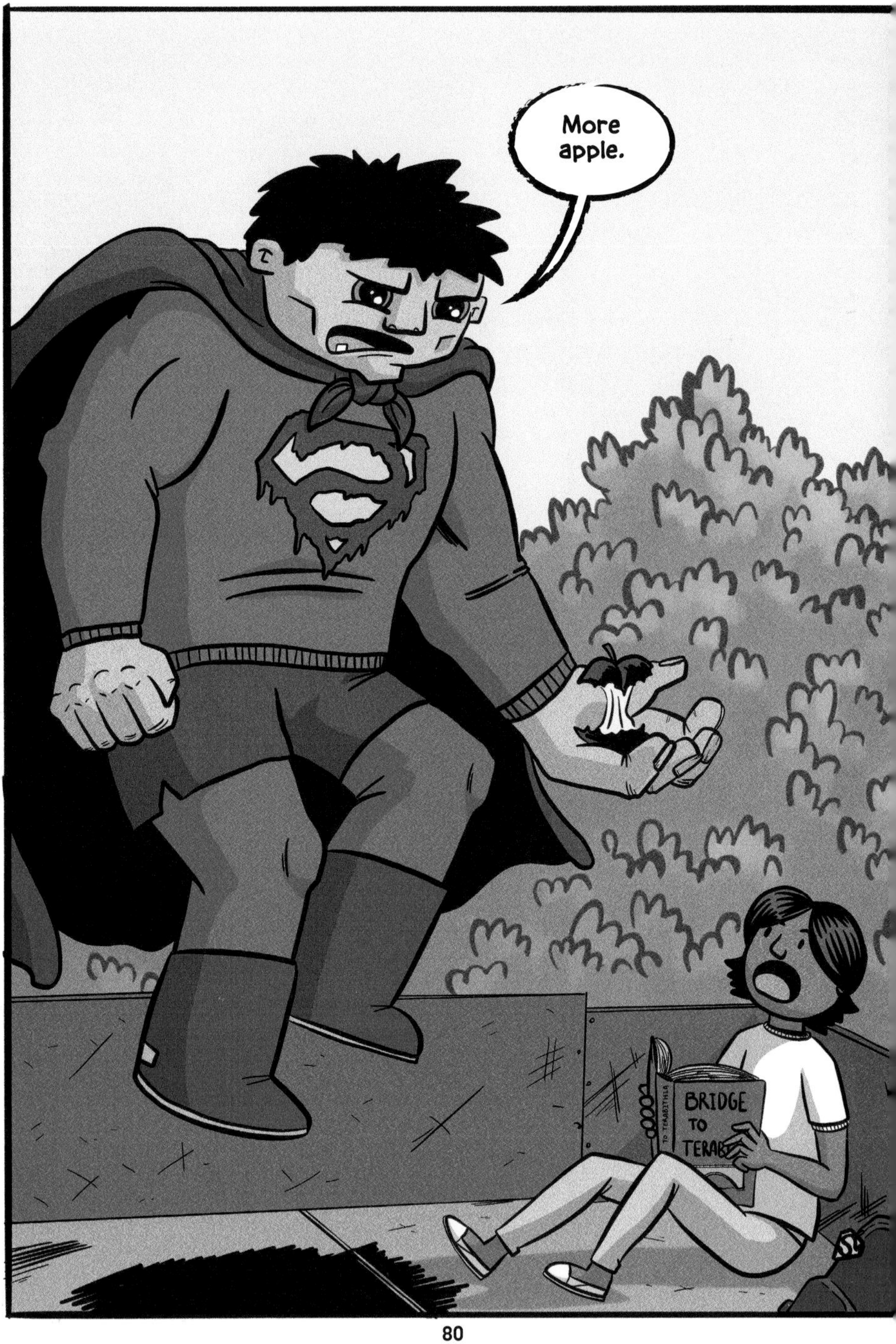
More apple.
BRIDGE TO TERAB

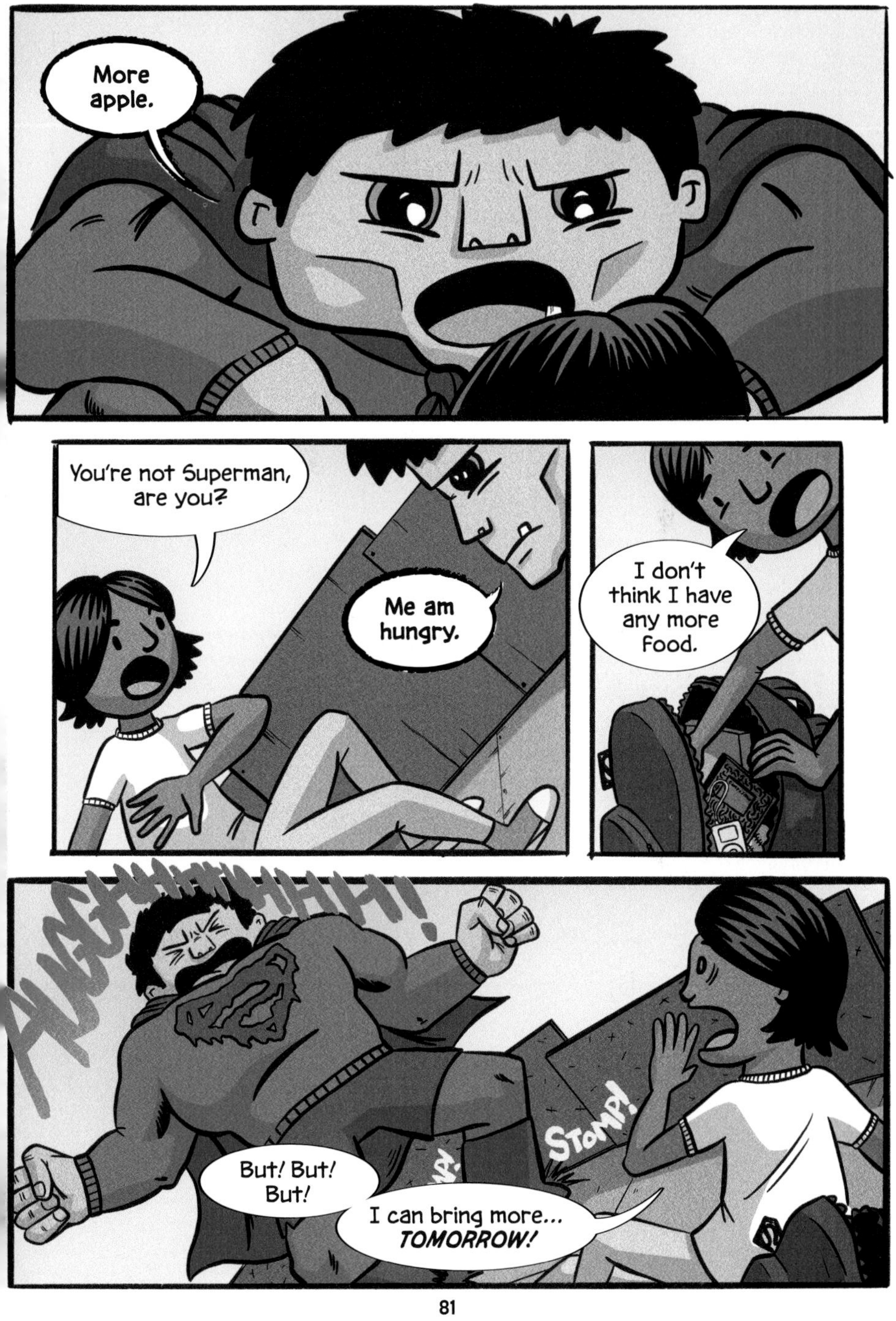

More apple.
You're not Superman, are you?
Me am hungry.
I don't think I have any more food.
STOMP!
But! But! But!
I can bring more... *TOMORROW!*

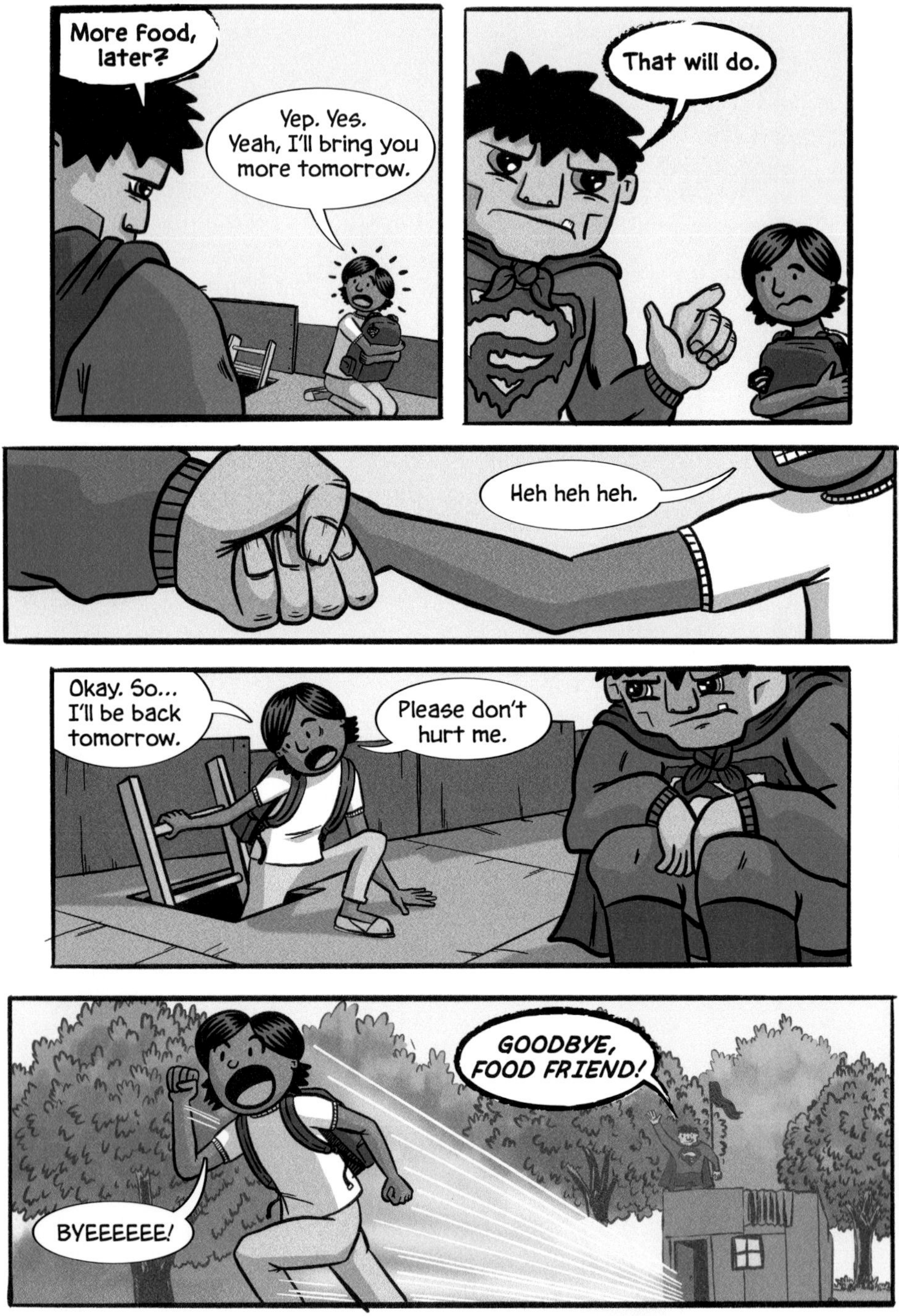
More food, later?
Yep. Yes. Yeah, I'll bring you more tomorrow.
That will do.
Heh heh heh.
Okay. So... I'll be back tomorrow.
Please don't hurt me.
GOODBYE, FOOD FRIEND!
BYEEEEEE!

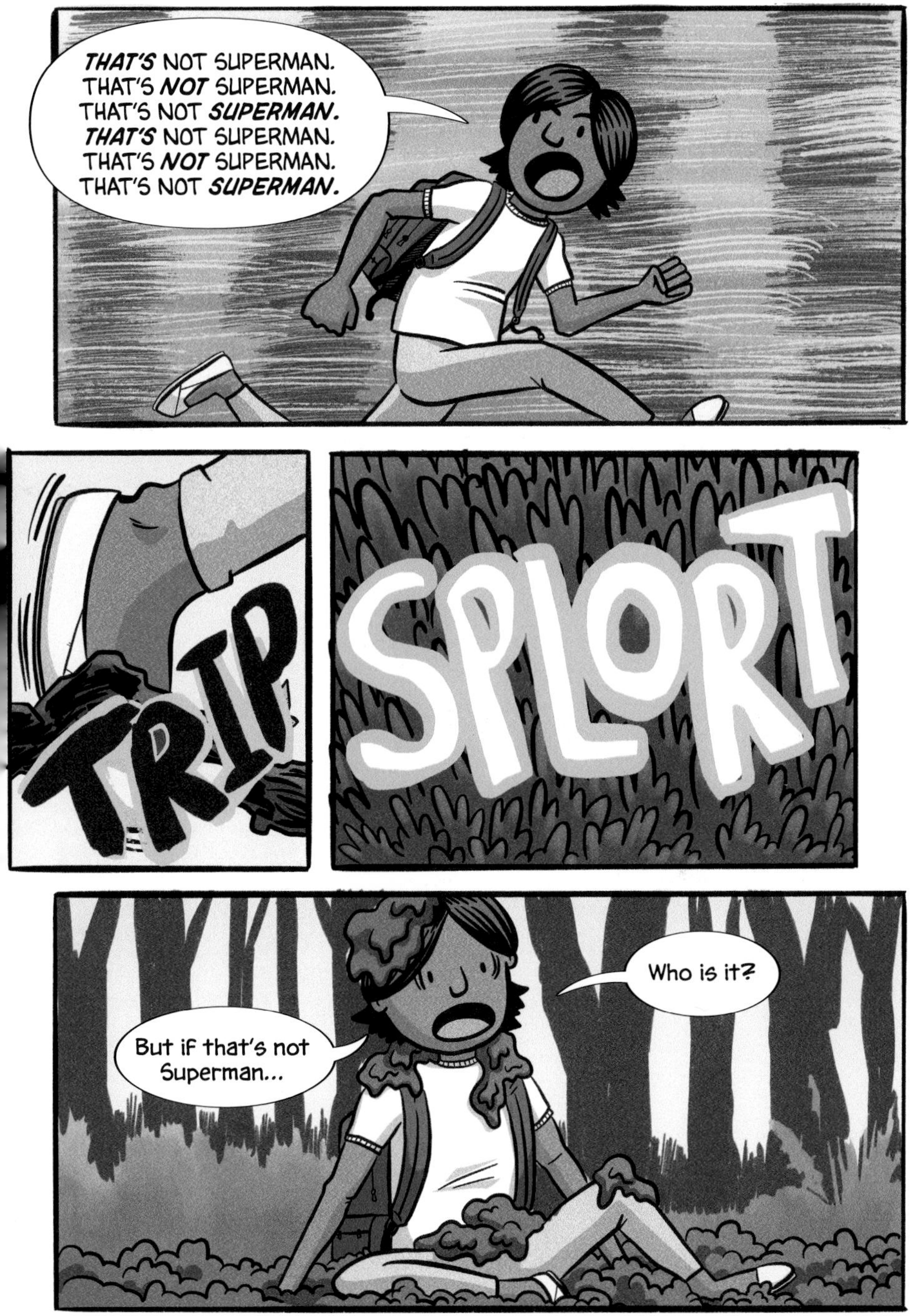
THAT'S NOT SUPERMAN. THAT'S ***NOT*** SUPERMAN. THAT'S NOT ***SUPERMAN.*** ***THAT'S*** NOT SUPERMAN. THAT'S ***NOT*** SUPERMAN. THAT'S NOT ***SUPERMAN.***
TRIP
SPLORT
But if that's not Superman...
Who is it?

CHAPTER SIX

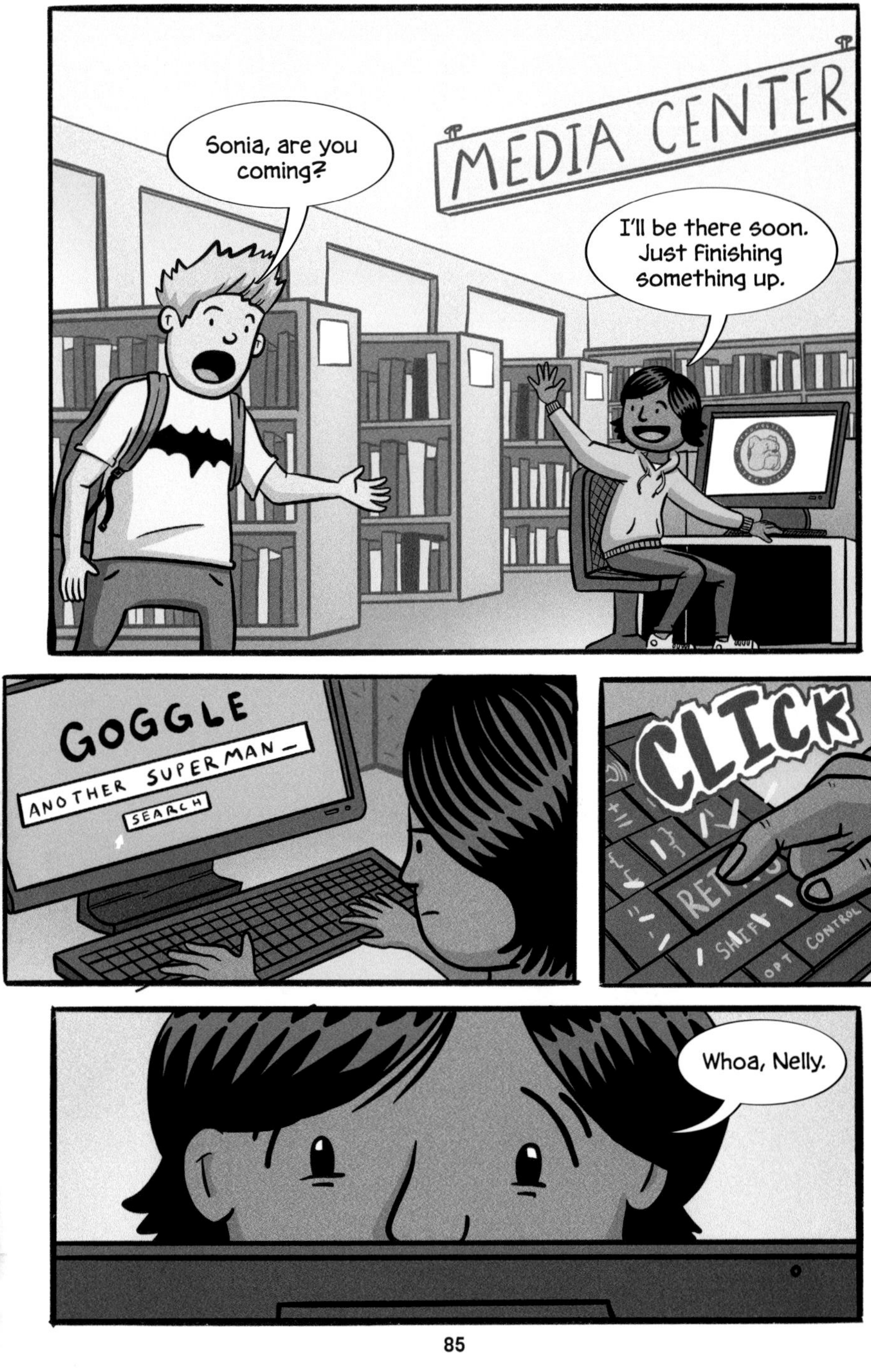
MEDIA CENTER
Sonia, are you coming?
I'll be there soon. Just finishing something up.
GOGGLE
ANOTHER SUPERMAN_
SEARCH
CLICK
RETU
SHIFT
OPT
CONTROL
Whoa, Nelly.

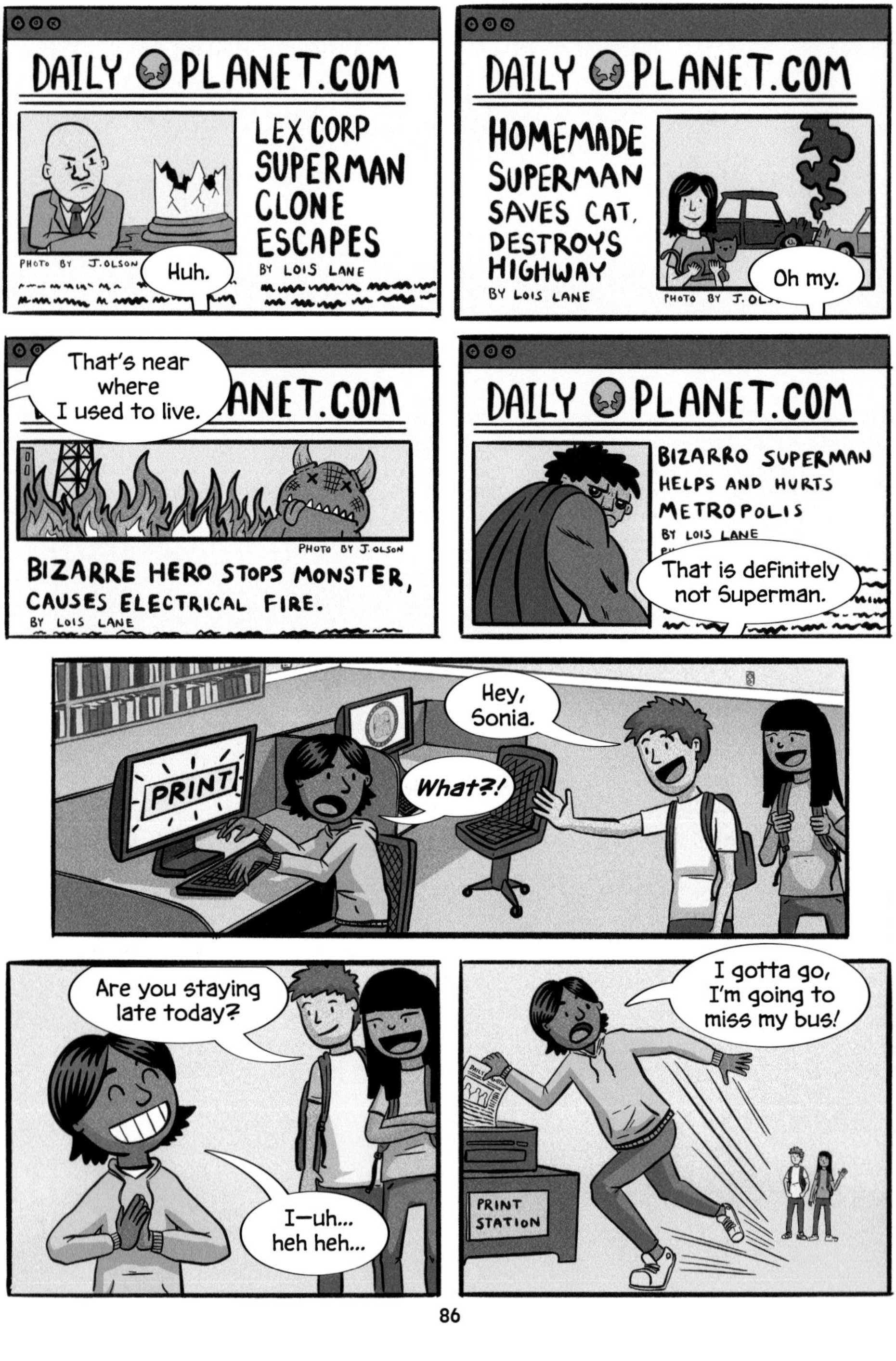
DAILY PLANET.COM
LEX CORP SUPERMAN CLONE ESCAPES
PHOTO BY J. OLSON
BY LOIS LANE
Huh.
DAILY PLANET.COM
HOMEMADE SUPERMAN SAVES CAT, DESTROYS HIGHWAY
BY LOIS LANE
PHOTO BY J. OL
Oh my.
That's near where I used to live.
ANET.COM
PHOTO BY J. OLSON
BIZARRE HERO STOPS MONSTER, CAUSES ELECTRICAL FIRE.
BY LOIS LANE
DAILY PLANET.COM
BIZARRO SUPERMAN HELPS AND HURTS METROPOLIS
BY LOIS LANE
That is definitely not Superman.
PRINT
Hey, Sonia.
What?!
Are you staying late today?
I—uh... heh heh...
I gotta go, I'm going to miss my bus!
PRINT STATION

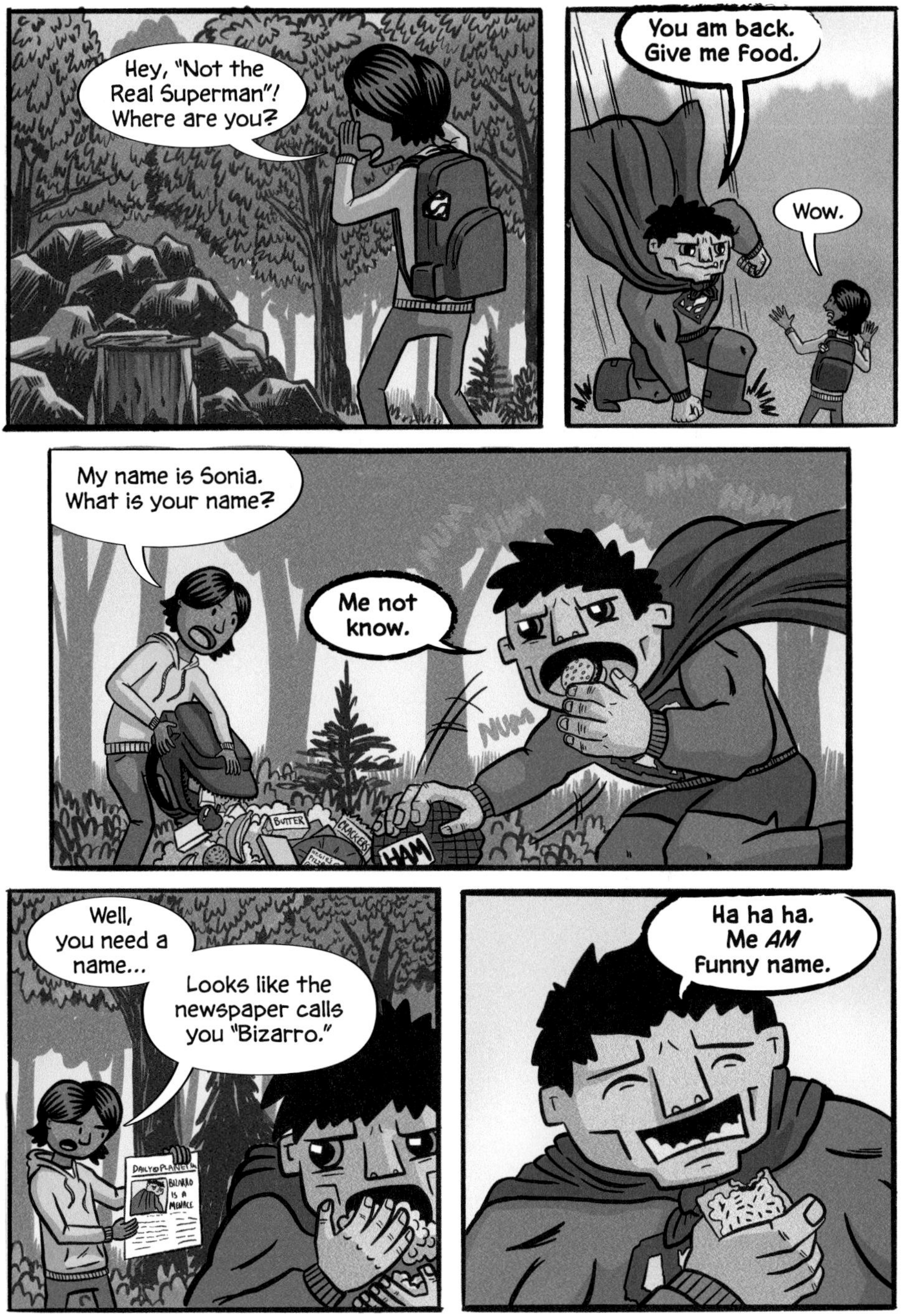
Hey, "Not the Real Superman"! Where are you?
You am back. Give me food.
Wow.
My name is Sonia. What is your name?
Me not know.
NUM
BUTTER
CRACKERS
HAM
Well, you need a name...
Looks like the newspaper calls you "Bizarro."
DAILY PLANET
BIZARRO IS A MENACE
Ha ha ha. Me *AM* funny name.

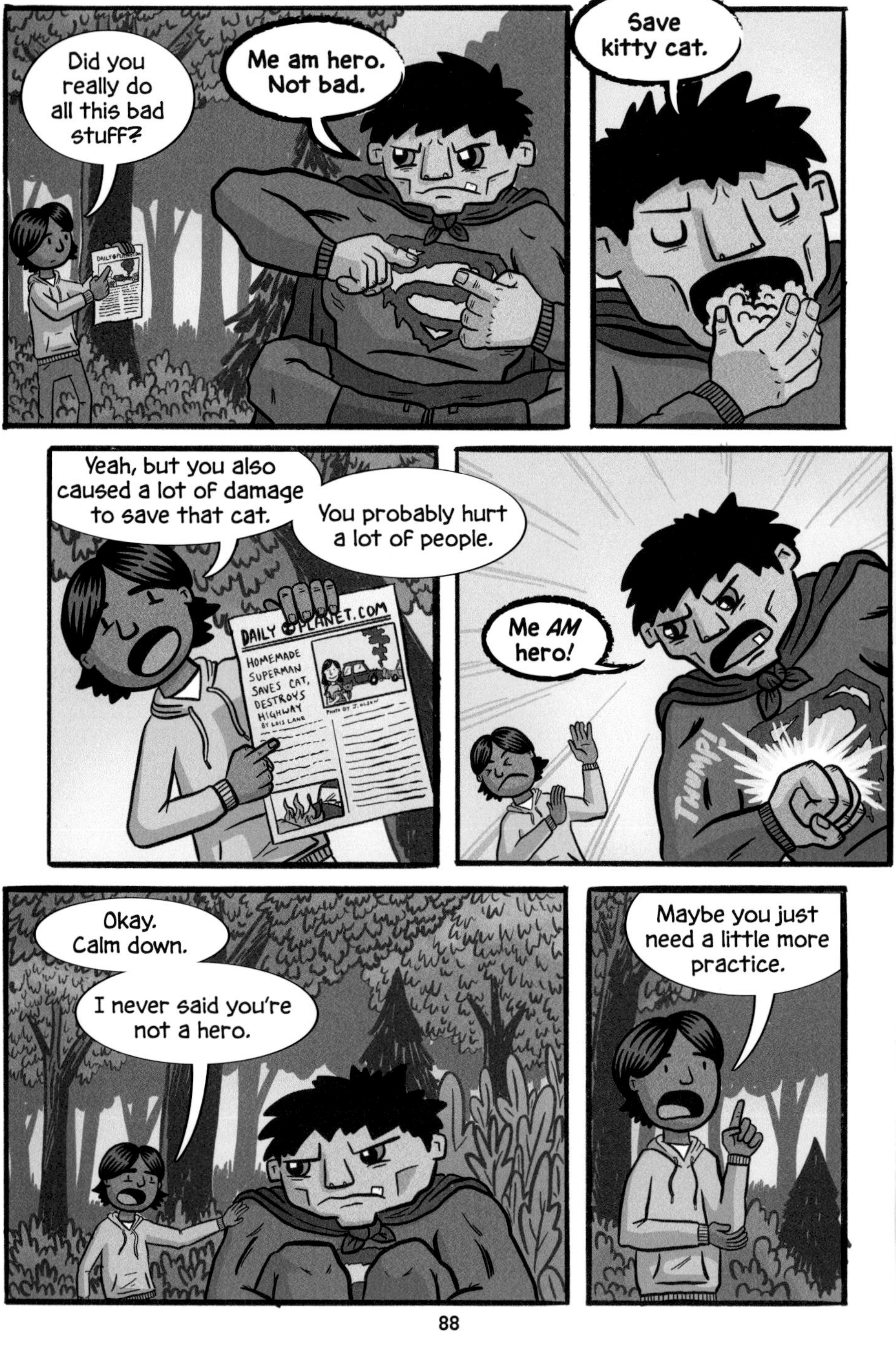
Did you really do all this bad stuff?
Me am hero. Not bad.
Save kitty cat.
Yeah, but you also caused a lot of damage to save that cat.
You probably hurt a lot of people.
DAILY PLANET.COM
HOMEMADE SUPERMAN SAVES CAT, DESTROYS HIGHWAY
BY LOIS LANE
PHOTO BY J. OLSEN
Me AM hero!
THUMP!
Okay. Calm down.
I never said you're not a hero.
Maybe you just need a little more practice.

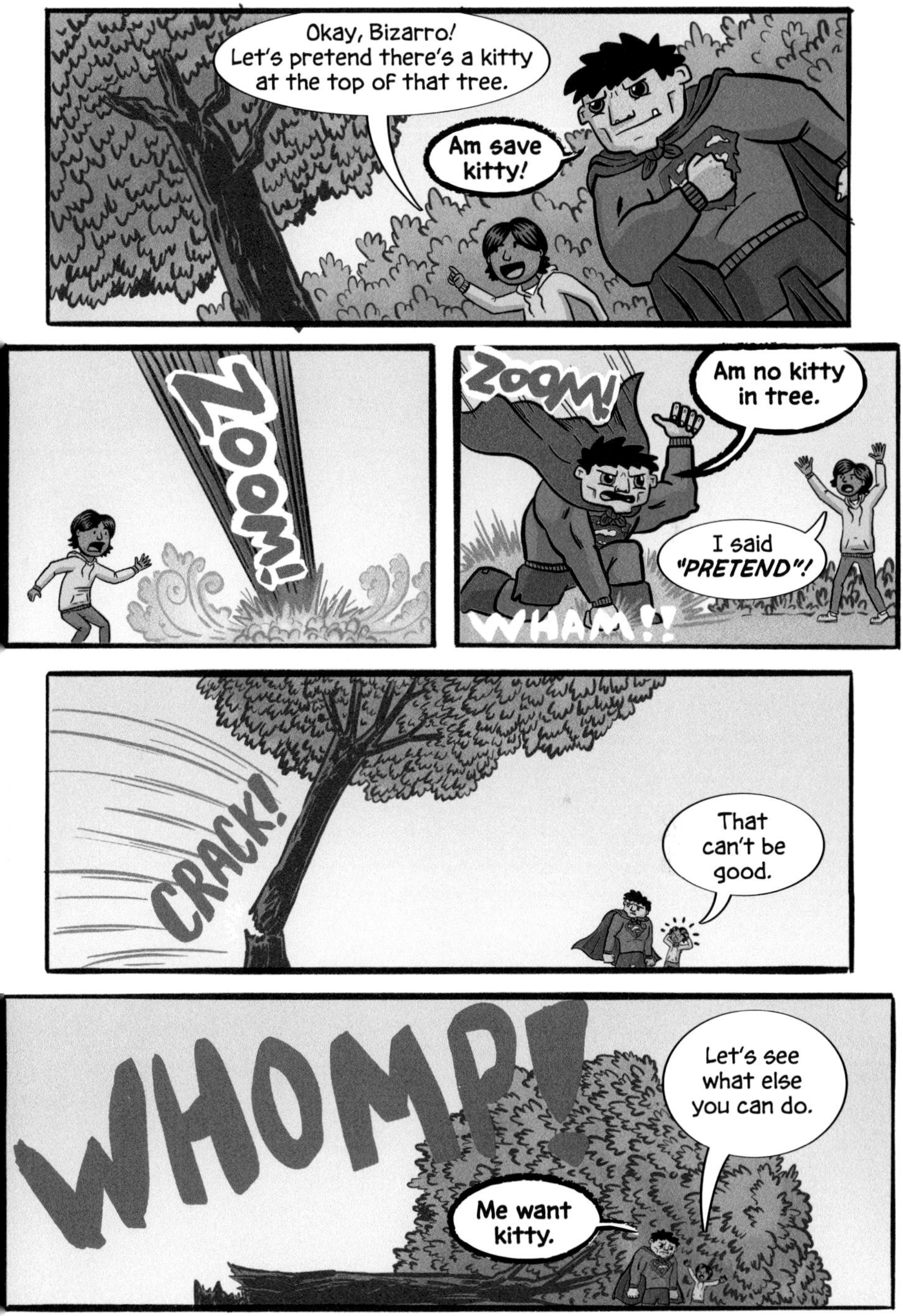
Okay, Bizarro! Let's pretend there's a kitty at the top of that tree.
Am save kitty!
ZOOM!
ZOOM!
Am no kitty in tree.
I said "PRETEND"!
WHAM!!
CRACK!
That can't be good.
WHOMP!
Let's see what else you can do.
Me want kitty.

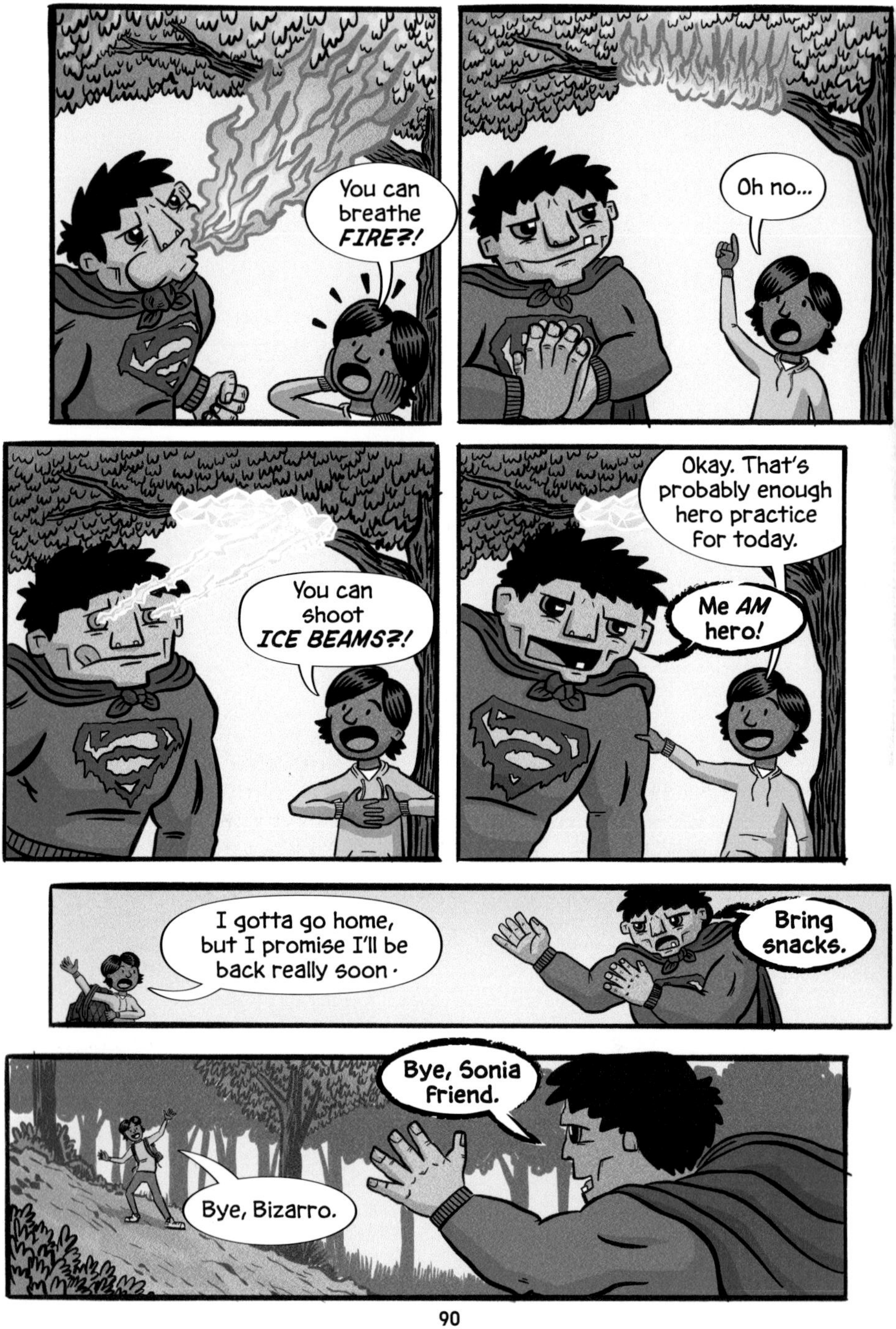
You can breathe FIRE?!
Oh no...
You can shoot ICE BEAMS?!
Okay. That's probably enough hero practice for today.
Me AM hero!
I gotta go home, but I promise I'll be back really soon.
Bring snacks.
Bye, Sonia friend.
Bye, Bizarro.

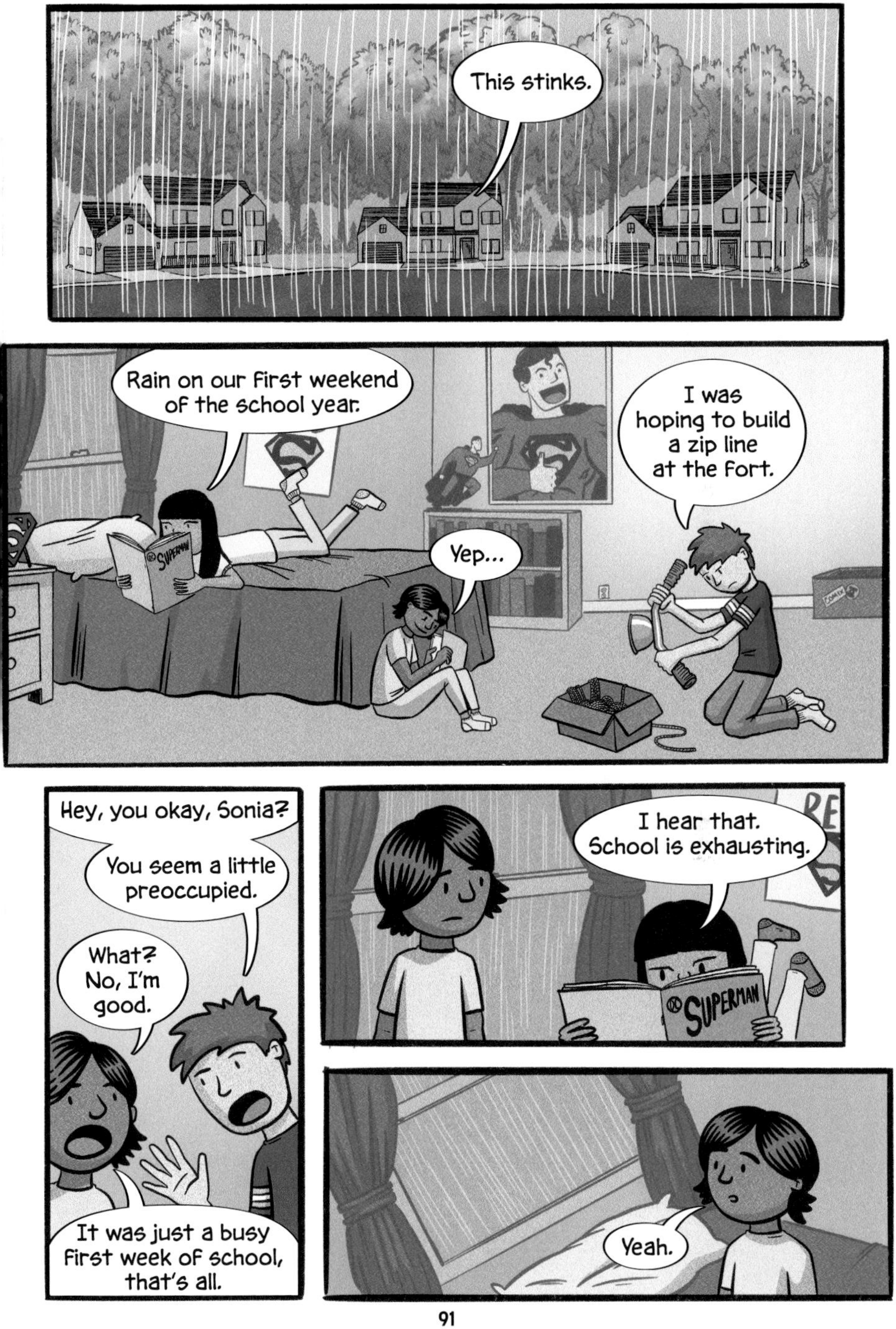
This stinks.
Rain on our first weekend of the school year.
I was hoping to build a zip line at the fort.
Yep...
SUPERMAN
Hey, you okay, Sonia?
You seem a little preoccupied.
What? No, I'm good.
It was just a busy first week of school, that's all.
I hear that. School is exhausting.
SUPERMAN
Yeah.

MONDAY

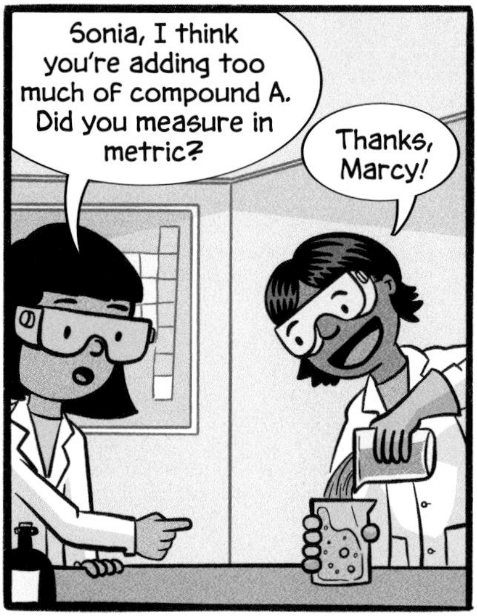
Sonia, I think you're adding too much of compound A. Did you measure in metric?
Thanks, Marcy!

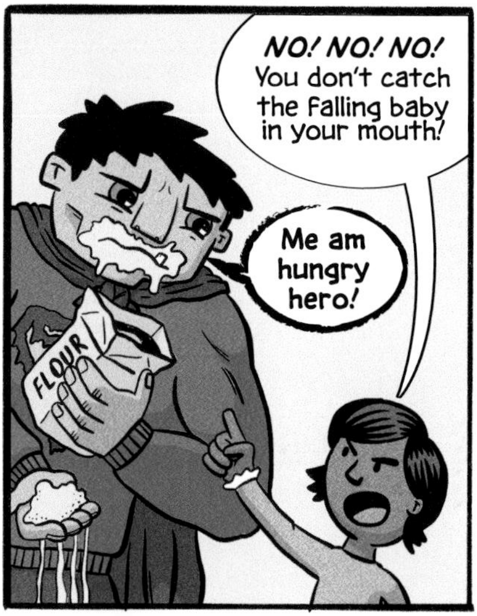
NO! NO! NO! You don't catch the falling baby in your mouth!
Me am hungry hero!
FLOUR

TUESDAY

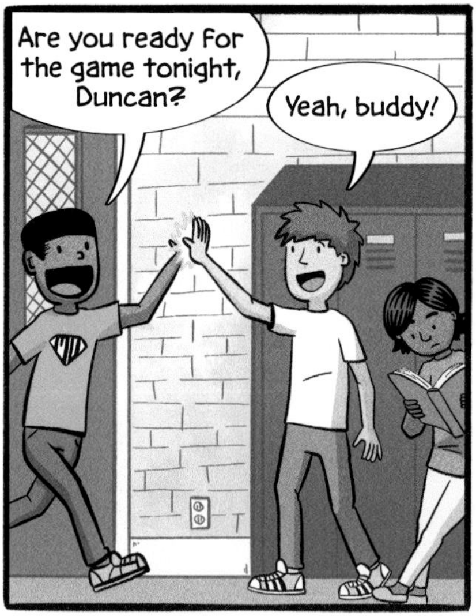
Are you ready for the game tonight, Duncan?
Yeah, buddy!

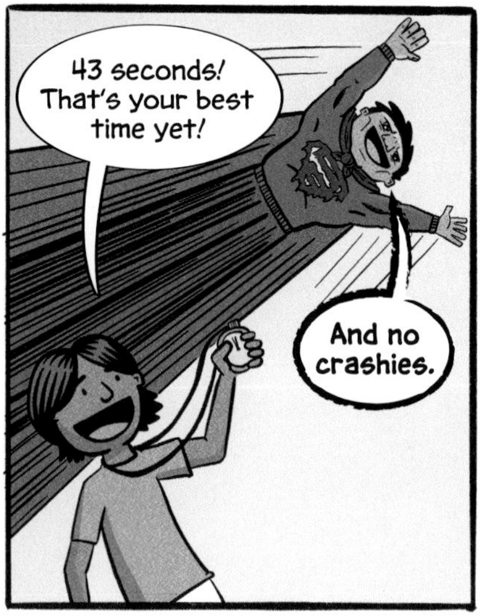
43 seconds! That's your best time yet!
And no crashies.

WEDNESDAY

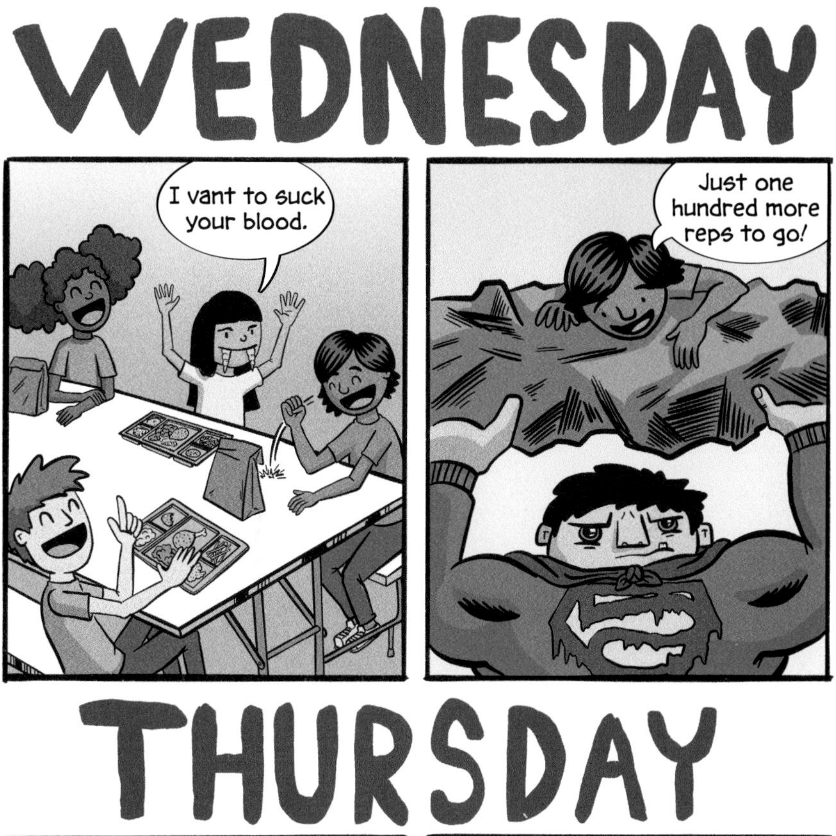
I vant to suck your blood.
Just one hundred more reps to go!

THURSDAY

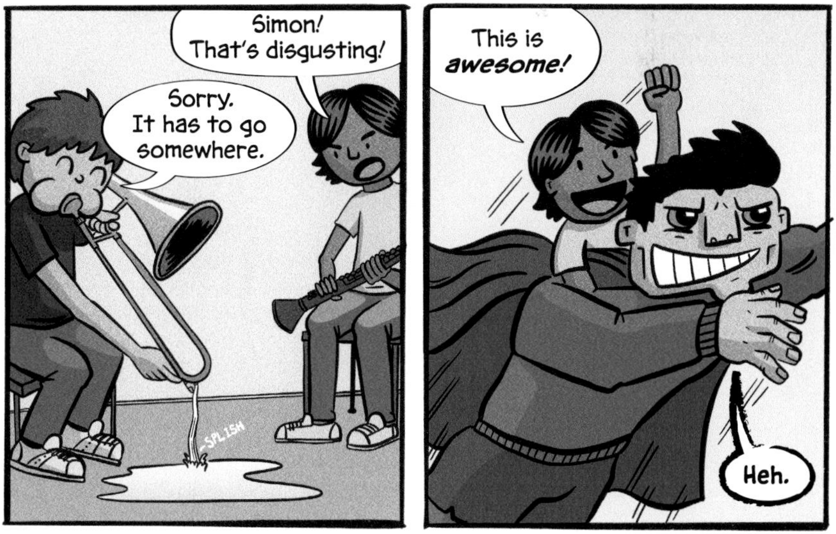
Simon! That's disgusting!
Sorry. It has to go somewhere.
SPLISH
This is *awesome!*
Heh.

FRIDAY

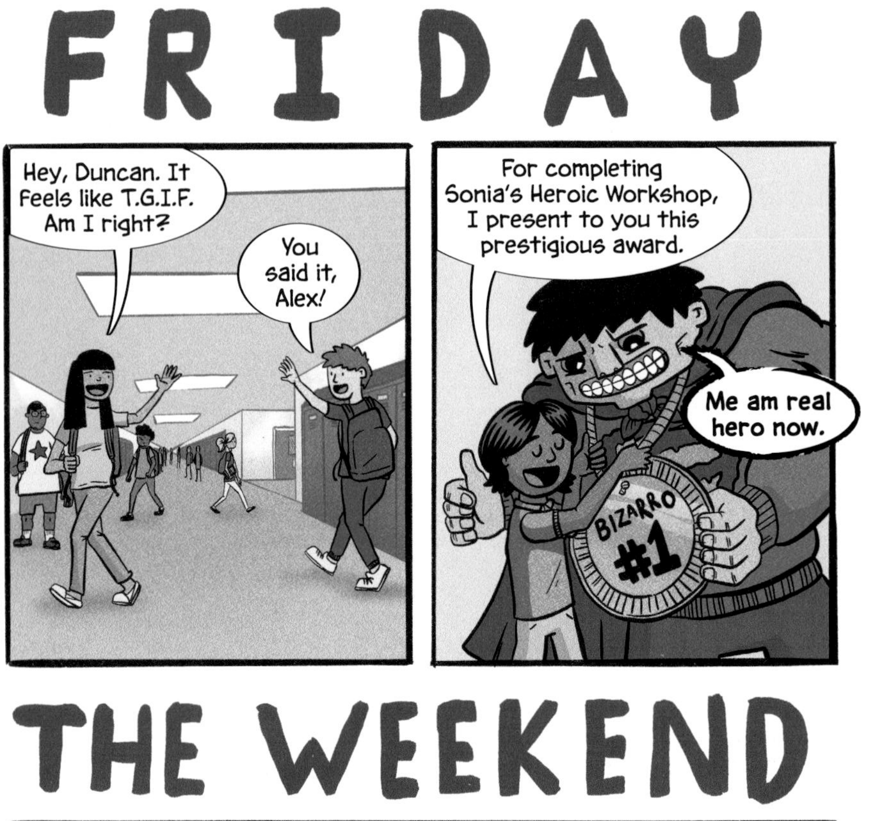
Hey, Duncan. It feels like T.G.I.F. Am I right?
You said it, Alex!
For completing Sonia's Heroic Workshop, I present to you this prestigious award.
Me am real hero now.
BIZARRO #1

THE WEEKEND

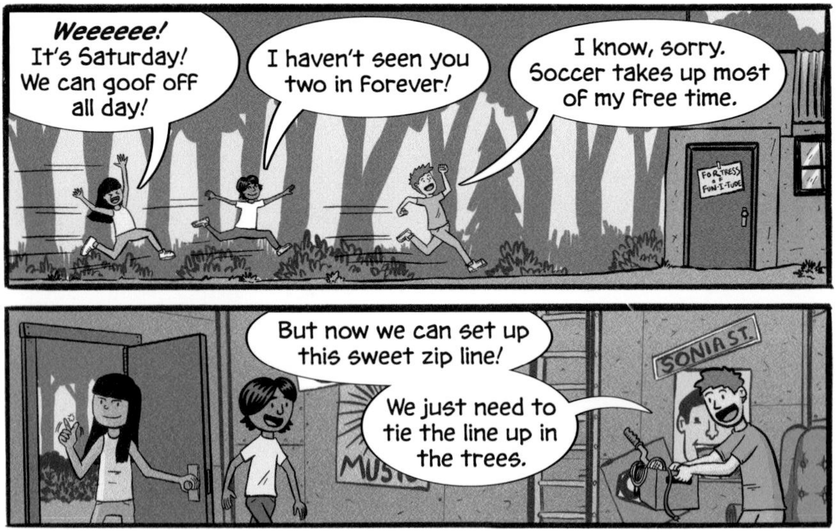
Weeeeee! It's Saturday! We can goof off all day!
I haven't seen you two in forever!
I know, sorry. Soccer takes up most of my free time.
FORTRESS OF FUN-I-TUDE
But now we can set up this sweet zip line!
SONIA ST.
We just need to tie the line up in the trees.

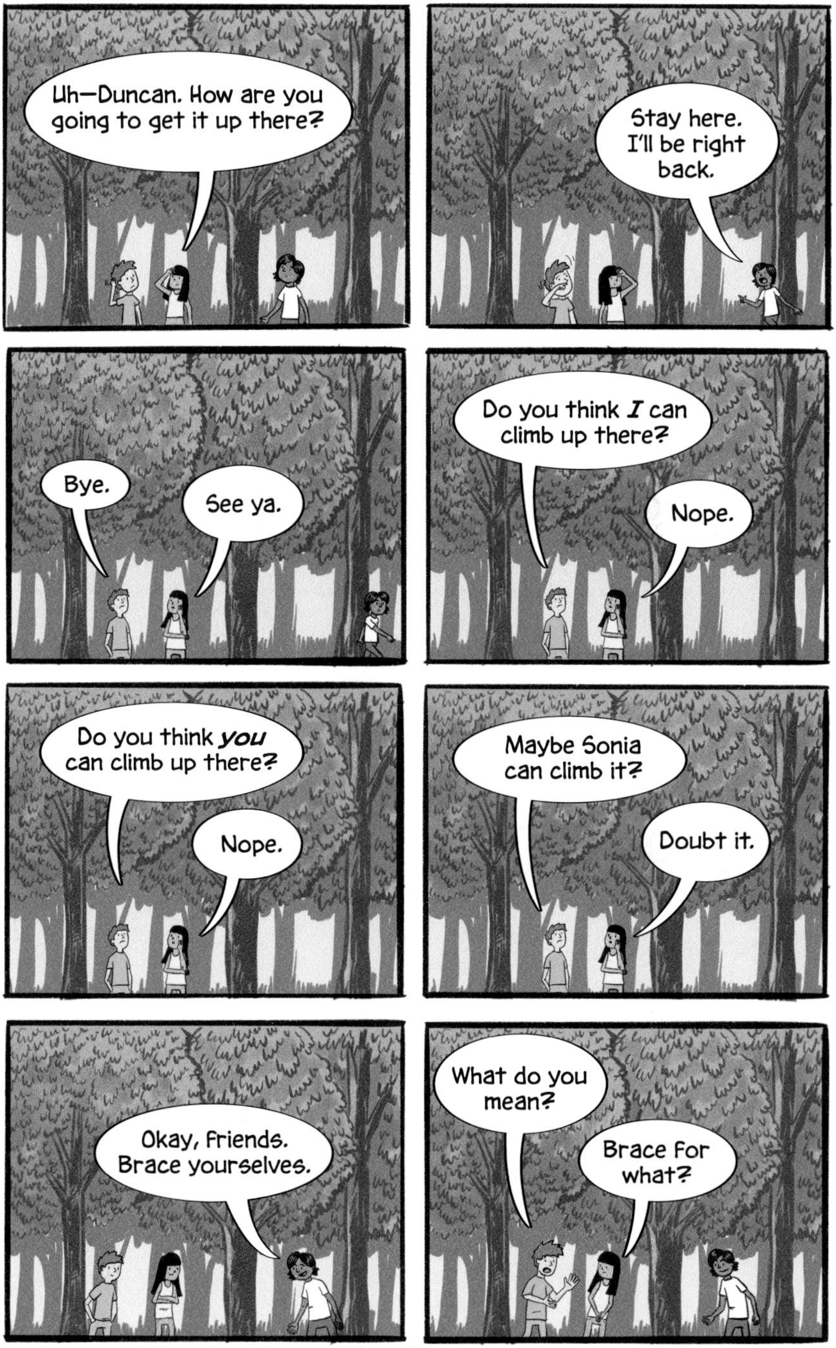
Uh—Duncan. How are you going to get it up there?
Stay here. I'll be right back.
Bye.
See ya.
Do you think *I* can climb up there?
Nope.
Do you think *you* can climb up there?
Nope.
Maybe Sonia can climb it?
Doubt it.
Okay, friends. Brace yourselves.
What do you mean?
Brace for what?

WHOMP!

AUGH!

AUGH!

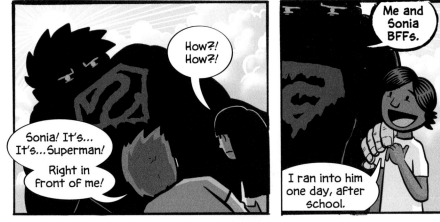

How?! How?!

Sonia! It's... It's... Superman!

Right in front of me!

Me and Sonia BFFs.

I ran into him one day, after school.

Mr. Superman, sir? Could you help us with our zip line?

We need to tie this up in a tree, but none of us can get up there.

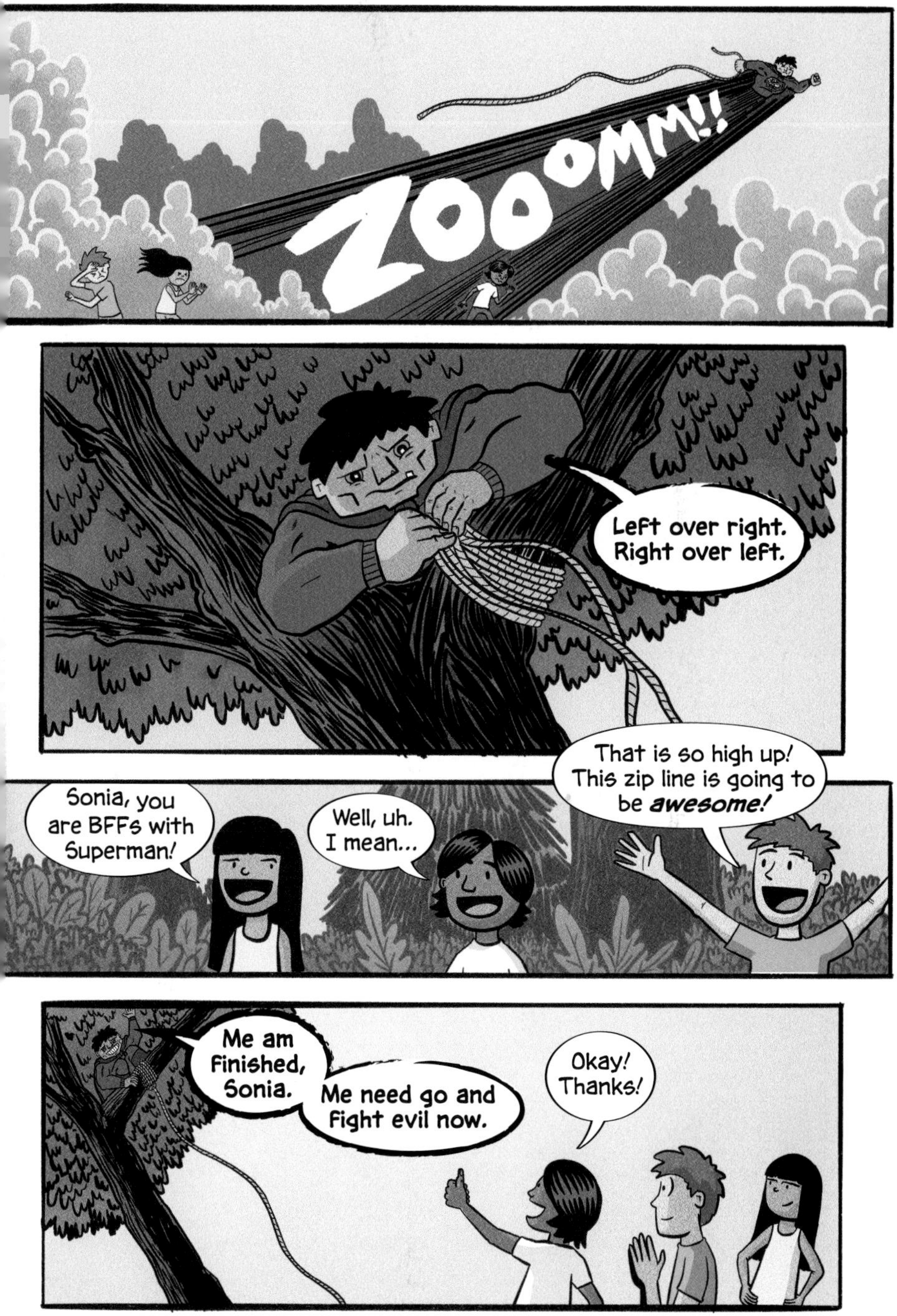
ZOOOMM!!
Left over right. Right over left.
Sonia, you are BFFs with Superman!
Well, uh. I mean...
That is so high up! This zip line is going to be *awesome!*
Me am Finished, Sonia.
Me need go and fight evil now.
Okay! Thanks!

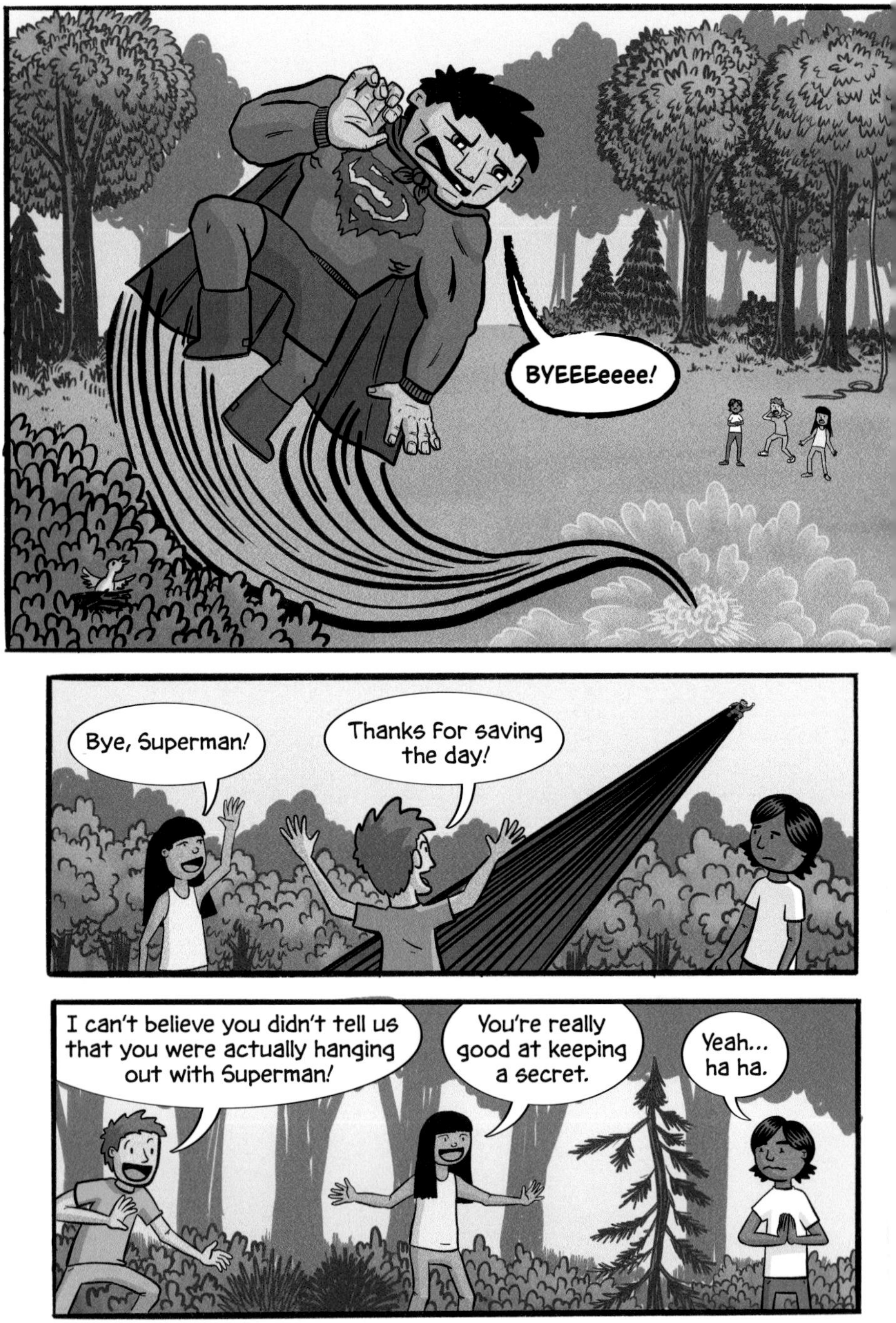
BYEEEeeee!
Bye, Superman!
Thanks for saving the day!
I can't believe you didn't tell us that you were actually hanging out with Superman!
You're really good at keeping a secret.
Yeah... ha ha.

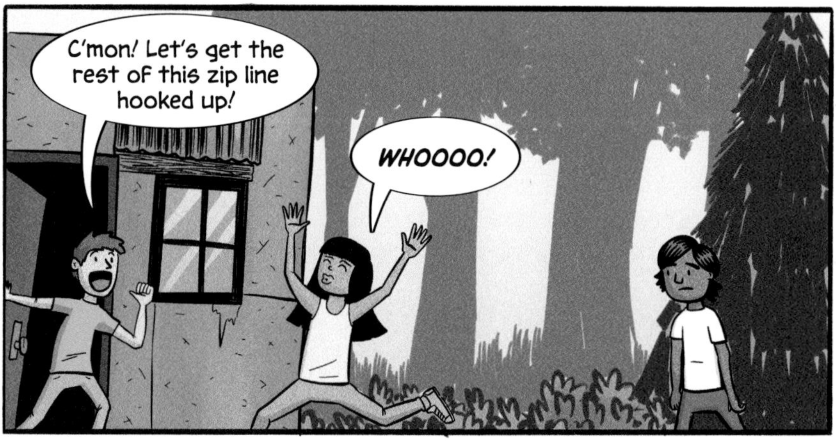
C'mon! Let's get the rest of this zip line hooked up!
WHOOOO!

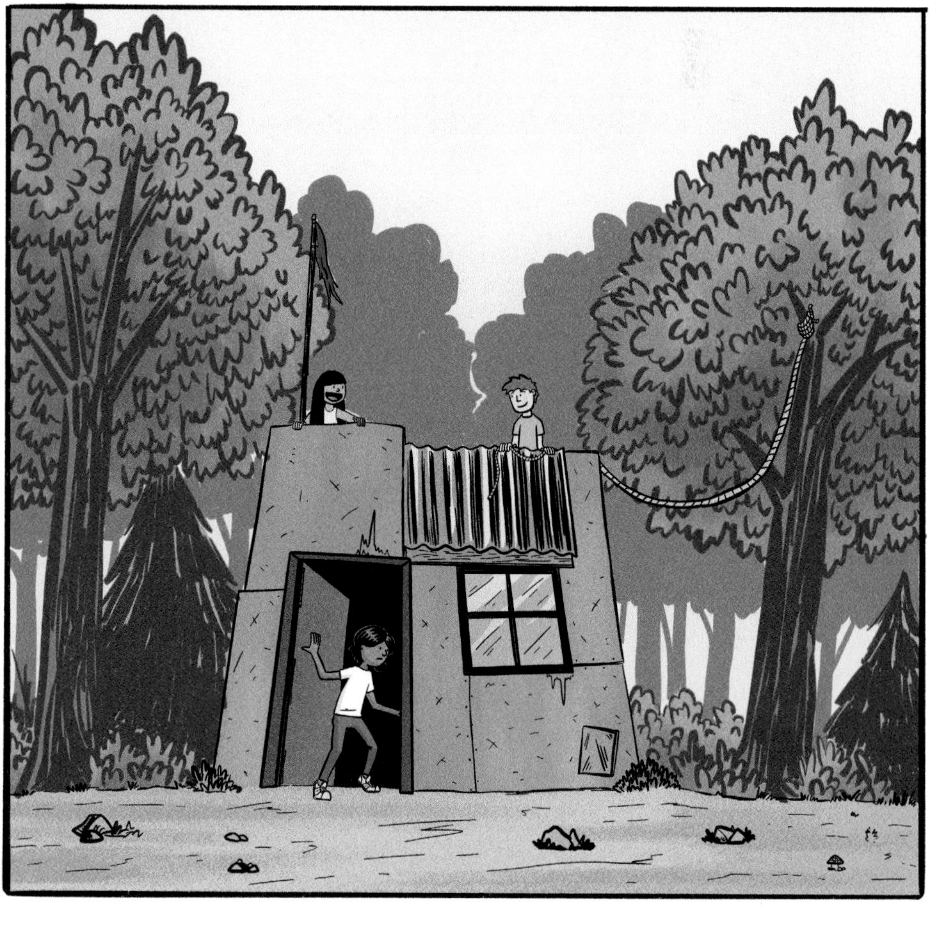

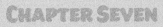

CHAPTER SEVEN

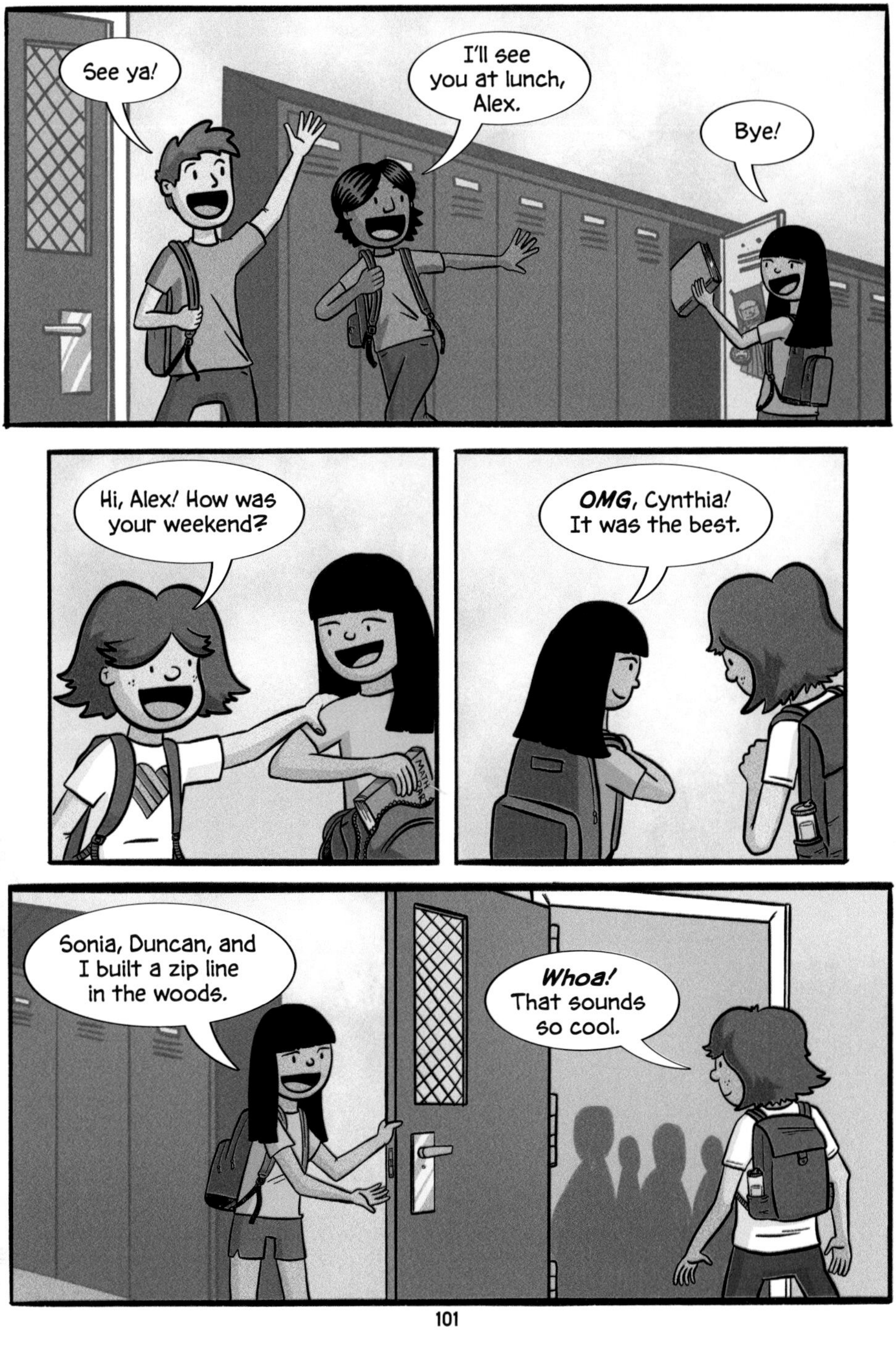
See ya!
I'll see you at lunch, Alex.
Bye!
Hi, Alex! How was your weekend?
OMG, Cynthia! It was the best.
Sonia, Duncan, and I built a zip line in the woods.
Whoa! That sounds so cool.

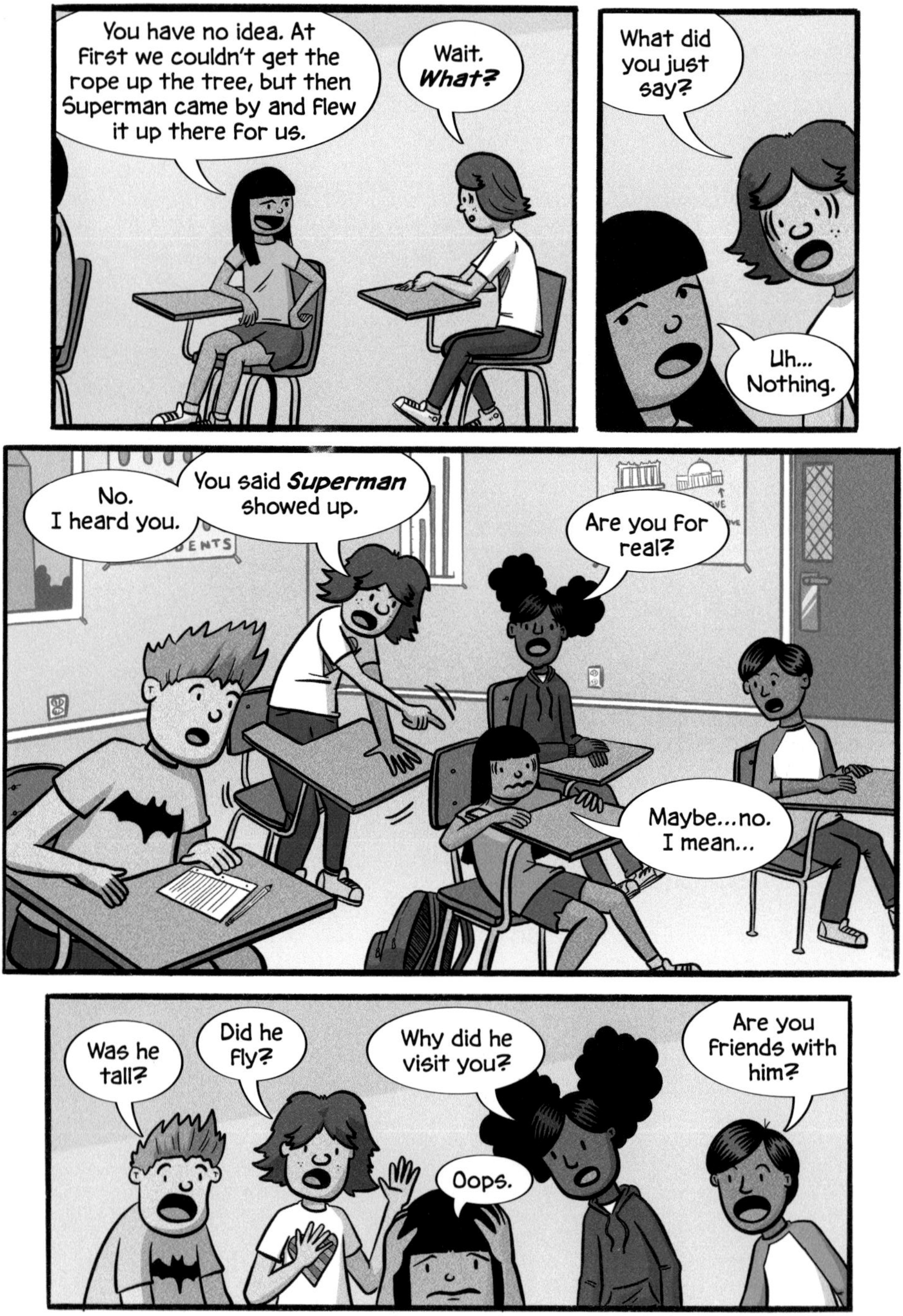
You have no idea. At first we couldn't get the rope up the tree, but then Superman came by and flew it up there for us.
Wait. ***What?***
What did you just say?
Uh... Nothing.
No. I heard you.
You said ***Superman*** showed up.
Are you for real?
Maybe...no. I mean...
Was he tall?
Did he fly?
Why did he visit you?
Oops.
Are you friends with him?

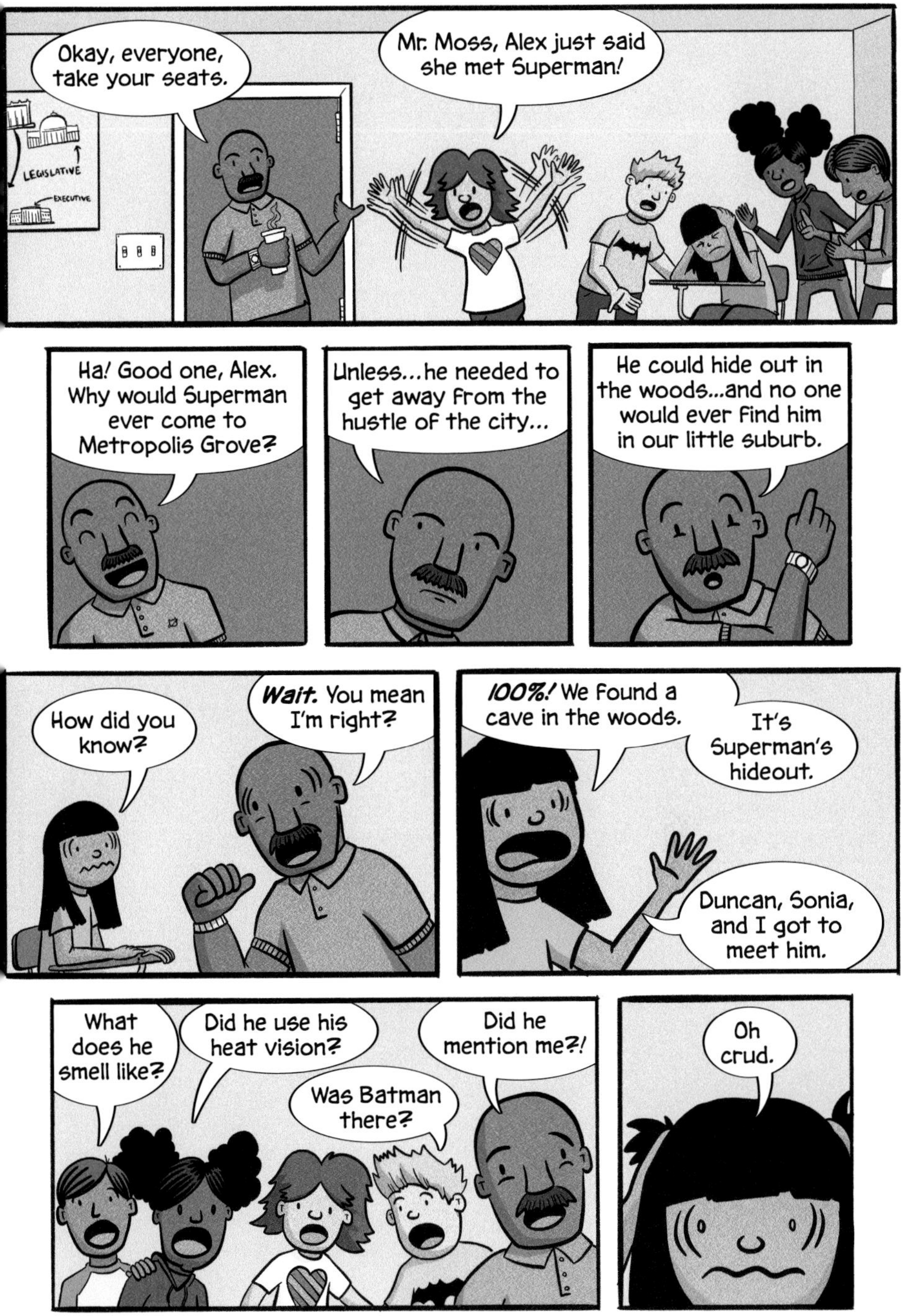
Okay, everyone, take your seats.
Mr. Moss, Alex just said she met Superman!
LEGISLATIVE
EXECUTIVE
Ha! Good one, Alex. Why would Superman ever come to Metropolis Grove?
Unless...he needed to get away from the hustle of the city...
He could hide out in the woods...and no one would ever find him in our little suburb.
How did you know?
Wait. You mean I'm right?
100%! We found a cave in the woods.
It's Superman's hideout.
Duncan, Sonia, and I got to meet him.
What does he smell like?
Did he use his heat vision?
Was Batman there?
Did he mention me?!
Oh crud.

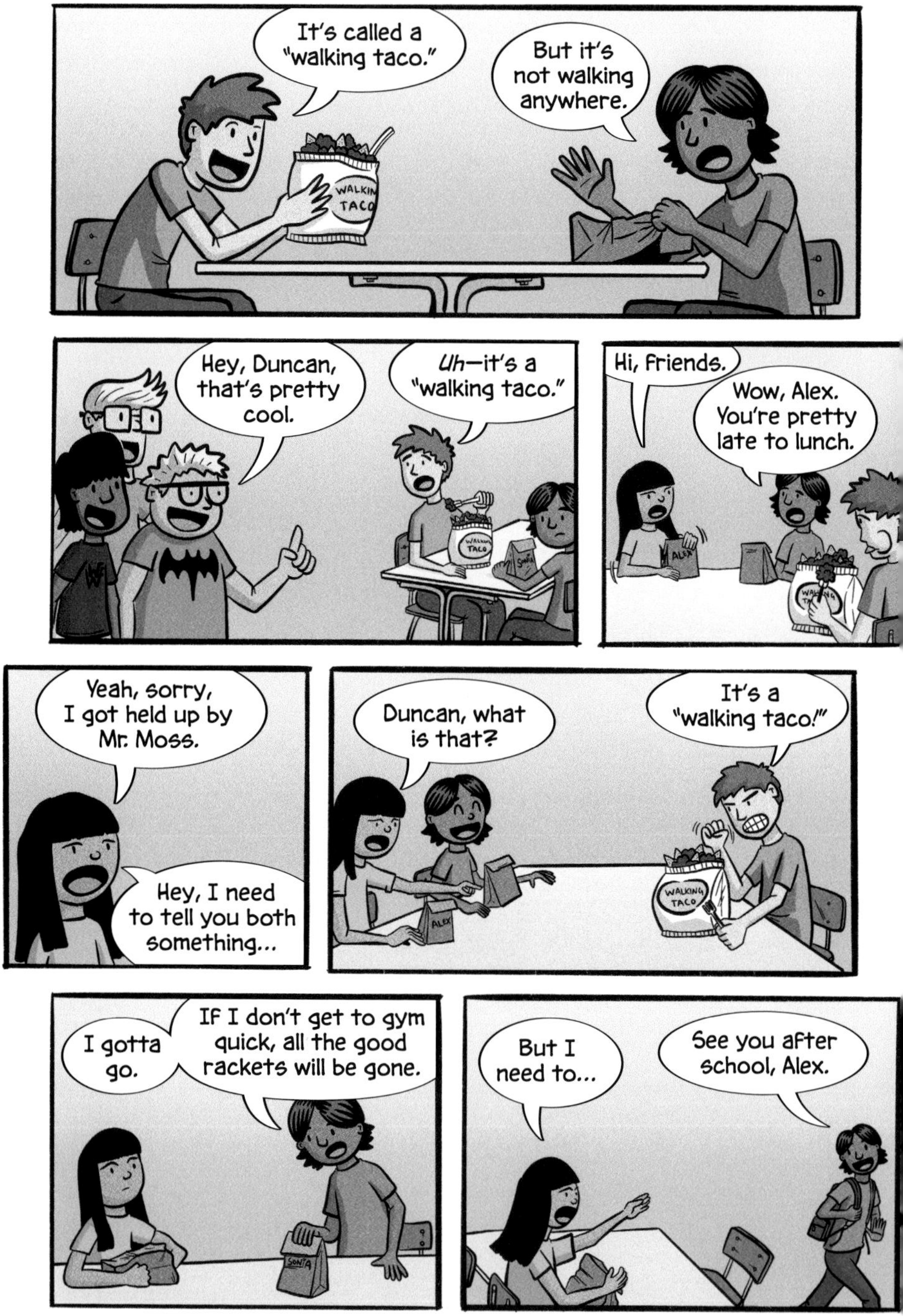

It's called a "walking taco."
WALKING TACO
But it's not walking anywhere.
Hey, Duncan, that's pretty cool.
Uh—it's a "walking taco."
WALKING TACO
SONIA
Hi, friends.
Wow, Alex. You're pretty late to lunch.
ALEX
Yeah, sorry, I got held up by Mr. Moss.
Hey, I need to tell you both something...
Duncan, what is that?
It's a "walking taco!"
WALKING TACO
ALEX
I gotta go.
If I don't get to gym quick, all the good rackets will be gone.
SONIA
But I need to...
See you after school, Alex.

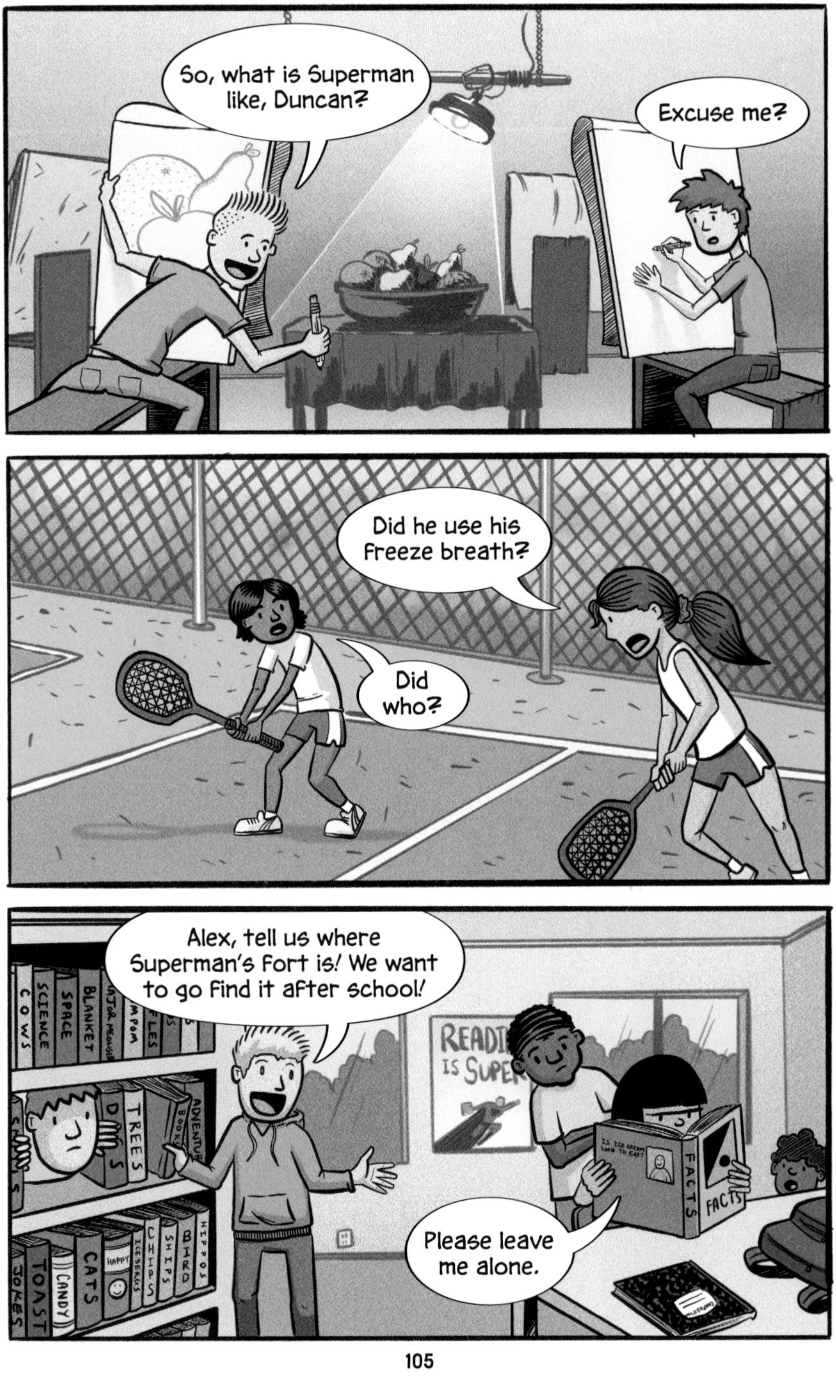
So, what is Superman like, Duncan?
Excuse me?
Did he use his freeze breath?
Did who?
Alex, tell us where Superman's fort is! We want to go find it after school!
Please leave me alone.
READI
IS SUPER
FACTS
COWS
SCIENCE
SPACE
BLANKET
TREES
CATS
CANDY
HAPPY
SHIPS
BIRD
HIPPOS
TOAST
JOKES

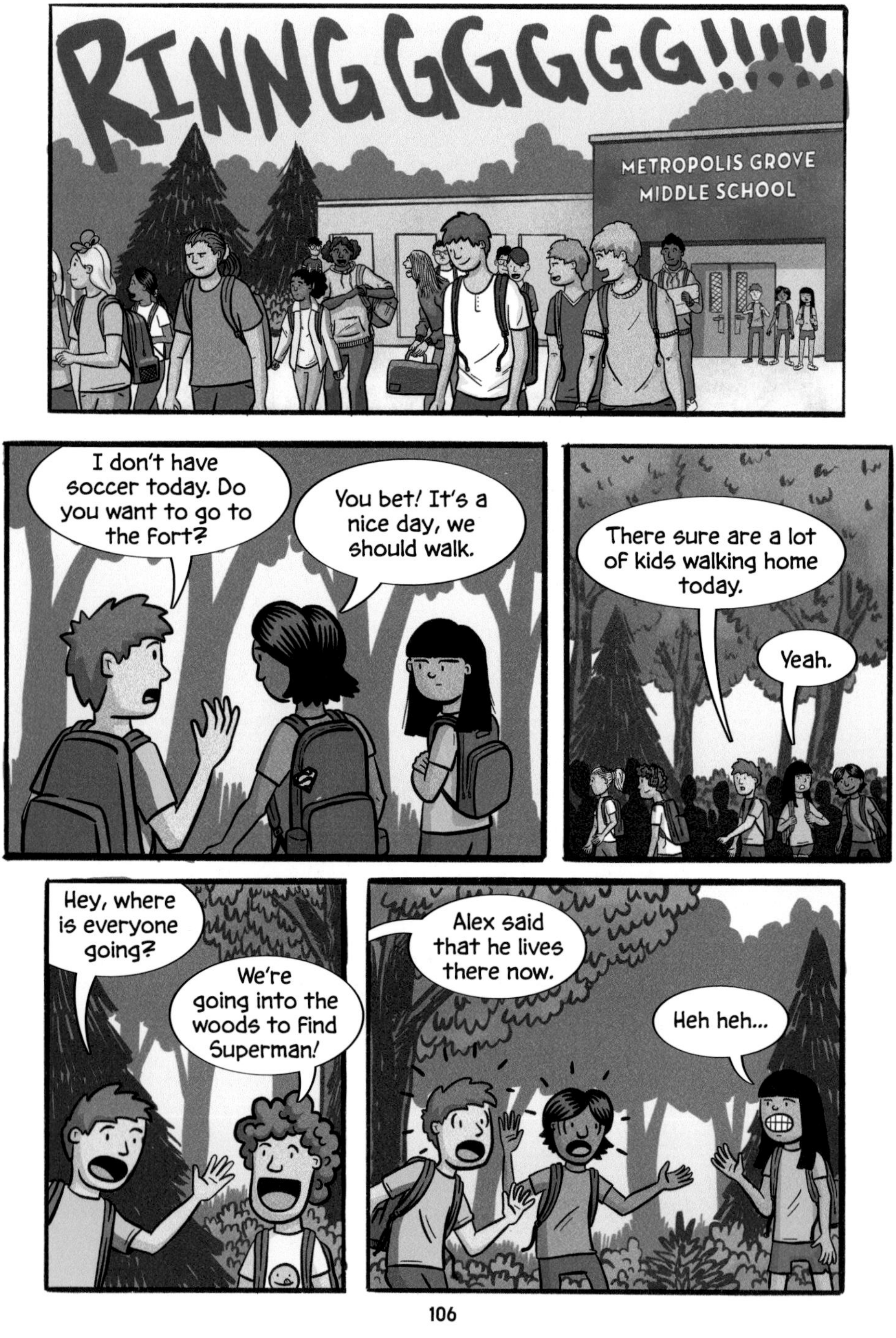
RINNGGGGGG!!!!!
METROPOLIS GROVE
MIDDLE SCHOOL
I don't have soccer today. Do you want to go to the fort?
You bet! It's a nice day, we should walk.
There sure are a lot of kids walking home today.
Yeah.
Hey, where is everyone going?
We're going into the woods to find Superman!
Alex said that he lives there now.
Heh heh...

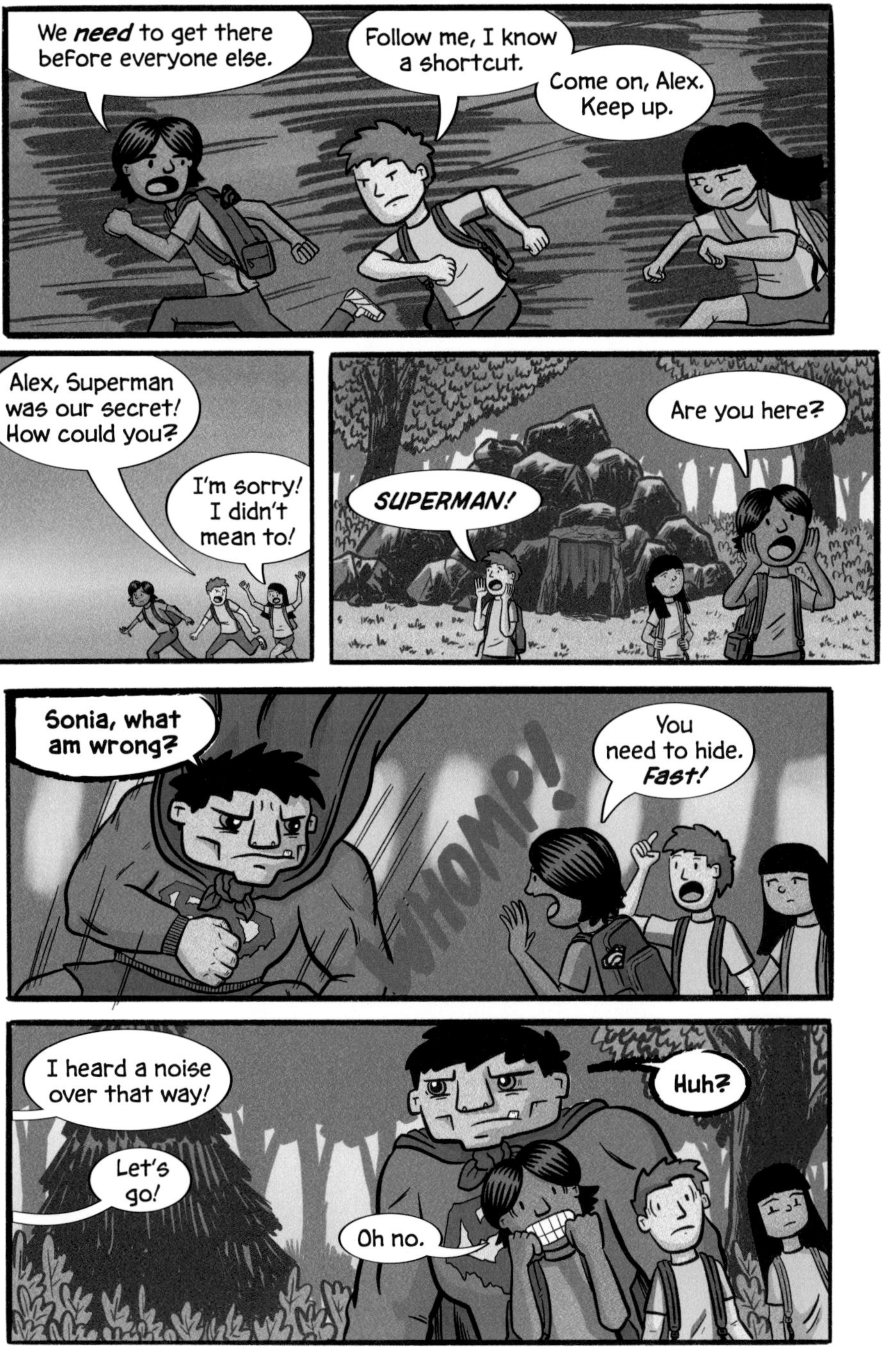
We *need* to get there before everyone else.
Follow me, I know a shortcut.
Come on, Alex. Keep up.
Alex, Superman was our secret! How could you?
I'm sorry! I didn't mean to!
Are you here?
SUPERMAN!
Sonia, what am wrong?
WHOMP!
You need to hide. *Fast!*
I heard a noise over that way!
Huh?
Let's go!
Oh no.

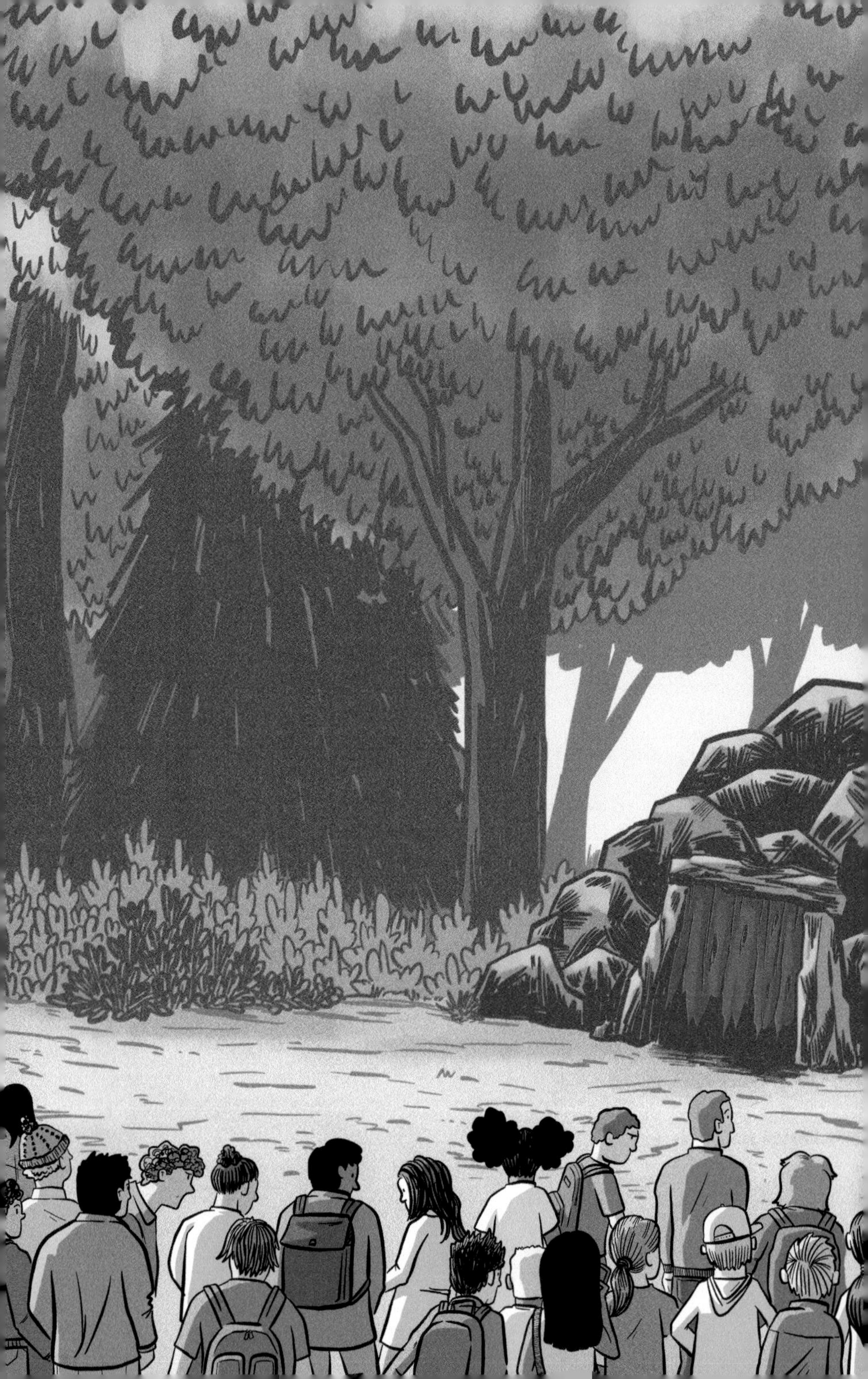

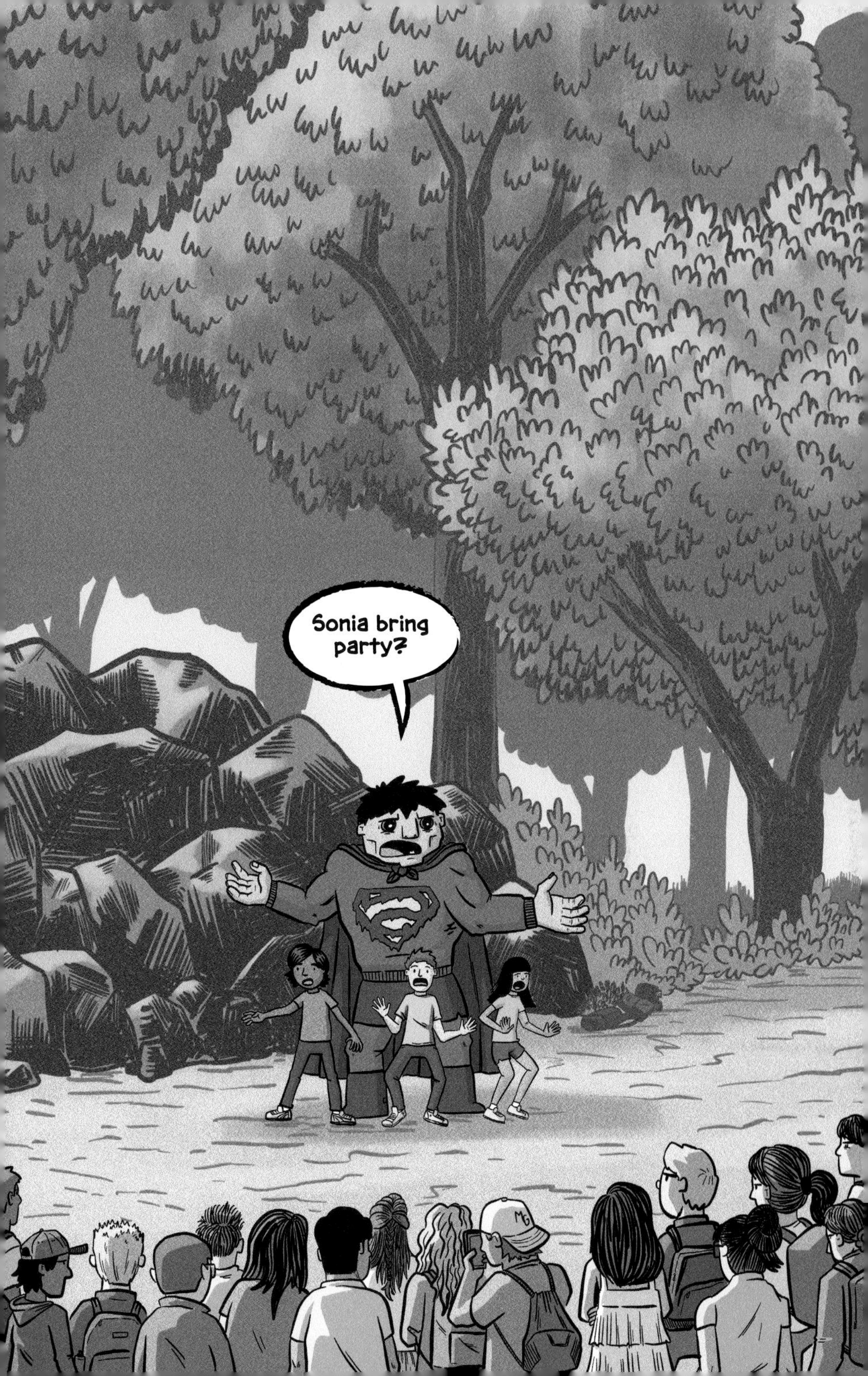
Sonia bring party?

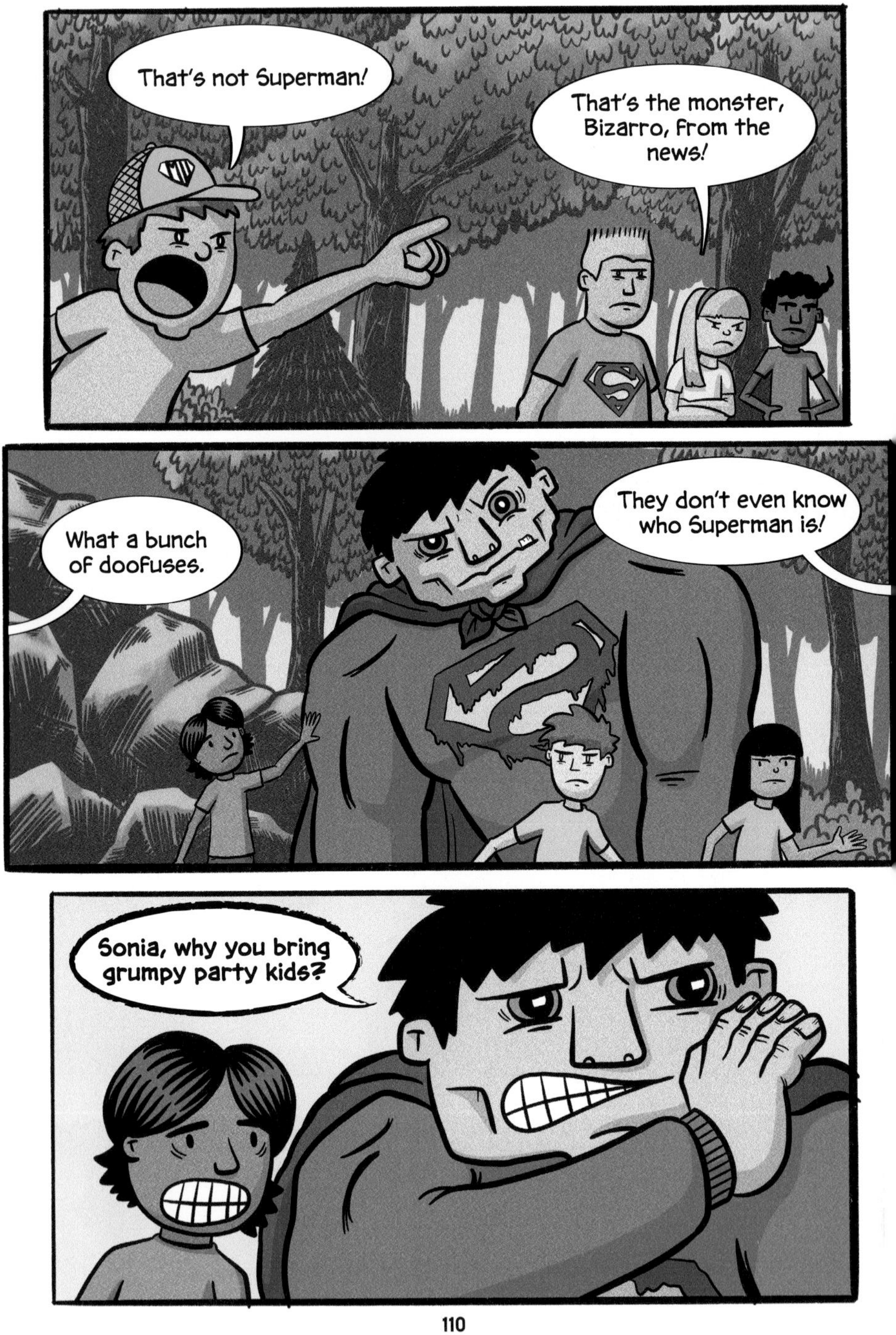
That's not Superman!
That's the monster, Bizarro, from the news!
What a bunch of doofuses.
They don't even know who Superman is!
Sonia, why you bring grumpy party kids?

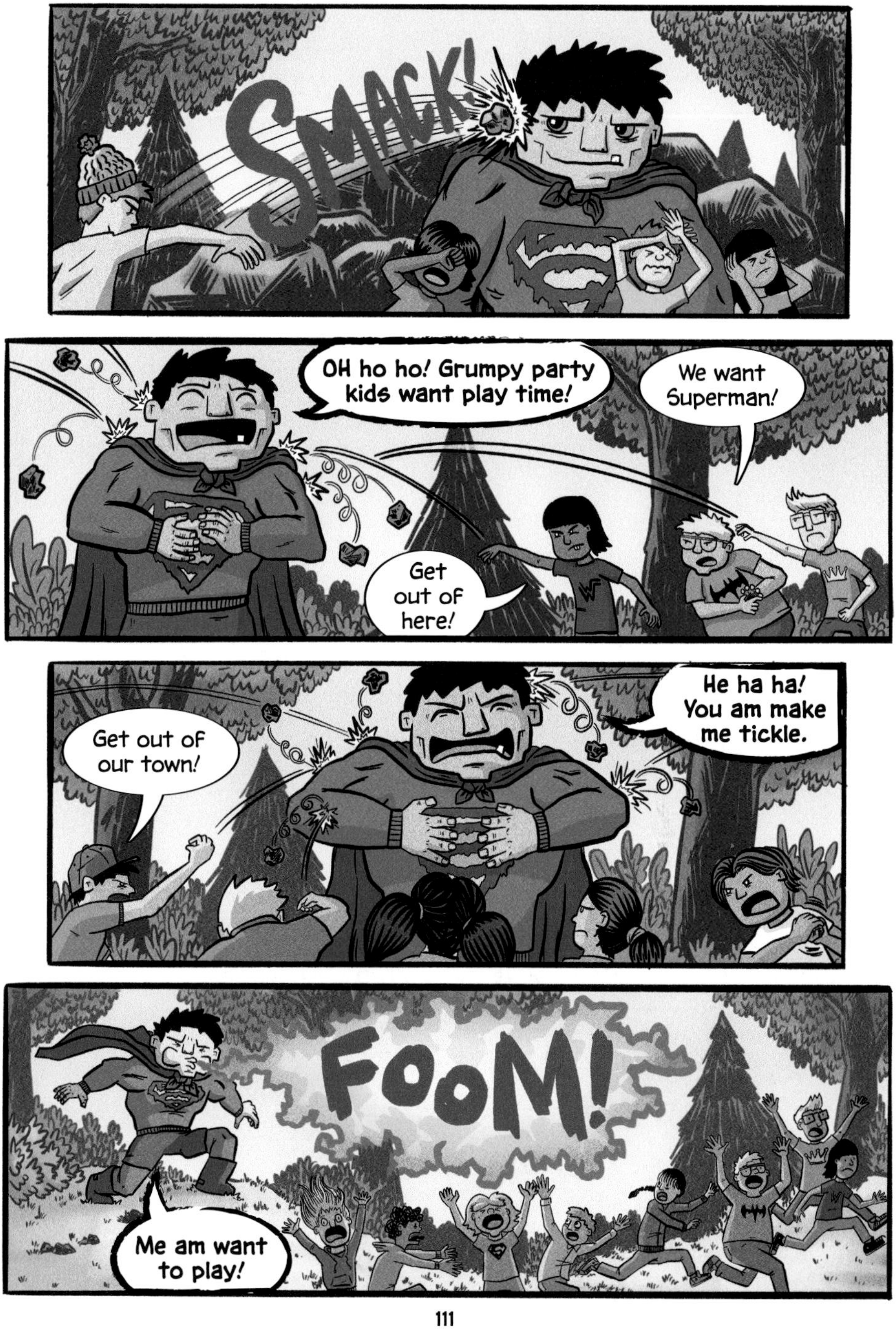
SMACK!
OH ho ho! Grumpy party kids want play time!
We want Superman!
Get out of here!
Get out of our town!
He ha ha! You am make me tickle.
FOOM!
Me am want to play!

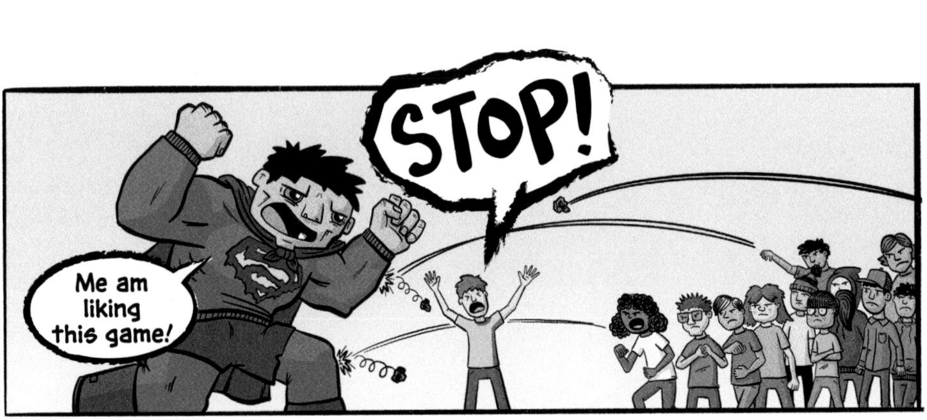
STOP!
Me am liking this game!

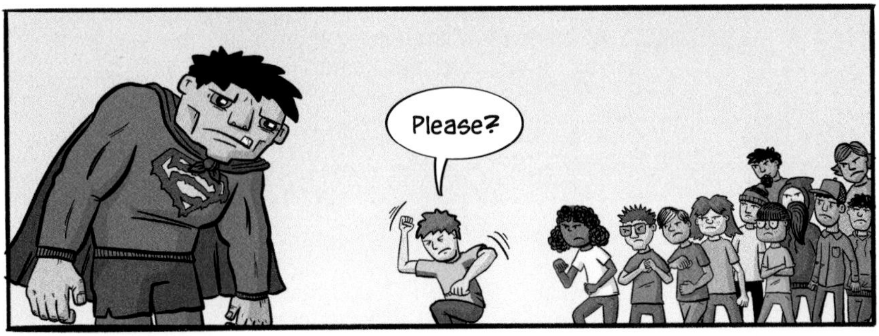
Please?

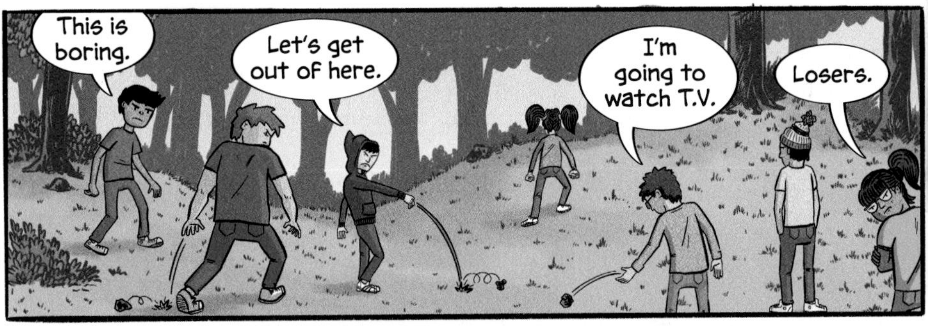
This is boring.
Let's get out of here.
I'm going to watch T.V.
Losers.

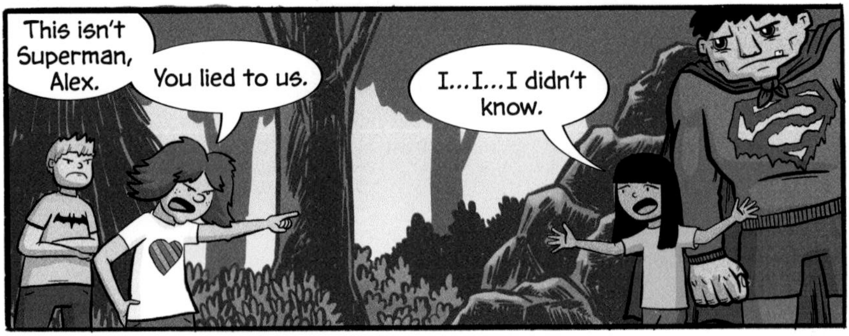
This isn't Superman, Alex.
You lied to us.
I...I...I didn't know.

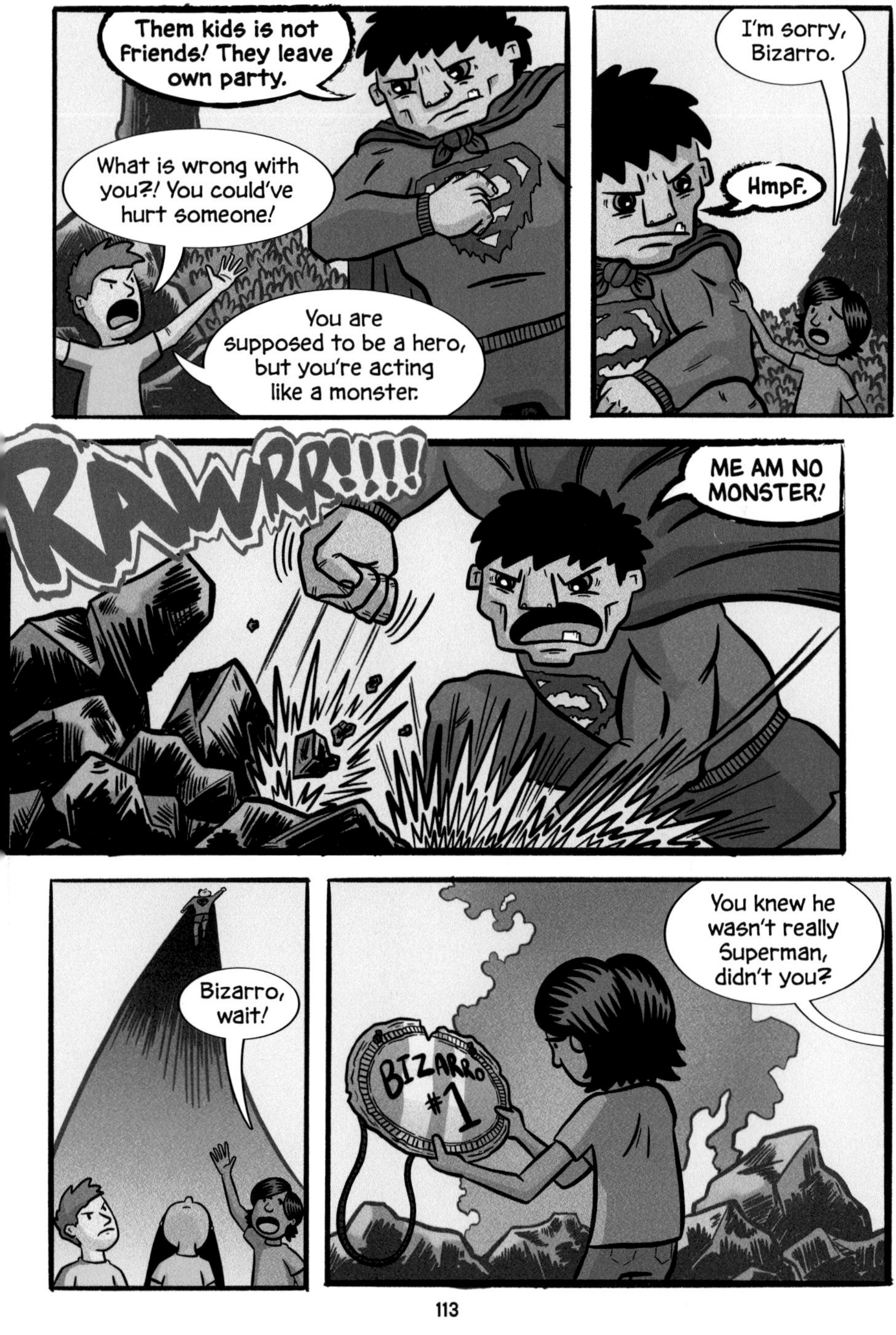
Them kids is not friends! They leave own party.
What is wrong with you?! You could've hurt someone!
You are supposed to be a hero, but you're acting like a monster.
I'm sorry, Bizarro.
Hmpf.
RAWRR!!!!
ME AM NO MONSTER!
Bizarro, wait!
You knew he wasn't really Superman, didn't you?
BIZARRO #1

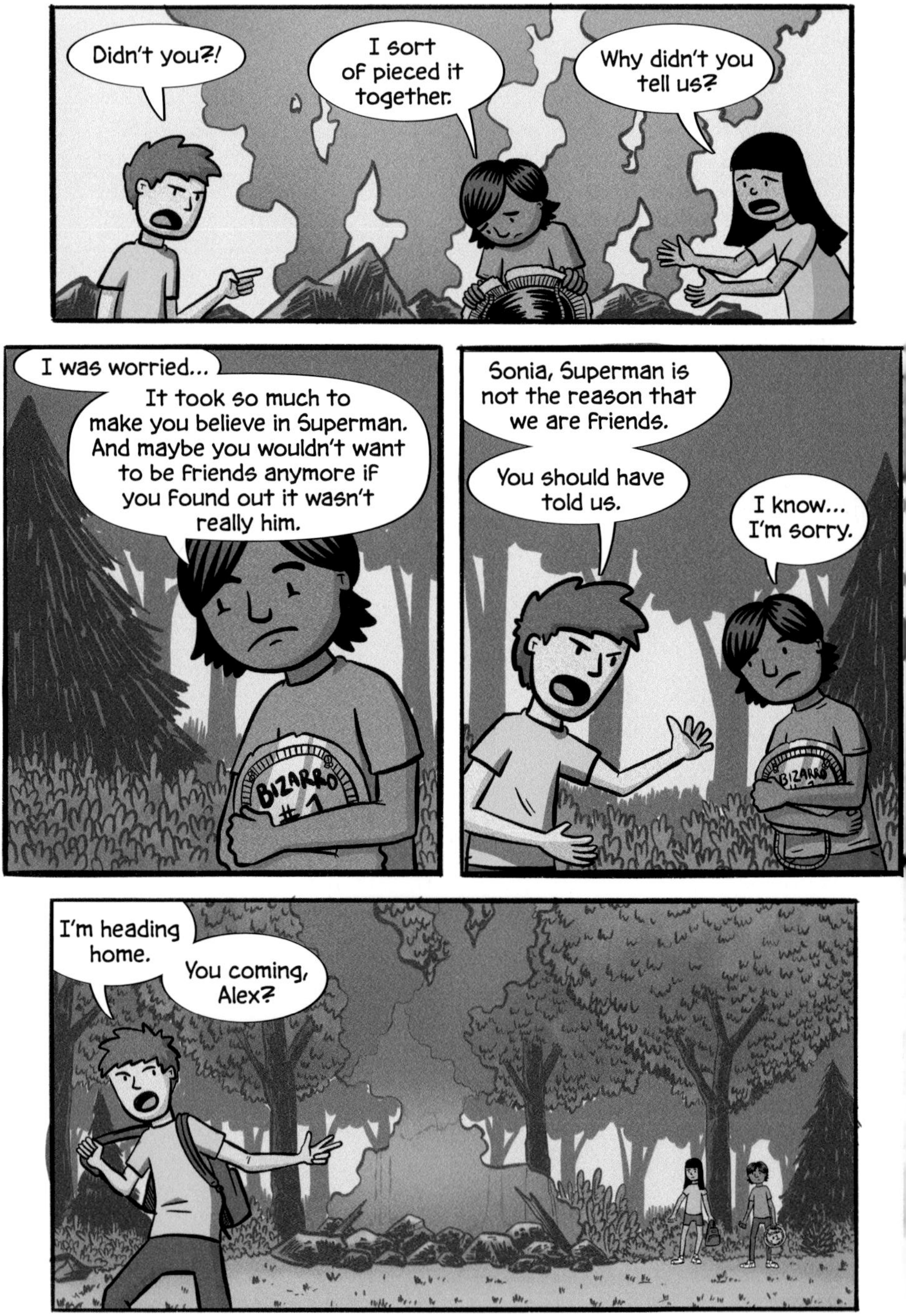
Didn't you?!
I sort of pieced it together.
Why didn't you tell us?
I was worried...
It took so much to make you believe in Superman. And maybe you wouldn't want to be friends anymore if you found out it wasn't really him.
BIZARRO #1
Sonia, Superman is not the reason that we are friends.
You should have told us.
I know... I'm sorry.
I'm heading home.
You coming, Alex?

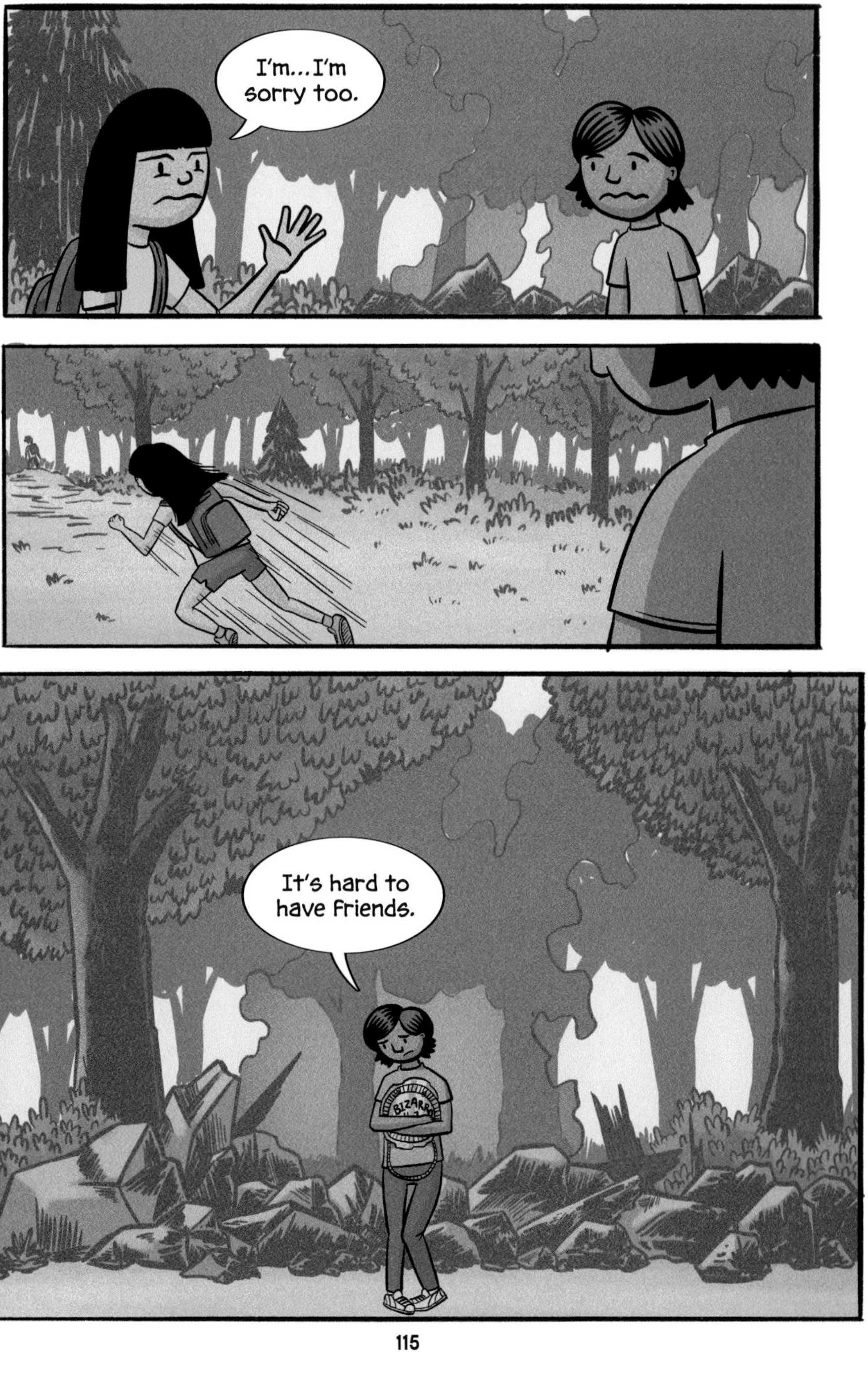
I'm...I'm sorry too.
It's hard to have friends.

CHAPTER EIGHT

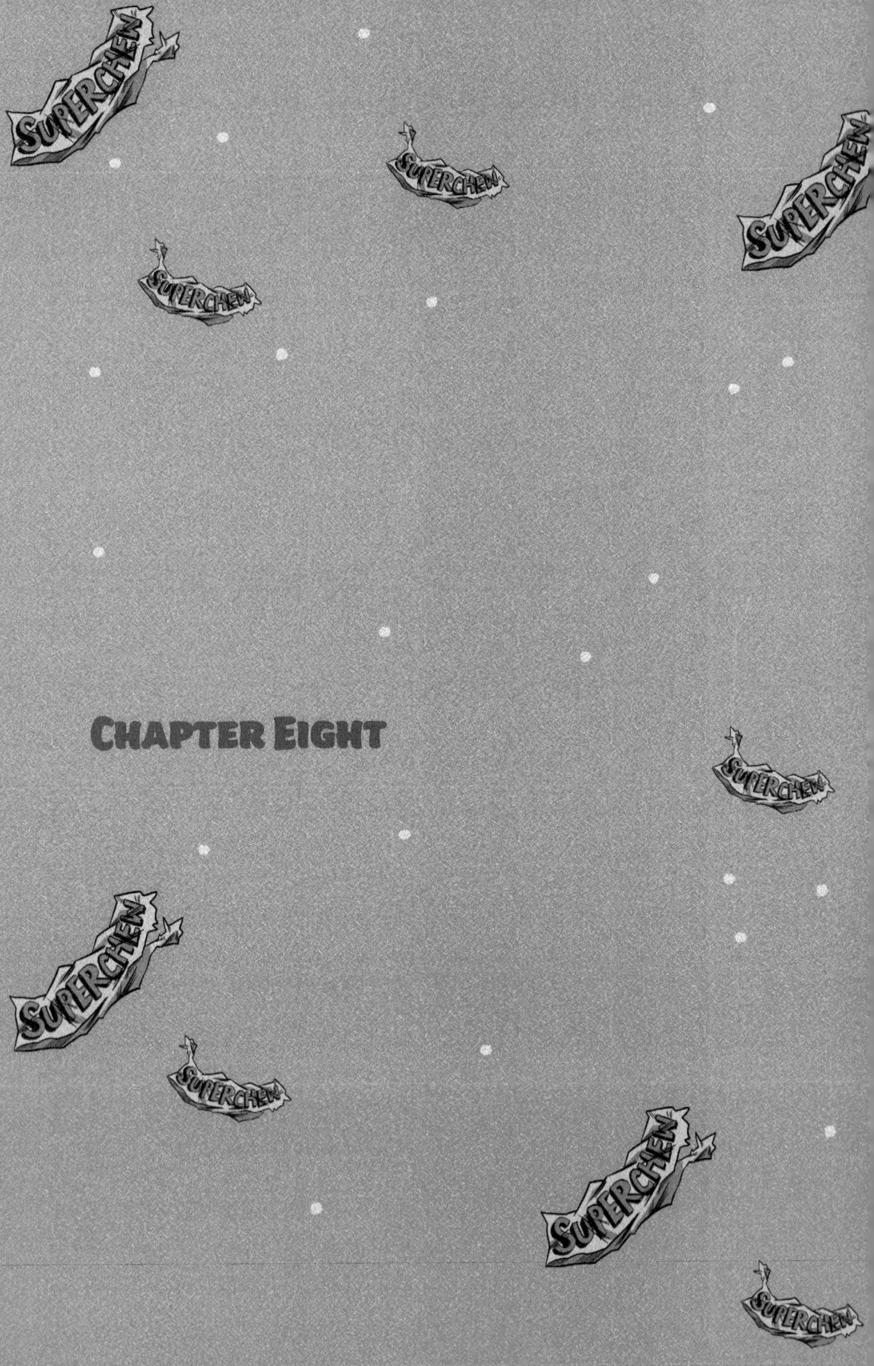
SUPERCHEW
SUPERCHEW
SUPERCHEW
SUPERCHEW
SUPERCHEW
SUPERCHEW
SUPERCHEW
SUPERCHEW
SUPERCHEW
SUPERCHEW

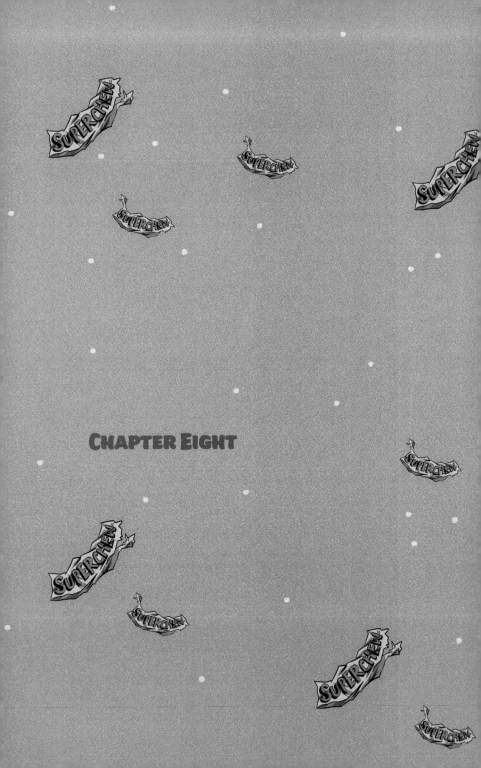

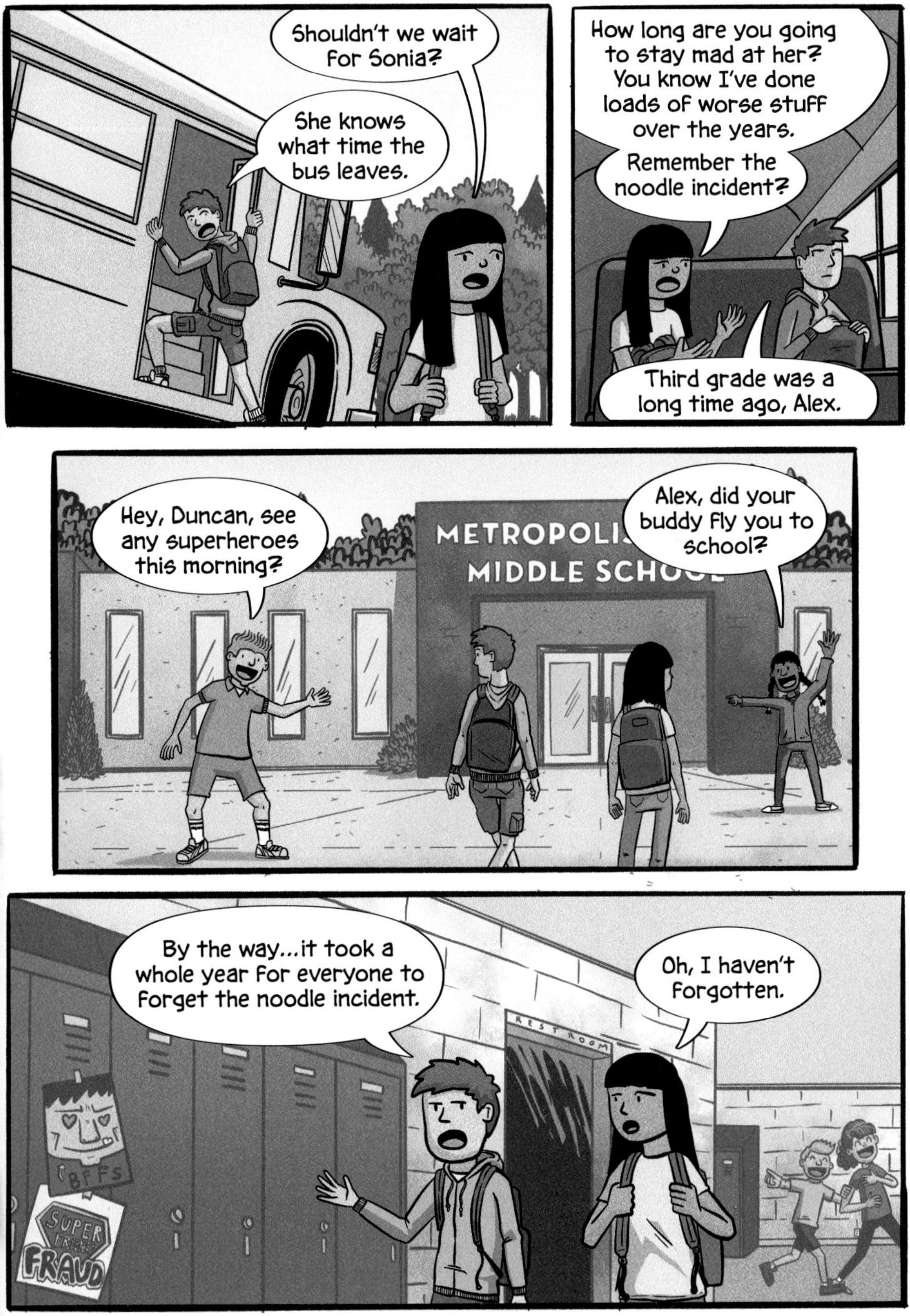
Shouldn't we wait for Sonia?
She knows what time the bus leaves.
How long are you going to stay mad at her? You know I've done loads of worse stuff over the years.
Remember the noodle incident?
Third grade was a long time ago, Alex.
Hey, Duncan, see any superheroes this morning?
METROPOLIS MIDDLE SCHOOL
Alex, did your buddy fly you to school?
By the way...it took a whole year for everyone to forget the noodle incident.
Oh, I haven't forgotten.
REST ROOM
BFFS
SUPER
FRAUD

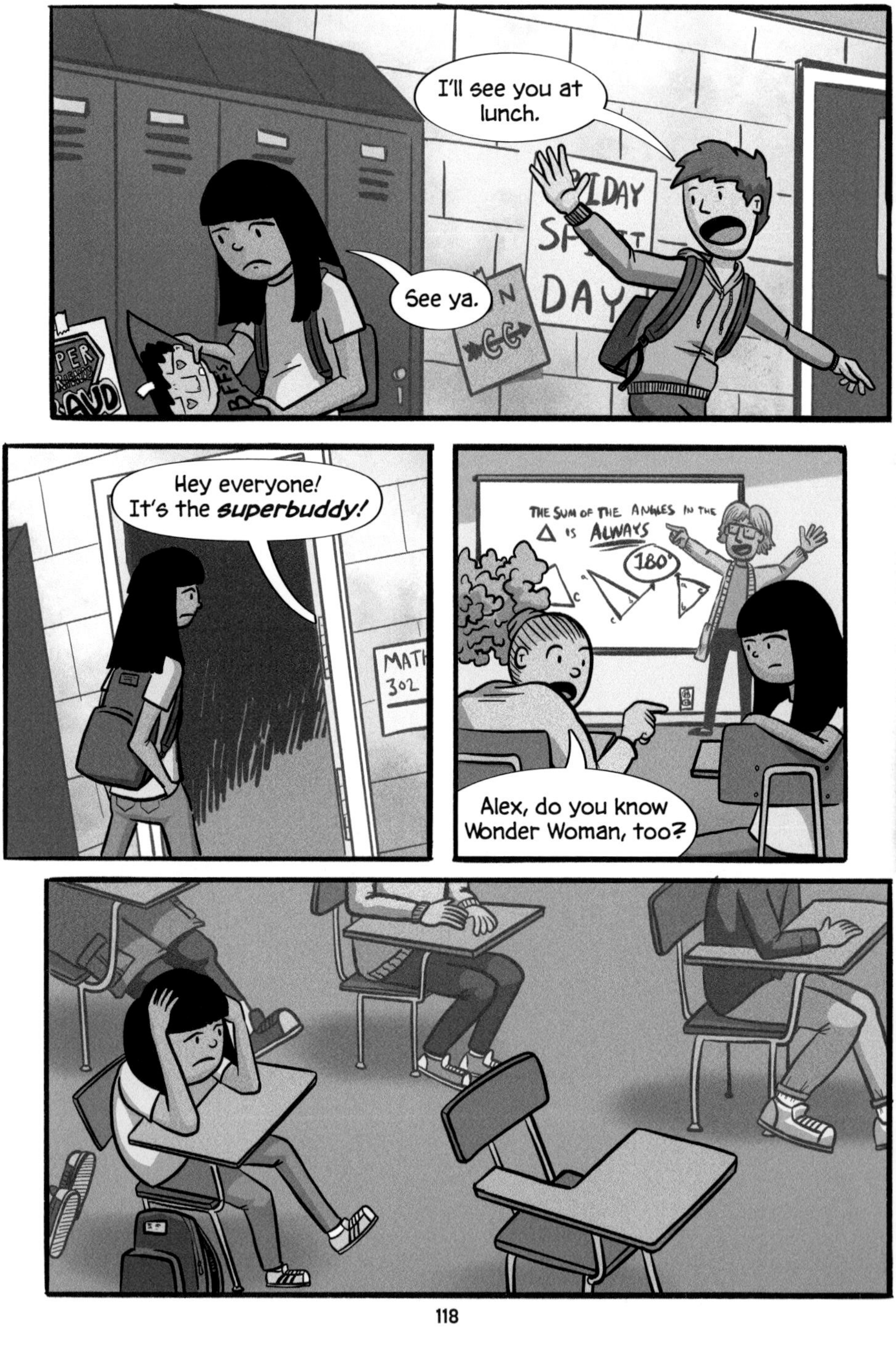
I'll see you at lunch.
See ya.
Hey everyone! It's the *superbuddy!*
MATH 302
THE SUM OF THE ANGLES IN THE △ IS ALWAYS 180°
Alex, do you know Wonder Woman, too?

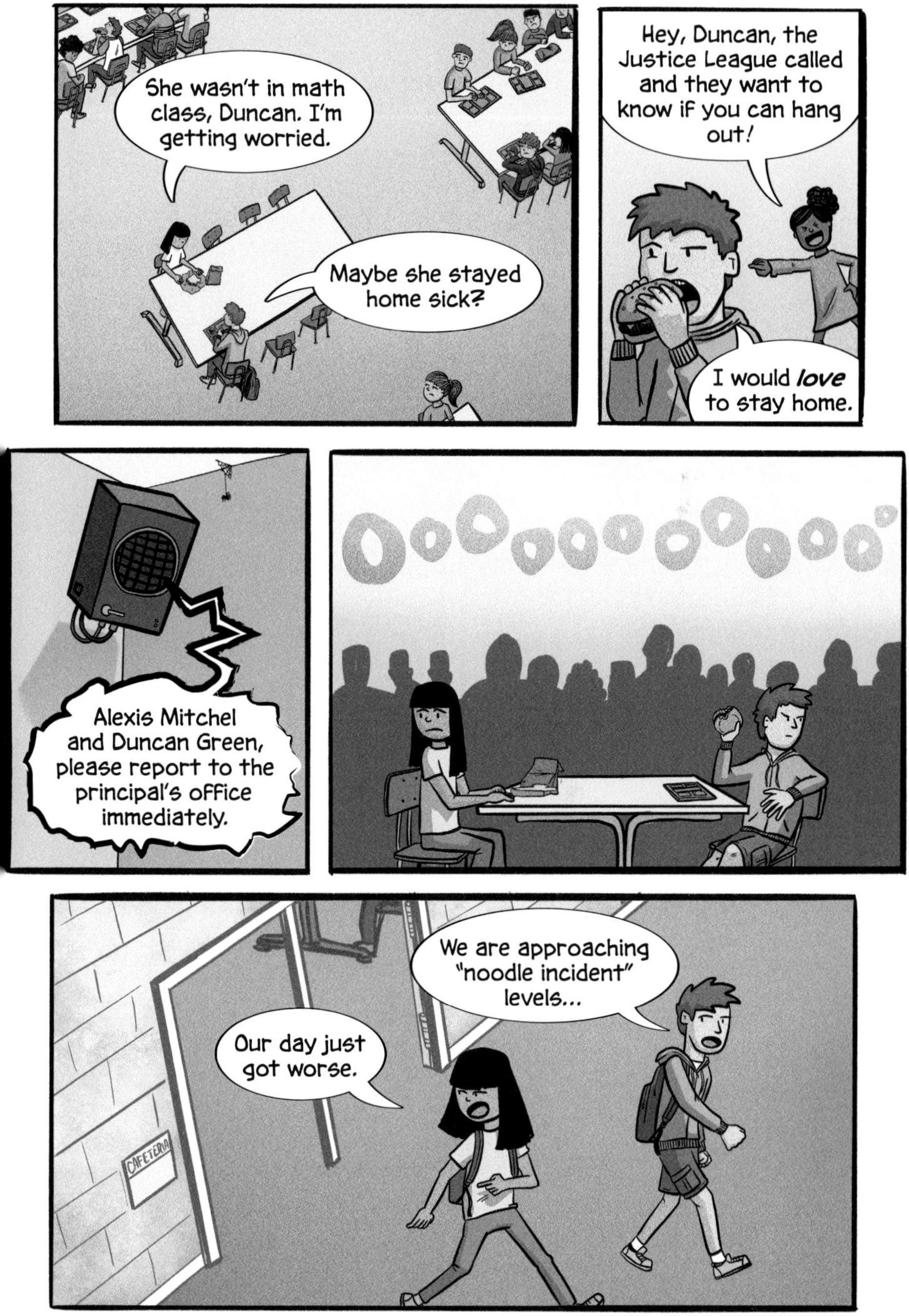
She wasn't in math class, Duncan. I'm getting worried.
Maybe she stayed home sick?
Hey, Duncan, the Justice League called and they want to know if you can hang out!
I would *love* to stay home.
Alexis Mitchel and Duncan Green, please report to the principal's office immediately.
We are approaching "noodle incident" levels...
Our day just got worse.
CAFETERIA

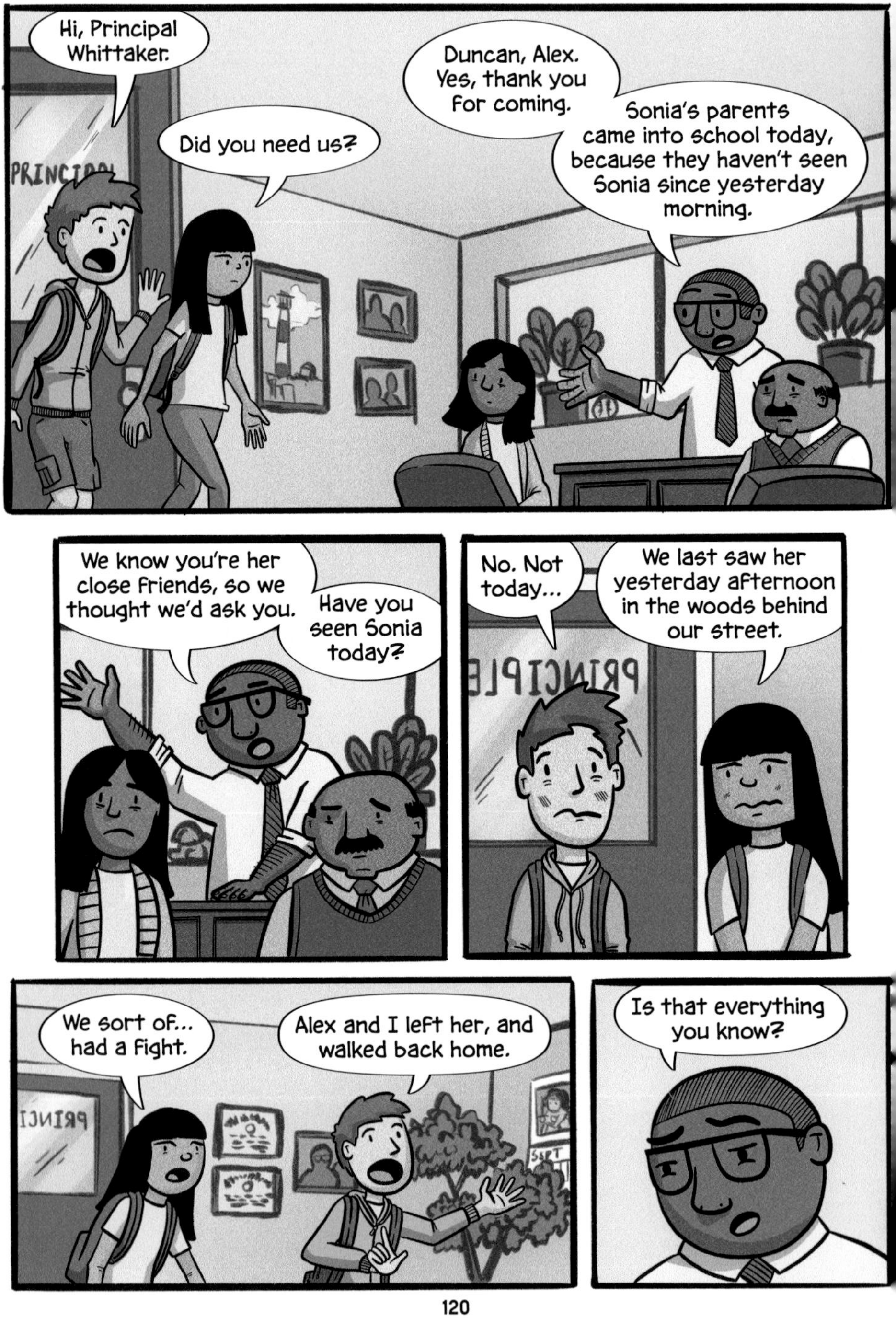
Hi, Principal Whittaker.
Did you need us?
PRINCIPAL
Duncan, Alex. Yes, thank you for coming.
Sonia's parents came into school today, because they haven't seen Sonia since yesterday morning.
We know you're her close friends, so we thought we'd ask you.
Have you seen Sonia today?
No. Not today...
We last saw her yesterday afternoon in the woods behind our street.
We sort of... had a fight.
Alex and I left her, and walked back home.
Is that everything you know?

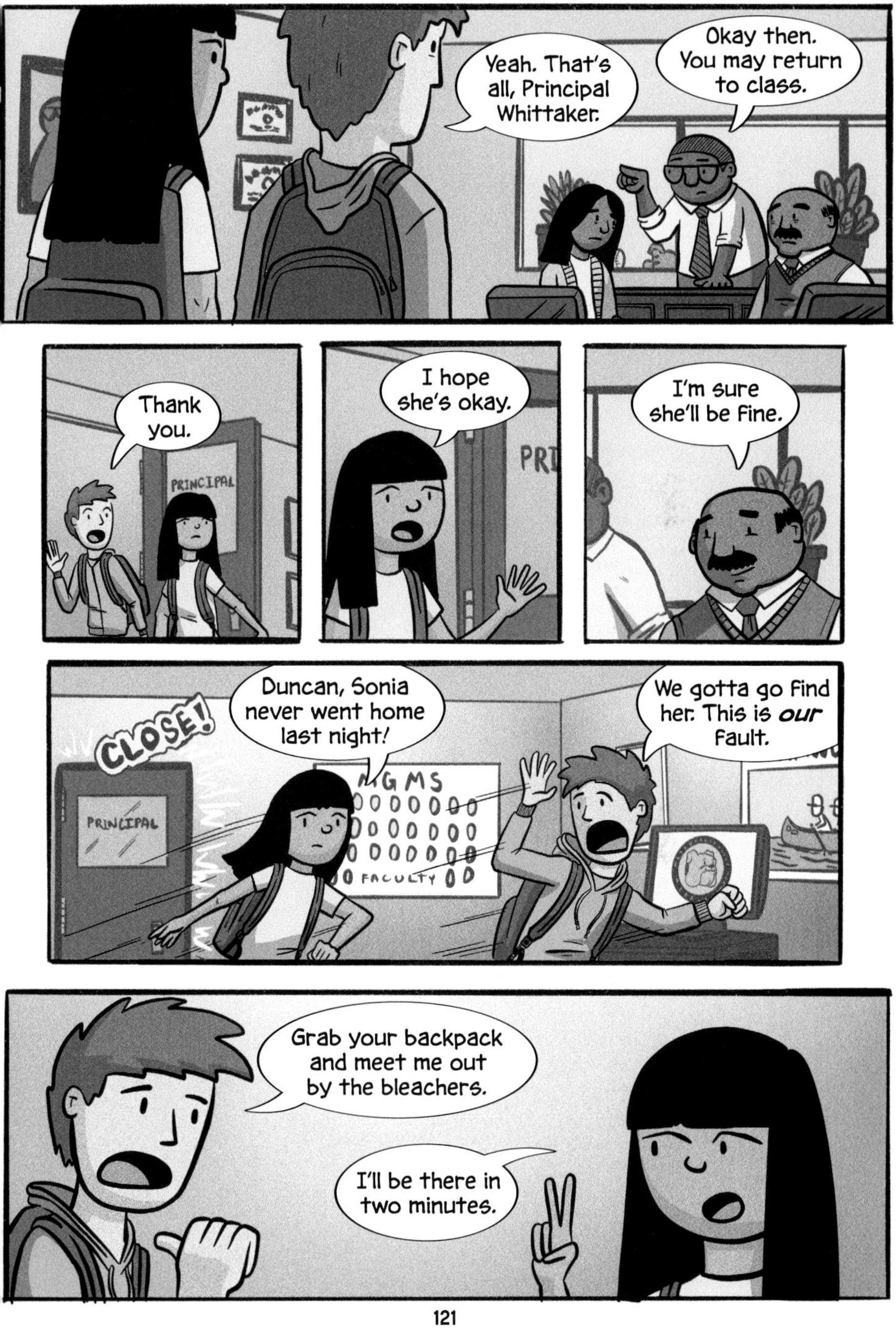
Yeah. That's all, Principal Whittaker.
Okay then. You may return to class.
Thank you.
PRINCIPAL
I hope she's okay.
PRI
I'm sure she'll be fine.
CLOSE!
PRINCIPAL
Duncan, Sonia never went home last night!
MGMS
FACULTY
We gotta go find her. This is ***our*** fault.
Grab your backpack and meet me out by the bleachers.
I'll be there in two minutes.

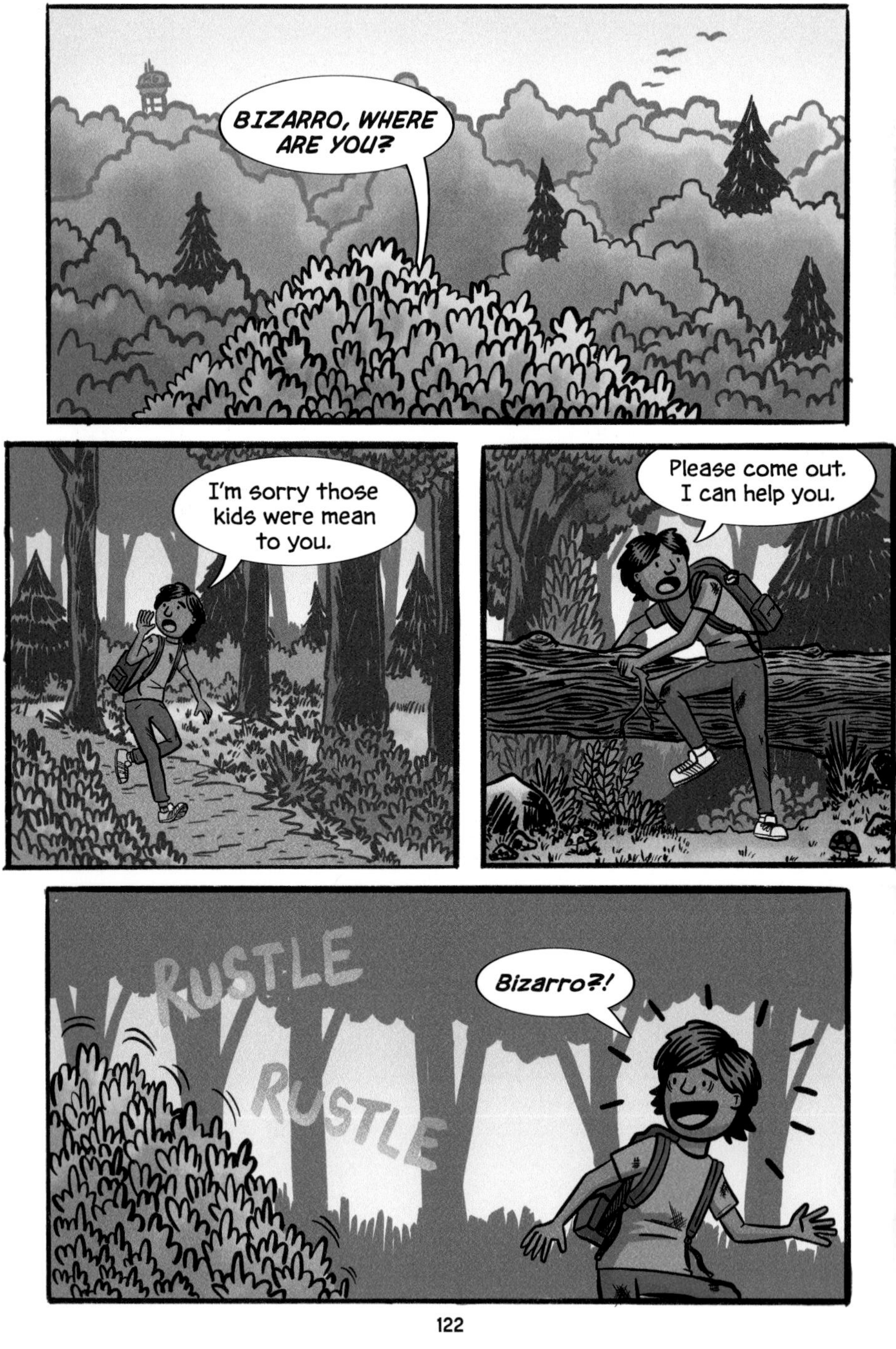
BIZARRO, WHERE ARE YOU?
I'm sorry those kids were mean to you.
Please come out. I can help you.
RUSTLE
RUSTLE
Bizarro?!

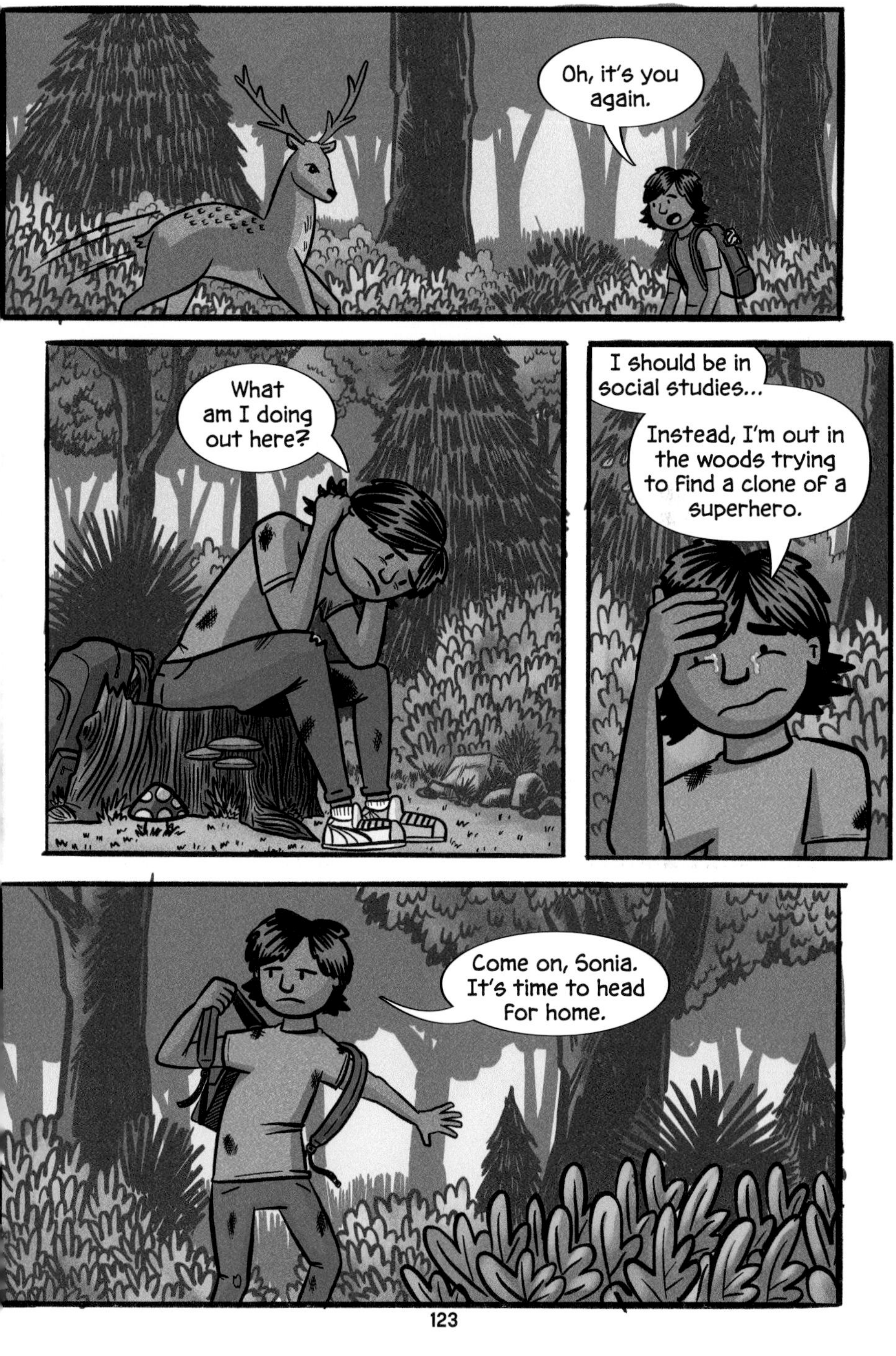
Oh, it's you again.
What am I doing out here?
I should be in social studies...
Instead, I'm out in the woods trying to find a clone of a superhero.
Come on, Sonia. It's time to head for home.

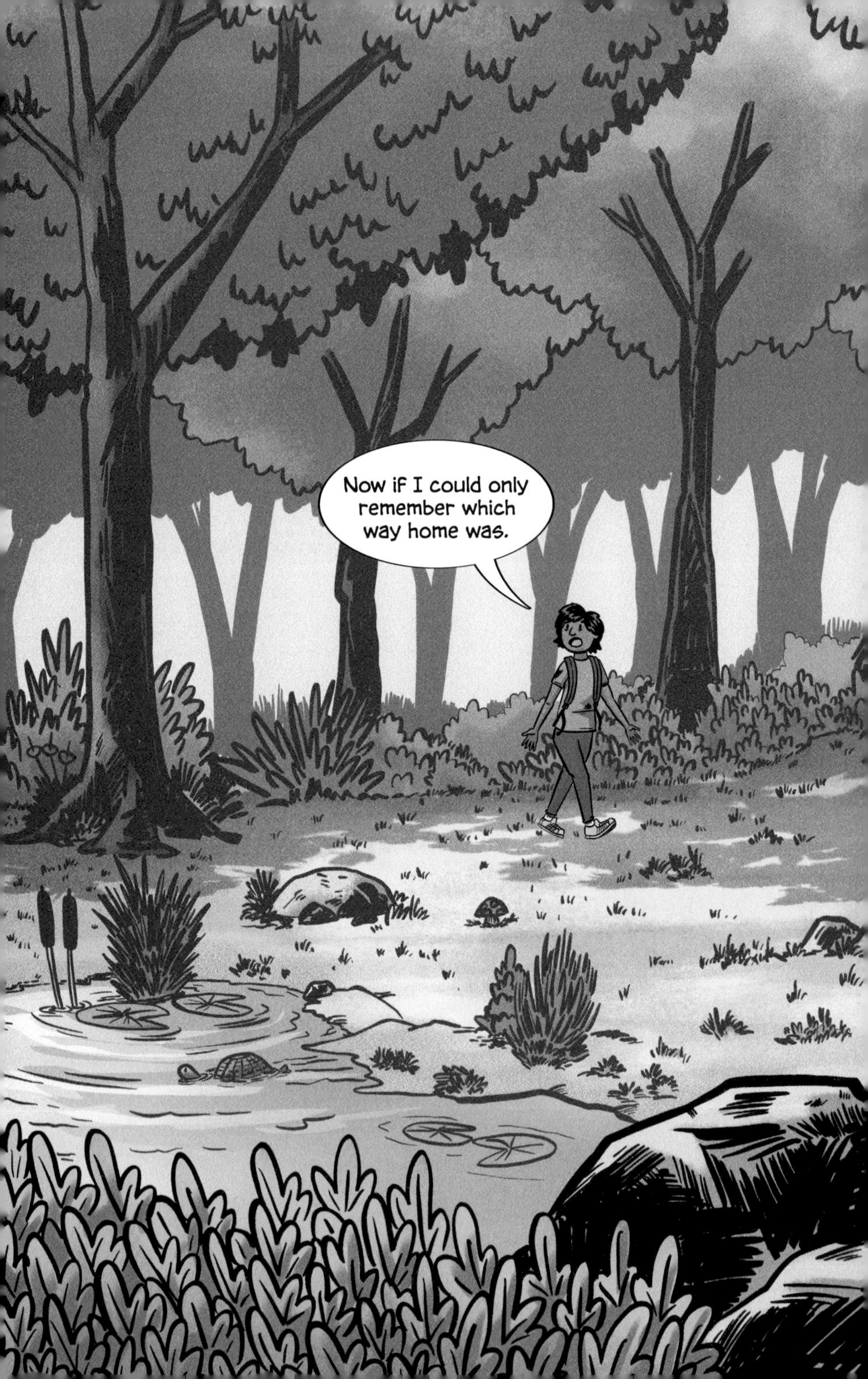
Now if I could only remember which way home was.

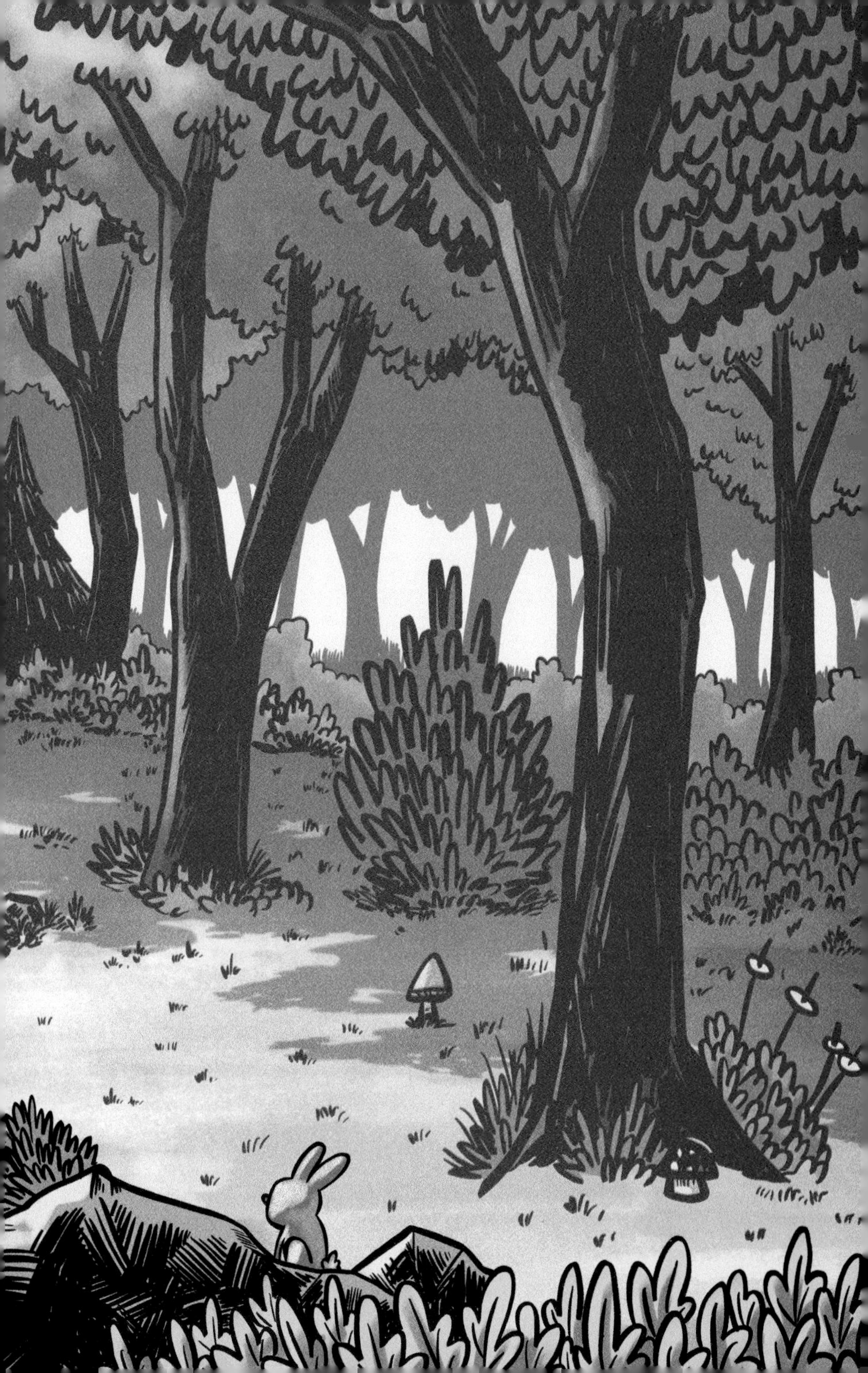

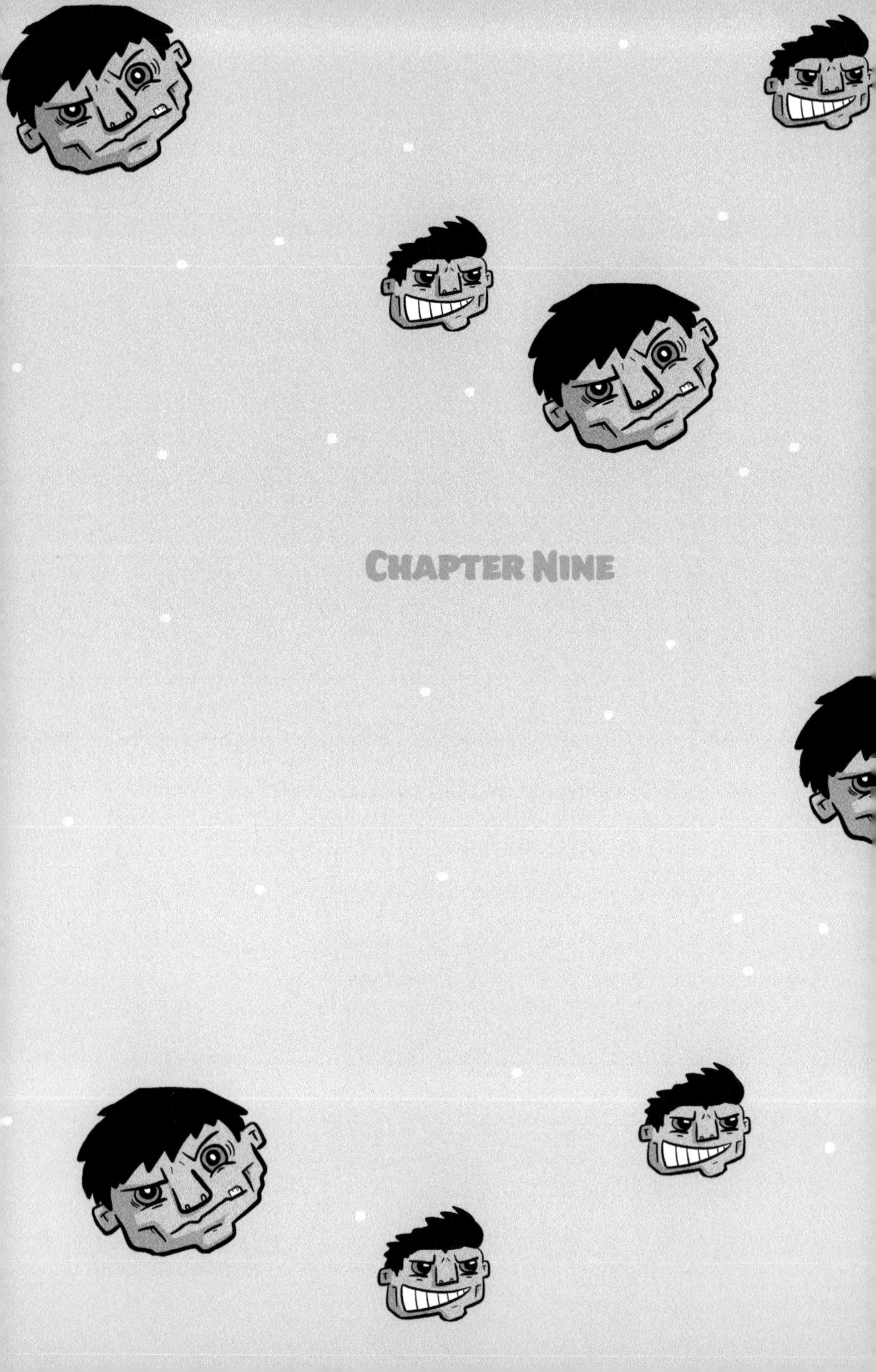

CHAPTER NINE

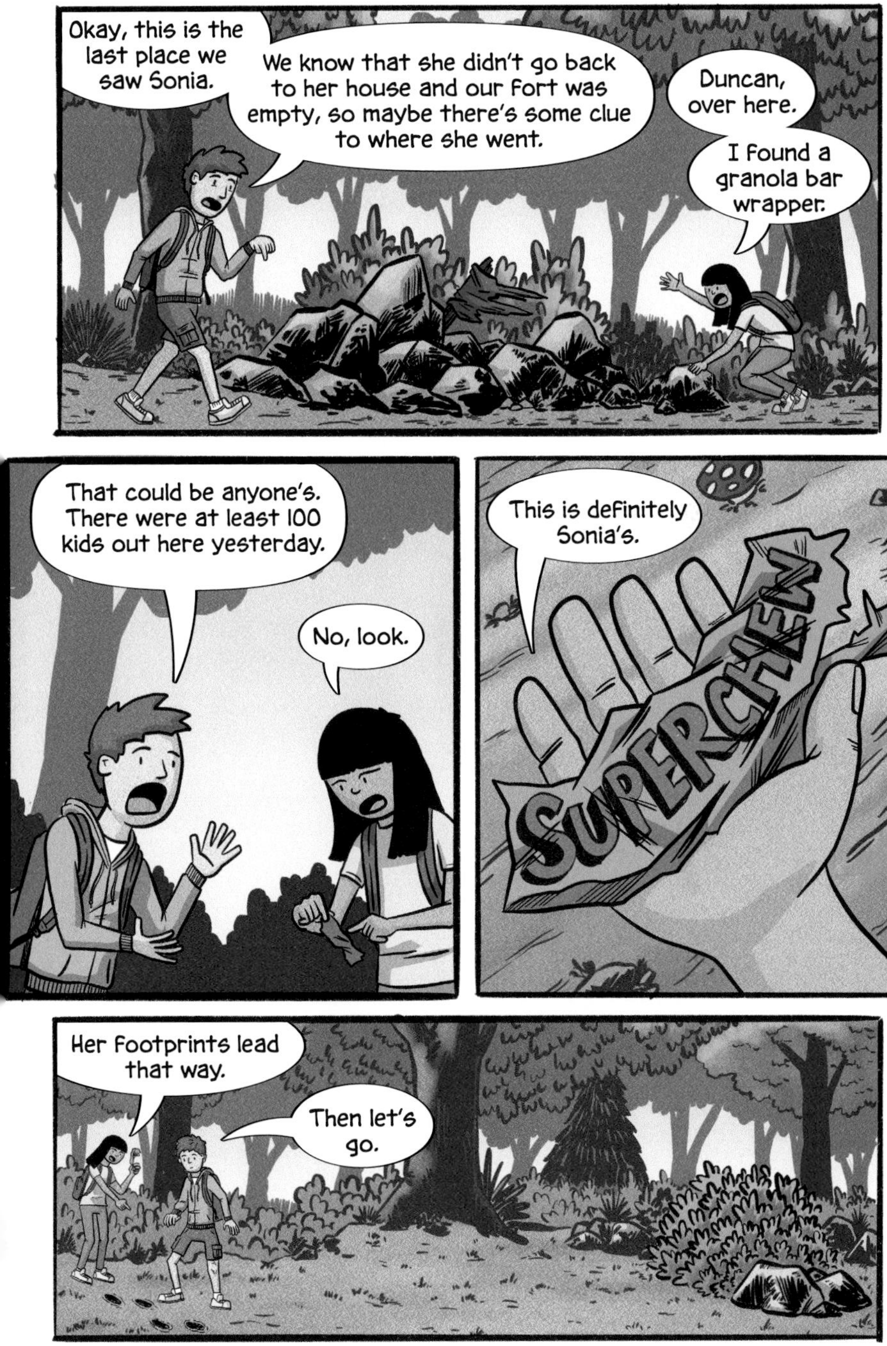

Okay, this is the last place we saw Sonia.
We know that she didn't go back to her house and our fort was empty, so maybe there's some clue to where she went.
Duncan, over here.
I found a granola bar wrapper.
That could be anyone's. There were at least 100 kids out here yesterday.
No, look.
This is definitely Sonia's.
SUPERCHEW
Her footprints lead that way.
Then let's go.

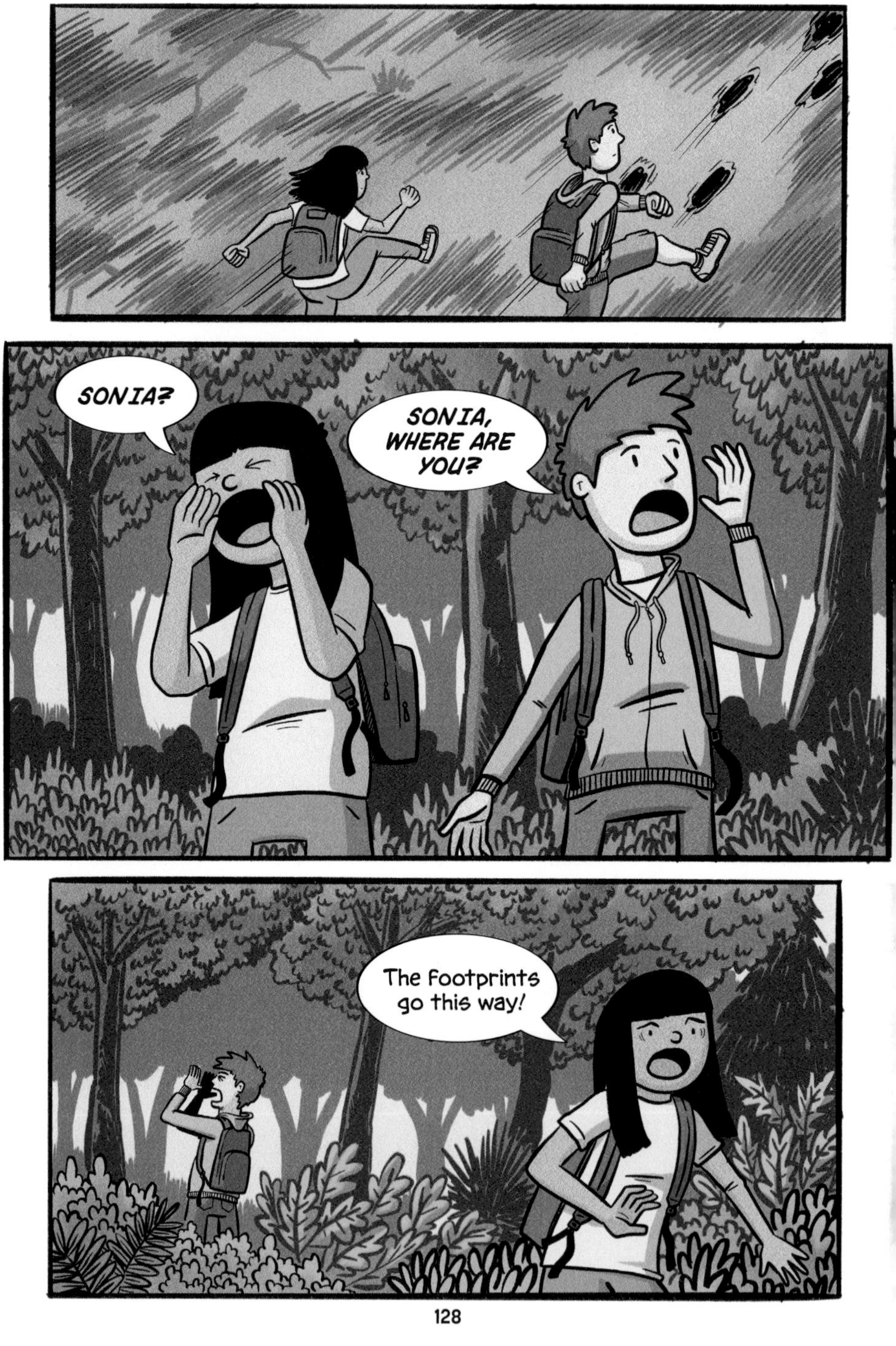
SONIA?
SONIA, WHERE ARE YOU?
The footprints go this way!

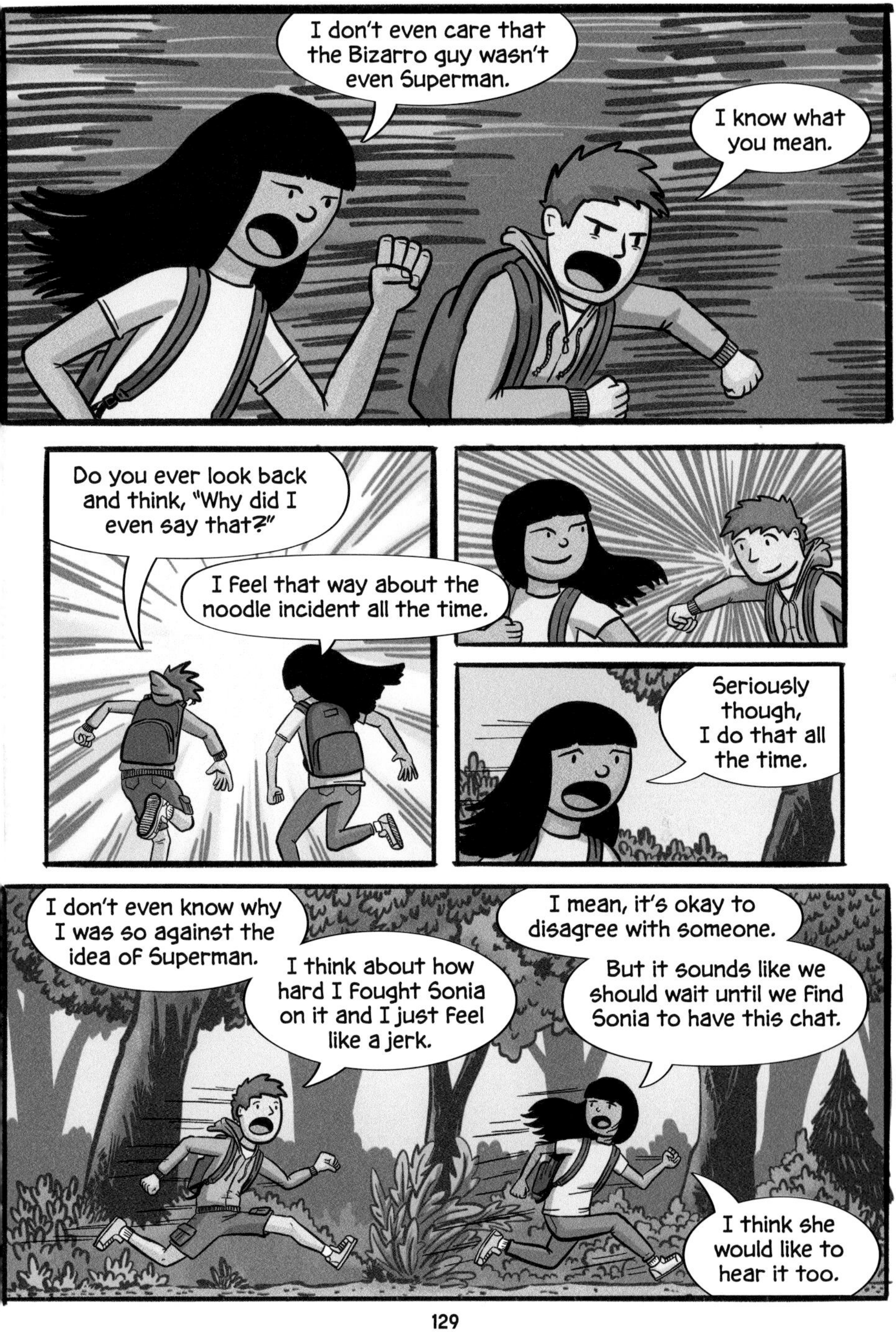
I don't even care that the Bizarro guy wasn't even Superman.
I know what you mean.
Do you ever look back and think, "Why did I even say that?"
I feel that way about the noodle incident all the time.
Seriously though, I do that all the time.
I don't even know why I was so against the idea of Superman.
I think about how hard I fought Sonia on it and I just feel like a jerk.
I mean, it's okay to disagree with someone.
But it sounds like we should wait until we find Sonia to have this chat.
I think she would like to hear it too.

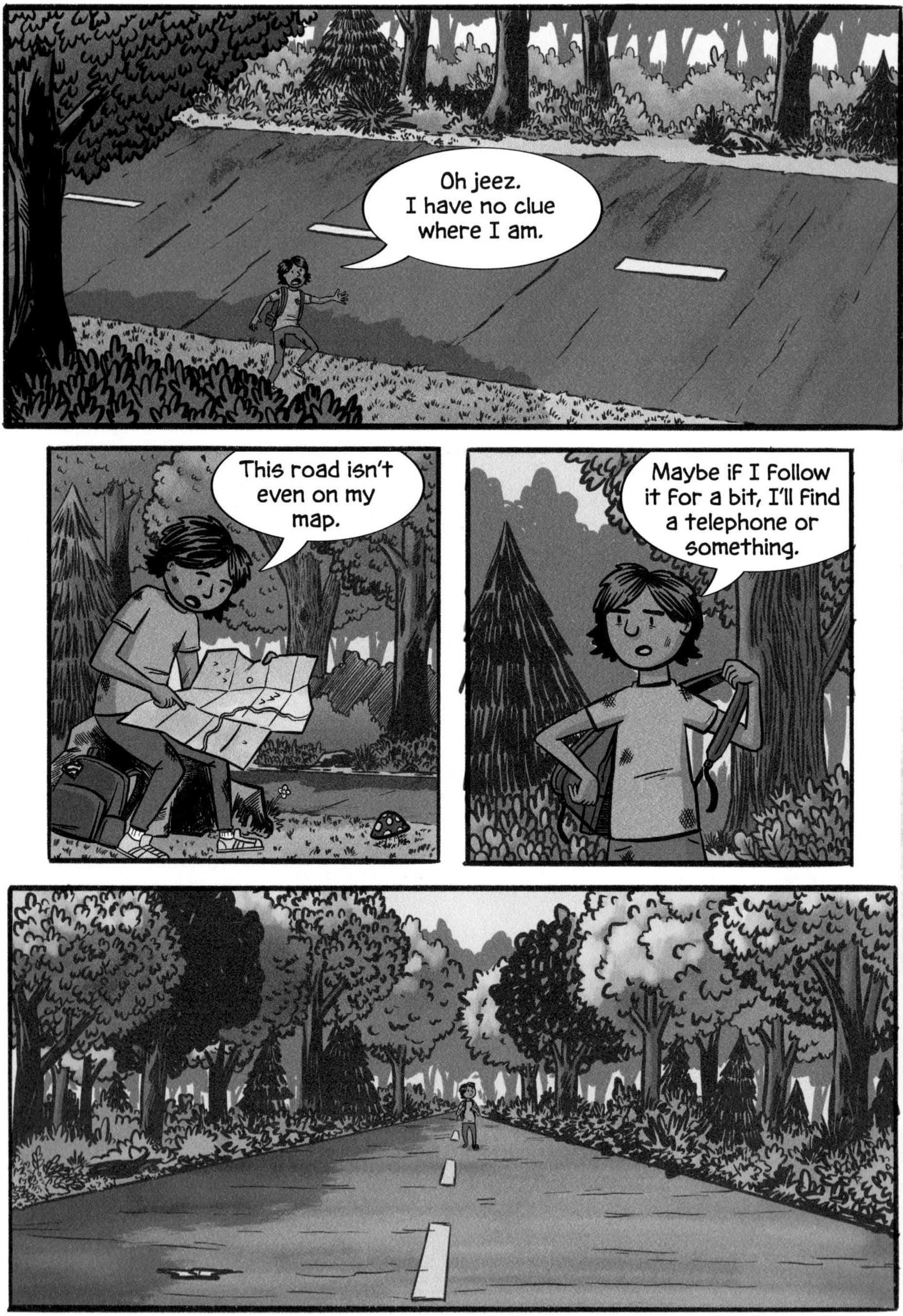
Oh jeez. I have no clue where I am.
This road isn't even on my map.
Maybe if I follow it for a bit, I'll find a telephone or something.

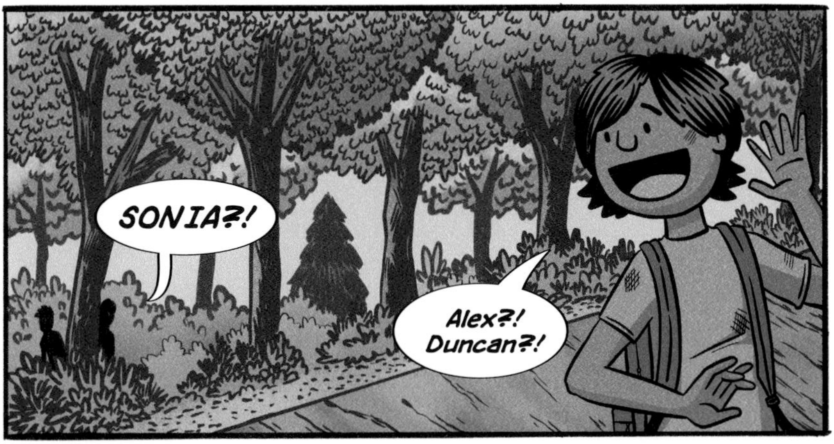
SONIA?!
Alex?! Duncan?!

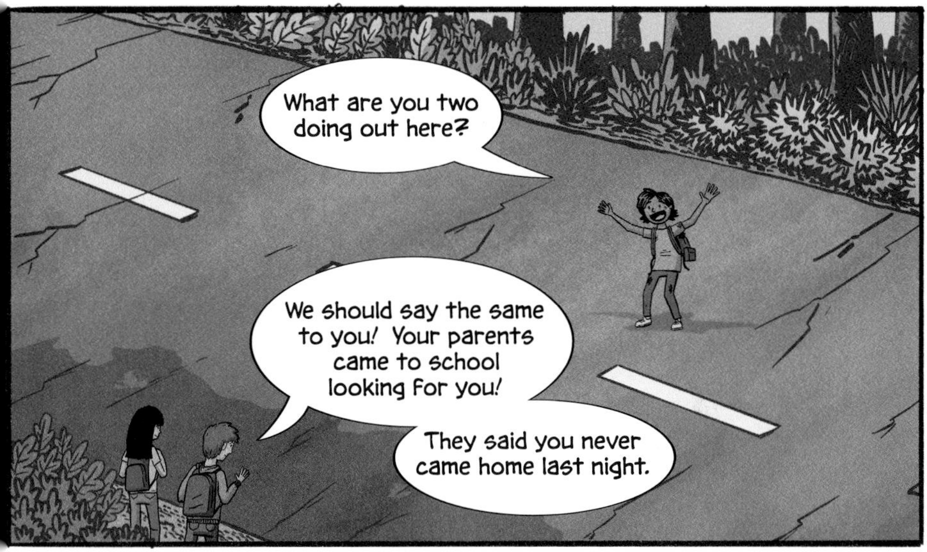
What are you two doing out here?
We should say the same to you! Your parents came to school looking for you!
They said you never came home last night.

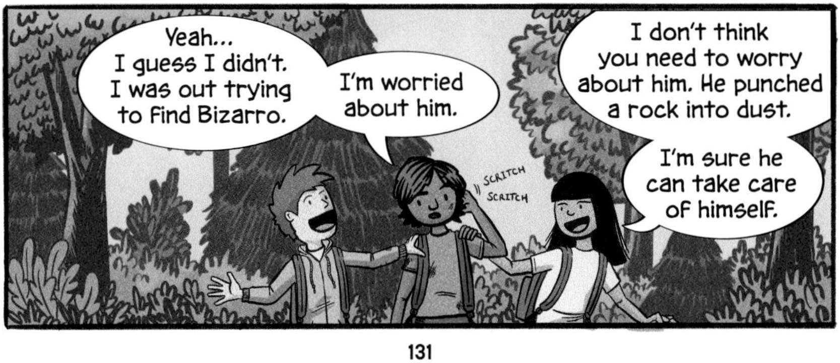
Yeah... I guess I didn't. I was out trying to find Bizarro.
I'm worried about him.
SCRITCH SCRITCH
I don't think you need to worry about him. He punched a rock into dust.
I'm sure he can take care of himself.

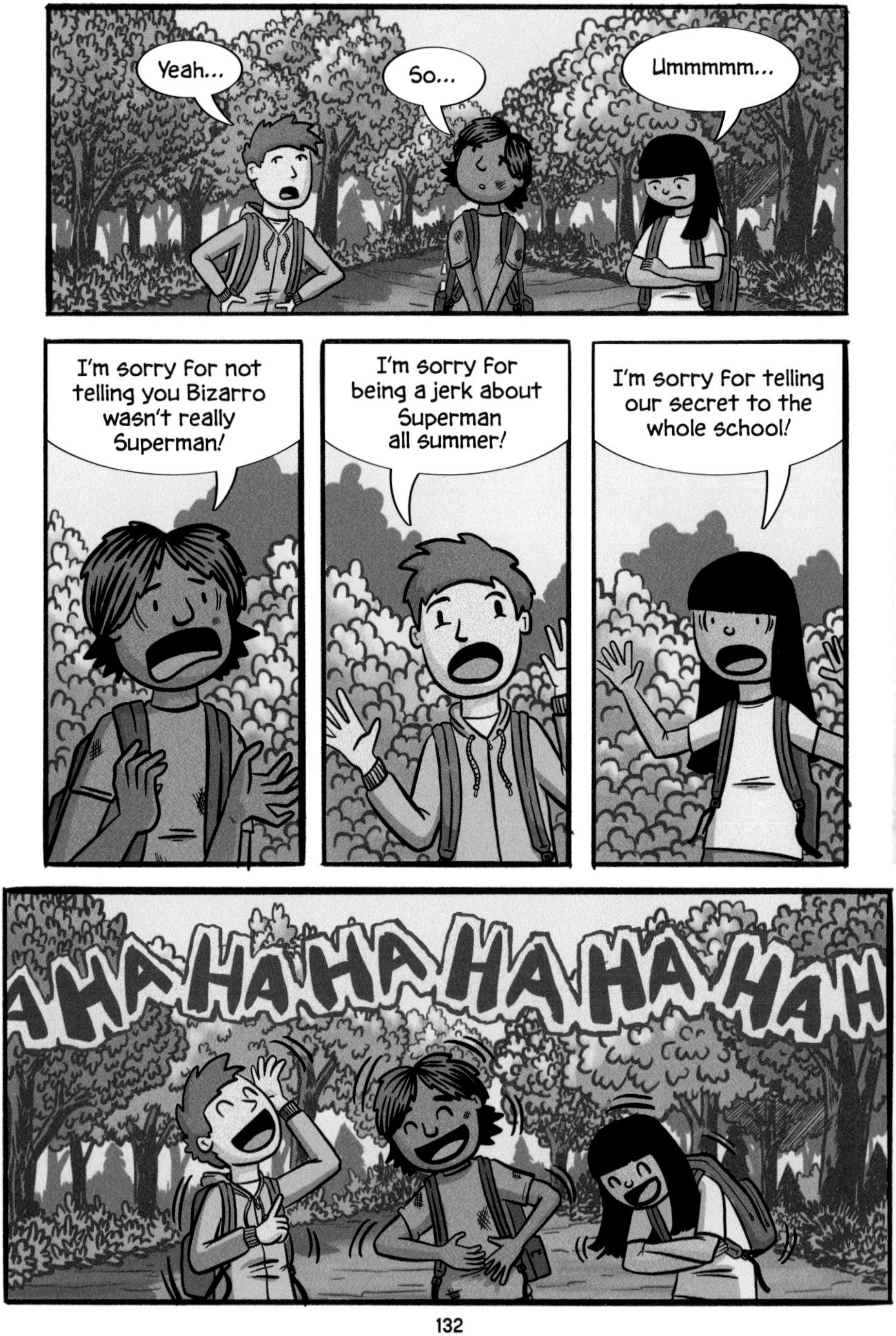
Yeah...
So...
Ummmmm...
I'm sorry for not telling you Bizarro wasn't really Superman!
I'm sorry for being a jerk about Superman all summer!
I'm sorry for telling our secret to the whole school!
AHAHAHAHAHAHAHAHAH

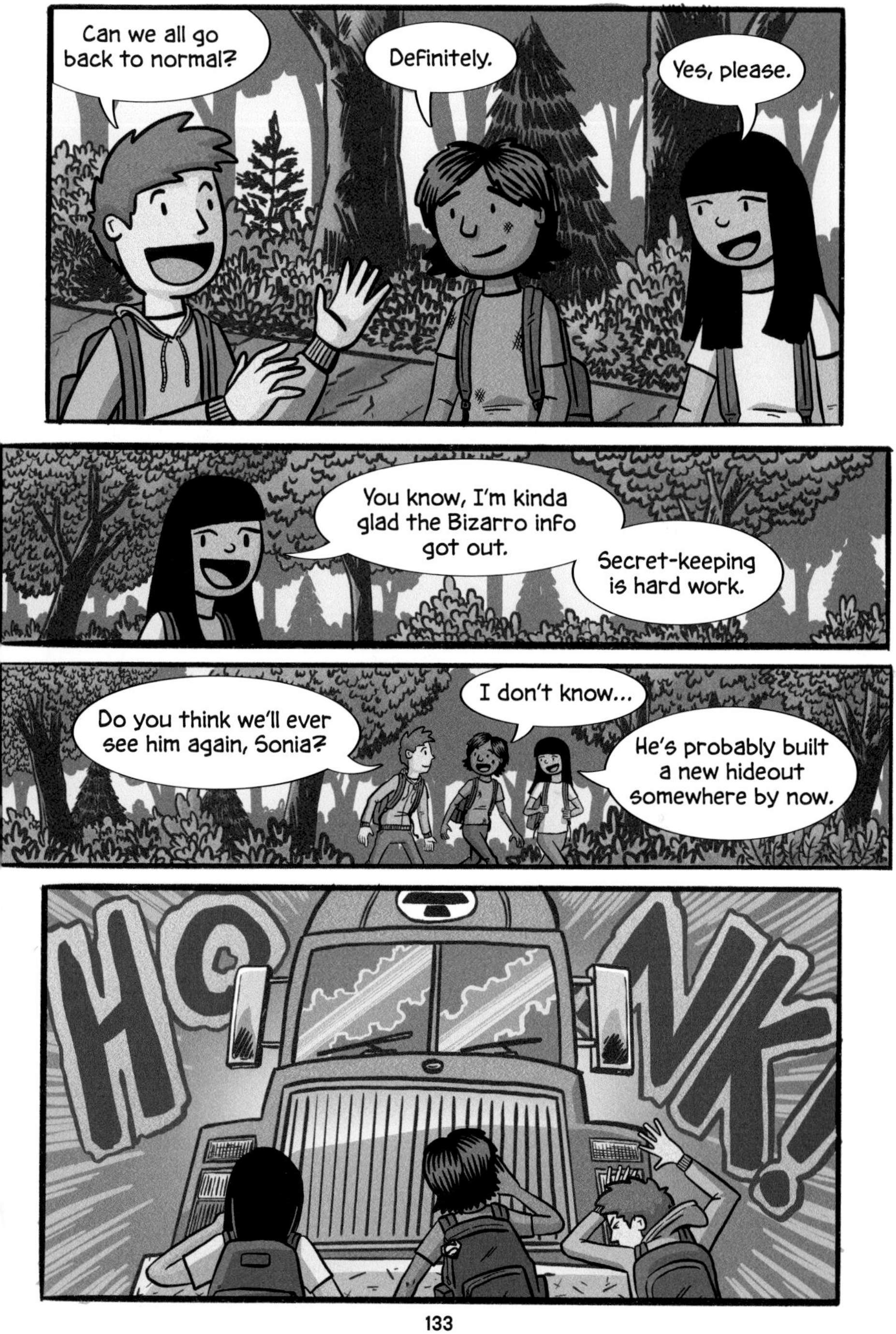
Can we all go back to normal?
Definitely.
Yes, please.
You know, I'm kinda glad the Bizarro info got out.
Secret-keeping is hard work.
Do you think we'll ever see him again, Sonia?
I don't know...
He's probably built a new hideout somewhere by now.
HONK!

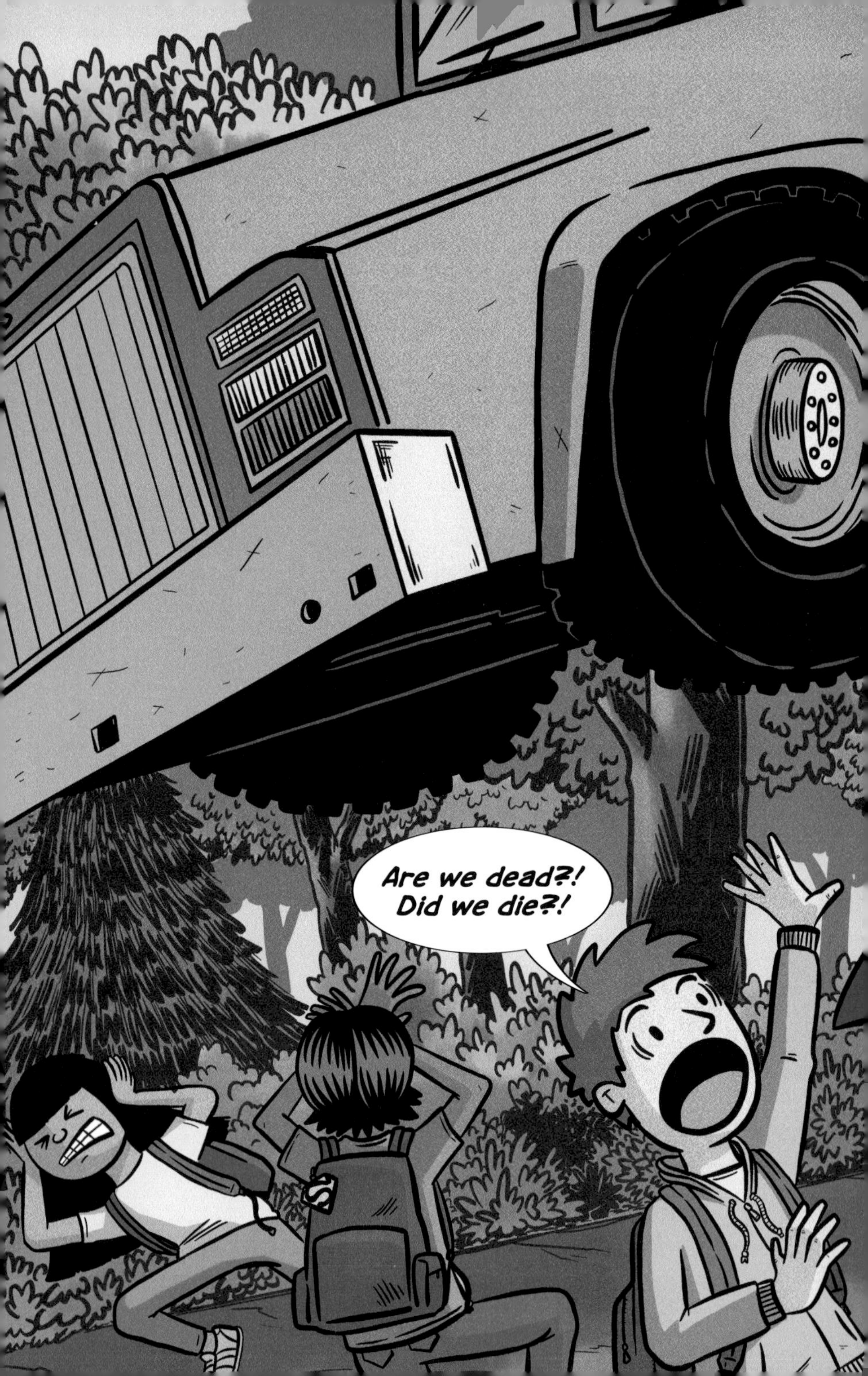
Are we dead?! Did we die?!

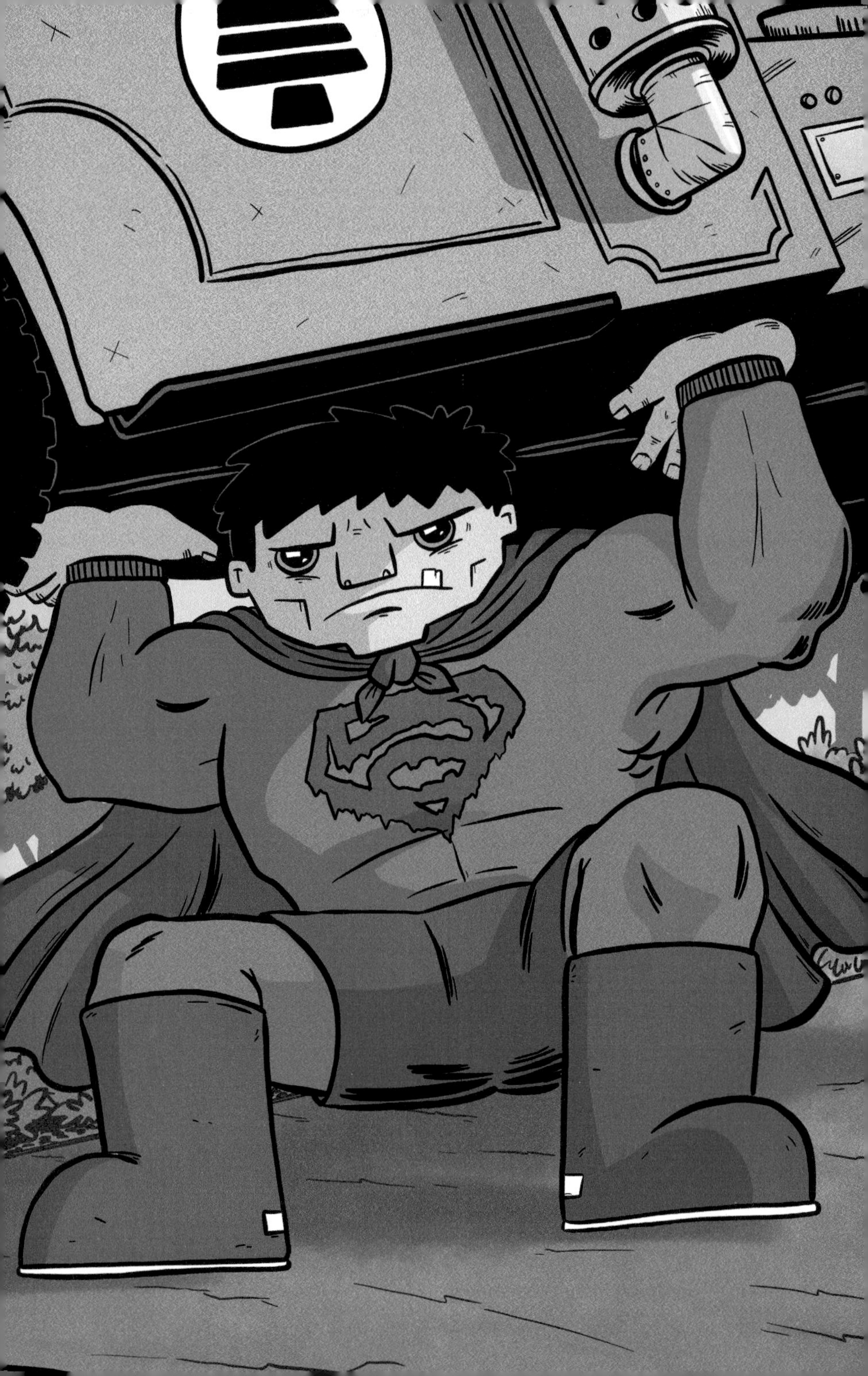

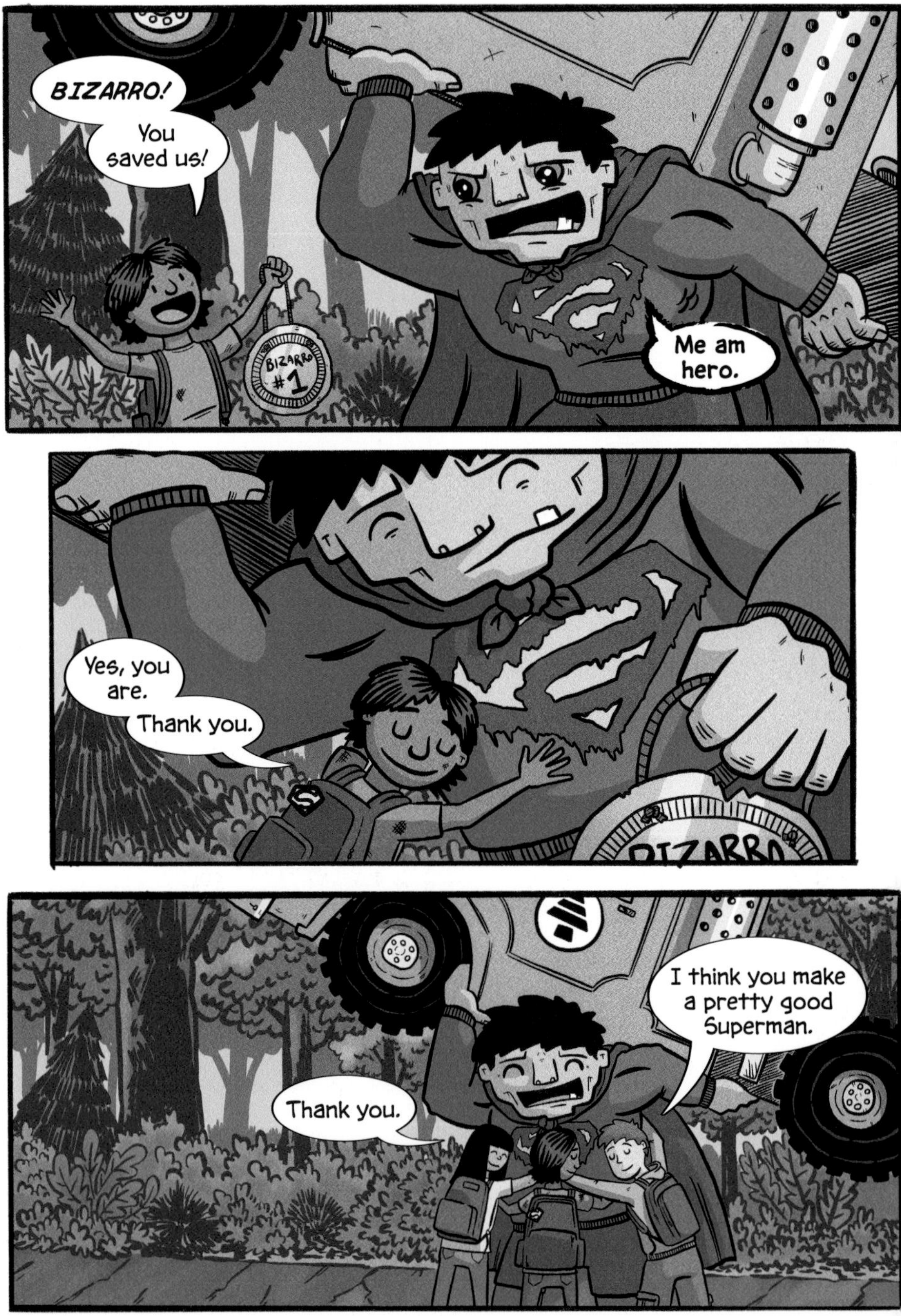
BIZARRO!
You saved us!
Me am hero.
BIZARRO #1
Yes, you are.
Thank you.
I think you make a pretty good Superman.
Thank you.

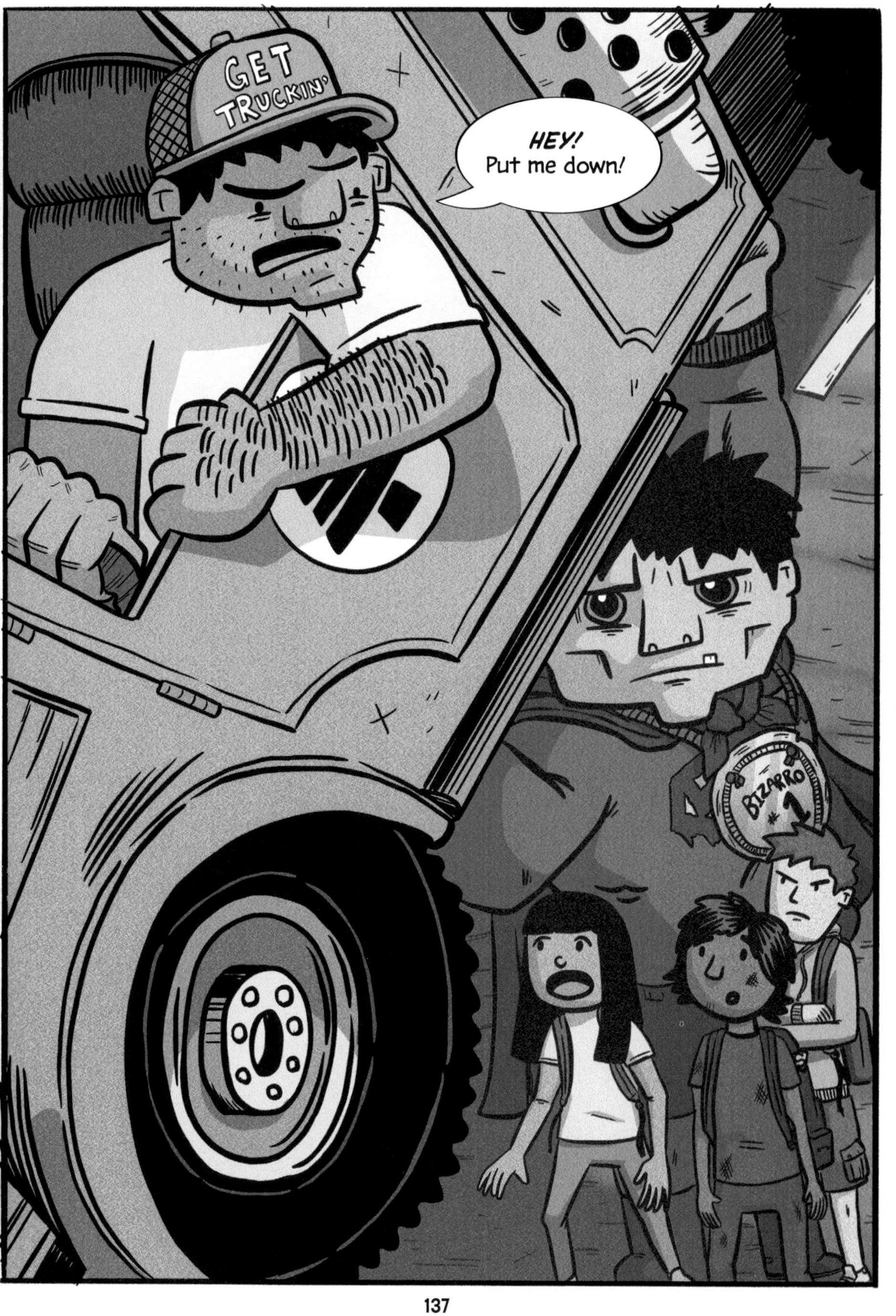
GET TRUCKIN'
HEY! Put me down!
BIZARRO

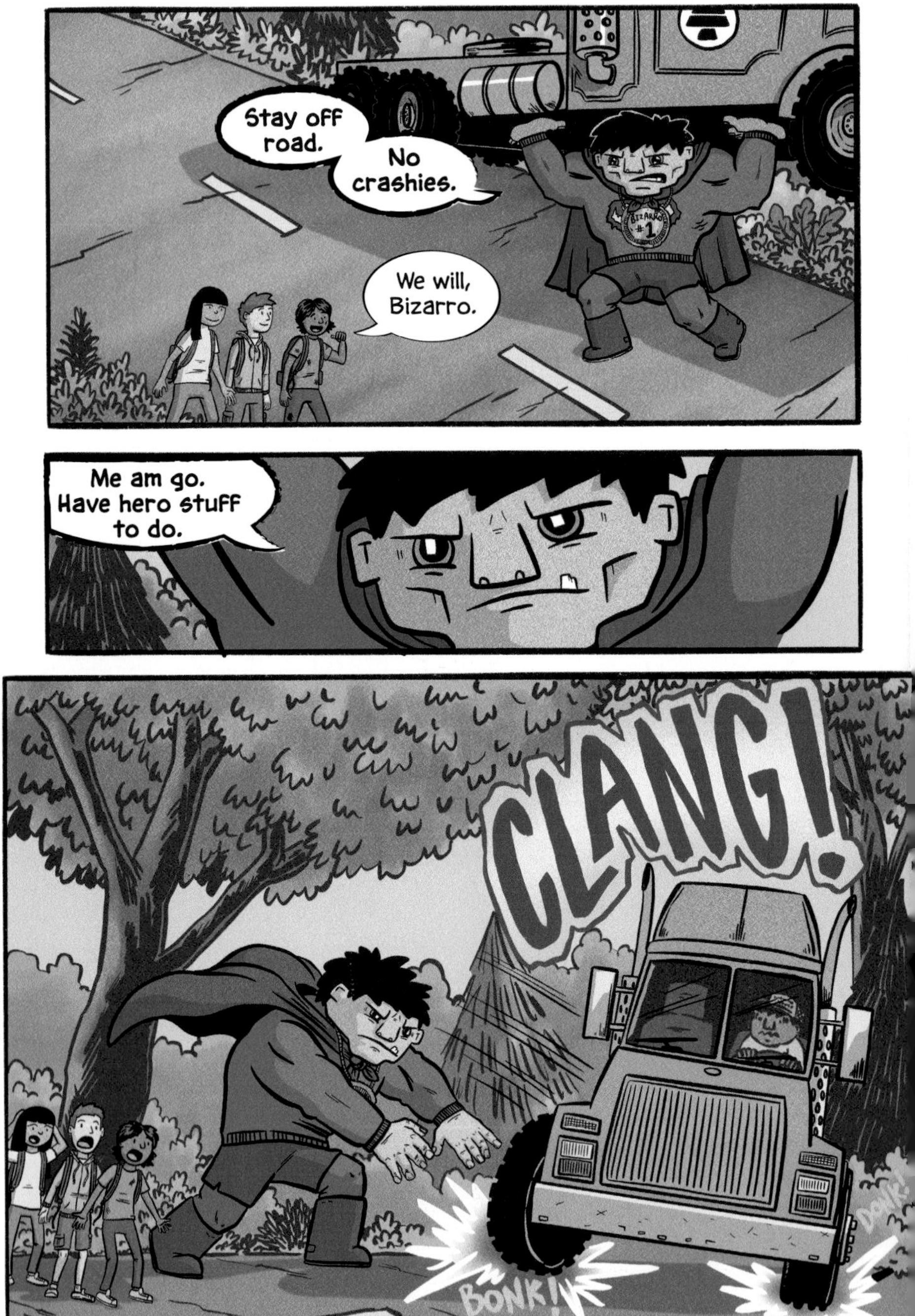
Stay off road.
No crashies.
We will, Bizarro.
Me am go. Have hero stuff to do.
CLANG!
BONK!
DONK!

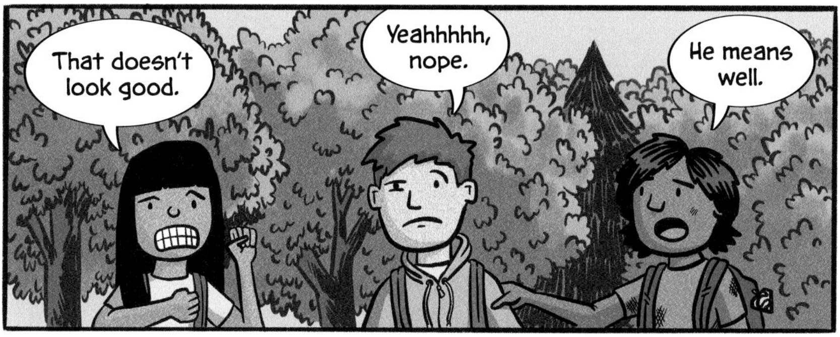
That doesn't look good.
Yeahhhhh, nope.
He means well.

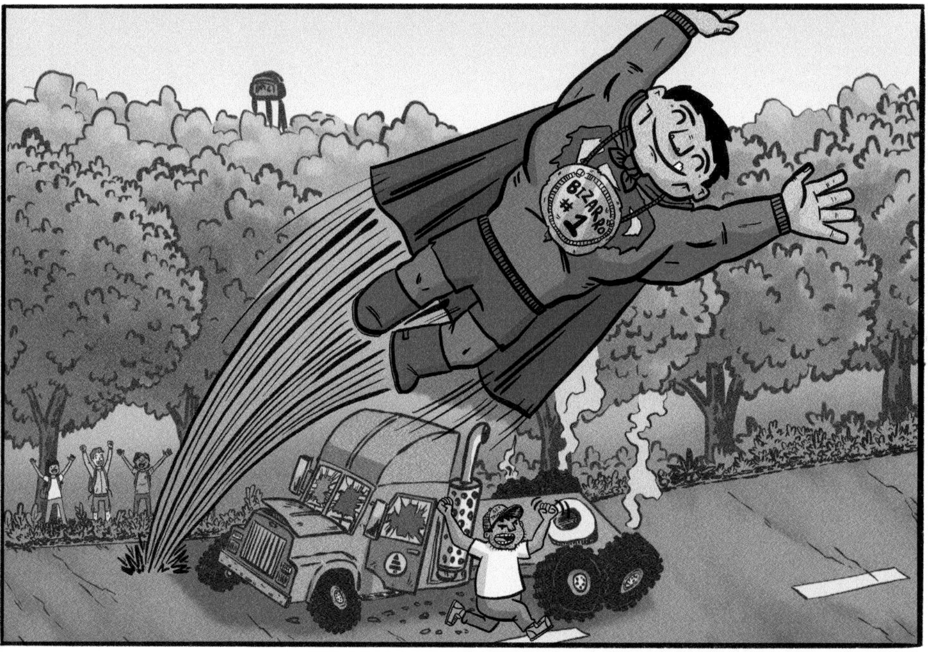
BIZARRO
#1

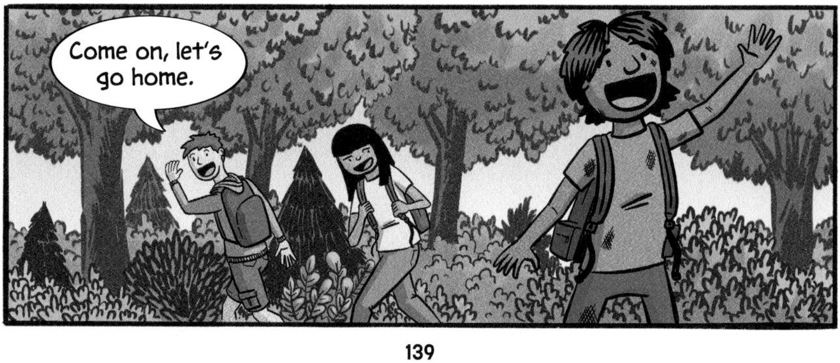
Come on, let's go home.

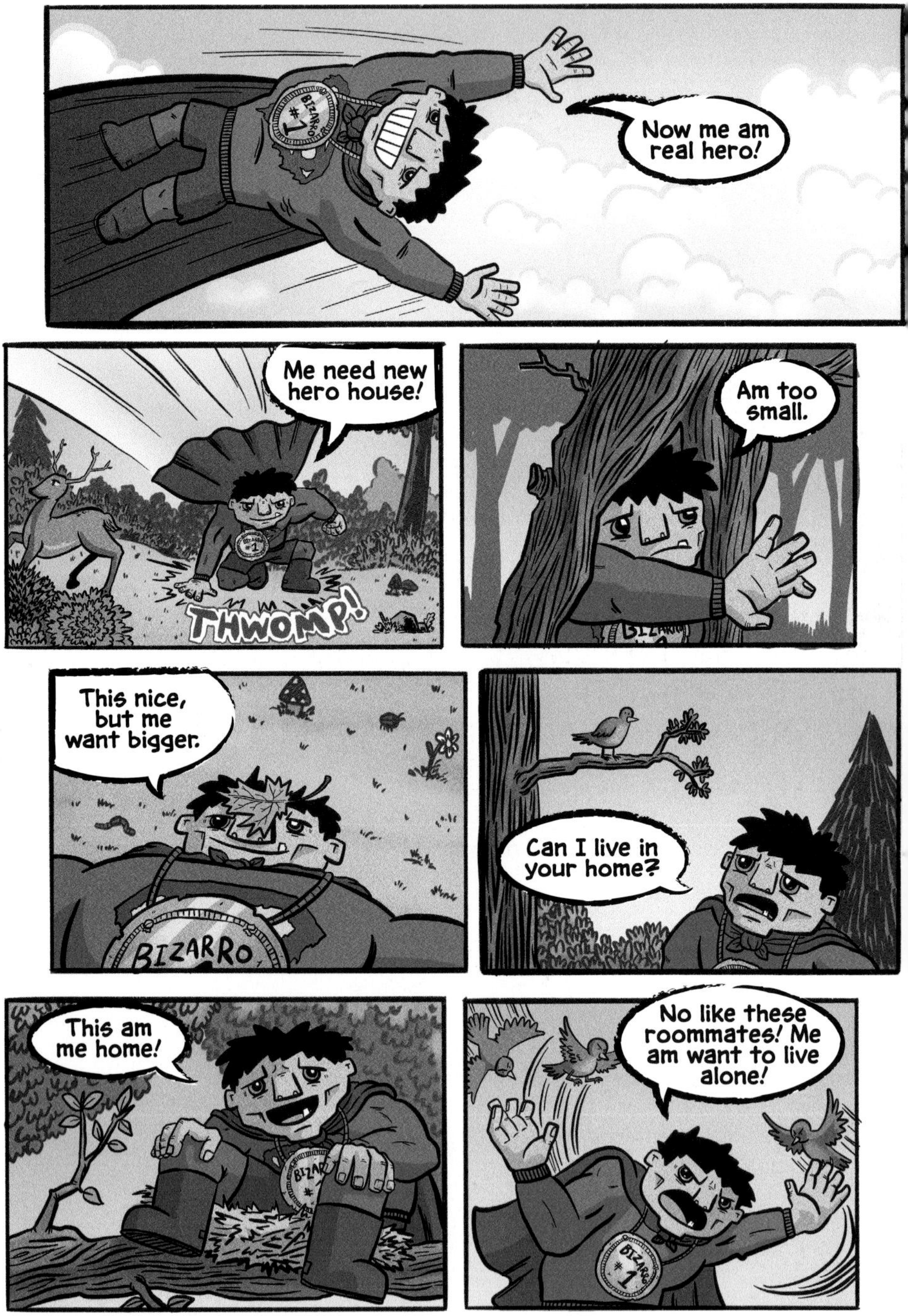

Now me am real hero!
Me need new hero house!
THWOMP!
Am too small.
This nice, but me want bigger.
BIZARRO
Can I live in your home?
This am me home!
No like these roommates! Me am want to live alone!

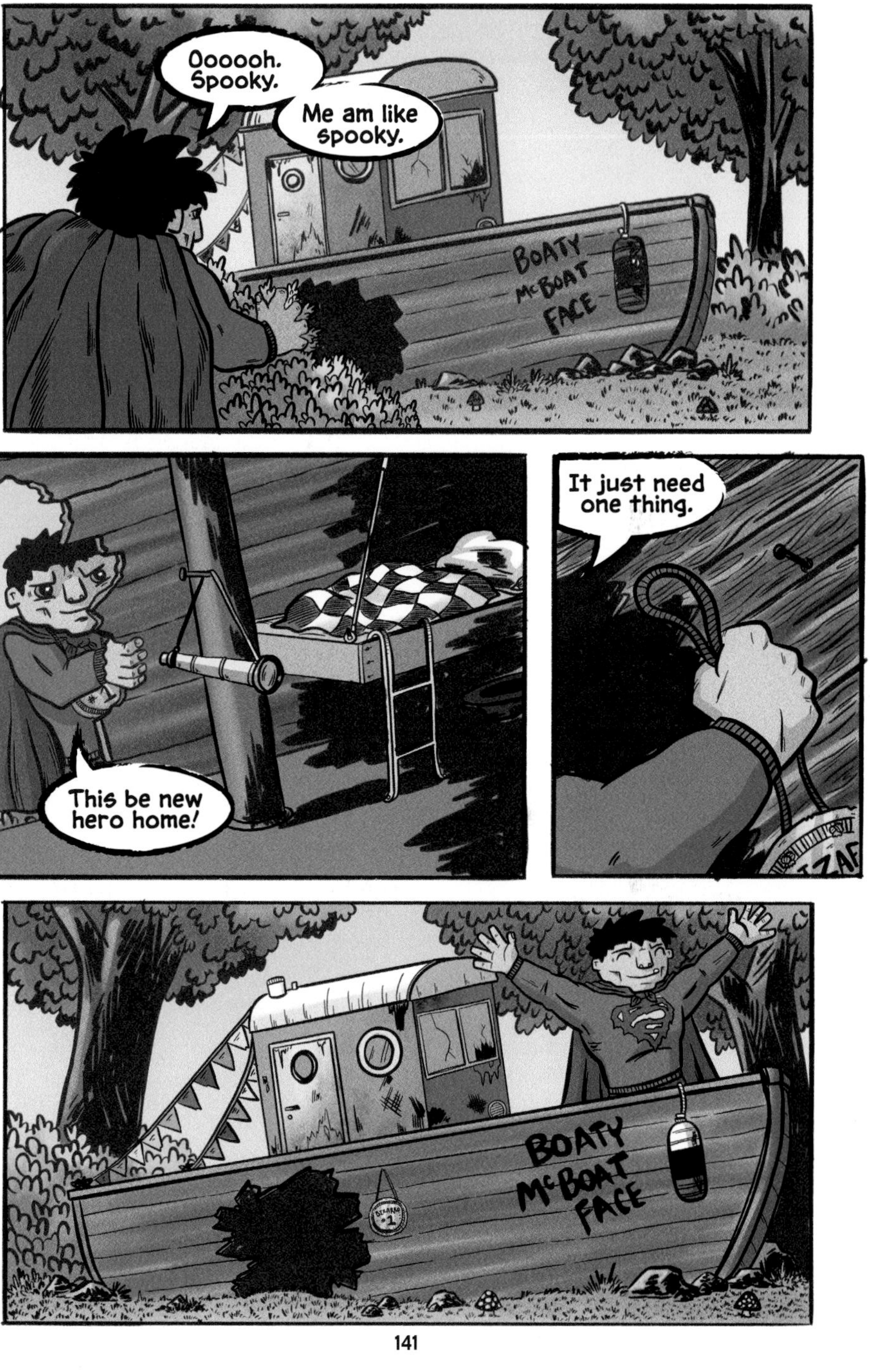
Oooooh. Spooky.
Me am like spooky.
BOATY McBOAT FACE
This be new hero home!
It just need one thing.
BOATY McBOAT FACE

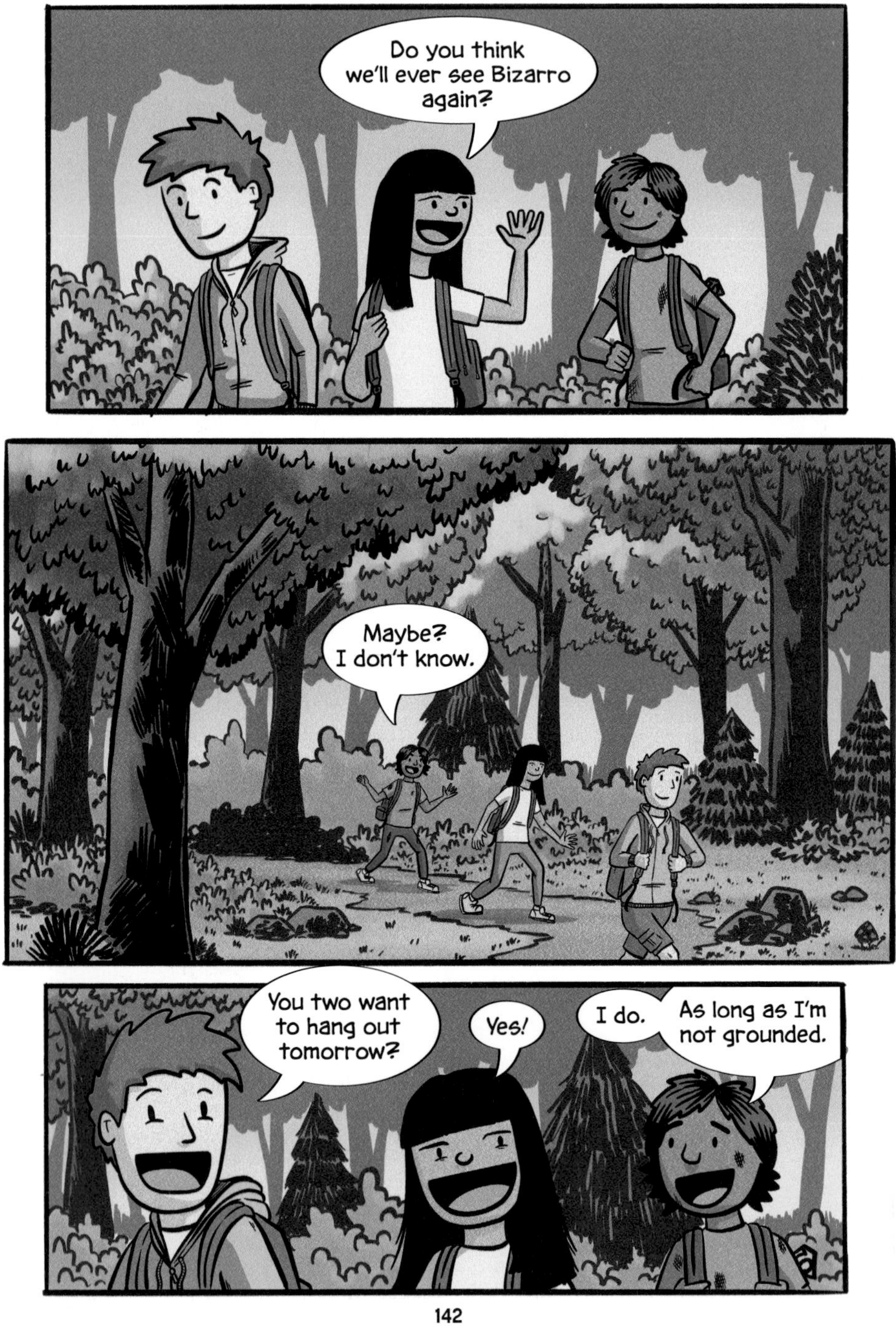
Do you think we'll ever see Bizarro again?
Maybe? I don't know.
You two want to hang out tomorrow?
Yes!
I do.
As long as I'm not grounded.

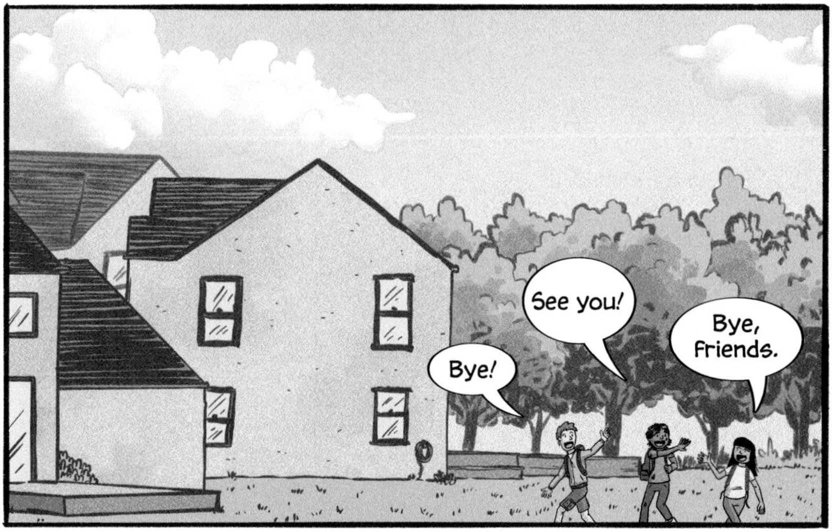
Bye!
See you!
Bye, friends.

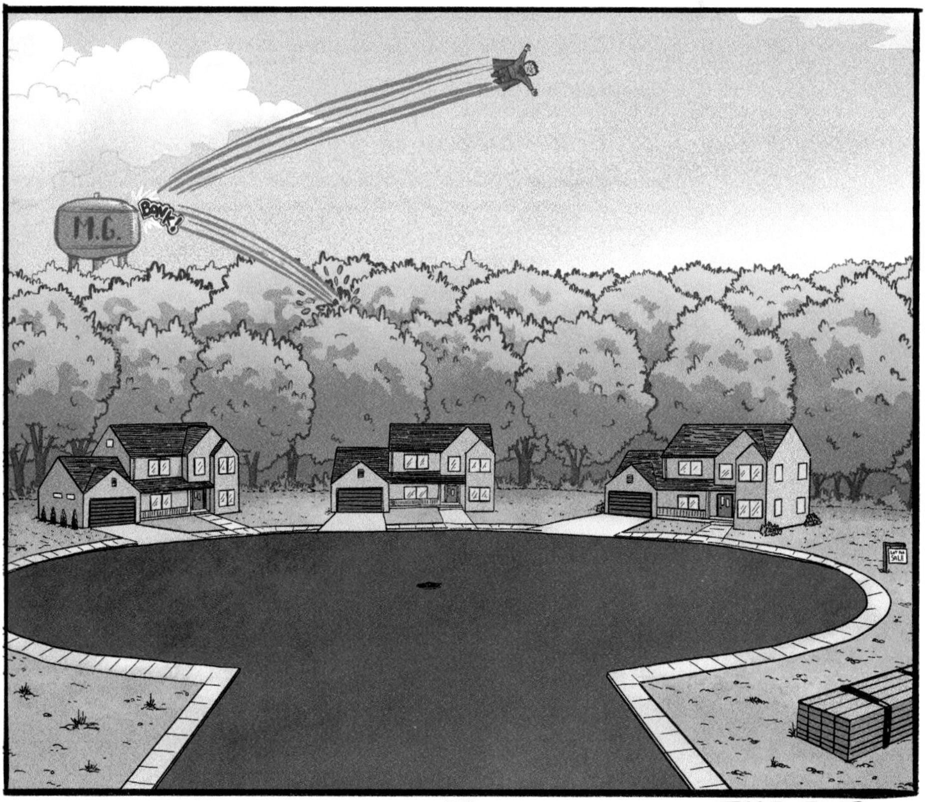
M.G.
BONK!

THE END

DREW BROCKINGTON

is an author and illustrator, and he lives in Minneapolis, Minnesota. His other books include *Hangry* and the CatStronauts graphic novel series. He works at his drawing table and loves to use pencils until they are tiny little nubs. You can find out more about Drew's artwork at: www.drewbrockington.com

The Tip Line of Evil is open!

NEW YORK TIMES BESTSELLING AUTHOR MICHAEL NORTHROP
DEAR SUPER-VILLAINS
ILLUSTRATED BY GUSTAVO DUARTE

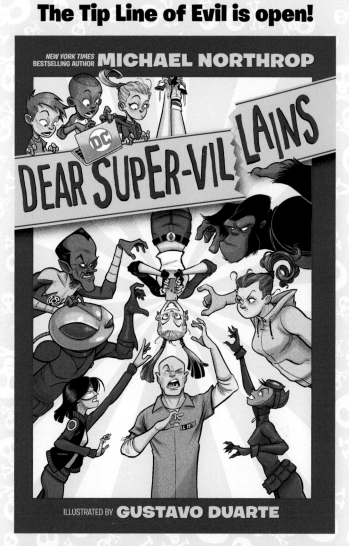

Lots of kids wrote to superheroes in *Dear Justice League*, but there are certain questions that can only be answered by a super-villain. If you, too, are curious about life on the dark side, *New York Times* bestselling writer Michael Northrop and artist Gustavo Duarte have teamed up in a super-fun story about characters who are so good at being bad.

Keep reading for an evil sneak peek at

DEAR DC SUPER-VILLAINS!

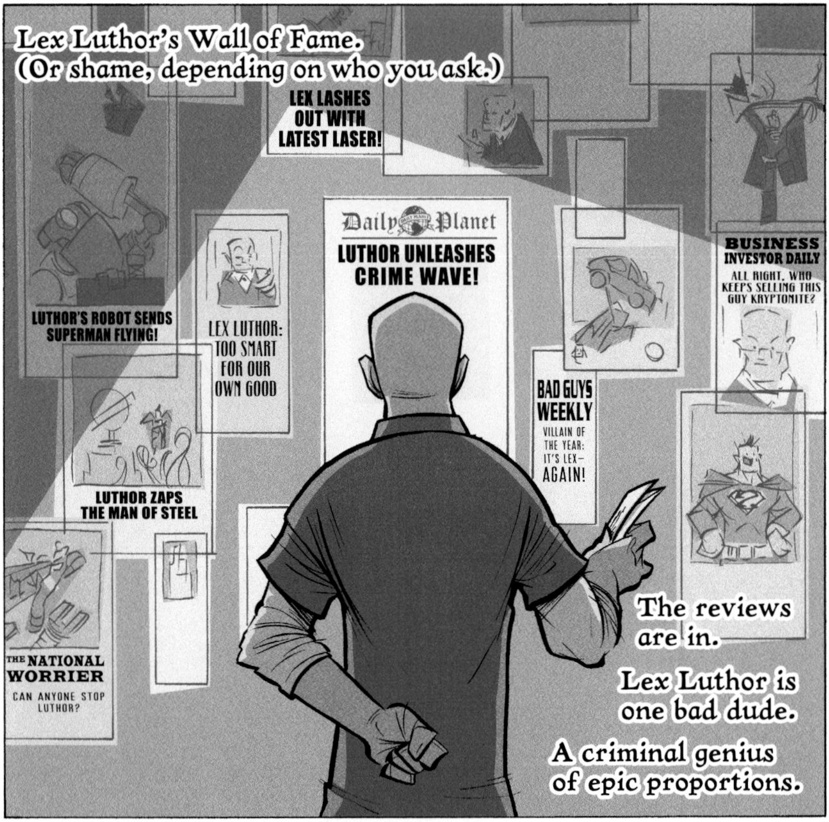
Lex Luthor's Wall of Fame.
(Or shame, depending on who you ask.)
LEX LASHES OUT WITH LATEST LASER!
Daily Planet
LUTHOR UNLEASHES CRIME WAVE!
BUSINESS INVESTOR DAILY
ALL RIGHT, WHO KEEPS SELLING THIS GUY KRYPTONITE?
LUTHOR'S ROBOT SENDS SUPERMAN FLYING!
LEX LUTHOR: TOO SMART FOR OUR OWN GOOD
BAD GUYS WEEKLY
VILLAIN OF THE YEAR: IT'S LEX—AGAIN!
LUTHOR ZAPS THE MAN OF STEEL
THE NATIONAL WORRIER
CAN ANYONE STOP LUTHOR?
The reviews are in.
Lex Luthor is one bad dude.
A criminal genius of epic proportions.

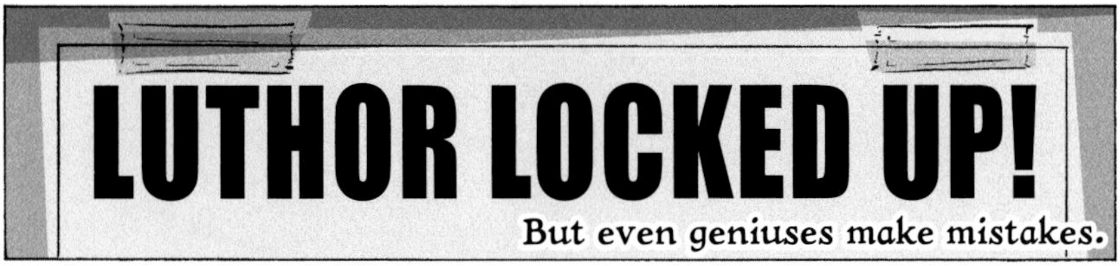
LUTHOR LOCKED UP!
But even geniuses make mistakes.

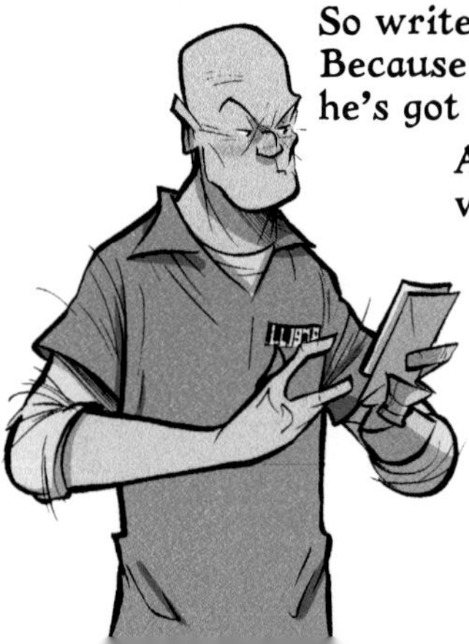

So write now.
Because right now,
he's got time on his hands.

And, at least for the moment,
we know where to find him.

Dear Lex Luthor

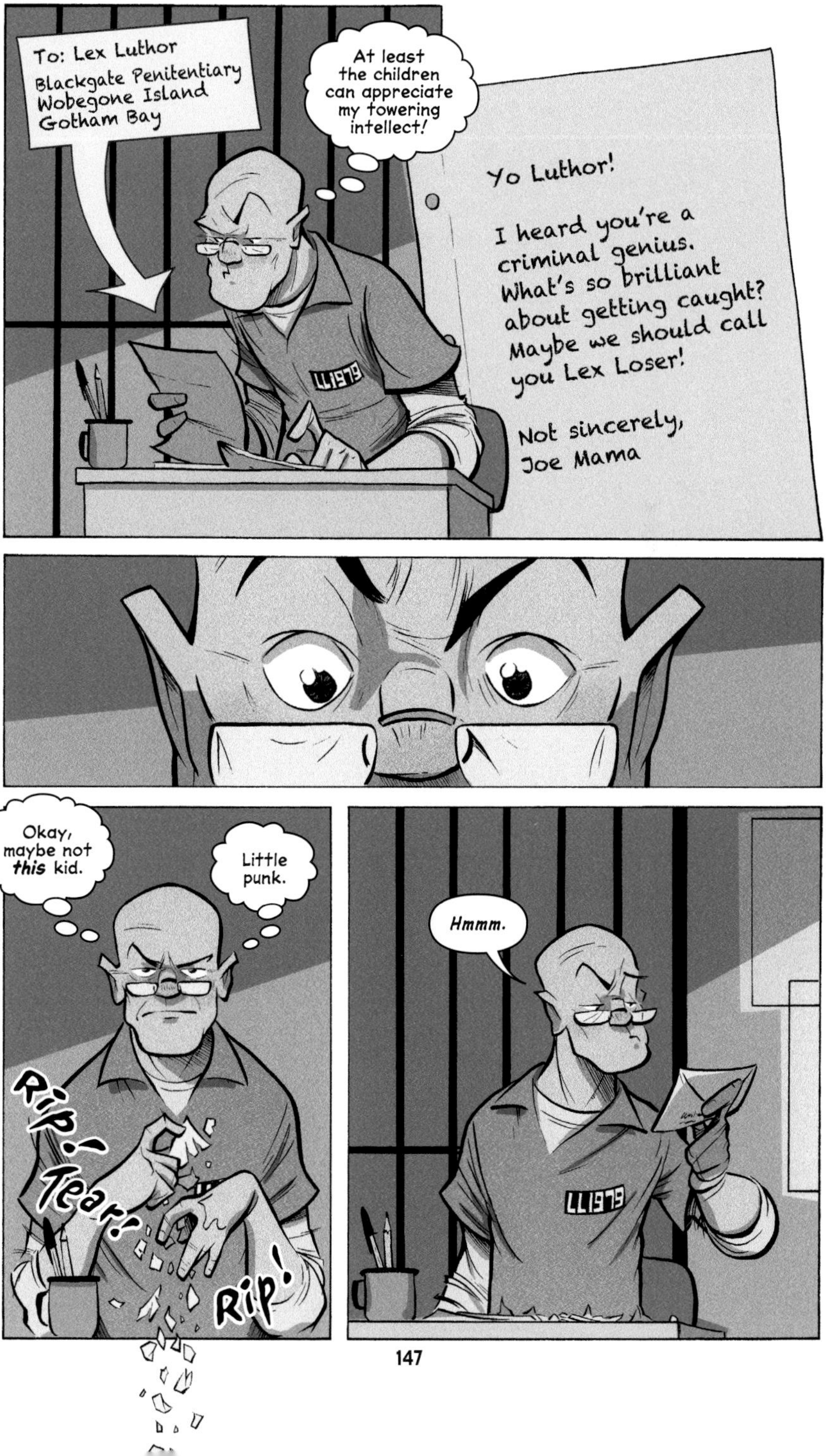
To: Lex Luthor
Blackgate Penitentiary
Wobegone Island
Gotham Bay
At least the children can appreciate my towering intellect!
Yo Luthor!
I heard you're a criminal genius. What's so brilliant about getting caught? Maybe we should call you Lex Loser!
Not sincerely,
Joe Mama
LL1979
Okay, maybe not *this* kid.
Little punk.
Rip! Tear! Rip!
Hmmm.
LL1979

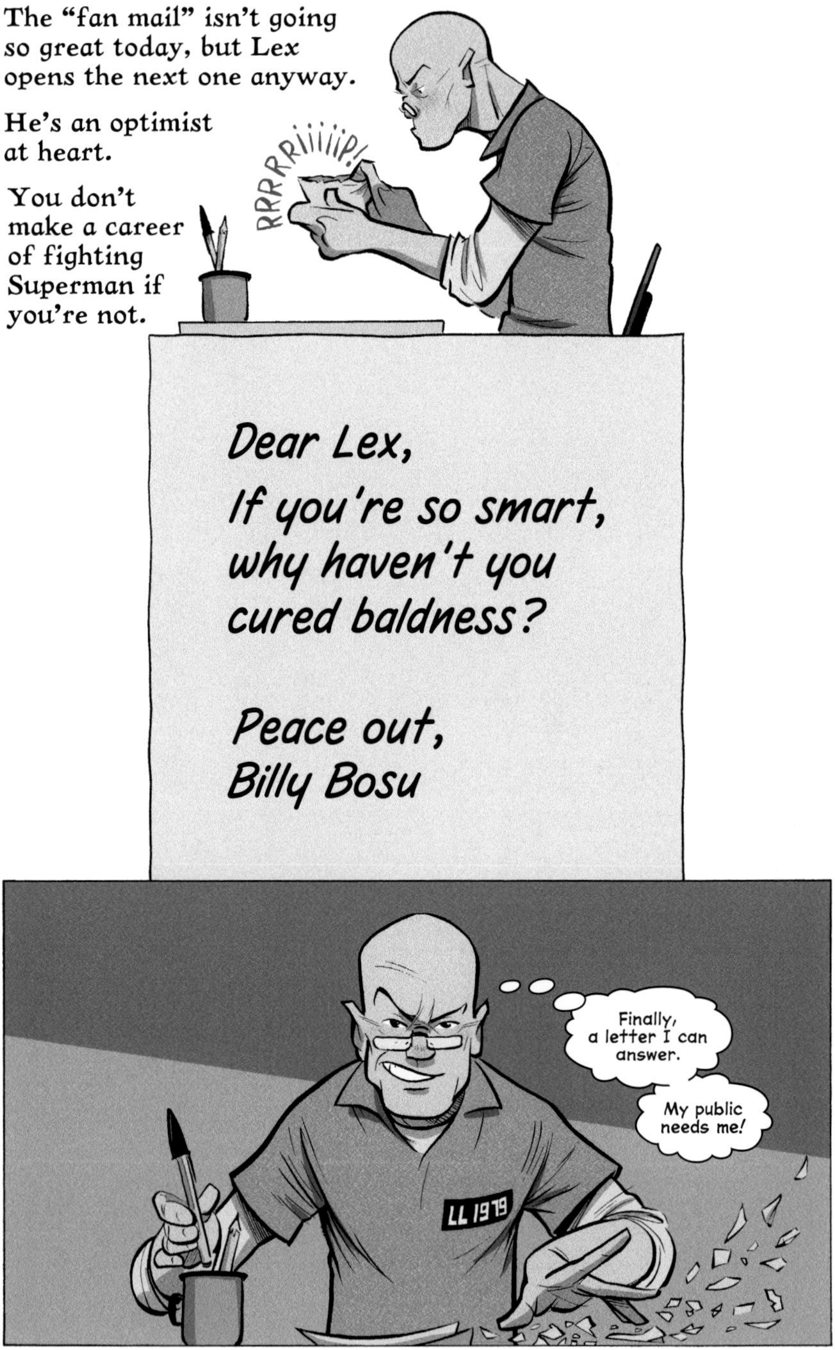
The "fan mail" isn't going so great today, but Lex opens the next one anyway.
He's an optimist at heart.
You don't make a career of fighting Superman if you're not.
RRRRRiiiiiP!
Dear Lex,
If you're so smart, why haven't you cured baldness?
Peace out,
Billy Bosu
Finally, a letter I can answer.
My public needs me!
LL 1979

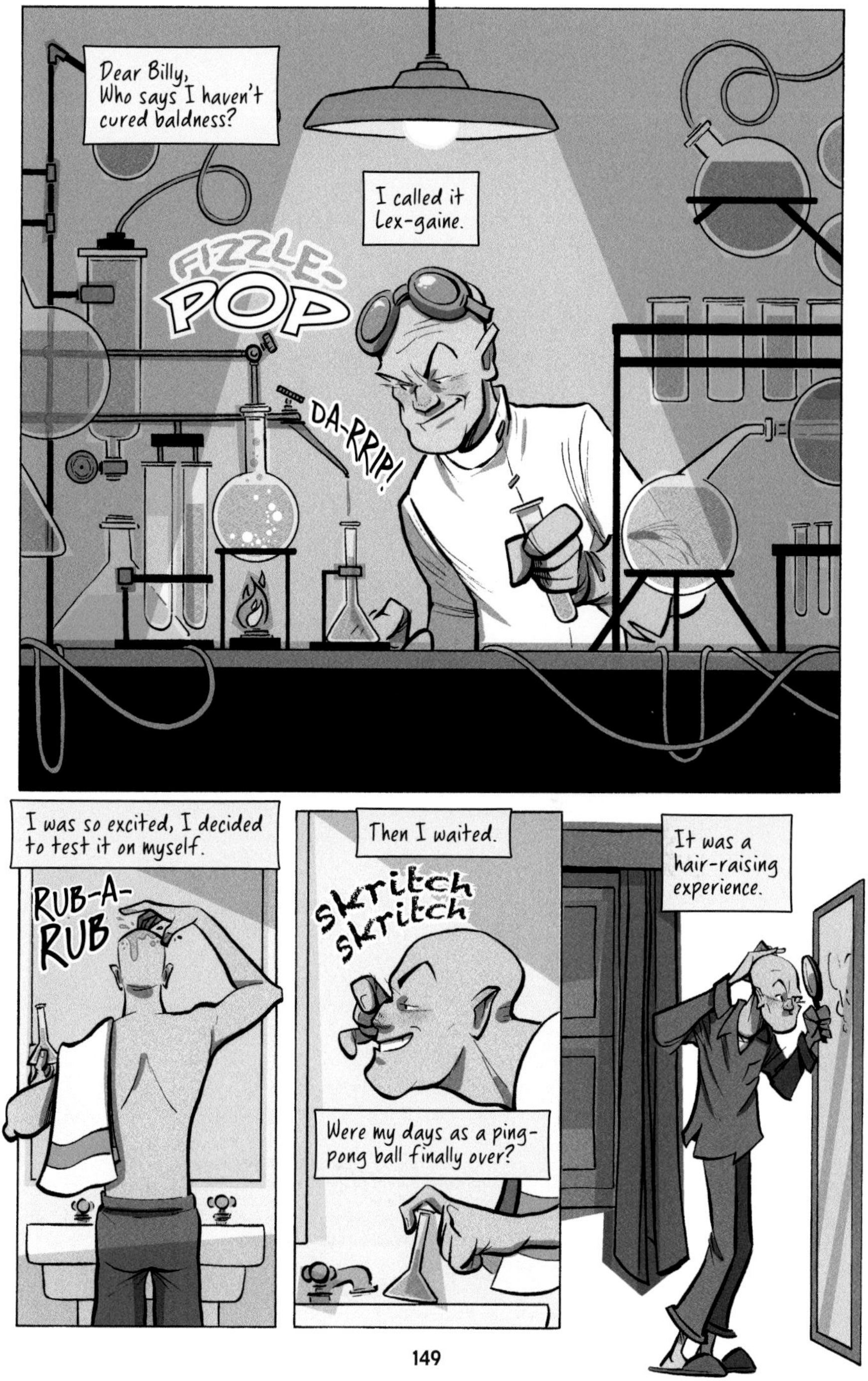
Dear Billy,
Who says I haven't cured baldness?
I called it Lex-gaine.
FIZZLE-POP
DA-RRRIP!
I was so excited, I decided to test it on myself.
RUB-A-RUB
Then I waited.
skritch skritch
Were my days as a ping-pong ball finally over?
It was a hair-raising experience.

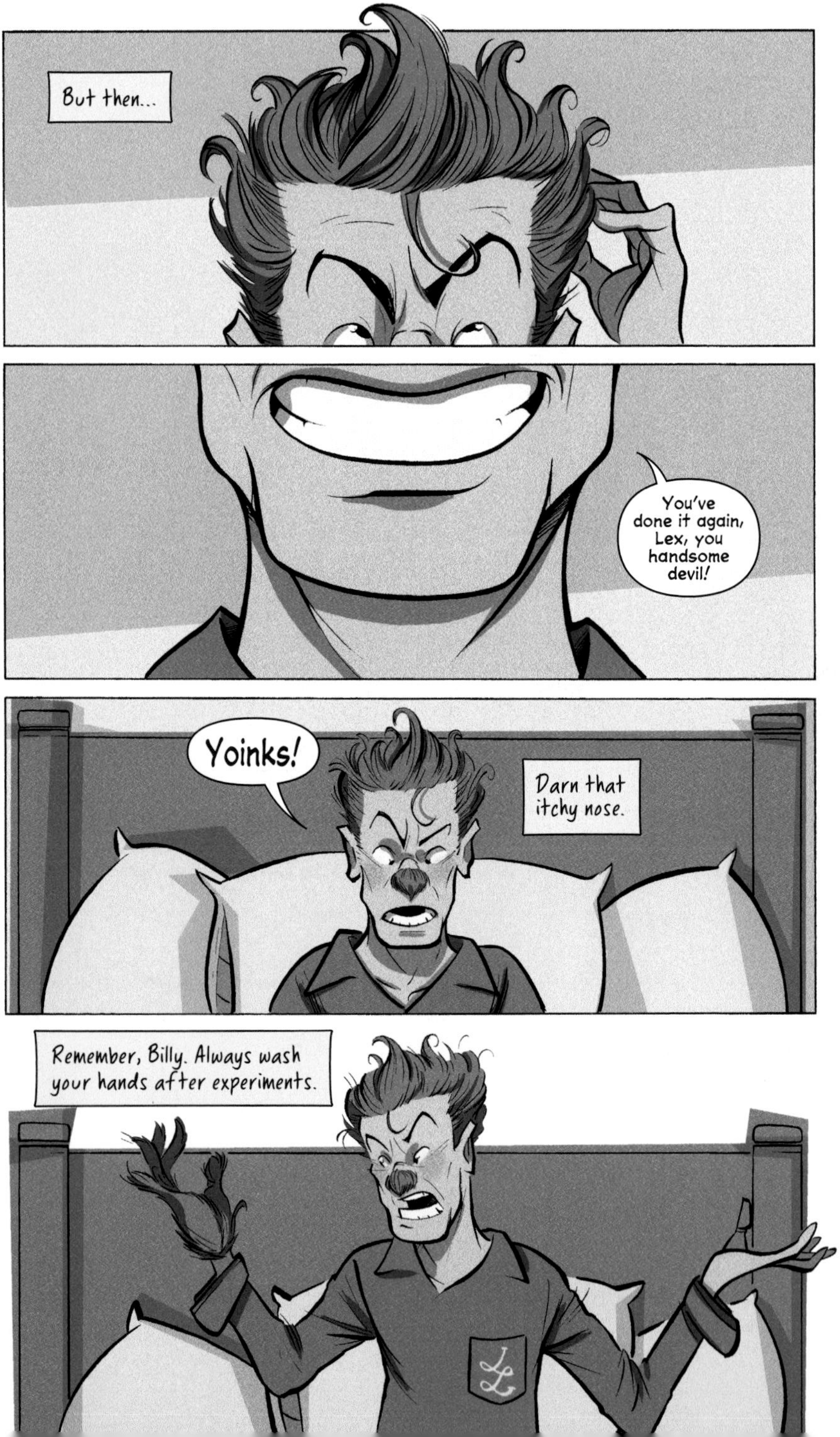

But then...
You've done it again, Lex, you handsome devil!
Yoinks!
Darn that itchy nose.
Remember, Billy. Always wash your hands after experiments.

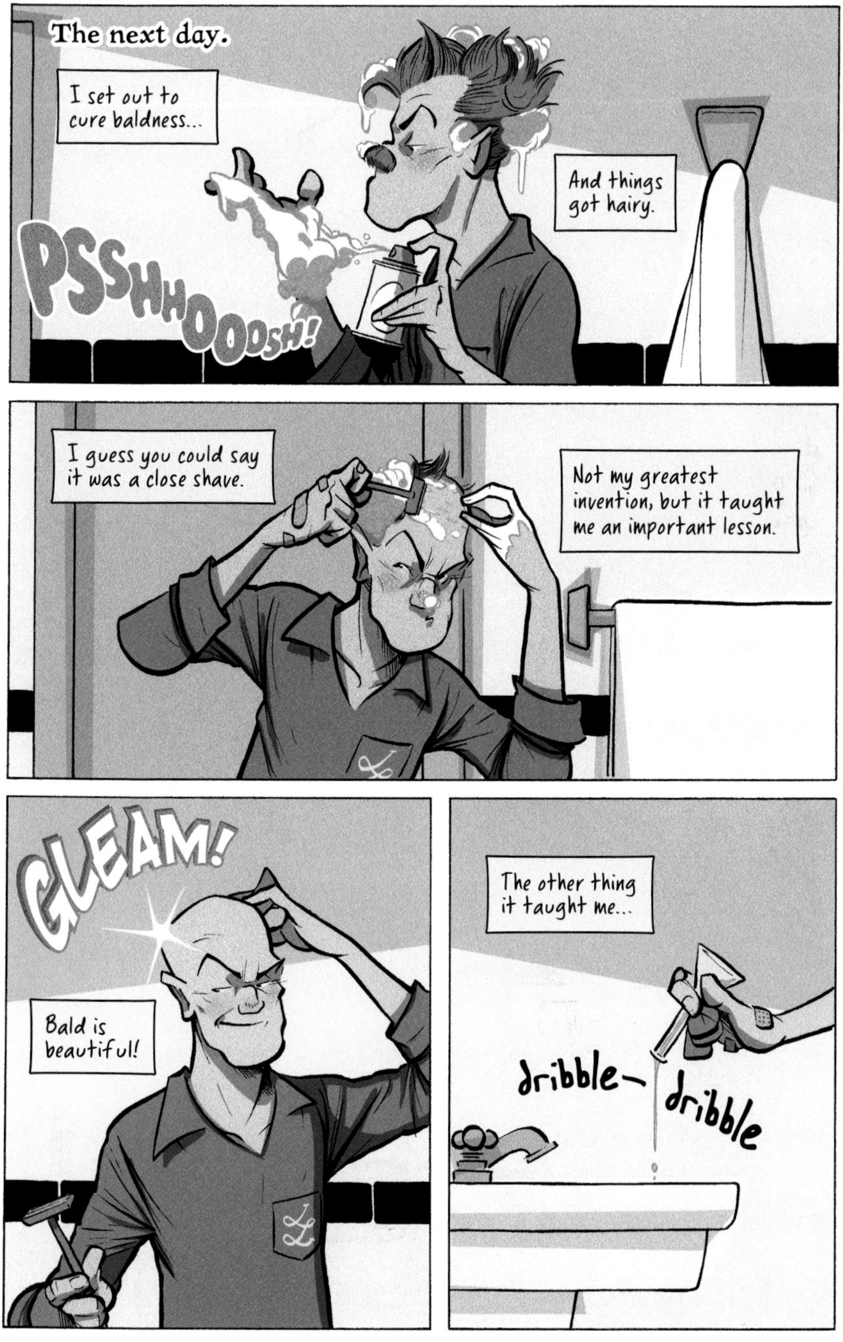
The next day.
I set out to cure baldness...
PSSHHOOOSH!
And things got hairy.
I guess you could say it was a close shave.
Not my greatest invention, but it taught me an important lesson.
GLEAM!
Bald is beautiful!
The other thing it taught me...
dribble-
dribble

The bathroom sink shares a pipe with the shower.

AAAAH!

The bathroom sink shares a pipe with the shower.

Sincerely,

Lex Luthor

P.S. Tell no one. Or I will find you.

P.S.
DEAR DC SUPER-VILLAINS IS AVAILABLE NOW!